INHERITANCE

BOOK TWO OF THE SEEKERS SERIES

J. A. WEBB

INHERITANCE (THE SEEKERS SERIES, BOOK 2), BY J. A. WEBB

Lonely Rock Press, LLC

Lonely Rock Press, LLC edition: March 2025

Print Book ISBN: 978-1-965915-05-9

eBook ISBN: 978-1-965915-03-5

Audiobook ISBN: 9798228465398

Paperback ISBN: 978-1-965915-04-2

Cover design by Jenneth Leed, InkMarker Design

Editing by Deirdre Lockhart of Brilliant Cut Editing

To learn where to buy this book or for more information about this and the author's other books visit: jawebbauthor.com

Library of Congress Cataloging-in-Publication Data:

Webb, J. A.

Inheritance (The Seekers, #2) / J. A. Webb 1st ed.

Printed in the United States of America

NOTE FROM THE AUTHOR:

Thanks for choosing this book, the second in The Seekers Series!

Although this novel can easily be read as a stand-alone story, the reader's enjoyment will be more complete if the series is read in sequence. So I'd urge you to stop now and read *Fragments*, book one of the series, before this one.

Better yet, go to jawebbauthor.com and get your copy of the free prequel, *Fugitive*, in your choice of ebook or audiobook and available only to my newsletter subscribers. Then follow that with the remainder of the series, in order.

Either way, I hope this tale thrills and blesses you. Let me know what you think by sending a comment at jawebbauthor.com. And please share your review on Amazon or Goodreads for other readers.

J. A. Webb
March 2025

"Thrilling Christian fiction . . . where the seen and unseen worlds collide."

CHAPTER 1

If only those stalking him would delay their assault until sunup.

"One more day. Please one more day." Hilkiah whispered the automatic prayer as he hiked, exhausted and sweaty, through this bone-white desert, continually moving inland toward the Great Salt Sea. He was far too old for this mission. But he had accepted the hardship, had insisted, in fact, knowing the necessity if his son were to escape in the opposite direction.

How long could he feign ignorance of the shadows moving on his back trail? How long could he convince them his behavior was consistent with his cover story, a desert sabbatical?

And how long before his body, or his nerve, would fail him?

Jaw set, he exorcised such thoughts. They would only weaken him. Could only dilute his already faltering resolve. So, he soldiered on, back aching and legs worse. But most troubling was his flagging strength.

"Only one more day." He staggered up the dusty rise. "You must endure. Jeremiah needs but one more day."

Late in the afternoon, he arrived at the intended camp and collapsed at the lip of the cave overlooking his back trail's rocky downhill slope.

The blistering sun receded, and in the course of a single heartbeat, the world around him changed, came into strange focus, his perceptions heightened. Now, the colors painted on that desert sunset were so intense as to be almost painful. He savored the sensory banquet, becoming one with the glory of this creation. The feather brushstrokes of those vibrant yellows, brilliant pinks, cutting blues lifted him into euphoria. Heart and mind expanded, and he soared into those heights, to so nearly grasp the mystery and power behind all things seen or sensed. Then he snapped back to himself, sitting on his rock, the evening breeze's caress on his neck familiar, like the invitation of a long-dead lover, bearing the warm scent of desert sage.

Euphoria deserted him and exhausted desperation returned. "Please," he whispered to that wind, "one more day, for Jeremiah's sake."

The baking heat faded. Soon frigid air descended from the starry black sky, penetrating his thin shirt, straight to his core. He shivered and levered himself to his feet, groaning with the darts of pain, the stiffened joints. Then he hobbled into the cave.

He struck flint to tinder and nursed the blaze until the flames rose, cheerful in the deepening darkness. Its yellow reflection danced on wind-smoothed limestone walls. Its comforting heat loosened muscles, dissolved aches, while outside the chill became biting. How extreme, how mercurial, the moods of this place!

He rolled on his blanket, his back to the fire, the sky in view. As his night vision returned, pinpoints of light appeared, grew more vibrant, a multiplicity of violet hues on full luminous display, the Milky Way cutting across it as a billowing cloud of light.

Far down the slope, there came a surreptitious movement, almost too subtle to be noticed, and he sucked in his breath. What was that? He waited, holding that breath, not daring to move. There it was again. Several men scuttled toward his position.

Adrenaline sped through his veins. He rolled deeper into the cave, careful not to look at the fire. He couldn't be blinded in the dark now. He grabbed his walking stick and pack, his precious cargo. Hands shaking, he gripped the stick tighter, knuckles turning white. Why this unreasoning fear? This was no surprise. This was the plan—*his* plan.

No other option now. He took one last deep breath. Then he squeezed through an opening in the cave's rear and into a labyrinth of water-carved passages. The flickering firelight threw his misshapen shadow on the uneven floor.

Where the main tunnel angled left, he stood on a fallen boulder and lifted himself onto a high shelf and through a crack hidden there.

He picked through the inky dark along the narrow passage, the slit of stars above his only guide. On this hidden escape route, not a tunnel but a fault through the bluffs to the Salt Sea, he'd pinned his hopes. If they assumed he remained in the cave network, they may delay long enough for the plan to work.

He exited into the open air and, without pausing, climbed a goat trail up the nearly vertical rise, fingers and toes scrabbling for purchase in the loose scree. Once on top, he dug deeper, searching for hidden reserves, forcing speed from his old tired muscles. Hadn't it been said that, when a person thought they were using all of their physical capacity, they were still holding back? Now, he must commit everything, even his very life force if such were possible, for his son and their secret.

His legs churned, stumbling over the rocky ground. He grit his teeth against the pain stabbing his joints and pushed his numbing legs on, footfalls echoing the thumping of his heart.

He must lose his pursuers in the dark and buy one more day. Just one more day to guarantee Jeremiah's escape.

Wobbling on legs beginning to fail, breath ragged, he clutched to that last memory of his son. Strength flowed from remembered love and imbued reserves muscle and bone could no longer provide.

On their parting, Jeremiah had insisted they flee together, taking the secret with them, protecting it as a team as they always had. Unable to convince him, Hilkiah asserted his authority, saying, "Jeremiah, you are a Keeper, the son of a Keeper, in a line of Keepers reaching back past living memory. Our people have safeguarded the Truth through war, invasion, enslavement, persecution, and even genocide. As the last living Keeper in our line, it is your time to do the same. You are bound by your oath. I now call on you in the name of that oath. Go and fulfill your mission. Know I love you and I would be with you if I could. I will meet you again over the sea."

Now Jeremiah was on his own, somewhere out there.

Just one more day, please, Lord. One more day.

Hilkiah continued staggering parallel to the cliff's edge.

Far below and to his left—a bowl of light where the stars reflected on the Salt Sea's glassy surface.

To his right—the inky night of the bluff top, blanketed in a dark the like of which could only be experienced here, deep in a moonless desert.

Even as the last of his strength flagged, hope flared. There was no sound of pursuit. Perhaps he'd evaded the hunters. Then bright lights flared at him from three directions. He had nowhere to go, teetering at the edge of a sheer three-hundred-foot drop.

If he allowed himself to be captured, he would soon betray the plan. There was but one price sufficient to purchase time for Jeremiah. He whispered, "I am sorry, my son. My final words to you were a lie."

He tipped his face toward the perverse comfort of those cold, piercing lights. So unreachable, so heart-achingly distant in that vast, unending void, an aspect of the infinite set in deepest blackness, sculpted in rock and in fire and in ice, that mortals might glimpse something of eternity. Might glimpse something of Him.

Hilkiah spread his raised arms in defiance, in worship, in prayer, or perhaps in welcome of what was to come. He pushed off, falling backward, seeming to hang in midair for a slice of endless time before accelerating toward the rocks.

He plummeted, smiling, drinking in that miraculous starry wonder. "Thank You, Elohim, for this last blessing, Your handiwork on display in the heavens."

CHAPTER 2

Shoulders wedged between two crates, Phillip braced against the jolts. Sunlight stabbed bright spears through the car's splintered wooden siding. The shafts of light illuminated the hot dust billowing through the floorboards.

Since receiving an emergency message from the other side of the world, he'd journeyed nonstop. He was now traveling as a diplomatic courier for Nob, a nation secretly friendly to the Seekers. With fast air travel reserved for high-level officeholders, his handlers somehow arranged air transport into the country, but couldn't gain his passage to his destination city. From Nob's capital, he'd ridden to the coast hidden inside this freight shipment.

And his contact, perhaps intentionally, failed to mention the fifty kilometers of unpaved dirt tracks. When the wheels left the asphalt and rolled onto the flat desert dust, the trip, until then uncomfortable, became unbearable.

Privation and pain were no strangers, though. His memory held few years not filled with such. He'd been but a grade-schooler when the Order executed his family. Abducted him to be trained in the terrible secret ways of the Eye.

But his parents had educated him as a Seeker. Even then, he'd known much and, by the power of that knowledge, had withstood the

Eye's indoctrination. By that and the remembered love of those parents the tyrants had stolen. The childhood they'd taken. Defiled.

He never revealed this, biding his time. Once he earned his first solo mission, he'd disappeared.

In the years since, he'd remained a primary target for the Eye.

And they, his.

Three loud thumps slapped the bulkhead, his signal to disembark. He stood, tightened his tactical pack, and clambered up the crates and out the trapdoor onto the roof. Outside, he lay flat and relatched the door as the wagon train approached an ancient iron bridge, the girders projecting skyward, the lone feature in the flat arid land.

He crawled to the side, ensured a safe landing place, and alighted with bent knees. As intended, he halted at the gulley's lip. This depression led toward his destination. He ran in the dry creek bottom, boots crunching dusty gravel. Crouched low, he used the raised banks to shield his movements.

Ahead, the ditch widened and emptied into the river. He crabbed on one bank. Beyond a scrub sage, a watercraft rocked in the bridge's shadow. At its bow hung the assigned signal—a yellow T-shirt, tied to the flagpole and flapping in the breeze. He fished a yellow kerchief from his pocket, his talisman. He tied it around his neck, ensured no observers lingered, then dashed into the concealing darkness below the bridge.

As he neared the seemingly unmanned craft, a head of wind-tousled blond hair popped up from behind the captain's chair. The young man waved. "Hello, cousin."

"Hello, second cousin." Phillip gave the agreed pass phrase and vaulted the gunwale. They grasped forearms and slapped backs.

"Welcome aboard, David. I am Jonathon."

Phillip had taken the name David for this mission. After so many years, to again converse in his native tongue touched something long dormant, buried somewhere deep, warmth now spreading from that inner place as long-forgotten memories resurfaced.

Then he shook himself. No time for such while on mission. "Have we confirmed the package's contents? The last message I received suggested this might be a portion of the True Text."

Jonathon untied the boat and pushed off as he started the engine. Once motoring toward the main current, he grinned at Phillip, his tanned face crinkling. "Not just a portion. Are you ready for this? Sitting down? I'm told we're to rescue a team of Keepers . . . who've guarded a complete copy of the *entire* True Text. Thirty-nine books in all."

Phillip rocked in his seat as if from a blow.

No one alive had ever seen a single intact book of the True Text, much less a complete collection of all the books. "Have they made it to the extraction point?"

Jonathon grimaced. "That's the bad news. We've had no communication from either individual. Word is the Order has caught Hilkiah, the father, far east of here, near the Salt Sea."

"How did he get clear over there? He was moving in the wrong direction."

"That's not the worst of it. Sources indicate he had with him a collection of scrolls. The Eye may already have stolen the True Text."

LEIF LIFTED his face to the sky, the sun warming his skin, penetrating deep to loosen long-tensed muscles around his eyes and jaw. He stopped and basked in the sheer joy of it. Then he laughed and spread his arms wide as if to embrace all creation.

This terrain was so strange, these conical hills like some mysterious fantasyland, rising as if by magic from the surrounding plains. Who'd expect to see such here, and only scant miles from his hometown? Who'd have thought he'd be *paid* to hike such an idyllic landscape, the Burr Oak Moraine?

What he now walked through was primordial forest, dark and green, full of life, his footsteps cushioned by thick loam, fingertips playing along rough trunks awaiting his soon-to-be logging crew. The nut-producing trees once planted here now offered thousands of acres of prime hardwood. They'd harvest these marvelous specimens, enabling his family millwork to transform them into prized heirloom furniture.

This deal of a lifetime would save his family's generations-old business, one sorely in need of saving. Advisor Haman already threatened to seize the enterprise, along with Leif's parents' home, if they didn't produce dramatic results—and soon.

With the stakes this high, he refused to fail.

He crested a hilltop, stopped, and leaned his back against the warm rugged hide of an oak. Far below, the blue of the sky, the white of the clouds, and the greens, yellows, and reds of the foliage reflected in the sparkling silver bowl of an abandoned sand quarry, the riot of hues broken into a shimmering kaleidoscope. The breeze carried crisp air, redolent of earth, sunshine, and growing things. He laid his head against the massive old bole as the sky peeked through gaps between its dappled leaves. With the green glow of sunlight shining through so inviting, he lost himself there, rising as if on the breeze now lifting those leaves, ruffling his hair.

An arrow slammed into the tree, vibrating its ominous note mere inches from his neck, and a clear, high voice called out from his right. "Don't you move, or the next one's between your eyes."

A deep, hoarse voice came from his left. "Keep your arrow nocked, girl. I'm moving up."

An older man in patched camouflage entered Leif's field of vision, bow held ready, the razor-sharp broadhead pointed at Leif's chest.

He inched his hands into the air. "I mean no harm. I was just hiking."

Gray stubbled cheeks twisted into a smirk. "Seems to me your hiking here *was* the harm. You're trespassing. Don't tell me you didn't see the signs on the road?"

He'd paid them no mind. "I'm here on business for Advisor Haman."

A lie, but one they couldn't disprove.

"Ain't that nice? Might do you some good if Haman was advisor in these parts, but he ain't. Get on your belly and put your hands behind your back. We'll go see Administrator Warren, and he can file the charges. Might let you off with a warning if you pay the fine in cash." The man's smile showed gray teeth, brown stains between each. "Lots of cash."

Leif gulped. "No wait. You don't understand. I'm here to negotiate with the stewards of this land."

The man's lip curled. "Negotiate what."

"For the timber rights. Haman wants to harvest the hardwoods." Another lie that would soon be true. He *hoped*.

The first speaker—young, maybe early twenties, and striking with dark-auburn hair cascading down her back, a light-olive complexion, and golden-brown eyes—moved into view, bracketing him from the right with her bow. Those eyes flashed with dangerous heat at the mention of harvesting lumber.

"Well, ain't that interesting," the man drawled. "Seems I should know something about that since I *am* the owner of this land, and there'll be no logging here. Not ever!"

MARIPOL, a zealous soldier for his god, responded without hesitation when duty called, no matter the difficulty. No matter how unpleasant.

Now far from home, battered by the desert sun, choking on dust, he continued his hand-over-hand descent of the rope ladder. Below him, the advance team stood over the broken remains of a man. The body so inconveniently dangled on this high cliff ledge it had taken a team of climbers half the morning to rig ladders for the official party.

His right foot found solid ground, then his left. He let go of the ladder, unclipped his safety line, and surveyed the body. It already stank, flies buzzing where blood congealed in oily pools on the rocks. Three Order officials stood in a half circle around it, eyes flat and uncaring.

He glared at the local section head. "Why, in the name of the Eternal, did you leave him lying here?"

The head licked chapped lips. "Sir, pardon, but we were following explicit orders. We were to touch nothing until you arrived."

"What is that under his body?"

The man shifted his feet, looking at the crumpled remains, and then away again. "It appears to be a backpack, sir."

"Is it possible the artifact we seek is in that pack?"

A satisfied smile. "That has been our assumption, sir."

Maripol mirrored the smile with a wider one. "Oh, wonderful." He dropped the sneer. "Is that blood I see running down his clothing, pooling beneath him?"

"Um, yes, sir?"

He gritted his teeth. "Do you think the blood may have found its way into the pack? May well be destroying that which we have taken such great pains to acquire?"

The section head faltered and backed up a step. "Uh, I don't know, sir?"

Maripol ground out an oath. "Get the pack off that body this instant!"

As a competent man, he appreciated competence in others. But so many were insipid order-takers, unwilling to risk independent thought. People like this man caused the downfall of the Hegemony. Now, they were ruining the Order.

The head issued crisp commands, and men hauled the pack to Maripol's feet.

The wind blew bellowing gusts off the salt flats, alkaline dust stinging his eyes. He lowered himself onto a boulder, turned his back to shield his prize, and peered into the bag's dark interior. Then he inched his hand into the opening and pulled free a round leather case, blood-soaked and dripping.

Holding his breath, not daring to hope, he untied the cords and unwound the protective outer layer, exposing multiple cylindrical objects, scrolls with strange crablike geometrical text. He shot to his feet. "Tell the chopper to pick us up. Move! We must get this to the university."

CHAPTER 3

Leif lay on his stomach, chin burrowing into the loamy ground, twigs and acorns grinding into his torso. The man wrenched his arms behind his back, forcing his shoulders to within a hairsbreadth of dislocation. He tied his hands together with what felt like sharp wire. A knee in his kidneys drove the air from his lungs while a palm on his crown rammed his face deeper into the soil. Did the man intend to smother him?

Fingers plucked at his right cargo pocket. Then his head bobbed free. He spat leaves, gasping, grit sticking to his tongue.

"What kind of fool travels this far from home with no cash?" The man folded a wad of bills into his shirt pocket and threw the empty wallet at Leif's face. With him unable to block the blow, it slapped his forehead.

"But I have cash." He craned his neck to see his captor better.

"Check again." The man snorted. "That billfold's empty as can be. Guess you're gonna need to pay your fine another way."

"Uncle, stop this." The girl scuffled closer, somewhere behind. "We're arresting a trespasser, not robbing him."

"Hush, girl. They put me in charge here, not you."

The girl growled, low and deep, like the feral cats on Grandpa's farm.

The man's toe poked at Leif's ribs. "Son, maybe I have been too harsh. I'm thinking you and I can make a deal, keep the middleman out of it. Why involve the authorities, right?"

Maybe he'd get out of this in one piece, after all. Leif rolled to his side and beamed his best, most disarming smile. "Uh, yeah. What kind of deal?"

"That's the problem—you having no cash. What else you got for trade?"

No reason to point out who'd relieved him of his money. "Nothing of value."

"That's not exactly so. What size boots do you wear? Those you got on look mighty nice."

When Leif made it back to the road, he searched to the north, then south, but his bike was nowhere to be seen. After three more passes, kicking through the tangled brush, he came to the small tree he'd been looking for. The cable lay cut on the ground, the bike gone.

Had a freight tug not happened by, he'd never have been home before nightfall. As it was, he had to endure the driver's constant jokes. But who could blame the man, given the way he'd found Leif, walking the country road, far from anywhere, wearing nothing but socks and boxer shorts?

When he arrived home, his four young children were hungry and filthy, dashing around the house and fighting like maniacs.

A teenage girl lay stretched on the living room couch, chewing a fingernail. One leg dangling, she played with an earring while immersed in a battered romance novel, a relic from the days of Hegemony.

He jerked back before the girl could see him in his skivvies. Once he'd recovered his coveralls from the garage and slipped them on, he reentered the house. The babysitter had not moved, even to recover the now crying baby.

Leif scooped him up and quieted him with a kiss to the cheek. "Where's Diana?"

The babysitter shrugged, folded closed her novel, and held out her hand.

He reached for his wallet before remembering his stolen money. "Diana will have to pay you tomorrow, sorry."

She rolled her eyes, then abandoned him to the trashed house and screaming children.

By late evening, he had them fed, bathed, and bedded down. He tried to skip their nightly ritual. But there'd be no peace until they were satisfied, so he lay in their beds, one by one, their little hands held in his as he sang each their special lullaby. Putting down the calls for "one more song," he kissed them and blew out the candle.

He padded downstairs, wincing at every step. That barefoot walk had left tender bruises on the balls of his feet. Hands on hips, he turned a circle. What a mess. He should pick up, but he was too shot. He made himself a drink, downed it, and poured another. About to turn, he snagged the bottle as an afterthought, then limped back upstairs.

As the whiskey washed all cares away, left the twinges in his feet fading, he blew out a long breath. Forget the office work tonight too. His freelance business was even more demanding than the old job, and he'd been working so many hours. Lately, he and Diana had enjoyed no time alone.

Hopefully, she'd return soon, wherever she was. They'd spend a quiet evening together. That'd be nice.

He washed and stretched out in bed with his drink and a book, waiting for her.

She couldn't be much longer, no matter what errand she'd run.

Could she?

Father Curtis, former priest of the Order of the Eternal and now a fugitive, again found himself in a familiar dream that long plagued him. It first came when he still enjoyed life as a parish priest. Long before he'd been falsely accused, convicted, and sentenced to death by corrupt powers within the Order. Even before his mentor, Professor Reuel, had hidden him here.

In those untroubled times, the dream had been like a dark storm cloud, a harbinger of the trial he'd soon face. Now it came for who knew what purpose?

Red desert sand, scorched and lifeless, blew in drifting tendrils across the cracked plain. The moaning of that arid wind offered the only sound beneath a low ceiling of roiling yellow-gray clouds.

This shattered rocky terrain blurred to the horizon, broken only by pyramidal heaps of debris. He stood on the summit of one, a crowd at the base—people he loved, his parishioners, his adopted family.

He suppressed a sob at seeing those familiar faces. Would he ever be with his people again? Ever again minister to these precious souls he loved so?

As always, he stood watch, focus on the far horizon. The expected dark form appeared, a writhing black cloud, low to the ground, spilling across the plain with unnatural speed. Moving so fast, nearly upon his people now.

The power of the thing vibrated the earth, pulsated the air, thrummed his being.

His hand numbed where it gripped the lantern, his fingers turning white. He let it fall. This darkness was unaffected by any such light.

He called for his people to gather to him, and they crowded in his direction, panicked eyes looking to him for salvation. But how was he to help them when he couldn't help himself?

They scattered before the looming darkness, and that darkness overwhelmed. Within the murky cloud, those remembered twisted shapes threatened. They darted ever closer, now on the heels of the slowest of his flock. An invisible fury buffeted his soul, a sense of inhuman rage, of insatiability, a desire to devour and destroy.

Down the slope, the lantern rested on a ledge where it had rolled. Now, the advance of that oily black cloud absorbed its light as if it ceased to exist.

He cast about for another weapon. Anything to save his people.

At his feet was an object, suddenly familiar. A wide belt, shining with some inner light, a light which, to someplace deep within his soul, sang a familiar song. A song of Truth.

He raised it above his head, and the light shone out. He begged his people to gather close, but they ignored him. Each scurried toward other heights, climbed to escape from the inky swelling flood in his own way.

The churning mass closed in. The forms clawed, clutching and pulling the slowest and weakest into its depths.

The wind rose to a scream. Sand and rock pelted him backward, threatened to push him from the precipice to the surging forms below.

On the adjacent heaps, people scrabbled for the summits, kicking, dislodging their fellows in their panic. He shouted to them, pleaded with them to aid one another. But the gale swept away his words.

His body lifted on the wings of the hurricane. Blown higher and higher away from his flock, he uttered a despairing prayer.

Anguished screams rose from his people's throats as they were rended, torn, and consumed, their death throes hidden in the mists.

He woke and lifted shaking hands to wipe cold sweat from his brow. The dream had come again.

But why, after all this time? What could it mean? Hadn't he already found the truth? Found Creator God? Accepted his lot, his mission?

Then why, still, would he be tormented by such nightmares, so long after he'd been wrenched from the arms of those he loved?

And why, for the first time since he'd accepted the existence of Creator God, did fear for those dark entities again overwhelm him?

He huddled in his quilt, back tight to the cold unyielding wall. He peered about the room, this long, windowless concrete box once a de facto prison, but now his home and sanctuary.

The fireplace lit the bare floor in a circle of orange light. The firelight a dull sheen highlighting the carved lion's paws on the oak table's massive legs, claws looking as if they'd sunk into the stony floor. Beyond, the metal bookshelves rose, visible only as hints of bridge strut geometry, the huge, hammered rivets giving an occasional glint as the flame tips flared yellow, then died back again.

He squinted. Was it his imagination, or was someone lurking in the deeper shadows beyond the row upon row of shelves? But the firelight possessed too little power, and those shadows remained impenetrable. Even so, those unseen corners couldn't harbor any threat. Had there been, Dantes, the black cat he'd adopted, wouldn't be curled into his belly, unconcerned.

Curtis ran one hand down Dantes's side, the sleek black fur fine and silky. Dantes stretched, pressed forepaws into his breast, and purred. Then the hair of Curtis's scalp rose in a wave of goose bumps. Dantes flashed to his feet, claws digging into cloth, fur on end, hissing toward that darkness. A terrible urge to rise twitched Curtis's limbs, and he vaulted to his feet, gaze darting, hands up to defend against a blow as he sidestepped toward the fire.

His back to the wall, he fed kindling to the coals, then another log. The light brightened, grew, the yellow circle now flooding past the table to encompass the nearest bookstacks.

He grabbed the candle from the bedside and lit it in those resurgent flames. Then, with Dantes at his side, Curtis prowled, knees bent, to the rows of shelving. He held the candle high until they reached the far corner and circled back.

The room was empty, as far as his eyes could testify. But a part of him still knew, could still sense, he was not alone. The rocker grated as he slid it to the corner nearest the fireplace. Then he hung the teapot over the coals and retrieved a cup from the sink. He'd not be sleeping again this night.

Thick cushions took his weight as he perched, feet planted on the floor. Ready to move at the slightest threat. While he waited for the water to boil, he whispered a prayer.

As he did, the nature of that prayer altered as if of its own accord. He now prayed for whomever the enemy stalked this night. For he had a new sense that this imminent danger, which had wakened him, which had come to him in that cursed dream, was not to himself. It was to another, somewhere out there. Someone he knew. Someone he loved.

Someone who had no protection. Had not the truth.

Dantes took position at his feet, his legs tucked beneath himself, haunches tense and twitching.

Ready to pounce.

CHAPTER 4

An identical pair of little blond terrors bounced on Leif's bed. The morning sun glared through the window. With only a sliver of the yellow orb visible above the horizon, it set fire to his already raging headache, the half-empty whiskey bottle on the nightstand explanation enough for that.

There was no sign of Diana. She must already be up.

He grabbed the two children and wrapped them in a bear hug, adding whisker burns to the kisses he lavished on their soft necks.

Two other youngsters, having heard the fun, bounded down the hall. One was a toddler, just having learned to walk, followed by a girl a few years older than the twins. They mock wrestled until the four defeated him, each holding down one arm or leg like a band of Lilliputians. "We've got you. We've got you. You can't move!"

Proving them wrong, he lifted all four little bodies into the air, dumped them on the bed, and made his escape. "Diana?" He tramped downstairs, heart singing even over the lingering hangover. He'd get the morning with his wife for a change. When last had he taken time to breakfast with her? Well, he was going to today. Coffee would taste great while looking into those smiling green eyes, and boy, did he need that coffee right now.

She wasn't in the kitchen or anywhere in the house.

"Where's your mom?" he asked the children, getting blank stares.

The tightness crept back into his neck, and he massaged it as he checked the house again. He was searching the basement when the garage opened. He dashed upstairs and met Diana entering the kitchen. Her hair tangled, her makeup smeared, she wore a sports jersey several sizes too large. A man's name was stenciled on the back. A man he knew.

"Where have you been?" That came out more harshly than he intended. He was about to rephrase when she sniffed, contempt on her face, and pushed past him into the room.

Head floating, disconnected from his own body, feet a mile away, he heard himself saying, "I asked where you've been." This time, the heat in his voice wasn't accidental.

"Out."

"I can see that. What in Hegemony do you think you're doing?"

She spun. "I can do whatever I want. You're not my father."

"No, I'm your husband. You can't keep acting this way."

"Or what? I'm doing nothing wrong."

"No, I mean yes, you are. This"—he waved his hands up and down, indicating her state—"is wrong."

"Says who? I'm a good wife." She leaned in, her finger stabbing at each word. "I do my job, no thanks to you. I take care of this house. I take care of the kids. What I do for fun is my own business."

He stood, hands frozen, mouth working but producing no words. What she was saying was wrong. He knew it at some bone-deep level. But how to prove it? His opinion bore no weight with her.

There had to be an objective measure of right and wrong he could appeal to, but what? The Writings? He scoffed. Those milk-toast writings weren't even consistent. But what else was there? "The Writings say so!"

She sneered. "You don't even read them. I know them better than you, and they say nothing of the sort. Anyway, aren't you late for your precious work?"

Her back to him she began making coffee. The fake, flavored kind she knew he hated.

Lars grinned as, without knocking, Leif breezed into the office, breathing heavily as if he'd been running. "Hey, brother. I thought you had meetings all week?"

Seeing Leif here at all, much less so early in the day, was strange.

Leif plopped into the old upholstered chair beyond Lars's desk and rubbed his forehead as if massaging a headache. "Something came up. When does the next freighter head to Capital? I need to send a message to Advisor Haman."

"Why don't you use the landline in German's office?" County Administrator German, a family friend, had one of the few landline telephones in the area.

"Nope. Too sensitive. This has to be a sealed letter, delivered by messenger, into his hand. Who's taking the next load down?"

Lars hesitated. The temptation to make this trip was almost enough to pry him from the mountain of work on his desk. He'd been wanting to see Father Curtis ever since their nighttime expedition to Two Rivers. Curtis's words still echoed: "There's no way to say what I have to tell you in a short time, but I'll do my best. Dear boys, dear friends, know this—the Writings are not holy writ as I once believed. I know this is shocking, but the good news is there is a God in heaven. He is real, of a certainty. You won't find Him in the Writings, but you can find Him if you try."

Father Curtis, their priest, helped them study the Writings and taught them to obey the Eternal. Now he was disavowing that? Why would he drop that on them and then disappear? Such questions burned like acid in Lars's insides, waking him in the night.

Phillip had given him and Leif a note with instructions on how they could contact Father Curtis. Phillip had said, "Read. Burn."

Leif had shown no interest. But Lars studied the procedure until he'd imprinted it into memory. Then he'd burned it. Now, he'd take action.

"A load's headed down this morning. Give me your message."

Leif handed over a sealed envelope addressed to Haman. Lars gripped it, but Leif didn't let go. "He needs to get it by tomorrow."

"Okay, it'll get there." Lars tugged on the message Leif still held. "I'll take it myself."

Leif released it, then slumped into the chair, and pressed his palms into his eyes. "Thanks."

"No problem. You okay?" His brother looked anything but okay with dark circles smudging the skin beneath his eyes, skin that otherwise had too much gray in it.

Giving his eyes one last rub, Leif stood. "Yeah. Just be sure it gets there." And he left, head down and shoulders hunched.

Lars opened a book and consulted it as he wrote his own coded message, sealed it, and addressed it. He slipped both envelopes into his briefcase and grabbed his jacket.

He was going on a trip.

The wagon train—a series of wheeled wooden wagons that mimicked trains from a bygone era when the world ran smoothly—stopped at Mazkelon Terminal. Jeremiah stood from his seat and slung his backpack to one shoulder.

A mass of people crowded the aisle, barely moving. Why were they taking so long to file out?

The press of bodies began to squeeze the breath from him. Someone shoved the pit of his back, and he stumbled, nearly toppling over the short man ahead. The crowd inched forward, and he shuffled, holding back those behind.

At last, he stepped off the gangway and onto the concrete apron. Guarded police barricades funneled new arrivals through a checkpoint.

Here was the reason for the delay.

Surely, he could slip out of the cordon. He stretched his upper back side to side. Using the movement as a cover, he glanced around. But no, too many guards watched too closely. No chance there.

Signs instructed passengers to have their documents ready for inspection. He approached the guard booth, only third in line now, and his heart lurched. His and his father's photos fluttered where they were pinned to the sidewall.

Hands jittering, he slipped sunglasses out of his pocket and donned them. Could this feeble disguise, along with his newly acquired hair color, be enough?

Another uniformed officer arrived and tapped the duty man's shoulder. "Your break time." He slid into the narrow booth, then jerked a thumb toward the photos. "You hear they caught these guys?"

Now Jeremiah was next in line. The moment of crisis was upon him. He held his breath and presented himself, false ID next to his face.

The new man didn't even look at him but waved him past as, with the breathlessness of a born gossip, he continued the story of Hilkiah's capture.

Jeremiah stumbled, hand cupping mouth to stifle a sob. Willing his tensed shoulders to loosen, he walked away, alert for the imminent shout of recognition, the blast of a cop's whistle, the jolt of a rough hand on his arm. He kept moving, walking as fast as he could without attracting notice.

And then he was out of the terminal, half a block away, then a block. He turned a corner, lost himself in the press of the busy sidewalk, and let the flow of bodies carry him along.

He'd escaped. Then he winced at the relief flooding his limbs, his body traitor to his heart. His father was in peril. He should go back, find him, help him. Somehow.

He wandered through the city, not seeing the streets through his jumbled thoughts. He should have stayed with him. Father was too old for this.

He straightened and walked with renewed purpose, jaw set. He'd find out where they had taken his father.

He ground his teeth and clenched his fists.

He *would* find him. He *would* rescue him.

But then his memory evoked a vision, unasked, and his steps faltered. It was his father's face. Stern. Resolved. Loving.

"Go now, and fulfill your mission," his father's parting admonition echoed anew.

He'd taken an oath, hadn't he? He wouldn't—*couldn't*—dishonor his father by breaking it. He'd follow through with the rendezvous, would keep this final promise. He'd pass his information to his father's contacts, fulfilling the spirit, at least, of his vow.

That duty discharged, he'd then find and free his father. No matter the risk.

He nodded, wiped his eyes, and marched toward the great Temple of the Eternal at the city center.

AFTER LARS DEPARTED to courier the message to Haman, Leif went to his home office to work on some estimates, but unable to focus, he gave up and leaned back in his chair.

He needed help. Help from someone with connections, maybe his old friend, German. No one was more familiar with the workings around this territory than that old man. It was near the lunch hour, but maybe Leif could catch him in the office.

He swung onto the borrowed bicycle, hunched over the handlebars too short for him, knees knocking with every revolution. Passersby stopped to stare at the bright-pink Diana had chosen for her bike. That first commission check was buying a new bike, no doubt about it.

German was still in his office, making notations on a pile of paperwork, the rest of his staff having abandoned him for the lunch break. No big surprise, the man was nothing if not devoted to his work.

Leif took a seat opposite the pile, and German set down his pen, peering at Leif over wire rims, mouth set in a pinched frown. "Yes?"

Leif related yesterday's assault.

The white brows furrowed. "Do you intend to press charges?"

"Oh no." Leif waved. "I want to get in good with these people. I need them. I thought you'd know 'em, maybe put in a good word?"

"Hmm. What business might you have with *them*?"

"Can we keep this between the two of us?"

"Of course."

"I'd hoped to negotiate timber rights. There's some prime hardwoods in those hills."

"I see." German pursed his lips. "You may want to abandon any designs on that timber. You'll not get anywhere with that clan."

Leif's heart skipped a beat. "Why not? Why would they pass up a lucrative deal?"

German rolled his pen across his papers, caught it with his other hand, and rolled it back again. "You know there were estate issues when old man Tunne died?"

"Died? The crook I met wasn't him?"

"Oh, dear me, no. That was Junior, his youngest son. The young woman must've been the old man's granddaughter, Katrina. Kat was helping Tunne reestablish grazing herds when he died. Her grandfather had wished for her to take the stewardship, but Advisor Fegan brought Junior in, handing it to him. You'll want no dealings with them, trust me."

"Why?"

German skittered the pen sideways. "Just you stay clear of that lot, boy, if you know what is good for you." He stood to greet a man who had entered. "My next appointment is here. Sorry, Leif. Best find lumber elsewhere."

Leif exited the offices and walked the cursed pink bike to the lake where he sat, throwing rocks into the foamy surf. He ignored the chattering squirrels, a family of them chasing circles about the trunk of an old silver maple.

Why did everything have to be so difficult? Why couldn't things go his way, just once? Everything hinged on his family getting access to that timber. His competitors at Artisans had better buying power. Once word got out about the contracts he was negotiating, they'd move in and underbid him, use their price advantage to destroy him.

His only hope was to secure this locally sourced lumber. Material he could produce at a fraction of the going price, even of the price paid by Artisans.

From the west, a line of rolling dark clouds approached, a squall line moving rapidly. A cold downdraft blasted out of that leaden sky, and he hunched his shoulders, blond hair whipping about his face. The squirrels dashed high into the tree, disappearing somewhere in the branches. A single fishing boat was in the center of the bay, now tossed about by whitecaps. On the far shore, the treetops, so recently soaking up the pleasant afternoon sun, now whipped before the gusts. Leaves ripped free and receded into the distance.

With an aching tightness in his chest, feet dragging with every step, he rose and made the slow trip home.

Where could he borrow enough money to buy a new bike?

His first commission check no longer seemed such a sure thing.

CHAPTER 5

Hadn't an hour already passed? When Lars claimed this bench outside of the terminal, the sun had been overhead. Now, it cast the first of the afternoon shadows, testimony to time spent twiddling his thumbs. Time he didn't have.

On arrival in Two Rivers, he'd taken his message to the college and handed it to the head librarian, a spinsterly woman with a pinched face, but kindly eyes. She slipped it into her sweater, then returned to her reading. Per Phillip's instructions, Lars then came here to wait.

The two-hour window he'd set for this meeting was almost over. He'd be forced to depart for Capital when the next southbound express arrived.

He searched for any sign of Curtis, eyes squinted against the midday sun on concrete, knees bouncing. He couldn't stop shaking. What if Curtis never got the letter or something happened to his friend? What if the Order intercepted it and was surrounding Lars, even now?

A dirty old woman approached. Her shapeless coat much too warm for this weather, the hood shadowed a smudged face turned groundward. She pushed a tattered baby carriage, the contraption piled high with jumbled possessions, and Lars had to lean far forward to see past it. One of the unfortunates who had fallen out of society, she mumbled to herself, arguing with an invisible companion.

He had sympathy, of course, but was ill-equipped. He squirmed on the bench, gaze darting everywhere but at the woman. As she shuffled closer, he leaned further forward, intent on his vigil.

A pain rammed his sternum. His hand flew to the spot, and he checked for blood. An object now lay in his lap, a square of fabric tied about a stone. Why would that old lady hit him with a rock?

He untied the rag and unfolded a slip of paper inside, the words stark—*Wait a few minutes, then follow me. Keep your distance. C.*

MARIPOL SLAMMED a fist on the desk, toppling an untidy stack of books. He closed his eyes and breathed, then reopened them to glare at the man across from him.

The man, a professor of languages, trembled. But to his credit, he repeated the message. "I'm sorry, sir, but these are not ancient texts." He tensed, shrinking in on himself, neck retracting into his starched white shirt collar, but when Maripol failed to strike him down, he unwound. "I've made a perusal of the scrolls and prepared an advance summary. It will, of course, take many days to make complete translations."

He slid a document across the desk toward Maripol, pushing it with a pencil, apparently attempting to stay out of easy reach.

Maripol scowled at the report. "Grandma's recipes?" He shot the man a look. "This has to be some sort of code."

"That is, of course, possible. Cryptography is not my field of study. I'm only expert in ancient languages, but I doubt that to be the case."

"Why?"

"Each scroll is in a different hand, and all appear to be of various ages—but each is a copy of the same text, which can best be summarized as 'Grandma's Recipes.' The beginning of each scroll is by an unpracticed hand but gradually improves with fewer mistakes and corrections. My initial guess would be we are looking at lesson work done by young students of the language."

Maripol gritted his teeth, maintaining an unmoving demeanor. Of late, for the first time in his long career, that had become difficult. Where had his icy core gone? What had happened to the man who could be moved by nothing?

They'd been duped, and even though it hadn't been *his* mistake, he'd pay for it if he didn't correct the course soon. This fiasco, on top of his failure to track down that cursed priest, Curtis, were career-ending errors. In this line of work, there was no such thing as being put out to pasture. Unless being buried under one counted.

Before Maripol's arrival, the local Order chief had concentrated only on tracking Hilkiah into the desert, planning to seize the man when he had recovered these supposedly ancient manuscripts from a cave. The locals had made only a cursory effort to watch Jeremiah, the son. Sloppy work, that was, and now Jeremiah had slipped away. Had evaded the watchers.

When Maripol arrived, he had, out of habit, enacted protocols to locate the young man. Loose ends were not to be tolerated, no matter how insignificant.

Now, all his hopes were pinned on those efforts.

He shouted for his attaché. When the man swiveled from his post guarding the door and into the office, Maripol raised a hand to halt any greeting. "Get me immediate updates on the search for Jeremiah."

"I received word he's been located in Mazkelon, a city on the coast of Mare Nostrum." At Maripol's dark look, the attaché paled. "I hadn't wanted to disturb you, sir. This information is less than five minutes old."

Maripol slapped the desk again. The last of the books hopped into the air, then tumbled, joining their fellows. He scraped back his chair, its wooden legs grating on stone tiles. "Get our best code breakers on those scrolls. Professor, our team will coordinate with you. Complete the full translations and make yourself available to the crypto team."

To his attaché, Maripol said, "Alert the chopper. We'll be leading the capture of Jeremiah. Get me a direct link with the team on the ground. Make it clear: They're to take him, but take him *alive.*"

LARS FOLLOWED the old woman away from the terminal and into a residential neighborhood, the street overshadowed by mature trees. He stayed a block or more behind, keeping an eye on his quarry.

He lost sight of her as she topped a rise and descended out of sight. With her moving so slowly, he didn't bother to hurry and catch up. He wasn't losing her.

When he crested the same ridgeline, ahead was nothing but empty sidewalk, descending for a ways before again rising up a gentle slope. The woman had vanished.

Heart skipping, he dashed uphill, searching in both directions. He pulled abreast of a tree-lined alley, and movement flashed to his left. There she was, opening an old-fashioned swing-up garage door and pushing her perambulator inside. She glanced toward him and limped into the garage, motioning him to enter.

He followed, then stopped short of the door, and peered into the dark interior. Was it wise to be trapped in there and with an unbalanced person?

A hand grabbed his collar and hauled him through. The door slammed on his rear. The woman straightened and smothered him in a hug.

He stiffened, arms at his sides. He'd known it. This had been a mistake. If she'd let go, he'd make a run for it. He struggled to break the grip, so strong for such a derelict, but the arms wrapped him even tighter.

Lips next to his ear, she said, "Son, it is so good to see you."

That voice. It was a man's voice. The arms let him go, now gripping him by the upper biceps and holding him at arm's length. He looked into Father Curtis's dark eyes. Lars grabbed his friend and scooped him into another embrace. "Father, oh thank Eternal."

When the backslapping bear hug ended, Curtis dug out a ragged lawn chair. He dusted it and offered it to Lars, then sat on a crate across from him.

Lars gestured to the jumble. "Is this where you live?"

"Oh no. We often use such abandoned homes for meeting places. Don't worry. Other men are watching the area. We'll be warned if danger approaches."

"Father. What in the Hegemony is going on? Why have you disavowed the writings? The Eternal? I thought you believed!" Lars gasped a slight sob at the last. Not until this moment had the full force hit him, how shaken he'd been to hear his trusted mentor had thrown over their shared faith.

"Son, I'm so sorry for the pain this has caused. If I could take that pain for you, I would. I struggled long, deciding what to tell you." Curtis gripped Lars's forearm. "You deserved the truth, though I wish we had been less rushed, had taken the proper time to work through it together. But I was unsure if I'd ever see you again." Now Curtis's voice choked, and he released Lars and sat up straighter as if to regain composure.

"Oh, I do want to know the truth, of course. But I don't understand."

Curtis sighed a long sigh. "Perhaps one day I will tell you all. Or not." He laughed to himself. "What is truly important, I'll tell you now. I already told you I learned the Writings were a lie, the Eternal was a false god, yes?"

"Yeah." Lars rolled his eyes. "And do you have any idea what a state I've been in since?"

Curtis snorted. "I can guess. I was in a similar state myself, but tell me about your struggle, what's going on in your mind, having heard these things?"

"My mind? I feel like I woke up from a nightmare to a world I don't recognize and learned the nightmare wasn't a dream at all." Lars swallowed, struggling with his jumbled thoughts while Curtis sat in silence, patient as always. "I liked to study the Writings. Following the teachings, serving the Eternal, I felt like a good person. It made me feel safe, made me happy."

Curtis slapped a knee. "I, too, valued these things, but isn't it better, more important, to serve a real God, to serve the truth?"

"What god? You said there is a God in heaven and asked me to pray to and seek the Creator God, whoever that is. But I don't know Him. How do I *know* this new god is real? Where are His writings?" Lars stood and paced as he talked, arms animating his speech.

Father Curtis came and placed hands on Lars's shoulders, stilling him. "I'll answer your questions, but I won't be able to tell you, at least yet, how I know these things. Can you trust me? Trust what I say is true?"

Tensed shoulders relaxed under Curtis's hold. "Of course I trust you. And I do want to know."

"Understand that, once you hear this, you can't unhear it and to possess this truth is dangerous. The Order will consider it high heresy. If they learn you harbor this secret, they'll hunt you down and silence you."

There was no consideration. Lars's heart burned. "Tell me."

"Very well. Sit and let me tell you a story." Curtis sat, head down and eyes closed, perhaps praying. "Long ago, beyond living memory, there were many religions. Powerful men unified the world politically and economically, but they didn't control the various faiths. They well understood that politics is downstream of culture, but culture is always downstream of theology. To have dominion over the world, they needed to do so through religion. So they took the most popular elements of the world-belief systems and created a new one. One of their own making. One serving their agenda. Thus was born the Writings and the Order."

Lars squirmed in his seat. This couldn't be true. No, all he'd ever believed couldn't be a lie, one made by evil men to amass power? No way everyone in the world would accept such a lie. He opened his mouth to object.

But Curtis lifted a hand. "Follow along. I'll answer your questions once I've told you the full story."

Curtis leaned in, eyes intense beneath those bushy dark brows. "Trust me when I tell you this is true. Believe me when I say I've seen the evidence. The Writings are false, but I now know the true God, Creator God. I've also seen enough to know that, before the Order had banned it and destroyed all existing copies, there was a book, the Scriptures of one of the old religions. It taught of Creator God. It taught truth. There are those who attempt to recover those writings, the True Text."

He seemed to reconsider whether he should continue. Then a new gravity weighted his voice. "This group is known as the Seekers, and I am now one of them."

JEREMIAH ENTERED the brightly lit cathedral. Even in his distress, the high arched ceiling, all glass and steel was a marvel. The streaming daylight made the ornamented white edifice, six stories tall, almost too bright for unshielded eyes.

He squinted. Row after row of seating marched across the expanse. In a far corner, the raised dais held an altar, and above it on the wall hung the huge symbol of the Eternal, at least twenty feet across and also gleaming white. Where were the confessionals?

Jittering with unspent adrenaline, muscles twitching, he shaded his eyes. To remain so exposed, in such a public space, was suicide. His photo was still plastered on every lamppost, even on this building's front door. Was that priest, the one chatting with the group to the left, sending furtive glances in his direction? Was that couple in the back row staring at him?

Maybe he was at the wrong temple? Or his father had been given bad information? Intentionally? A trap? It was time to get out of here, go to ground somewhere, anywhere, until he could figure things out. He turned to go.

But there, on the right-hand side, was a row of enclosed booths, painted the same blinding white as the walls, blending in as the glare obscured them. He lowered his head and slipped toward the second from the left, the appointed place.

He checked his watch. Good, still on time, thank heavens. The local operative was to be here for the same two-hour window every day. His belly churned anew. But what if he wasn't?

He opened the door to the closet-like space and knelt on the low padded bench. An impenetrable screen separated him from the priest who, assumedly, waited on the other side. Was anyone there? Was the *right* man there?

He was trapped in this tiny booth. What if they had waited for him to lock himself in? Maybe he should get out now, while he still could.

He took a deep, shaky breath. No, he was here to fulfill an age-old oath. *Oh, Lord, guide and protect me.*

He then recited the prearranged words. "Forgive me, Father, for I have sinned. I have sinned against the Order as has my father and his father before him, for generations without number."

From the unseen priest came the answering pass phrase. "The Eternal will forgive all, my son, as will the Order, as long as you seek."

"But I cannot forgive the Order."

A latch clicked.

Jeremiah flinched and reached for the knob that would allow him to open the booth entrance, to flee.

But a panel separating him from the priest swung wide. Beyond it, an older man in black robes beckoned. "Come. Hurry."

Frozen in place, Jeremiah glanced toward the priest and then the door, his path to freedom. But something in the priest's eyes, something kind, something gentle yet strong, reminded him of his father. He couldn't distrust such eyes.

Spurring his still frozen limbs to action, he squeezed through, and the man latched the panel into place, then twisted both decorative finials on the carved chair where he'd been sitting.

The rear wall swung away to a narrow, rough-hewn stairway descending into stony darkness.

CHAPTER 6

Lars struggled to gather himself.

He'd had so much to ask Father Curtis, and now everything in his head was ajumble. He couldn't get a single thought to hold still long enough to grab hold of it.

And then there was no more time. The cursed whistle sounded. It wasn't fair. So much still didn't make sense, but the warning whistle blew again, the final call. He hugged Father Curtis, snagged up his pack, and ran, nearly flying down the steep slope.

He'd delayed too long. When he was halfway down the hill, the train became visible where it rested in the yard. The last passenger boarded, and the conductor closed the doors.

Lars blew through the terminal entrance, slid across the polished concrete floor, and ducked through the passenger gate as the conductor was closing it. The man snagged him by the sleeve, only releasing him when Lars showed his ticket. With a reproving look, he relented. Lars climbed into the passenger car, and the wagon train pulled away, headed south to Capital. He stood in the narrow aisle, panting and sweaty, gripping a handhold.

With no open seat, he and one other late arrival spent the entire miserable trip on their feet, bounced and jostled by the potted road.

The straps of his pack dug into his neck, its weight stabbing deeper with every bump.

The physical misery was barely a match for the mental turmoil. How was he supposed to deal with this? His head understood, of a sort anyway, what Father Curtis had told him, but his heart couldn't keep up. Probably didn't want to.

Worse, Father Curtis's answers weren't answers at all, just more mysteries, not anything from which a body could gather any sort of clarity. For sure, not him. He was lost and blind in the wilderness with no map, and the only advice Curtis could give him was to "ask Creator God"? Really? How was he supposed to do that? Where was he supposed to find this god of Curtis's?

Upon arrival at the hotel, he collapsed onto his bed, still fully clothed, and clunked his pack to the floor.

He almost wished Father Curtis never turned his world upside down. Almost.

But something was going on deep inside him, some sort of thrill, like the one when he broke a trail into the wilds, going somewhere he'd never been before, unsure what wonderful new thing he might discover.

Still, something was missing, and he didn't know how to find it. Father Curtis had been no help. Really? Ask Creator God? Lars would love to if someone would point Him out, offer directions to His meeting room.

But lacking a guide, someone to teach him, how was he ever going to understand?

His limbs grew heavy. His mind began to cloud. He whispered to the lengthening shadows. "How will I ever get answers? How will I ever know Creator God if no one shows me the way?"

He closed his eyelids, just for a minute. Just to ease his burning eyes, still whispering those same questions over and over.

Wouldn't someone, somewhere, offer some answers?

~

Phillip waited at the safe house Jonathon set up in Mazkelon. He'd prowled the floor plan, moving window to window until he knew how many steps it took to get between any one of them. If he paced any longer, he'd wear paths deeply enough into the floorboards to guide his steps in the dark. Handy, that'd be if the evening grew any darker. He'd not be lighting any candles this night.

For hours now, the fine hairs on the back of his neck had tingled. Jonathon was too long gone. Had something gone awry? Was a strike team even now about to breach the door? Phillip again checked the approaches, peering through slit drapes, standing well back to ensure his moving shadow wasn't visible from the street.

The not knowing caused muscles to ache, too long primed for a fight. To wait, inactive, unable to engage in that fight was even worse. Members of his team could be out there in need. While he did nothing.

He raised the handheld radio to his lips, then for the hundredth time, let it fall to his side, the mike unkeyed. He'd been the one to order radio silence, except in an emergency. He'd not be the one to betray it.

But he'd never sent men into peril, only to hole up in safety like some fat overseer, shirking duty. He'd always been in the action. The danger. Doing something about it.

The men he'd been tasked to transport were twenty-four hours overdue. If the rumor was true, one of them had been captured and could be leading the Eye here. A certainty, in fact, if he was still alive.

He prowled the room to check the windows again, glancing at his watch as he did so. Twenty-four hours and thirteen minutes late.

A flickering shape outside moved toward the rear entrance. The door banged open, and he crouched, ready to repel attack. Jonathon rushed in, dragging a pale young man with shockingly black hair, an obvious dye job, and badly done. Locking the door behind himself, Jonathon watched through slit curtains.

Apparently satisfied, he turned, still panting as if from some marathon sprint. "David, this is Jeremiah, the boy we've been looking for. We're in a bit of trouble."

DIANA HAD BEEN PAYING the sleepless price of her late-night antics, so when Leif arrived home from work so early, she left him to watch the kids while she took a nice nap. What luxury, no kids yelling for her attention.

She woke, the dull pain in her temples gone and fresh energy buzzing in her veins. Too bad, she didn't get this treatment every day. Her stomach growled, and she padded downstairs to find something to eat.

Balancing her sandwich and a glass of wine, she walked onto the deck and sat at the patio table. Leif and the kids were in the backyard, Leif in a lawn chair, a tumbler in his hand while the kids played on the swing set. When he saw her, he stood and climbed the deck stairs toward her. His walk was steady, but his unfocused eyes betrayed his inebriation.

She rolled her eyes. "Can't you watch the kids for one hour without getting tanked?"

He set his jaw, pivoted, walked into the house, and slammed the patio door behind him.

"The heck with you, buddy," she muttered. She didn't need to put up with this. She was tired of Leif, tired of him working all hours, ignoring her, and taking her for granted.

He always assumed she'd be there, waiting whenever he decided to play husband, and lately, he never bothered to do that. On the rare occasions he *was* home, he spent his time brooding and drinking.

She refilled her wineglass and walked to her room to get ready. She was going out. He could deal with the kids himself for a change.

PHILLIP LOOKED THROUGH SLITTED BLINDS, watching the empty street. How long would it remain so? If Jonathon was to be believed, someone had kicked an anthill, and the ants were swarming this way.

"My contact with local operatives verified it," Jonathon said.

"Order forces are crawling over the city, and more troop transports are arriving by the hour."

Phillip nodded. "And you were spotted extracting Jeremiah from the cathedral?"

"For sure. If not for the priest's efforts, we'd be in custody."

Now, all routes in or out of the city had been blocked. Phillip studied the map in his head for an alternate escape route, for any tool he might use.

Jonathan poured himself a cup of water and gulped it down. "Can we still use our original plan?"

That plan had called for Hilkiah, Jeremiah, and Phillip to board a luxury yacht and sail across the sea, eventually arriving back in the Republic.

Could they? Phillip closed his eyes and rubbed them. "The boat's docked in the civilian marina, and the place is a perfect trap. The seawall protecting the harbor has only one tight passage to open waters, an ideal choke point. Order forces can block any escape."

Yet he could find no better option.

At a hint of movement outside, Phillip motioned Jonathon to protect Jeremiah, then stationed himself behind the door. It inched open. An unfamiliar face poked through. Phillip grabbed the man's wrist and took him to the ground, knee to his neck, only releasing pressure when the man offered the correct passcode.

Once on his feet, the messenger dusted his clothes. "Authorities have begun sweeping the city door-to-door, searching for Jeremiah, starting at the eastern outskirts and moving westward. At the current rate, they'll arrive here just before sunup."

Phillip smacked a fist into an open palm. "Looks like they're forcing us toward the sea, whether we want to go that way or not." And the time to implement an alternate scheme was fleeting. He began gathering gear. "Pack up. We leave just after midnight."

Jeremiah didn't share fluency in Phillip and Jonathon's native tongue, and his own was unintelligible to them. Prior to the Bad Times, Common Tongue had been the language of worldwide trade and was still the default international language, as well as that of the

Republic. Through trial and error, they had established that all three spoke that tongue, if painfully.

Phillip framed his first question to Jeremiah, the most pressing. “Hilkiah have scrolls?”

Jeremiah scrunched his brows in seeming incomprehension. Then his eyes widened. “Yes. Has scrolls.”

Although expected, the answer hit like a physical blow, driving breath from Phillip’s lungs with an audible *oomph*. The rumor was true. Hilkiah had been captured with the precious texts. If only Phillip had gotten the message sooner. Had only arrived more quickly. He pushed those feelings aside, bringing that part of himself under control until the mission was accomplished.

Time enough for self-incrimination later.

He was honor bound to bring this young man to safety, that mission now more pressing than ever. Jeremiah was the only living man the Seekers had ever discovered who’d studied actual copies of the True Text. Even though the scrolls were lost, or especially because of that, the knowledge in this young head was invaluable. He must be brought safely out of this trap at any cost. Any cost, including Phillip’s own life. Thus was the path of honor.

He whispered to Jonathon. “We move together to boat. You two on board are to be. I then start fire in boat far from seawall, a diversion this is. You then sail fast. I take out guards at choke point before you are there. Is best I know to do.”

Jonathon shrugged, palms up, and after an abortive attempt to find words, abandoned Common Tongue for their own shared language. “A wonderful plan, except I have never operated a sailing craft. More of a motorboat guy myself. And where am I to go? You’re the one with the contacts across the water. You take the boat. I’ll take out the guards.”

But Jeremiah’s head had begun jerking, coal-black locks flying. He set his jaw and hugged his pack to his chest. “No leave without Father.”

Phillip held up a hand. How to explain in Common? “You in

country take up Seeker resources. Can't free father while keep you safe."

The boy sullenly assented, but he extracted a promise that Hilkiah would be rescued at all costs.

Phillip won out with Jeremiah but lost the argument with Jonathon. Phillip would pilot the boat while Jonathon took out the harbor guards. A suicide mission at best, a terrible compromise. He, Phillip, again sitting idle while another took physical risks on his behalf. There had to be some other way, but what?

Midnight came and went. In the early morning hours, they slipped across a public park, gliding like shadows over the patchy grass, keeping to what cover they could find in the palms bordering the open spaces. Phillip's nerves were charged, blood singing in his ears, eyes identifying every shadow, mind calculating angles of approach and lines of sight as they ran.

Beyond a wide street running parallel to the beach, the moonlight reflected from foamy breakers. They crossed the pavement, affecting a casual stroll, and approached the chain-link fence surrounding the marina. A sign announced that no unauthorized craft would be allowed to exit the harbor.

But the guards continued to sit at a table near the fence, playing cards, paying them no mind. They passed the gate and onto the boardwalk.

It made sense. They wouldn't care who entered the marina. Many people lived on craft here, coming and going. They'd be watching the seaward side.

His guts clenched tighter. If only he could mitigate the danger Jonathon was about to face there.

Inside, Jonathon led the way along the wide wooden walkways. He turned aside onto one of the many slips and pointed to their sailboat, the *Tikvah*, a sleek red-hulled craft smaller than the surrounding boats. About thirty feet in length, sizable enough for ocean travel, if barely, but also manageable without a large crew.

Jonathon climbed the ladder to the main deck and made a quick sweep of the boat, then signaled Jeremiah up. Phillip was about to follow when the boardwalk vibrated with the passage of booted feet. He vaulted aboard, then crouched, and spun left, then right.

Men were closing on them, handheld lights swinging as they ran. There were at least four squads, forty-eight men or so. Too many to take on in a fight.

The soldiers closed, weapons raised, hemming them in.

There would be no escape.

CHAPTER 7

Father Curtis yawned and stretched, then pushed aside the documents he'd been studying.

He did a double take at his watch. How had so many hours passed and without him noticing? But it was so easy to lose track in his windowless hideaway home. Even more so when absorbed in this work, this study that consumed his days since his arrival.

With another glance at that pile, he laughed. To the Order, possession of these documents would convict him of high heresy. Ironic, then, that a wrongful accusation of the same heresy had been the impetus for his flight from the Order's hunters and brought him here, to this.

As a result, once innocent, he was now quite guilty and glad of it, even if this current task seemed a hopeless one.

Across the table, Professor Reuel bent his white head over his own work. The furious scratching of his pen on paper and the fizzling candlewick offered the only sounds.

"I'm ready to give up." Curtis ruffled again through the mismatched documents. "We're never going to reassemble the True Text from this mishmash." He tossed the papers back to the table. "We need full copies of the originals, not these fragments."

Dare he ask the question that had pursued his every thought since Phillip's departure? "Is it possible Phillip might recover authentic documents?"

Professor Reuel's pen stopped, and the customary smile curved his wizened face. His twinkling blue eyes sparkled from deep in their spiderweb pockets. "Oh, my boy, how can you be so impatient? Only weeks ago, you accepted the false Writings as holy writ. Now you expect to reassemble the True Text, lost for generations, in days?"

He wagged his pen at Curtis. "You swore your oath as Seeker knowing full well this work has taken many decades and will likely take many more. If there are no more Keepers, no more original copies of the True Text, our work is the only hope. If we fail, the world will never again know the truth, never again be able to learn about Creator God."

A flush spread up Curtis's neck. So many had devoted uncounted years, sometimes sacrificing their very lives for this effort. Who was he to insist on fast or easy? "I still pray Phillip returns with the True Text. After all, I served the lies of the Order all my adult life. Now that I possess the truth, now that I have some limited knowledge of Creator God, I'm anxious for answers."

He shivered, then wrapped a sweater tighter around his frame. But the shudders kept running deeper to his core. "I've said nothing, but my dreams are getting more disturbing. I sense an urgency, an impending danger. We don't have much time."

No doubt, these dreams had a meaning. Indeed, he was seeing such visions for a reason. But what?

If this was the only hope, he wouldn't give up the fight. He picked up his notebook. Ignoring his aching back, his burning eyes, he resumed reading.

The professor turned to his writing.

With a jolt, they both sat upright. He and the old man looked at one another and simultaneously said, "Phillip!"

"My dear boy, we must pray," the old man said.

Both slid out of their chairs, assuming a posture of fervent prayer, and there, they remained. Inexplicable tears ran down Curtis's face and in rivulets across folded hands and soaked shirt cuffs as, with no idea why, they pled that Creator God be with Phillip.

LARS WOKE, still fully clothed, hands shaking so violently it took two matches to light the bedside candle. Once the wick took, the expanding circle of yellow light revealed the musty hotel room, the worn floral coverlet.

He rubbed his face to expunge his dream, one in which Phillip was surrounded by armed men, men who would torture and then kill Lars's friend. He had at first rolled over, seeking the fading threads of sleep, but the dream was too disturbing to allow slumber to take him. Instead, his heart pounded, and the need to rise, to do *something* overwhelmed him.

And even now, the intensity of those dream-inspired emotions didn't abate as they should.

He fell off his bed, driven to his knees by a compulsion to pray. And pray he did. He prayed as he never had in his life, not with the memorized, rote devotions of the Eternal, but in words drawn from his heart, his thoughts, his deep yearning.

When, much later, time again began its normal progression, the whole of the experience remained imprinted upon his soul. But strangely, he couldn't recall a single word of his pleas for Phillip, though they must've lasted for hours, judging by the now melted stub of what had been a new candle.

What he did retain was a memory implanted into the fiber of his being, one of connectedness with the divine he'd never experienced. That very afternoon, he'd asked Father Curtis to show him who the real God was, and in this, his request had been answered.

He now knew the Creator of the universe with a knowing that couldn't be captured by mere words. In a flash, he lunged for the desk, pulling pen and paper from the drawer. He had to write this down, preserve it. Relate it in some way Leif would understand. Would accept for himself.

After dozens of abortive attempts, he dropped the pen. There was no way words could communicate that moment, this thing granted specially and specifically to him, a precious gift from Creator God. No way to impart this *knowing* to another.

He put his head on his hands and wept mixed tears—joy for what he'd experienced and agony that he couldn't give this experience to anyone else.

Phillip hunched beneath the almost physical sensation, the crushing weight of helplessness. Of defeat.

Bad enough that he and Jonathon had come to their end, but to lose Jeremiah and his irreplaceable knowledge? He must buy his escape, even if it cost Phillip's life.

He searched, his gaze flashing from the boardwalks to the water, then the walls. There was always a way if only he seized upon it in time. But there was nothing, not a single opening in the trap, no weakness to be exploited.

He placed his body in front of the others, facing the incoming threat. His death might buy them time, create an opening they could use. The only certainty, though, was that capture was no option. Anything but that.

Behind him, Jonathon shouted, terror in his voice.

Phillip whirled, ready to spring toward some new threat. Instead, he fell to his knees, the strength departing his limbs, the breath his lungs.

Three men, unnaturally large, stood on the boat deck. They shone with an inner radiance so bright he couldn't look directly upon them.

"Fear not!" the one in the center boomed. "Do not kneel before me. Stand and prepare for departure."

Another headed toward the front of the boat and shouted orders to the soldiers.

The uniformed men saluted, formed up, turned, then marched back toward the city.

Mechanically, as if in a daze, Phillip readied the craft to launch. Everything moved with liquid slowness, colors intense, sounds ultra-clear and yet distorted as if heard under water.

He fired up the inboard motors, the throaty murmur bubbling from beneath the hull, vibrating the soles of his boots, and nodded for Jonathon to untie the moorings. They navigated the maze of slips, then toward the seawall and the sole exit.

What about the soldiers guarding that exit? Surely, they'd open fire? But when they neared the narrow break in the concrete barrier, the position was unmanned. They glided past and into the open sea.

Phillip gave Jeremiah the helm and plucked Jonathon's sleeve. He led him to the mainmast, and they unfurled the sail. Then, as if the fog enshrouding his mind cleared, he came to himself and paused. "Where did they go?"

Jonathon raised his brows. "I was going to ask you. I looked away. When I looked back, they were gone."

Pausing work on the sails, Phillip and Jonathon searched the ship. Nothing. The mysterious visitors had left as they had arrived, in the blink of an eye and seemingly from nowhere.

Phillip leapt up the companionway in two bounds. "Time for mysteries later. Now we make a run for it."

They raised the sail, and it filled, popping, the curve of the sheet pregnant with the captive breeze. The vessel heeled under, the deck surging beneath his feet, their wake now churning white foam. He took the helm and aimed the prow west, a fair wind off their port quarter. He glanced rearward, and the air, streaming with the speed of their passage, swept his hair forward to flap about his forehead. The twinkling shore lights receded astern until they were lost in the hazy blue distance.

Phillip turned away from the land of his birth, of his inheritance, and faced the place he now called home, the only place in the world where he was known, loved. Where he now had a new family.

He might even live long enough to see them again.

A great miracle that would be, indeed.

CHAPTER 8

Old Bob lived just past the south side of town. Leif rode his rattletrap bike down the gravel road, following the curving railroad tracks.

In all his years in Northwoods, he'd never been to this tree-lined lane. It was an isolated location, well off the beaten path and well concealed, tucked between rail lines, timber, and cornfields. Alert for the rusty saw blade, the sign by which he'd been told to recognize the turnoff, he continued to pedal, the chain grating with every rotation. It better not fall off way out here.

And there it was, on his left, an old circular blade nailed to a post. He turned off the road and onto the steep driveway. He walked the bike up the berm and stopped short of the tracks to take in the sawmill previously hidden from the road.

A thick tangle of trees to the west, the westbound railroad on the south, and the northbound on that border, bracketed a six-acre site wedged within those two rail embankments, which, having run side by side, now veered off toward their respective compass points.

A ramshackle cottage lay tucked into the trees on the west edge. Neat piles of logs were stacked next to a siding parallel to the northernmost line. On the eastern border stood a brick building with a tall smokestack, the kiln, backed by the timber overgrowing the parallel railroad rights-of-way. A low, open-sided structure with a rusted tin roof occupied the gravel yard's center.

Leif lay his bike in the ditch to hide it from the house. The rusty thing was less embarrassing than his pink chariot, but still. He walked, gravel crunching, toward the heart of the operation, the mill. He stopped outside of the open-sided building, surveying the complex assemblage of gears and conveyors.

The huge circular blade was at least five, maybe six, feet across. A foot-wide belt connected it to the power source, an old tractor mounted on a steel frame. A large pulley, the mate to the smaller one at the blade, replaced its one remaining rear wheel.

"Amazing piece, ain't it? Nothing else like it anywhere hereabouts."

Leif jumped. A man wearing faded canvas overalls and a checked flannel shirt had materialized at his elbow. Intent on the machine, Leif hadn't heard the approach. A little older than Leif, he had a gentle face beneath mousy brown hair. A lean hand, rough and steely in contrast to the face, reached for Leif's.

German had led him to expect a much older man. Leif shook the hand. "Old Bob?"

"Oh, lands no." The man chuckled. "Old Bob's my dad. I'm Young Bob. Pops asked me to show you round. He don't get out of the house much. Bad knees."

"So you know how to run this thing?"

"Sure. I've been helping Pops all my life. Don't run her much anymore, though. Fuel for the tractor, you know."

"Mind if I see it in operation?"

"Can try." And Bob did try. And try. And try. He got the old machine to cough a cloud of black smoke, but never started the engine.

After thirty sweaty minutes, Leif gripped Bob's shoulder. "Stop. Let's be real here. These machines need some work before they're gonna run. What'll it take to get everything here in working condition? By the end of the week, let's say?"

Bob massaged his chin, leaving a greasy handprint. "Not sure it can be done. She'd need spark plugs, maybe plug wires. Fuel, of course. I'm guessing that's the biggest problem. The gas I scrounged was old." He scratched under one overall strap. "I did strain it. Was plenty dirty, though. So prob'ly a fuel filter too, come to think of it. Tall order, all told."

Leif opened a pocket notebook and scribbled in it. He tore out the page and handed it to Bob. "Whatever you need, you put it on my account. Here's the authorization. I want a successful test run before we try to show this to Haman."

Young Bob's face lit. "Fair enough, Mr. Leif. I'll have 'er running like a top." He rocked back on his heels, gripping his overall straps. "It'll do Pops good to see the old mill working again. A bit of him died when he had to shut 'er down."

The sight of that authorization in Young Bob's hand, for all purposes a blank check, caused a momentary twinge. But you have to spend money to make money, right?

Besides, how much could a few little parts cost?

Lars woke early and wandered to the lobby café. He should have been fuzzy from lack of sleep, but he felt rested and sharp. Didn't even mind the fake eggs and ersatz coffee, much. Though why would anyone eat this stuff, given a choice?

Fueled and caffeinated, he opened a book at the hotel room desk. Referring to it repeatedly, he composed a coded letter to Father Curtis. It read simply: "I have met who you told me to seek. Please tell me how I can learn more about Him."

He addressed and stamped the envelope and dropped it at the front desk as he exited the building. He walked through the early morning streets, his step springy, the rising sun glorious, the crisp fall air refreshing, the sounds of a waking city a symphony. It was as if he had gone to sleep in one world, two-dimensional and gray, and awakened to this full-color three-dimensional wonderland.

He rounded the corner to the administration building, low and squat. Even these new eyes of his couldn't make that place look good.

Time to deliver this message to Haman. He shuddered. That man warranted a wide berth.

At the reception counter, he stated his business. The young desk clerk eyed him dubiously. "Name?"

She then repeated it into the mouthpiece. Her eyes widened before she replaced the receiver in the cradle. "You'll find the advisor's office if you—"

Lars held up a hand. "Been there. Know the way."

Once up the multiple flights of stairs and down the well-remembered corridor, the carpet so thick he was afraid he might lose a shoe in it, he brushed his knuckles on the doorjamb.

The powerful man lifted his head, hand resting on a sheaf of paperwork. "Ah, young Lars, so nice to see you again." Haman didn't stand but pointed to a well-padded leather chair opposite his own. "To what do I owe this pleasure?"

Lars stammered and in answer pulled the message from his briefcase and slid it across the desk.

Haman picked it up and turned it over before slitting it with a letter opener. He read the message, refolded it, and slipped it back into the envelope. "I am scheduled to arrive in Northwoods three weeks from tomorrow. I'll try to come sooner and might be able to make it up by Friday. Kindly inform your brother I shall inspect the sawmill at that time."

He rested the letter opener on Leif's envelope, point first, like a sword ready to plunge through a heart. "Assure him this *issue* will be dealt with."

PHILLIP SAT at the helm facing backward where the purple hues of the predawn sky brightened, then the huge, red wavering ball of the sun began to crest the endless perfect arc where ocean met sky. The horizon, that flaming orb, were so massive, on a scale beyond anything ever experienced by land dwellers, much the pity. And the colors! Indescribable.

He raised his face to that sky, eyes closed, the better to luxuriate in the soft breeze playing on his neck. Warm. Gentle. Almost loving. The quartering wind had continued all night, almost as if shepherding them home.

He searched again. No land. No other vessel in sight. Unbelievable no pursuit had appeared, no intercepting gunship plowed through the waves. Just them, the water, and the open sky.

Jonathon pushed through the hatch and climbed onto deck.

"Sleep well?" Phillip asked, his mother tongue rolling free.

The dark bags under Jonathon's eyes were answer enough. "Worried they'd be tracking us down."

"No sign of them yet." Phillip waved toward the bow, indicating the empty waters. "Hey, what's your real name, anyway? We might as well dispense with the aliases. Mine's Phillip."

He reached to shake hands as Jonathon said, "Mine's Thaddeus. Nice to meet you, Phillip." Thaddeus stared for some time, watching the burbling foam in their wake. "What was I thinking?"

Phillip raised an eyebrow.

"Why did I stay on the boat?" Thaddeus waved rearward. "Now how do I get home? To my family?"

Running fingers through his wind-tousled mop, Phillip grimaced. "Things were so confused back there. I hardly thought of it. Trying to stay alive took all my attention, I guess." That strange feeling, like the world had changed, like time had expanded. "And I was in a fugue for a while there. It's all fuzzy now."

Lips pursed, brow wrinkled, Thaddeus nodded. "I guess that's it. I wasn't thinking, either. Just acting, my only thought to get Jeremiah clear."

Phillip fisted Thaddeus's shoulder. "We can get you transport once I make contact with my people. All you have to do is enjoy the vacation while we sail across the wide blue ocean." But Thaddeus's expression hardly looked any more cheerful, so Phillip punched him again, then patted that shoulder. "No second-guessing. Your focus was where it needed to be. Neither you nor I mattered as much as getting Jeremiah to safety. With the scrolls gone, what he knows is all we have left."

Thaddeus didn't answer, just stared rearward, fine blond hair whipping about his face. "What, exactly, happened last night?"

Phillip pursed his lips. "I've been wondering the same. But you saw them too. Right? Those three big, shining . . . whatever they were."

A grunt escaped Thaddeus. "If you saw them, I guess I did too. Though if you'd claimed it was all my imagination, I'd have believed you." Another long pause. "So if they were real, please explain what they were. What they were doing there? Why in all the world did they help *us*?"

Great questions. Why? But Phillip had seen similar before, hadn't he? That night, the one of the Garden of the Lion. He'd never understood the meaning of that episode either, and now this?

Jeremiah popped his head out of the hatch. "Breakfast for anyone?"

He held a skillet full of scrambled eggs. The aroma shook Phillip free of his reverie, and he accepted a heaping plate, then hoisted a generous spoonful toward his mouth. The eggs may have been powdered, but they seemed like ambrosia. How had he not noticed how hungry he'd become? Surviving certain death added such renewed zest for life.

As he and Thaddeus wolfed down the second round of man-sized portions, Jeremiah raised his hand like a shy schoolboy. "Where best place to make safe scrolls?"

Phillip put down his half-finished plate. The problem with this kind of work was the language barrier. It made his head hurt. Give him mortal threat any day. For that, he had all the tools he needed, but for this? "Make safe what?"

"Place safe for scrolls."

"You say father has."

Jeremiah squinched up his face as if searching for words. "Yes, he has. But I have." Obviously frustrated by his inability to make himself clear, he raised a finger, then laid open his pack to remove a leather case. With reverent care, he unwrapped the outer covering. Inside were many scrolls.

For the second time in a day, Phillip's breath left him as if he'd been punched.

"Real scrolls," Jeremiah explained. "Scrolls of Keepers."

LARS ARRIVED home from his whirlwind trip, exhausted but exhilarated. He had to share his experience, this incredible new knowledge of God. Once Leif heard the truth, he'd want to know God. He'd have to. Nothing better to stop the downward spiral of his brother's life.

He walked from the rail terminal to Leif's house, not even stopping at the office to shed his briefcase. Leif was in the backyard, reclining on a deck chair as the last violet-streaked clouds of sunset faded. He cupped a tumbler in one hand, a near-empty whiskey bottle on the table next to him.

Lars mounted the steps. "Hey, where are the kids?"

Leif waved his hands, wobbling in his chair. "Pfft, who knows? Diana got all crappy and ran off to her mom's or something." He squinted at Lars. "Wanna drink, li'l bro?"

A sinking feeling swirled in Lars's belly. But he'd come on a mission. "No, and I wish you wouldn't either. I have something important to tell you."

Leif ignored the second, choosing instead to take offense at the first. "You an' Diana, whas' your pro'lem? H'gemony. Act like issa crime fer a guy to relax a li'l."

"I didn't say that, but since we're on the subject, can't you see how your drinking is screwing up your life? You're either drunk or hungover every time I see you. You can't function like that. Your work is failing, and your marriage is falling apart."

"Hah. What marriage?"

"See? That's what I mean. You're destroying your life. You're destroying *yourself*."

"So's my fault she's such a pain?"

"No, but what you do *is* your fault. Sin is crouching at your door and wants to own you. Get yourself under control before it's too late." Where did that come from? Didn't matter. It was true.

Leif was closing down, though, turning in on himself like he always did, going into a brood. Lars had to snap him out of it. "I met with Father Curtis. I have something big to tell you."

Leif didn't budge, his arms crossed, his gaze focused on the deepening twilight.

"Brother, look at me." Lars moved into his line of sight. "This is important."

Leif uncrossed his arms. "What?"

"This has to stay between us. You can't repeat this, even to Diana."

"Whatever."

"I'm serious. Swear to me."

"Okay, okay, I swear. Whash so important?"

"Father Curtis has learned the Writings are a hoax." Lars dropped the bombshell, then paused for Leif's shocked response.

Instead, Leif blinked at him, expressionless, then put back his head, and laughed. "Hah. Took long enough. I coulda tol' him that. Besides, he said that in Two Rivers, remember?"

"No, you don't understand. The Order forged them."

Leif slapped his thigh. "Yep. What I've been saying all along."

"This is serious. Listen to me. Father Curtis says there are writings the Order has suppressed and they tell of the true God."

"Yeah, yeah, whatever. You were fooled once, li'l bro. Don't be fooled by the same scam a second time."

"This isn't a scam. We're looking for the truth!" We? When did this become we?

Leif poured the last dribble of whiskey into his glass, shook the bottle, then looked up the open neck as if he might find more hiding there. He cast it over his shoulder to clatter on the deck. "Good. Look for the truth. I'm gonna go to the tavern to look for whiskey. Let's see which of us finds it first."

Halfway home, Lars stopped in his tracks. He'd forgotten to tell Leif of Haman's upcoming visit. He ought to skip it. It'd do no good for Leif to hear the news tonight, the bender he was on.

But then he huffed and spun back around. A promise was a promise. Back at Leif's house, he scribbled a note and left it on the kitchen counter for his brother to find when he sobered up. He then started home, alone in the dark. Why did Leif have to be so unreasonable? Why was he so set on ruining himself?

Lars would write Father Curtis for advice. He had to get through to his brother before it was too late.

CHAPTER 9

Severe weather, unanticipated by any forecaster, forced Maripol's chopper to ground. He resorted to land travel, but during the journey, he'd been cut off from all wireless communication, a failure no one had yet explained. Vague mumbling references to "unusual atmospheric conditions" were the best he had gotten.

Now he'd been informed that the chief of all Order security forces in this region, General Zelek, had escorted the fugitives onto a boat and out to sea, had orchestrated their escape. "Where is this man now? I want him before me!"

The local bureau man stood before him, head lowered, literally studying his toes.

"Speak up! Where is he?"

The man braved a glance up. "Um, that's the thing, sir. He is currently in Nob."

"He returned to Nob already? How? We were unable to fly. How could he?"

Now the man's gaze returned to his shifting feet as if readying for flight. "According to the general, he hasn't been anywhere near this area this whole week. He is annoyed at our questions."

"Oh? Are we annoying him?" Maripol pointed at the bank of monitors. "Make a copy of the footage from the marina. Send it to him with an invitation to appear before me. I can see his face on that boat. Can't you?"

"Yes, sir, and the officers on site identified the man as General Zelek. But, sir—"

He chopped the air. "No buts. Get him here now."

The chief steeled himself, squaring his shoulders and raising his head. "Sir, you should hear this first. There's more to the story."

"What could you possibly add?" Maripol again waved toward the still screen, the general's face in close-up view.

"Pardon but the general wasn't here, no matter the evidence. He was returning from Midrash with our bishop and a party of twenty others. Like you, their plans to travel by air were interrupted, and they instead chartered a bus. I have received confirmation from Nob. The man at the marina couldn't have been the real General Zelek. Would you like to interview the bishop yourself?"

The thought of crossing a bishop tempered Maripol's burning desire to get his hands on this general. He ground his teeth. "I'll speak to the bishop at a more convenient time." More convenient for the bishop. "But you're certain of this? There can be no doubt?"

"No doubt at all, sir. I'm sorry."

Now what? With nothing but a mystery, an impossibility, and one failure to apprehend the suspects, the dagger had now turned. He must get this situation back under control and the fugitives in custody before someone decided to use that blade. If he failed to provide his superiors a better target, there was little doubt as to whose breast it would be plunged into. "And the fugitives? Are we tracking them? Has the navy gotten shore radar back online?"

"We have no way to locate the vessel at this time."

"Navy chase craft?"

Obviously tired of being the bearer of bad news, the man soldiered on. "Still disabled, sir."

Maripol never admitted defeat, rarely had even been at a loss as to what to do next.

Now as he stared at the status board, impotent and without a clear path forward, an uncomfortable chill iced his spine. Was that the cold breath of failure he felt, creeping ever nearer even now?

After vacating his corner office, Leif had set up digs in an unused storeroom adjacent to the shop break room. Some may have seen this as an embarrassing rebuke. Leif, however, wanted to be far removed from Dad's kingdom, so this suited him just fine.

He was working there when Young Bob entered at a half run. "Mr. Leif, we have a problem."

Leif resisted his first impulse and bit back his retort. Could anything be more irritating than people bringing a problem without providing detail, much less potential solutions? He breathed slowly in and out. "How can I help?"

"The guys down at the store won't let me have the parts. After you left yesterday, I checked the whole operation from end to end. I need bearings for the conveyor and some odds and ends for the loader, besides the stuff we talked about for the tractor. But they told me to pound sand, won't give me as much as a nut."

The papers in Leif's hand rattled in his aborted move to throw them. If he tossed them across the room, he'd have to pick them up. "Did they say why?"

Bob shifted, gaze to the floor. "My credit isn't so good. We been struggling."

"I gave you authorization on our account."

Lips tight, Young Bob stared at the floor.

"You showed it to them?"

He nodded.

"They still refused? Why?"

He shook his head. "Said I needed to come back with cash."

Bob in tow, Leif visited German's office and related the story. "So I hoped you could persuade them to work with us, give us the parts we need."

German pulled his lip. "I thought we agreed you were giving up the whole timber idea?"

"Haman sent me a message, told me it was a go." A pang shot through his belly at the half-truth. But this was no time for reservations, only for action. "He's coming to inspect the mill, maybe as early as Friday. "We need this thing running, and fast." German sat unmoving, expression bland, so Leif added, "This could mean a lot of money for the local economy."

German cracked a smile. "Trying to incentivize me with self-interest? Well, it is the best way to inspire a politician to action, I suppose."

He wrote a note, folded it into an envelope, and sealed it before handing it over. "Take them this. You'll find them eager to assist."

The manager of the parts store paled when he read German's note and was most cooperative, then. Not willing to trust anything to chance, Leif stayed to ensure Bob's entire shopping list was filled without exception. It wasn't.

"Where are the spark plugs?" Bob asked after inventorying his haul.

The manager licked his lips. "Hard to come by. We'd have to send to Two Rivers for that. Sorry."

Unbelievable. Was everyone dragging their feet? "How long will that take?"

"Can't say. I can send an order by post. We usually get things within a few weeks. If they have them in stock, that is."

Leif pivoted to Bob. "Is it going to run without new plugs?"

Bob hugged his paper sack full of parts as if afraid the store manager might take it back. "No, Mr. Leif. I pulled 'em. Two are cracked. We never had the money to do maintenance the last few years. We got by with what we could scrounge."

Leif gave a mock sigh. "Well, then, I have to be the bearer of bad news. I'll go tell German we failed in the mission he assigned us. It's gonna be ugly, but at least, it's not *my* fault."

"Now hold on. Hold on." The store man blubbered. "Just so happens I have a boy who can run and grab them right now. I see a wagon train forming up. I'll have him hitch a ride, and he should be back with the parts by nightfall. 'Course that comes with a bit of a cost."

Leif waved that off. "Put it on the account."

Success was the only concern.

PHILLIP LOUNGED in the captain's chair, two fingers on the helm's big wheel.

Thaddeus dropped onto the starboard bench. "You make piloting a ship look easy."

Phillip ran one finger along the steady wheel. "Strange it's never taken more effort than this." A marvel. "And this with no autopilot, no control systems at all."

He kept waiting for a swell or an errant gust to lurch the craft, to change the rudder pressure, but not so. Since their escape, the sails had been set, the rudder trimmed, and that had been the end of it.

"I could take my hand off the wheel altogether." And for a moment, he did just that before he returned a finger to the wheel. Something in him refused to cast all caution to fate.

"Please don't." Thaddeus held up a palm. "Someone best stay here, hands on the controls, just in case. Jeremiah and I'll continue to spell you, as we have."

"Yes. The worst always happens eventually."

But not this night, at least not yet. The hull sliced through calm waters. Foam trailed in their wake, luminescent beneath a moonless sky. The stars overhead so crystalline bright as to be almost painful. The breeze blew the hair from his forehead soft, warm, like the hand of a beloved father offering a blessing.

They fell quiet, and he took advantage of the peace to meditate. That there was a Creator God, that the supernatural world was real, he'd always believed. That there was an unseen war between good and evil? This he also believed, though his experience of warfare had been rooted in this world, the evil quite corporeal. But he did believe.

His first brush with the unexplainable had been the night Curtis had gotten himself in trouble, the night of that strange and powerful vision. The night of the lion. Coincidence? Possibly. But what had happened at the marina? That was no coincidence.

Thaddeus cleared his throat. "This borders on the creepy. You know."

Phillip did. "The quartering wind is one thing. The absolute invariability of it is another. One might explain it as the luckiest streak in the history of sailing. . . . "

"And that?" Thaddeus nodded beyond the starboard hull, then gestured all around.

Indeed. "One cannot explain *that*." Day in, day out, beyond a hundred-yard area, the rest of the world experienced different conditions.

There, in that world, yards from their hull, the gentle east-southeast wind they sailed before was instead racing from the north, as evidenced in the foam blowing from whitecaps swirling on twelve-foot seas.

"How?" Thaddeus whispered. "How is it that the *Tikvah* isn't rocked by those waves?"

They sailed in calm seas, almost glassy, the perfect radius of their localized weather moving with them, stilling the waters and bending the wind within their protective bubble.

"If that isn't enough, there's the matter of our progress." Phillip reached for the sextant, then pulled his hand back. What was the point? It would be no different the sixth time. There was no explanation for it. "We're traveling at a speed physically impossible for any vessel of this sort." He waved to the sails rippling in the breeze. "I'd guess the wind's at five knots by the feel of it. So how are we moving many times that rate?"

Thaddeus whooshed out a breath, then slapped Phillip's back. "I've studied the unnatural, considered the impossible, and have no choice but to accept them as real."

Phillip grunted. But what in all creation could explain such a thing?

"It must have something to do with Jeremiah and those scrolls of his." Those precious scrolls. But who'd heard of anything like these unnatural things, miraculous things, now occurring? "It can only be the hand of Creator God. There's no other explanation."

Yet what, exactly, did He have in mind for them? What next?

After Leif abdicated the project management department, the responsibility defaulted to Dad. Ever since, there'd been a gnawing in Lars's belly, worsening whenever he thought about it. Phase one shop submittals for the new Capital Events Center were due, and as far as he could tell, no progress had been made. Everything rode on this, the largest contract they'd ever attempted. The lack of progress created an actual weight on his chest, pressing on his heart, worse because he had no oversight of the department. Had Lars or Leif been in charge of the effort, Dad would be breathing down their necks. Instead, Dad seemed unconcerned.

Best Lars satisfied himself he was worrying about nothing. Then he could get back to his overstuffed inbox without this distraction.

He approached the office Leif so recently vacated and knocked on the open door. Velde, the new engineering manager, sat behind the desk. His brother, Hector, leaned back in an executive chair, midstory, while Hector's girlfriend, a junior draftsman, massaged Velde's shoulders.

"Hey, guys." Lars stopped in the doorway. "I was curious how the submittals for the Events Center are coming? They're due next week, right?"

Velde took a deep martyred breath. "What of it?"

Velde had been a trainee draftsman only weeks ago, but Dad had appointed him to this position, vaulting him over other men with more experience. Lars couldn't explain the choice, but maybe Dad knew something he didn't?

"Just worried. Are they done?"

"Will be."

The rats gnawing his guts were getting bigger. Maybe one of them was named Velde? "If they're not done yet, how are you going to have them reviewed and corrected in time?"

"Don't you worry yourself."

"But—"

Velde reached up to grip the doorknob. "Do your job. I'll do mine." He slammed the door. Had Lars not drawn his fingers out of the frame, they'd have been crushed.

Yep. Definitely rats.

CHAPTER 10

Captain Simon woke from unpleasant dreams. He couldn't remember them, but the heart-pounding terror lingered. Not like the momentary fear of ordinary nightmares, the kind that evaporates on waking, but a persistent unease, a dread, a certainty of some impending doom. A man about to be keelhauled would feel this way, waking the morning of his sentence.

He shook his head to clear the fog. He rolled, but was pulled up short, arms and legs wound tight in damp sheets.

Damp sheets? That wasn't right.

Oh, he'd slept plenty of nights in humid bedding as a crewman. The lower decks on most merchant vessels were poorly conditioned and stuffy, heavy with night dew, river air, and stagnant bilgewater. But as captain of this towboat, he had the privilege of his luxurious upper-deck berth, complete with air-conditioning and central heat, courtesy of the ship's systems. Not that his crew didn't enjoy the same. Stern master and generous benefactor, that was the way of a tightly run ship.

He threw the sheets away and sat on the edge of his bunk. Sweat flew from his arms in splattering arcs.

Wow, that must have been a bad one. He'd never sweat his bed like this.

Breathing deep and stretching away the last of the dream fog, he stood to strip the fouled linens. Still, it lingered—the vague sense he was forgetting something, something he was supposed to do, something urgent.

A flashing recall played, a scene from his recent nightmare. It was more like a memory of something he'd done, than the recollection of a dream. So vivid, so real.

In this dream, he'd taken the tender to the delta and met three men, brought them back to the towboat. Strange. He'd never done any such thing. Couldn't imagine needing to.

A light knock rapped at his door.

He checked the time. It was still midwatch, a little abaft of four a.m. Visitors at this hour never boded well.

He threw on a robe, preparing for bad news. He popped the latch. The companionway's dim red light outlined his first mate. "Everything okay, First?"

"Eh? Oh yeah, fine. No problems to report. Couldn't sleep, so started my rounds early. Found this in the wheelhouse." Jespers handed over a clipboard.

Simon studied the manifests. "We got our barge assignments early? Good. It'll be a balm to set sail."

Jespers nodded. "Sooner the better."

But his movements were uncharacteristically jittery, his eyes shadowed, brow furrowed.

"All good, First?"

Jespers jerked his head as if to shake off an unwanted thought. "Yep. Good to go. Just want to be underway. Being at anchor makes me itchy."

Simon handed back the clipboard. "You know the drill. Get this tub moving."

There came a wave of unreasoning panic. Something was telling him not to give this order. He shoved aside the irrational thought, strode to his comms panel, pressed a button, and spoke into the mouthpiece. "All hands, all hands. Prepare to make up tow."

And the lights went out.

Jespers, always prepared, clicked on a flashlight so Simon could see to dress. Together, they went to wake the chief engineer, but his cabin was empty. They found him belowdecks, inspecting the generator controls, two assistants standing by and holding flashlights.

Simon crowded his shoulder to view the readouts. "What's the problem, Chief? We lost power."

"I darn well know we lost power, for crying out loud. What do you think I'm doing here at four a.m.? Taking a midnight stroll?" The chief closed his eyes and took a deep breath. "Sorry, Cap'n. That was out of line. The short answer is that nothing is wrong, or I should say I can find no reason for the outage. Everything seems to be fine, except it's not working."

Simon's craw was itching, his teeth clenching, but he forced the heat down. A captain never let them see him sweat. Or swear. "Either there's something wrong or there isn't. Which is it?"

"Both. We have no power. But nothing's wrong with the systems. The turbine is spinning, the generator is engaged, and we're reading good power outputs. We have correct voltage at the distribution panels." The chief's forefinger stabbed a gauge. "The juice is there, but it's not doing what it is supposed to do."

"You're telling me we have electricity, but nothing electric is working?" Simon resisted the urge to pound the bulkhead. *Cool head, old man. This dream hangover is making you a bit off beam.*

The chief had no such inhibitions. His face red, eyes bugged, he *did* pound the bulkhead. Twice. "I'm sayin'—" He lowered his voice. "I'm saying I can find no mechanical or electrical problems to explain the outage."

"You must have missed something." When the chief's face reddened further and he began to speak, Simon held out a hand to forestall the eruption. "You're tops at your job. But it's easy to miss something under fire, at four a.m., in the dark." He gripped the man's shoulder. "Bear up and recheck everything from stem to stern, slow and careful. You'll find it. There's no man jack on the water better at this."

A frown still darkening his expression, the chief engineer glanced at his assistants and bid them to follow with a jerk of the hand. "Aye, Cap'n."

Simon called after him. "I'll be in the wheelhouse. First with me."

Five minutes later, in his big swivel chair, Simon was reviewing the logs when the duty officer brought him a note. "Message from *Ursus*, sir. They've been hailing us. We've not received their calls, obviously. They sent over a runner. They're next in line to make up tow and are asking when we plan to undock. We're holding up the fleet, sir."

The furrows between Simon's brows felt like they now approached unfathomed depths. "Bilge rats. How many behind us in the queue?"

"Four, sir."

He pulled his lip. "If we lose our spot, we wait another day, sitting here like a derelict." He turned his back to the men, staring out the wide starboard windows. How to stall those swabs?

He swiveled back to face the wheelhouse. "Send a runner to *Ursus*. Say we'll undock within the half hour, ask pardon for the delay and all that."

He kept his gaze dockside. Soon, a young crewman sprinted down the gangway ramp, making for the *Ursus*, where he disappeared on the tugboat's deck. He reappeared moments later. Simon uttered a string of oaths under his breath as the *Ursus* withdrew their gangway and cast off, moving toward the barge docks.

The messenger returned, panting. "Sorry, sir. They've reported us to dock control. Told 'em we're inoperable."

Simon scrawled a hasty note and handed it to the lad. "Take this to control. Keep them from bumping us clean out of the schedule if you can. Get cracking, son." As the messenger ran, Simon watched him speed across the docks on swift legs. "Oh, to be young again."

"You were young once, a long time ago." The first mate spoke from where he leaned in the corner. "But if memory serves, you could never run like that."

Simon gave him a smile he didn't feel. "True that. This body weren't made for running at any age."

They sat watching dockside. Nothing else to do on the dark inert ship.

The messenger reappeared, sprinting their way. He entered the wheelhouse. Now sweating and breathless, he handed Simon a sealed message before bending over, hands on knees.

Simon slipped the flimsy out of the envelope, read it, then handed it to the first mate, who shook his head and announced to the crew. "We've been bumped to last in line. Guess Chief has a full day to fix whatever broke."

The lights came on. Instruments whirred, their rising whine accompaniment to the bangs and clangs of the ship's machines so eerily silent moments before. Sound echoed all about, the deck plates vibrating with the renewed life.

He suppressed another string of curses. "Five minutes sooner, and we'd be making tow right now. Bilgewater!" He stomped out of the wheelhouse ready to know what the chief engineer had to say for himself.

The first mate dogged his heels through companionways and down ladders to the generator room. There, the chief engineer was standing with hands on hips, face red, shaking in silent fury. His assistants had crowded to a corner near the entry hatch, the point furthest from his reach.

After Simon spent over twenty years on the water with this man, he couldn't mistake the signs, so he waited as the chief gathered his self-control, stage by stage, until it seemed the man was again coherent. "Glad you found the problem, Chief. I knew you would. What was it?"

The chief engineer looked like he'd slipped backward a notch in the battle with his ire. He snorted out a series of growling noises before answering. "There was no cause, and we fixed nothing. I'm tellin' you, Cap, we checked everything three times. There—was—no —problem. I was standing right here, no one was touching a thing, and then—bingo!" He slapped his hands together. "The old girl lit right back up. No reason."

Simon grimaced and massaged the base of his neck. "Well, something happened." He lifted his arms, then let them fall limp. "Anyway, we've been bumped. We've got the day at dock. You've had a tough morning, but I need you to go over her again, find the gremlin. If this'd happen when we're steering through a bridge . . . "

The chief scowled. "Oh, I'll find it all right." He marched off, then called over his shoulder. "Boys, with me."

Simon nodded to Jespers. "He'll find it, and tomorrow, we'll be on our merry way."

A dark look passed over Jespers's face, and he turned away, muttering, probably thinking his words inaudible. " . . . pray to Eternal it don't end like that dream . . . "

LEIF LEFT HOME EARLY MORNING, dawn not yet even pinking the horizon, the chill air cutting straight through his thick flannel shirt. He kept his speed low, barely pedaling, moving as quietly as he could, the grinding of the chain and the irregular thump of bent wheels on pavement the only sound in the empty streets.

Today was the test run, and he'd been wide awake before five, nerves afire and stomach burning.

He topped the mill driveway and descended, greeted by the floodlights encircling the yard and the low, sweet murmur of idling engines. Young Bob, standing in the compound's center, beamed at his handiwork.

Joy swelled, and Leif rode the scandal of a bike right into the yard, unthinking. Oh, who cared? What did it matter compared to this? He dismounted, the chest-expanding glow of achievement lightening the world and his burdens. "Everything ready to go?"

Bob spread his arms like a king presenting his domain, practically giddy. The tractor powering the sawmill burbled along. Next to the mill, the heavy thrum of a powerful engine resounded from a larger tractor. In place of a bucket, what looked like a pair of beetle mandibles outfitted it. Bob climbed into its cab, and with these metal jaws, he plucked a log from the pile, spun, and set it on the conveyor.

He scrambled down and moved to the sawmill controls. He throttled up the engine and pulled a lever. The circular blade whirred to life, spinning up until it emitted a deafening whine. After another lever released came a sound like marching boots, and the conveyor advanced. The log fed into the blade inch by inch. Then, sliced in two, it rested on another conveyor.

With the air of an orchestra conductor concluding a successful performance, Bob powered down the noisy contraption. "Woo-hoo!" He pumped a hand in the air. "I told you she'd be ready, Mr. Leif. I told you."

"Wow, just wow. Great job." What else would Haman expect to see? "The kiln." Leif pointed to the brick monstrosity. "It works, right?"

At Bob's crestfallen face, the glow expanding Leif's chest hardened to a ball of lead and settled in his stomach.

"Well, it ran years back." Bob tugged on one ear. "No moving parts to break or anything, but no way to test it till we get that propane tank filled. We'll hafta blow rust outta the lines and clean some orifices, but there's not much to it. May need to replace a few valves."

Stupid. Why didn't he ask about that sooner? Another obstacle to shut down his plan just when things were looking up. "Is there anything else, besides the kiln, that we need to be thinking about? Everything's got to be working in case he comes this week, no surprises."

Bob scratched that earlobe. "Well, best we talk to Pops. I never got to run this thing full time like he did. I just thought you wanted to see the saw running, not everything else."

Another voice, old and scratchy, came from the house. "Got all my old records in the kitchen, young man. You wanna bring this mill up and runnin', I can tell you what you'll need to do."

Leif turned. Standing behind him, the much older and grayer version of Young Bob extended an arm.

"Leif, meet my pops. Pops, this is the man I was telling you about who's gonna save our mill."

The codger squinted at Leif, then at his bike. Shaking his head and muttering, he walked into the house and banged the screen door closed.

CHAPTER 11

The guilt dragged on Lars, slowing his movements, making him groan as he stood, his feet scuffing the tiled office floor. Lying twisted his innards all the more when it was his mom. But what else was he to do? He wanted to visit Father Curtis, but he couldn't tell her about it, could he? Curtis's life depended on him keeping the secret.

He fidgeted at his desk, staring at the blank wall, not at his work, so deep in his thoughts he jumped when a hand landed on his shoulder. He spun.

But Mom stood behind him, her expression soft in concern. "What's wrong with you? You're getting as moody as Leif." Her brows rose. "You're worried about your brother, aren't you?"

Lars grimaced. He didn't answer. Where would he ever begin?

"Have you tried talking things over with the new priest?"

He'd never trust the priesthood again, knowing what he did now.

"I know you were close to Father Curtis." She must've misread his expression. "But the new man seems nice too. You should give him a chance."

He couldn't hold back. "You shouldn't trust that new guy. Don't tell him anything."

She assumed her scolding look, the one she used when she

caught him stealing cookies between meals. "Now, Lars, you show respect. I understand you disagree with what they did to Father Curtis. I don't believe he could have done all they're saying, either, but that will work itself out. The truth always wins in the end."

Lars scoffed, leaned back in his chair, and crossed his arms. "Maybe in some things, but not when it comes to the Order. They have power, and they use it to win. They don't care about truth any more than they care about you or me." He stopped short. He'd said more than he should have.

Mom sat and took a slow breath. "Maybe it's time you tell me what you've been keeping from me."

He gulped, fidgeting with his pencil. How was he going to get out of this? But he didn't want out of it, did he? Not really.

He laid the pencil on his desk and relinquished his hold on it with a deliberate opening of his grip. Then he related the recent weeks. The tension in his chest unwound. In its absence, it became clear how much keeping this secret from her affected him. And how he let it put such distance between them. The changes had been so gradual he hadn't noticed the increasing disconnect.

He was never going to create such a web of lies again, for any reason. Not ever.

She sat listening, no sign of judgment, only the occasional clarifying question. Then all she said was, "Okay."

His jaw dropped, and he gawked at her. "Okay? Is that all?"

"What do you expect me to say?"

"I don't know. I thought you'd be mad. Or shocked. Something."

She crossed her arms, eyes focused inward. "Hmm, mad?" She then patted his knee. "You were doing right in helping an innocent man. I'm scared for you and disappointed you didn't trust me, but not mad. As for being shocked, how simple do you think I am?"

"Um, what?"

"Do you think I can talk to a priest about life and things of the spirit for this many years and not have any idea what kind of man he is? Do you think I wouldn't recognize the power structure the Order has built? How they use it?" She rolled her eyes. "Please."

"So you don't want me burned as a heretic?"

Her chest bounced with her silent laugh, the one that made her blue eyes twinkle. "I should spank you for taking such risks, but I'm proud that, when the choice presented itself, you chose the path of honor."

"There's more. I need to tell you about Creator God."

And so he did.

For the second day in a row, Captain Simon woke rank with sweat, hand shaking with unremembered terror.

As was true the day before, he recalled little about his dreams, except taking the tender to pick up those three men. That part was imprinted clearly. And this day, that dream or memory or whatever it was, having been merely strikingly real the first night, was beginning to feel like a demand.

He growled and swung his legs out of the soggy bed, creating pooling footprints of sweat. He wouldn't be letting this drive him over the edge. Who took nightmares seriously? He wasn't one of those batty old women running to the Order priests with every bad dream, begging for charms and blessings to protect them from the evil spirits. He was a man, and he lived in the real world.

If he told anyone about this, they'd think he was crackers. If his men suspected him of weakness, he could write off his command. No one wanted a crazy man in charge of a battering ram weighing millions of pounds.

No, sir. Time to deep-six this thing for good. He dressed, ready to make for the wheelhouse, even though his blue luminous watch hands indicated only three a.m., much earlier than his normal time.

He popped open his cabin door and recoiled. His first mate, Jespers, was standing in the hall, hand raised to knock.

"What in Davy Jones are you doing here at this hour?"

Jespers looked him up and down. "Same as you, I reckon. Couldn't sleep. Want to make tow and get off this accursed dock?"

"Couldn't sleep?" Simon narrowed his eyes. There was something about the way Jespers had been acting. "Why, exactly?"

Jespers went still, his gaze averted. "Just couldn't. S'pose I'm a bit worried 'cause Chief never found the problem."

Simon grunted. Losing power under tow was a bargeman's worst nightmare. Even worse than these blasted dreams, the dreams that, for all the fire in tarnation, he couldn't remember.

They walked in silence to the wheelhouse. The image of his craft without power, millions of pounds of barge under his command, swept away, helpless in the current, colliding with some bridge, somewhere . . . Well, he couldn't get that picture out of his head.

In the wheelhouse, he took report from the officer of the watch. No barge assignments had yet been transmitted, so Simon settled in to wait with a fresh mug of coffee, reviewing the night's logs. A crewman arrived, carrying an envelope.

"The manifest, I hope?" Simon asked.

Once the man handed over the paperwork, Simon reviewed it, frowning. "A little light."

"They gave us the option to wait for more. But none are due in this morning, and other towboats are in line behind us."

He gave a jerk of his head. "Can't afford to wait. We'll take what we can get and hightail it."

He lifted the mike with an inexplicably shaking hand. He put his thumb on the key, then let go. What if . . .? But no, he was no fainting daisy, looking for ghosts where there were none. He keyed the mike. "All hands—"

The lights went out, the wheelhouse now illuminated by only the sliver of moon and stars, their cold light shining from so deep in those boundless heavens, so far away. The whining moan of gyros winding down, powerless, filled the compartment, their song a melancholy accompaniment to the hollow sinking of his guts.

He sat frozen in his captain's chair, his throne of worldly power, that power now helpless against the vagaries of the inexplicable.

LEIF HAD GOTTEN in the habit of sleeping in.

What freedom, to make his own hours, to decide for himself when he worked and when he lazed a few extra minutes in bed. He'd never before been able to enjoy such indulgence. Dad had always been so adamant that family members set a good example. "A good manager is always the first one in and the last one out."

Now Leif could work any way he darn well pleased. Wide awake now, he chose to remain in bed, luxuriating in the delicious freedom, the privilege of deciding whether he felt like getting up.

A pounding on the door interrupted his pleasure. He covered his head with a pillow. If he ignored whoever it was, maybe they'd go away. "Leif, where are you?"

Just great. Dad didn't sound happy.

Cursing, Leif rolled out of bed, working up some irritation to displace the thudding terror. This gut-deep panic, so familiar, always accompanied Dad's disapproval. How could it still affect him so, even now? Hadn't he left this all behind?

He slipped on a dirty T-shirt and sweatpants and padded downstairs. With the kids in the middle of a morning cereal mess, he collected sticky kisses on his way through.

When he opened the door, Dad stood sweating, trembling with ill-contained anger. He thrust a wadded sheaf of papers into Leif's chest. "Hope you're planning to pay these 'cause I'm not going to!"

Leif snatched at the falling papers before they could hit the ground. Spark plugs, machine parts, diesel fuel, gasoline, gas lines, and fittings, and on and on. With prices. Surprisingly high prices. He winced at the invoice from the fuel depot. Who'd have guessed a thousand gallons of propane cost so much?

A rising warmth edged out the panicked pounding in his chest. "You knew I was working on projects. What're you so mad about? This is an investment, a necessary investment, and pure chicken feed compared to the money we'll make."

"Projected profits don't pay the bills, and these have to be paid now. Do you realize I couldn't get the mechanic to fix the brakes you and your brother ruined? Do you want to know why?" Dad must've mistaken his silence for an eagerness to hear more. "I'll tell you why. Because I have to pay the parts store off"—he tapped the papers Leif held, finger thumping through them and into his chest—"before they'll give him our brakes."

Leif rolled the papers and used them like a baton to rap the imaginary head of the parts store manager. "That's not right. German guaranteed those charges."

Dad's lips went so tight they turned white. "German personally guaranteed that *I* would pay those charges. Me. And before you think to involve him in your schemes again, you'd better have another think. I'm going there next, and he will never, ever pull a stunt like that for you again. You want to blow a fortune, blow your own. Your name is off all the company accounts, starting now."

He whirled and stomped off. Leif stood where he was, arms limp at his sides. The heat that had risen to his chest gave over to an empty ache. How could this go so badly? He was giving this everything he had. How could his dad turn on him?

Then he spun and slammed the door. To Hegemony with him. If Dad wanted it that way, fine. Leif would run this show, and then Dad could *bid* for Leif's work. He'd be a rich entrepreneur, a huge success, free of Dad's control, placing orders where and when he wanted. And he'd flaunt that success at family gatherings. Dad would see what he lost, and he'd regret it. Just wait.

Leif marched back into the house and through the kitchen. Ignoring Diana's questions, he went upstairs and dressed for the day. He had an empire to build, and he'd start by checking with Young Bob. Time to verify everything was ready for Haman's visit.

It better be. The man could arrive any time. Leif's future, his family's future, rode on this meeting. His gut clamped tighter, so he stomped out the door and into the bright fall sunshine.

Yeah, bright. Just like his future. He'd be making sure of that.

CHAPTER 12

Diana kissed each child, hugged her mom, and stepped back to leave.

But Mom caught her arm. "You're still wearing it?"

Diana pulled the chain from under her blouse and fingered the gem-studded love charm her mother purchased, one supposedly blessed by the new priest. "I'm still wearing it."

"Good. That lump Leif seems immune, but it'll bring you luck yet. Lots of fish in the sea, you know."

"Mom! Stop it." She teetered toward the door, fighting the high heels. She rarely wore them, but her mom had insisted, decking her out in these along with pearls and a fur wrap.

"You are a beautiful catch. Flaunt it while you got it, girl."

She did feel magically transformed, her everyday drab replaced by this new exciting self she'd seen in the mirror. She'd gotten so blah, soul sucked dry by the day-in, day-out drudgery of her marriage. Tonight, she was alive again, and she liked it.

Good thing Mom was between boyfriends this week and happy to have the kids over. Diana's friend, Mindy, had been wheedling her to go to the temple social at Crescent Lake, a year-round resort area reserved for the ultrarich. "Come on. Do you want to sit around and get fat, old, and miserable with that guy, or do you want to have fun? Live a little!"

As Diana and Mindy now approached, Diana fingered the gemstones again. "I tell you we won't get in," she whispered.

"You're not going to start *that* again are you." Mindy grabbed her arm and hauled her along. "The hottest venue might be closed to the average person, but we're not average. Young pretty women can find a way when others can't. Watch and see."

The golden prongs pricked Diana's fingertips and she dropped the charm to suck at the wound. "I heard the temple limited invitations for this gala to the very elite of the elite."

"Leave it to me." Heels clicking, hips swaying, Mindy sashayed off and began working on one of the robed guards.

Diana hung back as a group of fashionably dressed men approached, laughing and joking, their libations well underway.

A guard shooed Mindy aside to wave the new arrivals through, greeting them with an obsequious deference that singled them out as either rich or powerful or both. Mindy sidled up to one of the men.

"Here now. I told you women to get out of here," the guard ordered.

"Hold on, there." A man stopped him. "By no means can we leave these lovely maidens languishing in the cold." He crooked one arm to Diana, and one of his friends put his arm about Mindy's shoulders.

The guard shrugged, unclipped the velvet rope, and ushered the party through.

When they entered the VIP balcony, her escort approached a man who stood as if the sun of this galaxy, these glittering people all revolving around him. Tall and regal, he wore a suit that must've cost more than Leif made in a year.

The man on her elbow made a half bow. "Mr. Mullman, sir. Thank you so much for the invitation."

Mullman inclined his head and patted him on the shoulder, eyes aloof. Then those eyes sighted her and widened, and there came a barely heard whisper, " . . . Marguerite . . . "

Her escort stammered, then drew her forward. "This is my new friend—" He turned to Diana, face reddening. "What was your name again, honey?"

But those eyes of Mullman's had captured her. So intense, that gaze. As if in a dream, she extended her hand toward this compelling man. "Diana."

Instead of shaking her hand, he bent to kiss it, then trapped it between his own. "I am Mullman, and it is my pleasure Miss Marg—Miss Diana."

The orchestra began a slow tune, fantastic in its composition, and he pulled her close. "May I have this dance?"

As they negotiated the crowd, moving toward the dance floor, snatches of whispered conversations followed. " . . . is that?"

" . . . can't be . . . "

"No, but looks so much like . . . "

But her nervousness and the effort of walking in these heels without tripping took all her concentration.

Once the dancing started, all else was forgotten. Never had there been a night like this, and never had she had so much fun. Had she, at last, met her prince charming? Mullman was handsome, attentive, and apparently rich. And those mysterious eyes of his, gray one minute, tinged blue the next, twinkling with mischief all the while. And his touch! How could a man's hands bring such a flush of blood wherever they happened to land? Feeling something she couldn't explain, had never experienced, she drank in the heady exhilaration.

Whatever it was, she wanted more.

Now, she leaned in closer as they danced. The light took on a peculiar, golden, liquid glow. Time slowed. Her every movement poised, their bodies glided in perfect counterpoint round and round the dance floor, her former awkwardness replaced, as if by magic, with an unconscious grace. How was it that the attention of this man transformed her so?

As the band completed the final song, he drew her close and whispered in her ear. "I wish you could be on my arm every night. May I see you again?"

A smile leapt forth, only to fade on her lips as the dreamlike bubble popped. What was she thinking? She was a married woman. She lowered her head.

But why not? Like her mom said, the Eternal loved her, wanted her to enjoy life. And she hadn't been, not for some time.

What did she owe Leif, anyway? Besides, would he even notice? Or care? He was too tied up with his true loves, his booze and his business.

She raised her eyes, lips nearly brushing Mullman's. "I would love to see you again."

What did she have to lose?

CAPTAIN SIMON AND HIS CREW, having again been bumped from the schedule, tore the boat apart.

Just as on the previous day, once they lost their barge assignments, the power was restored as mysteriously as it had failed.

Simon ordered all hands to report to the chief engineer and assist him in any way possible. The chief divided the men into teams, each led by one of his assistant engineers. They inspected every power distribution panel. Left no electrical connection unchecked. Isolated and tested every circuit. And tested. And tested again under his tyrannical eye.

Late in the afternoon, the first mate took Simon aside. "The men are gettin' antsy, Captain."

"Don't blame 'em. I'm anxious to get underway too."

"Not that, sir. A superstitious lot these men are. You see the charms they wear, the relics in their berths. How they run to the temple at every port to buy blessings from the priests." Jespers licked dry, cracked lips. "There are whispers, sir."

Before he could stop it, Simon's head jerked to look over his shoulder. Were the men watching, even now? He cursed himself. A captain was never spooked. By anything. "What kind?"

Falling foul of crew morale was worse than low water and more dangerous. One built morale slowly, painstakingly, over time, but crews could be taken by a wave of dissension, wrecked in an instant. And it all started with the misguided toss of the smallest rumorous pebble. Untold captains had been bankrupted, vessel stewardships seized, careers sunk in that way. Lives lost.

"The men are starting to think the tub is cursed, sir. We don't correct course—we'll have real problems."

Bilge rats. "Like we don't already? Never mind, I understand. We're doing all that can be done."

The mate pulled a face. Apparently, Jespers hadn't volunteered everything.

"What? Out with it."

Jespers blew heavily. "Don't want you to think I put any stock in this, sir, not like some of them men. But, well, there are the dreams."

Simon stiffened. "Come again?"

"The men, sir. They've had dreams. Seems all had the same one. Something about passengers." The mate waved the thought away. "I know that's crazy, sir. Forget I said anything."

Inwardly clenching his guts against a sudden churning, he kept his facial muscles placid, his body language casual. "Finish what you started. They all had the same dream? About what?"

Jespers raised his hands in the air as if to find the missing words there, then let them drop. He glanced around like a guilty child. "They think the spirits are telling them the boat is doomed if we don't bring three men on board. That if we find these men, the spirits'll bless us, if not, well—"

Simon looked askance at his longtime mate.

The mate reddened but straightened his back. "If the men get any more worked up, we'll be doomed for sure, spirits or no. Something needs be done." He snuck a peek over his own shoulder, then lowered his voice. "Between you and me, I've had the dreams myself, and let me tell you, they're no fun."

Simon patted him on the back. "Thanks for being straight with me, First. We're all getting a bit stir-crazy, sittin' at anchor so long. Best thing is to get this tub back under tow. That done, they'll forget this craziness."

They worked well past midnight until finally the chief growled his surrender. Every system had been triple-checked. There were no faults in any of them. At least, none that could be found. But if so, what caused the failures the past two mornings? Simon kept that question to himself.

He went to his bed, limbs dragging and knees throbbing. He was too old to crawl around those service chases. But at least he was too tired for any cursed dreams tonight.

But within a scant few hours of tormented sleep, he woke, more afflicted than ever, jerked awake when the first mate barged into his cabin without knocking. It took only a single glance at his face to know why. "The dream again?"

The mate nodded, red-faced and panting. "Me and all the men, and now we have a mutiny on our hands. I suggest you address the crew, sir—now."

CHAPTER 13

Phillip sat in the captain's chair, having turned to face Thaddeus and Jeremiah who shared the starboard bench. He now chanced letting go of the wheel, but wouldn't leave the helm unmanned, notwithstanding that he had as of yet, in all the days on the water, ever needed to adjust either rudder or sail. Who could explain such a thing?

Between them was a folding table supporting a chess set. He, Thaddeus, and Jeremiah had been playing a tournament all day. Other than cooking, they had nothing else to do.

But with Thaddeus tying up the board, it was getting harder to find any move that wouldn't lead to disaster. Phillip'd best buy time while he thrashed about for some sort of gambit. "You say you want to return. You mention family?"

Thaddeus's head jerked up. His gaze and concentration had been locked on the board. Now his lips drooped, his gaze fell, and his shoulders hunched as though against deep pain. "Yes, have family."

Phillip rocked backward. Thaddeus was old enough to be a father, but Phillip had yet to picture it. Especially in this line of work. "How many?"

Thaddeus's mouth screwed up, and a wrinkle formed between his brows. He shot Phillip a confused look. “One family. Mother, father, brother, two sister. Is this you ask? This language still not so good.”

“No, no. I ask you have how many children.”

“Ha.” The laugh burst like an explosion from Thaddeus’s lips, and he grinned, teeth white in that now sun-reddened face. “No. No children.” The grin evaporated. Something haunted overtook hooded eyes. “Though my Esmer and I, we think we maybe should wed. But this thing we do?” He gave a wide-armed shrug, indicating their surroundings. “Maybe this not so good? One day, I think no. Another, yes.” After a long silence, his gaze locked on the far horizon at their rear as if seeing something there. “If I ever see her again . . . ”

If only Phillip could do something for this young man. This loyal young man. But the best thing was to get to their destination. From there, he could ship Thaddeus home. Back to his Esmer. For now, perhaps distraction was the best Phillip could offer.

And there it was, the move he’d sensed had to be there but had been, until now, unable to see. He reached for his bishop and slid it across the board, glancing up to judge Thaddeus’s reaction. Did he see the impending jeopardy?

Thaddeus wasn’t watching the board. His gaze was focused far forward. He stood, finger pointing.

There, low on the horizon, was a dark line. It could be a squall, but no. Something about it was wrong, unnatural.

As it neared, much more rapidly than should have been possible, it grew higher into the sky. The clouds had a greasy cast to them, the colors somehow off, unnervingly so, and the movement in those clouds was dizzying. Stomach churning. They roiled, undulated. What looked like appendages formed, extruded seaward, only to retreat into the churning mass.

Thaddeus yelled, barely audible over the wind now screaming in the rigging. “Those be funnel clouds?” Those winds whipped his hair even inside their protected bubble.

Phillip leapt to his feet, knocking chess pieces across the deck. “Life jackets. Thaddeus, sails. Jeremiah, helm.”

A strange sensation now pulsed the air, thrummed his chest, a song of power and threat. And underlying it, a sense of rage, a desire to devour and destroy.

The sails, previously luffing, now swung wildly, popping, the sound like cannon-shot. The gusts buffeted them, threatening to blow him from his perch as he struggled to pull in the sheets, which moved as though animated by that menace. They fought him with violent jerks and landed seemingly intentional blows to his head.

The bubble of calm they'd enjoyed had evaporated. The deck bucked, the bow pitching skyward before diving into cavernous troughs. Phillip one-arm hugged the mainmast as he made fast a last tie about the sail. The violent motions slammed him against the spar. The wind-driven salt spray blinded him.

The boat dove into another trough, and even though Jeremiah was doing a sound job at the helm, the cresting water broke over the bow and washed the length of the boat, sluicing down the companionway. A few more of those and they'd founder.

Phillip pointed.

Thaddeus, nearer the hatch, let go of his handhold and dove to shut it. Another wave traversed the deck, knocking him from his feet. He went down, carried by the surge, about to be washed overboard. As he raced by it, he caught the steel helm wheel with two fingers, then disappeared beneath the swirling flood.

The dark wall of clouds was on them now, and the driven spray stung as if ripping the flesh from Phillip's cheeks. With it, the wind carried something new, an odor of rot, of death and sulfur, and of something else. He shielded his eyes, trying to pierce the unnatural black fog that accelerated toward them, about to engulf them.

Ahead of their craft, out on the water, something moved—a flicker of white against the oily darkness. There it was again, the form of a man, seemingly walking on the water, a white aura radiating from him so pure it hurt to look upon, growing in intensity until Phillip had to cover his eyes. Yet the afterimage still burned behind closed lids.

But with his eyes shut, the surrounding darkness pounced, rushing into his mind. His body shuddered with instinctive revulsion at the touch. He snapped his eyes back open, needing to see the vision again, the presence of that light. But the shining figure disappeared behind a towering wave.

A chorus of howls joined the screaming wind, all the hounds of hell released, baying furious joy for the hunt. In the darkness, now just ahead, shadowy forms coalesced, undulated, and reached, hungering for him. The roar of triumph from the unseen depths froze his heart midbeat.

As a Seeker operative, he'd faced mortal danger, had been under physical threat, had even endured torture. This dwarfed any peril he'd experienced. Those shrouded entities rejoiced, screamed in pleasure at his imminent annihilation, a ceasing to be that went far beyond the destruction of the physical body. Those shrieks carried with them a promise of unending agony. Whispers pried his mind with images, visions of himself, eternally consumed, drowned in this essence of corruption and evil, separated for all time from anything good or wholesome, from the light. And with those whispers came the certain knowledge, somewhere soul deep, that he could do nothing to stop them.

For the first time, Phillip knew true terror. His knees jellied, his throat closed, his mind dithered—all conscious thought lost, smothered in this blackout, this psychic overload.

And then, there it was again, that shining form, that man out there on the water. But now, it was not the form of a man, but of a great desert lion, terrible in its power. It charged toward the approaching darkness, then opened its maw with a deafening roar, vibrating the molecules of the air, of Phillip's being.

Time stopped.

Nothing moved, not the boat, the wind, or the water. The roiling clouds hung stationary inches from the bow, an oily black glacier. The appendages advancing from that darkness held frozen like the trunks of mammoths caught in sudden ice, reaching for a last gasp of air.

Then time surged ahead. The radiating blast wave of something —not force or even energy, but of intention—pulsed from where the lion had been. It flashed outward in an expanding sphere, not seen but sensed as it passed over the boat, over Phillip.

The dark beings, the greasy clouds, the sound and wind, rolled up like a scroll, receded, fled as if sucked into another dimension, moving at a ninety-degree angle from everything that could be felt and seen.

And then it was gone. The water was again glassy, the sun bright in a heart-achingly blue sky.

CHAPTER 14

The problem of Leif picked away at Lars's mind, distracting his focus. The question always right there, nagging just below the surface. How to get through to his brother before it was too late?

With Mom on his side, Lars prepared to depart for Two Rivers to meet with Father Curtis. He'd know how to approach Leif.

Why hadn't Lars thought to make an ally of Mom sooner? So many things were easier and felt better when not hiding them. He'd keep that in mind from now on, catch himself before he slipped into deception again.

Which made him think of Dad. Having promised himself no more secrets, keeping Dad in the dark left a queasy twinge in his belly.

He looked up from the briefcase he'd been packing and hugged his midsection. "Mom, how should I tell Dad?"

She smiled her secret smile. "I'll take care of that."

He shot her a questioning look, then opened his mouth. He had to be rid of this ball of ugly in his belly.

She interrupted with an upraised finger. "I'll tell him tonight. You know how little he loves the Order."

With that, Lars was moving. He hopped on the wagon train, now a paying passenger, and in one of those nice padded seats this time, thanks to Mom's help. What luxury.

He could get used to this.

~

PHILLIP CROUCHED where he had ridden out the storm, arms still wrapped around the mainmast. In some far-distant place, someone was wheezing. Then it came again, and things snapped into focus as if his spirit had wandered away and was now slammed back into his battered body. His cramped throat had painfully reopened. Now, his lungs spasmed, straining for the breath he'd been holding. For how long? Time had become unreliable.

He didn't move, didn't dare, but remained clamped to the mast, gaze darting in all directions in search of the next threat. When none materialized, he lowered himself to the deck, limp, empty.

A memory resurfaced. Thaddeus had been washed overboard. A steel band clamped his heart, and he jerked around, searching the aft deck. There they were, Jeremiah, and yes, Thaddeus, spread-eagled on the wet teak deck boards, chests heaving.

The sun beamed down from a cloudless blue sky and warmed Phillip's back, still chilled from the beating waves and wind. He forced cramped muscles to move and, with cold-numbed fingers, untied knots he finished tightening seemingly moments ago.

Thaddeus came to help, and they soon raised and set the sails. They collapsed into the benches next to Jeremiah, who had returned to his station, fingers clamped to the helm, face strained and white.

The fair quartering breeze they had come to enjoy refreshed Phillip's spirit as it rippled their shirts, the salty clean smell washing from them the scent of fear and death that had blown out of that dark place.

And then Phillip stood and shambled stiff-legged to the starboard rail, staring, moving as if in a dream. He *must* be dreaming, had to be, because what he was now seeing was impossible. There, on the far horizon, was a sliver of land. How could that be? They should be many hundreds of miles from any shore, but there it was, as real as the dried salt on his face. He blinked, then shook his head. But the mirage remained, much too solid to be some atmospheric vagary, some refracted illusion.

As the coastline grew nearer, he studied it through the powerful telescope. He silently blessed the nameless Seeker who provisioned the boat and seemingly anticipated their every possible need. "There's a harbor to our north, and that's something I don't understand. We traveled directly west for our entire trip. The first land we should encounter is the east coast of the old United Republic, but that coast runs north and south. This one runs east and west as far as I can see. Maybe we were blown into a large inlet, and what we're seeing is its north shore."

Thaddeus slapped the chart to trap it on the bench when the breeze lofted it skyward. He folded it and slipped it back into the waterproof pouch. "I agree. Only one way to know. We must make landfall to determine where we are."

Phillip didn't respond. Taking the *Tikvah* and her invaluable cargo into potential danger went against his better judgment. But the mission plan called for him to make contact with an operative on the east coast who could smuggle them across the continent and back to Republic. Without that aid, they couldn't travel.

No choice, then. To get where they were going, they must first find out where they were.

He went to the rear railing and leaned out to inspect the battered inflatable still tied to the stern platform, even after the wild ride. Whoever had prepared the craft had done a good job. The outboard motor had been dismounted and clamped to the stern rail, the tender standing upright in her mounts. But even as well as it had been stowed, some damage must've been done to the dinghy or motor.

Thaddeus came alongside him, lips pursed. "Think it's seaworthy? We took a real hammering."

"Let's find out." Phillip swung onto the ladder and descended to the platform.

Amazingly, some bent mounting brackets showed the only visible damage. They unshipped the dinghy and motor, placed the dinghy in the water, then clamped the motor in place.

Phillip filled the oil and gas, then instructed Thaddeus, "Say a prayer." He said one of his own and pulled hard on the starter.

The waterlogged rope snapped.

They located the ship's toolbox, battled the unfamiliar assembly, and replaced the rope.

He then braced himself and told Thaddeus, "Say a better prayer this time."

When he pulled, the motor sputtered and then went still. He closed the choke and tried again. It popped, emitting a dark puff of gassy fumes. With another adjustment, the engine settled into a happy purr.

Thaddeus flashed a thumbs-up. "A win for the team."

With no shortage of fuel, Phillip left the tender idling, afraid to turn it off lest it fail to start a second time. He reboarded the sailboat and stuffed gear into a pack.

"Hey, where are you going?" Thaddeus asked in their shared language.

"You stay here to protect the cargo."

Thaddeus put out his hand and closed the top of Phillip's bag. "I'm expendable. You're not. I wasn't even supposed to be on this boat. I have no idea how to travel through this land and barely speak the language. If we lost you, I'd have no chance of getting the package to its destination."

Phillip balked. In the end, he had to agree. But it rankled.

Soon, Thaddeus sped away, aiming at a point just outside the busy harbor. He'd motor close enough to see signs on channel markers or docks. Perhaps that would be enough for Phillip to divine their location.

Phillip and Jeremiah sat on deck, unmoving until the dinghy disappeared among the scattered vessels anchored closer to shore. Phillip knuckled a spot at the base of his skull. He needed to do something, anything. Sitting here, just watching and waiting, left him feeling useless, weak. Once again, he must accept the idea of someone else taking action, of being protected, when he was supposed to be protector.

With an oath, he stood and went belowdecks. There'd been fishing gear in one of the lockers. The chances of catching anything at a random anchorage were thin, but he had hours to kill. And it'd be a good distraction. Something to ward off the dark imaginings now plaguing his thoughts.

Besides, a man fishing would be less suspicious than a boat anchored so far out for no apparent reason, wouldn't it? He'd been trained to operate the boat but had never been a rich yachtsman. They did this kind of thing, didn't they?

He threw a line landward, watching for Thaddeus's return as he fished. His line had not more than touched the water before there came a sharp tug on his rod, then a harder pull, nearly yanking it out of his unprepared hands. He reeled in a nice-sized sea bass, its shiny blue-gray scales and pink-tinged gills glistening in the sun. Shaking his head, he landed the fish and went to find a container.

There'd been a portable ice maker in the gear, hadn't there? He unpacked the unit, filled it with water, and powered it up. Back on deck, he continued the charade. Obviously, this one fish had been lost. It'd make a nice dinner, but the anomaly wouldn't repeat itself.

Less than ten minutes later, he'd caught not just more fish, but too much. His cooler could hold no more. With each cast, his frustration grew. The hook would barely touch the water before the jerk of another strike transmitted through the line. He was never allowed to rest, and he needed rest after the storm. His arms ached, his back was tight with pulled muscles, and his side and legs were covered in bruises.

One never knew when peril would call, requiring action. To fail to recuperate, to be ready for that action was unconscionable, given the chance, and this was one of those chances, the sun ready to warm sore muscles, the boat's restful rocking a balm. If it hadn't been for these irrepressible fish interrupting the opportunity.

Growling at the most recent catch, a huge sea trout, he pulled out the hook and tossed it back with an oath.

He stripped the hook from his line, attaching only a lead sinker. He wouldn't have to worry about snagging anything now. With a satisfied nod, he cast far into the blue. As soon as he did, something took the sinker and started running with it. He reeled in another fish. It was holding the lead sinker in closed mouth, refusing to let go.

Phillip sighed, cut the line, and dropped the suicidal fish into the water. He went belowdecks and rummaged in the repair parts until he found a section of pipe six inches in length. This he tied to his line. Nothing would swallow such an outsized lure.

He cast again and eased his aching backside onto the deck chair, watching the coastline for the dinghy. His rod constantly bounced in his hands, the water boiling where line met water, but no fish could be large enough to take his improvised bait. Then he froze. Imagine what kind of monster it would take to swallow a six-inch pipe!

He was reeling the line back in, spinning as fast as possible. Was that a growing swell, even now following his approaching line? Some monster come to take his bet? Should he keep reeling or just throw the whole thing, rod and all, to the deeps?

A chuckle sounded from above and behind. There, Jeremiah's mussed hair was outlined against the bright sky, his head peeking over the forward deck.

"Hey. Have good nap?" Phillip called. He'd forgotten all about the lad he'd left drowsing topside.

"Not sleep. Nerves. Anyway, show too good. Funny."

"Yes, strange." Phillip again struggled to speak Common Tongue. "Have never seen such."

Jeremiah rubbed his chin. "No, not seen, have heard. Some scrolls make histories. Many stories like this. I show them to you. My father calls this thing ark effect."

"Strange word."

"Word from early time. First Word of God were carried in box called ark. If have box, serve God, blessed much. Many miracles."

Unconsciously, Phillip reverted to his native language. "Another good reason to keep you out of their grasp. We don't want to give the Order any blessings."

Jeremiah raised his hands in apology. "Understand this not."

In Common, Phillip said, "I see. Miracle, many miracle, with you. Never let Order get scrolls, get miracles for themselves."

Jeremiah shook his head, his expression grave. "Oh no. Is good miracle only for peoples who love God. Is bad miracle for peoples turn backs on God. These story, too, are in history." His lips flattened and eyes narrowed. "I like see Order have these bad miracles."

He gave a firm nod. "I think I like this very much."

CHAPTER 15

Once in Two Rivers, Lars delivered his note to the institute librarian—the same older woman with those same kind, playful eyes, the ones that seemed to know more than they were letting on. Then, his jacket tight against the blustering fall winds, he returned to the terminal and claimed a seat on an outside bench.

Scanning the street, waiting for Curtis to arrive dressed as an old lady, Lars gave a double take when a young man pedaled up on a taxi bike. "Lars, right? I was sent to give you a lift. Hop on."

While he puffed and pedaled uphill, the cabbie asked, "How do you know the professor?"

Lars pulled his lip. What was the safe answer here? Who was this professor guy? No way to tell for sure, so he deflected. "Oh, a friend of a friend. Are you a student?"

That should move them to a safer topic. After all, Father Curtis always said there were few things people liked to talk about more than themselves.

They pulled up in front of a brick hotel. His benefactor waved him in. "Stop at the front desk and give them your name. They have a room waiting for you."

Inside, the clerk handed him a key marked 215. "Up those stairs, second floor on your right."

Grinning, anticipation lightening his steps, Lars took the stairs two at a time to a landing, past a door marked Mezzanine Mechanical —Authorized Entry Only, and up more stairs until he faced a glass door for the second floor. At room 215, he inserted the key in the lock. Father Curtis was inside the cramped little room, sitting in a straight wooden chair, studying a notebook on his lap.

"Father!" Lars hurried across the worn burgundy carpet to give Curtis a bear hug. "I'm sorry to bother you, but I have so many questions."

"Not a bother, son. It does me good to see you. I miss you and all of your family." Curtis looked out the window, the dusty pane allowing the view of an alley and another brick wall beyond, a warehouse by the looks of it. The sight seemingly mesmerized him, his smile faltering. "You have no idea. I spend my days largely alone. Adjusting has been difficult." He let out a breath. "What questions can I help you with?"

Lars lowered himself to the lumpy mattress, facing Curtis. "I'm worried about Leif. He and Dad got in a blowup. Leif threw all of his work on Dad's desk and walked out. Quit."

Curtis frowned. "He no longer works at Northwoods?"

Lars toyed with the tassels edging the floral bedcover, kneading them through his fingers like prayer beads. "Oh, he came back, kinda. He's freelancing, still putting work through the mill, but now he's running his own jobs for commission."

A sideways nod. "That may be a healthy move. Give him and your dad some space to clear the air."

"Yeah, that's what I thought, at first." He let the tassels fall. "But it's not working so well. I mean, he's doing the job fine, but he's drinking harder. When he had to show up at the office early to please Dad, he kept the drinking under control." Lars rolled his eyes. "At least on work nights. Now he might go on a tear in the middle of the week or all week even. Things aren't good with Diana, either."

"Lars, I am sorry." Curtis seemed to lose himself, staring again out the dingy window, then wiped his eyes with a sleeve. "What can I do to help?"

Lars clasped his right fist in his other hand. "Tell me what to say. I tried to talk to Leif about Creator God, but I messed it up. He laughed and walked out, didn't care." The heat of tears threatened release. He held them back. "What do I say to get through to him? If he'd just try, he'd find God. Then he wouldn't want to drink anymore. Maybe he and Diana could get things working again, especially if I told her about God. That'd help, wouldn't it? How do I do it?" Now he choked on the tears. "How do I make them listen like you made me?"

Face reflecting the pain Lars felt, Curtis settled next to Lars, hand on his shoulder. "I wish I could give you those answers, but that's not how the world works. There are no secret words you can say to make someone listen or to make them stop doing bad things." He squeezed Lars's shoulder. "Believe me. I've tried so many times, but people only listen when they want to hear. They only quit doing those bad things, drinking, for instance, when they decide they want to quit. Until then, you and I are wasting our breath. All you can do is to be there, be a good influence, plant the right seeds, and be prepared to help them. When they're ready."

Lars peered into those kindly, dark eyes, searching for answers there. "What can I do to *make* him ready?"

In those eyes was a distant, growing sadness. "That's just it, son. You can't."

"Well then, when will he decide?"

Releasing Lars's shoulder, Curtis frowned at the window and the cheap floral curtains. "That's up to him. The answer is different for everyone. The sad news is some people never turn back from their dash toward destruction. That's the hard, cruel fact of it. You need to be aware of that. Without giving up yourself, be prepared to catch him when he falls."

Lars shuddered. He didn't want to see what falling looked like if it was worse than what was happening now. "What do you mean when he falls? How do I know when that happens?"

Curtis blew out a breath. "You keep looking for easy answers. I don't have any. Some people get to a point where the pain of consequences causes them to turn back. We call that hitting bottom. For some, hitting bottom results in terrible lifelong consequences. Some people never do. They die first."

Now, the tears broke free to splatter the carpet. "I don't want him to hit bottom like that. Why can't there be a better way?" He kept his face tipped down to hide those tears. His fingers again worked the bedspread. A tassel was missing, and a burn hole scorched a flower.

Curtis's whisper came as if from a great distance. "I wish I knew. Oh, how I wish."

PHILLIP SHADED HIS EYES, squinting. Was that movement nearer the shore? He retrieved the telescope and focused it on a craft weaving among the anchored boats. Yes, no doubt about it. Moving this way was the tender.

He called out to Jeremiah, who was again sunning on the foredeck. "Thaddeus on way back. Have passenger. You take pistol, hide in cabin, follow my lead."

Phillip checked the chamber of his own pistol and slipped it into his waistband, then assumed a relaxed waiting position, legs bent, knees absorbing the rocking of the boat, ready to spring if need be.

He waved as the dinghy approached. Thaddeus's returning grin augured no trouble. Still, when the craft bumped against the stern platform, Phillip didn't jump down to catch the line, electing to maintain the tactical advantage of his elevated position.

Thaddeus leapt to the *Tikvah* and secured the tender.

Phillip called to him in their shared homeland's language. "Should I be worried about this guy? Can he understand me?"

"He is no danger and seems to be limited to Common."

Phillip relaxed. A bit. "You checked him for weapons?"

Thaddeus gave a thumbs-up, then helped his passenger onto the *Tikvah*. Once they had climbed to the main deck, he made introductions, speaking in Common Tongue. The newcomer, Captain Simon, was a short, stout man, large with muscle and not fat. With his spiky crew cut and short burly arms, his appearance was reminiscent of that of a badger.

Once introductions had been made, Thaddeus said to Simon, "So you tell me you know I come, yes?"

"Yep. It's true." Captain Simon swigged at his canteen. "I was waiting for you folks. You see, I had this dream."

Phillip jolted. So many unexplainable things, and now this? "Excuse?"

Captain Simon capped the canteen, the sweat shiny on his forehead. "A very persistent and persuasive dream, you might say. I had it three times. First was two days ago. My crew and I had arrived at the grain terminal here—"

"Wait." Phillip then spoke to Thaddeus in their native tongue. "Where is here? Where are we?"

Thaddeus held up a finger toward Simon. "Pardon moment." Then to Phillip, in the same tongue. "You won't believe it until you see it. We hit the right continent, but the wrong coast. We are on the southern, not the eastern coast and are now sitting outside the Great River delta."

"Impossible. We would have run aground on the southeastern peninsula first. And we are another, what, seven hundred miles further west? None of that is logical."

Thaddeus shrugged. "Possible or not, it is true. I saw the proof myself. How many impossible things must we experience before we quit using that word?"

What was the point of guessing? Either they were where Thaddeus claimed, or they would learn otherwise soon enough. Phillip returned his attention to Simon. "Pardon to interrupt. Please tell story."

Simon started where he had left off, telling of the events of the past three days. "When I got to the docks, I knew it as the place from the dream, so I tied up. And here comes Thaddeus, just as I remembered him, cruising by in that dinghy. I hailed him, and here we are."

Laughing, Thaddeus slapped his thigh. "He yell '*Tikvah*, *Tikvah*,' waving to me like madman."

Simon drew back, brows furrowed and mouth in a mock frown. "To be sure, scared me to death to see you there, folk just walkin' out of dreams as you are." His gaze became distant. "Though the thought of *not* catching you scared me worse."

CHAPTER 16

Lars sobbed silently. He tried to stop, tried to apologize, but couldn't force the words past his constricted throat.

Curtis gave him time, made him feel it was okay and there was no hurry.

As his emotions ran down, Lars raised his head from his tear-soaked hands. "I'm sorry, Father. That's so embarrassing."

"No apology needed. If you knew the many nights I wept over the stubborn people I love, you'd not be embarrassed."

Lars wiped soggy eyes. "I'm just tired from all the traveling, and the dreams I've been having haven't helped one bit."

Now Curtis sat up, alert. "What kind of dreams?"

"Oh boy, howdy. I've never had such. You know how most times you wake up and everything is okay, no matter how scared you were while you slept? Once you're awake, you can laugh, and the next thing you know, you barely remember what the dream was, right?"

Curtis pursed his lips, gaze intense. "Yes?"

Lars rubbed his forehead, groping for the words hidden beyond reach. "Well, these dreams are more stubborn. They don't go away. Like the other night, I dreamed Phillip was on a boat somewhere and was gonna get himself killed. I couldn't get over it for anything. It took a whole night of praying before that one let go of me." He snapped his attention back to Curtis. How could he have forgotten? "Oh, hey. Did you get the note I sent? That very night when I was praying, I met Creator God."

Curtis cocked his head, tone seemingly nonchalant but posture stiff, betraying hidden tension. "What night did you say you had that dream, son?"

What night? What did that matter? "The night we met. Last week."

Curtis jumped to his feet, knocking over the chair, the back rapping on the carpet. "Wait right here. Don't move. I have someone you need to meet."

When Simon ushered the trio onto the towboat, the crew was in tumult, crowding about the gangway, fingers pointing, riotous voices raised. As they climbed aboard, the first mate kept the mob away, but exclamations followed, some men saying, "It's them. The men from the dreams!" And others muttering less-welcoming words.

The dark glances ratcheted Phillip's nerves, so he appreciated the promised privacy of a cabin, one on the upper decks away from the belowdecks crew quarters.

Leaving the main deck and the agitated crewmen behind, Captain Simon led up a flight of expanded metal stairs, or ladder as Simon called it. Their feet rang hollowly as they climbed around a landing, up a second flight, then through a metal hatch and into a companionway, its bulkheads, deck, and overhead all welded metal sheeting. A single porthole at the far end cast dim light into the gray space, revealing four more small stateroom doors, two on either side of the narrow passage.

Simon stopped before one and indicated the others with a jerk of his bristly chin. "My chief engineer, pilot, and assistant pilot are in the other three cabins. We moved the first mate below to clear this berth for ya." He opened the door and ushered them inside. "Sorry we couldn't fit a third bunk. Two of you'll have to hot rack, or one of you take the floor. Best we could do. My cabin is on the next level above. If you need me, you'll find me there or up top in the wheelhouse."

He stepped into the corridor, then turned, stubby arms braced on either side of the frame, crew-cut head poking into the cramped space. "First mate'll keep the crew clear of you, though you've naught to worry about. They're excitable, but they're all good lads. Soon, the novelty'll wear off. Mark me." And he disappeared down the passageway and out the hatch.

The cabin housed a metal desk and two bunks, so closely spaced even the slight Jeremiah had to duck his head when he sat.

But it hardly mattered. To be safely hidden in this space, away from prying eyes, not to mention hunters, was a blessing.

The deep rumbling of ship's machines intensified, the vibrations radiating through Phillip's boot soles. Outside the porthole, the concrete wharf-side began to slide past. He stepped outside and grasped the railing as chocolate-brown water churned and the docks shrank in their wake. No other craft gave chase, none as much as moved their direction. He let out a deep breath, willing tense muscles to release, his grip on the steel to loosen.

Thaddeus appeared at his side, his own body language still screaming high alert and something else. That same pall that shadowed his features since his accidental departure from his homeland. But what he said was, "You think Jeremiah's safe here?"

Phillip looped his arm around Thaddeus's shoulders, then squeezed after a comradely shake. "Seems so. But best we keep two at all times guarding the scrolls. We'll take turns getting a little air. Some exercise."

His body screamed for that after so long cooped up on the sailboat. What a joy it'd be to get a workout, practice a few forms.

And then, answering Thaddeus's unasked question, he added, "And once in familiar territory, I promise. My people will find a way to get you home."

Thaddeus stared at the receding gantry cranes, then returned to the cabin, the lines on his brow as deep as before, his eyes just as shadowed.

Curtis returned to Lars, a much older man in tow. "Lars, please meet Professor Reuel, my mentor and friend. Professor, please meet Lars, my young friend from Northwoods."

Professor Reuel shook Lars's hand and made a formal bow. "I am pleased to meet you, at last, my boy. It seems as if I have known you for so long, having heard so much about you from Curtis."

So this was the professor? Lars shifted, glancing at Curtis for guidance. "Thank you, sir."

"Oh, don't sir me. I don't even let my first-year students do that." The old man eased himself into the straight chair. "But tell me about your remarkable dream. Omit no detail."

Lars related the dream, his strong compulsion to pray, and the visitation from Creator God. "I don't want to sound proud or braggy or anything, but I know it was Him. Have you heard of such a thing before, Professor?"

The old man waved. "Oh yes, of course, my boy. But first, a question of my own." He turned to Curtis. "This was the same night, correct?"

Curtis nodded his affirmative.

Reuel rested his chin on his fist, blue eyes burning bright. "Interesting. We three had a similar experience, Lars, all on the same night. Of course, Curtis and I were awake and so did not dream as you did. Instead, we had a vision in which we, too, saw Phillip in danger. We had the same pressing need to pray for him, and so of course we did." He leaned back, eyes narrowing and growing distant. "Apparently, our friend was in need, and Creator God intervened by compelling *us* to intervene, you might say, through prayer."

Lars opened his mouth to repeat his question.

But the old man's raised hand forestalled interruption. "And yes, boy, before you ask again, I believe your experience was genuine.

Such an awareness of the divine presence is called an epiphany, and others of my acquaintance have enjoyed such, although I have never been so blessed."

He lowered his hand to his lap, gnarled fingers locking together as if grasping for something he couldn't hold onto. "It is rare, but it's recognized as a legitimate experience, albeit a subjective one, unprovable in worldly terms." He steepled his fingers before his lips. "Although, in the case of your dream, one could reasonably argue you have objective evidence, no?"

Smacking a fist into his palm, Curtis grinned. "Of course! We all had the same vision at the same time in separate locations. That's proof this was a genuine experience, based in reality and fact, validated by our separate witness. Amazing! I never thought to be able to count such experiences as objective evidence, but this could be counted as such, couldn't it?"

Lars rubbed at the shivers rising on his forearms. "So I really met Creator God? I was sure, but at the same time, I was afraid I was making it up, somehow." He hiccuped, the echo of a sob.

"My boy, Creator God is as real as this furniture." Reuel slapped the wooden side table. "Just because you cannot see Him doesn't make it not so. Can you see the wind? Is the wind therefore not real? No! You see the effect of the wind on the trees. Likewise, we see the effect of Creator God in this episode, as we can in so many other things."

He stopped to catch his breath, relaxing back into his chair. "Which begs the question you are about to ask me. Where is Phillip, and is he safe?" He shook his head, the wispy white fringe of his hair catching a ray of sunshine that somehow penetrated the dingy window. "I do not know. I make no promises, but I will risk a direct inquiry."

He levered himself against the table to stand. "At best, it will be many days before we can hope for any response, and I stress that this is the best case." He wagged his finger. "We must be patient and each do our respective jobs as we wait for word."

Lars piped in. "So, what's my job?"

Professor Reuel raised his brows.

Curtis stepped in, hand on Lars's shoulder. "It's your job to go home and help your family. Pray for them. When we know more, we'll tell you."

"And you'll tell me more of the True Text? I want to learn."

Professor Reuel opened the door to leave, chuckling. "You cannot stop a Seeker from seeking, my boy. I should know."

CHAPTER 17

Leif searched about the sawmill. Where was Young Bob? He was about to check the house when a muffled "oh, you nutterbutter" came from the other side of the yard.

He followed a stream of charmingly unblasphemous curses toward the kiln building. Outside the kiln proper, a paved ramp cut into the earth, terminating at the exposed stone foundation, inset into which was a wooden door. He stepped through. Inside, a pair of greasy overall legs stuck out from underneath a large metal frame.

"Bob?" he called, peering into the dark. He was about to lean over the housing when a *whumpfh* preceded a mushroom-shaped fireball. It ballooned out of the construct and spread dissipating flame over the blackened concrete ceiling. He yelped and danced back, rubbing his head, putting out stray sparks in his scalp. His hands came away black and smelling of burned hair.

Bob rolled out from under the contraption. He lay on a low four-wheeled cart, a pipe wrench in one hand. "Oh, sorry, Mr. Leif. You shoulda let me know you were there. Coulda got yourself hurt."

"I did tell you I was here, and what were you doing?"

"This old burner was being stubborn. Pa says she always had a mind of her own. He and she have a kind of hot-and-cold love affair, you might say." He yukked at his own joke, then climbed to his feet and peeked above the dish-shaped mechanism.

Leif followed more cautiously.

Inside the bowl was a flame, a perfect blue flower. The whole thing was nothing more than a burner like on a gas stove, but this one was at least four feet around.

"She's running sweet now, don'cha think?" He grinned at Leif. "Ole Mister Haman's gonna be impressed at what you done here, Mr. Leif."

The heat was building. Leif pointed at the flames. "Should we be staying in here with that?"

Young Bob led the way to a room abutting the kiln's main exterior wall, inside of which was a collection of valves and meters. He put a wrench on a lever and turned it. "This is the main. The other valves are set just where I want 'em. When the time comes, we can open the main and fire her up for Ole Mister Haman."

"I appreciate everything you've done here, Bob. I'm impressed."

Bob grinned. "Pa and I are tickled pink you're giving us a chance to get her running again. Looking forward to working her for you. Speaking of that, Pa has something for you in the house. C'mon." They walked to the old cottage, and Young Bob opened the screen door, gesturing Leif ahead.

Inside the dim interior, Leif stopped. Floral patterned paper from another century clung in wrinkled sheets to the walls. Soot stains formed a reverse waterline around the top patterned border. A kettle steamed atop an antique woodburning range. The pitted wooden lay counters bare, and cooking utensils hung on hooks covered the available wall space.

"You keep a neat kitchen, Bob."

From the doorway, Old Bob entered the room, carrying a cracked binder under one arm. "My missus, God rest her soul, would skin me alive if I let her kitchen go to seed."

"Hello, Old Bob." Leif leaned a hip against one of those spotless counters. "Young Bob said you needed to see me?"

"You bet. Told you I had these old notes." The older man patted his binder. "Got 'em right here. Copied off a few things you and Young Bob'll be needin'. Blank work schedules, toolin' lifespans, parts inventories, maintenance schedules, output figures for plannin', and the like." He handed over a thick folder.

Leif flipped through the handwritten papers inside. "This is awesome. It'll take a lot of guesswork out of things. I can't tell you how much I appreciate the both of you." He slapped Young Bob's back. "You should be proud of your boy. He's a real gem."

"No, Mr. Leif. It's we who appreciate you. Gettin' this old mill back on her feet is a lifelong dream, and because of you, I'm gonna live to see it happen." The old man shook Leif's hand, then snapped his fingers. He fished in the binder for another folder. "Almost forgot. Here's the labor requirements. You'll want to have your people trained well in advance. Can't have the yard fillin' up with timber and no crew to mill her out."

"Hadn't thought that far ahead, but thanks."

Old Bob worked his cud, squinting at Leif. Weighing him? "Can be a dangerous business. Get serious men, professionals. No drunks or jokers. Young Bob has a list of interested candidates, all eager given the pay we offered. Generous, that. And smart. You'll have your pick of the best men in the county. You can set up interviews whenever you're ready."

Leif pulled his mouth into a tight expression, hand to the back of his head, fingers digging deep into wind-tangled hair. "I wasn't planning on hiring *anyone* myself. I was just helping you get the mill going so you could run it."

Old Bob chortled and slapped a thigh of his patched coveralls. "Do I look like I have the money to pay a crew? Especially at that rate? Nope, you're the moneyman, just like you promised Young Bob. We'll make sure the mill runs like a dream for ya, show you what needs to be done." A gnarled finger pointed Leif's way. "Just bring enough men. We'll train 'em up for ya."

Leif nodded. But, in doing so, in the course of one day and with no assets, had he committed himself to becoming one of the largest employers in Northwoods? The highest-paying one at that?

He shoved aside his creeping unease. With Haman's backing, this is a sure thing. A guaranteed winner. He nodded again, then grinned, pumping Old Bob's hand. "You better believe I will."

How hard could it be to saw logs, anyway?

PHILLIP RESISTED the urge to glance at his watch. It was almost his turn to take a break, but *watching* the minute hand creep toward the top of the hour only made it seem to move slower.

As the guardians of the scrolls, he, Thaddeus, and Jeremiah had agreed that two of them should stay with their precious cargo at all times.

And that made it a long couple of days. The confined cabin was wearing on everyone.

Phillip's body thrummed, limbs jittery, and now, despite his so recent vow not to, he was glancing at his watch, counting down until his free time.

At least the crew had been steered clear of their space. That had been easily enforced once the strange happenings began to occur.

The first thing crewmen noticed was extraordinarily fast healing. When they received the cuts and abrasions—a normal part of a deckhand's rough work—those seemed to disappear overnight. This brought more muttered words, more dark glances.

But Captain Simon assured them there was no reason for concern. "They're a spooky lot, but solid men all. They'll keep to their place."

Phillip's watch ticked three p.m., then five after. Where was Jeremiah? He had a wristwatch. He was perfectly capable of telling the hour, so why was he stealing Phillip's break time?

But there Jeremiah was, opening the cabin door and making room for Phillip to exit, that same quiet smile on his face. Phillip winced. How could he let himself become so irritable and with this lad, of all people? He slapped Jeremiah's shoulder, bounded through the companionway, out the hatch, slid down the double flights of ladders, and strode into the bright sunshine. Arms spread, he embraced those warm rays.

But was that a disturbance near the forward railing? A cluster of agitated crewmen? He changed direction and slipped up behind to eavesdrop.

"Terrible thing to see," someone muttered.

"Lost me lunch, I did."

"And *that's* supposed to matter?" An older deckhand slapped the younger upside the head. "Andy lost his *leg*, he did."

"What coulda happened?" A stout man spat over the railing, then rocked back on his heels. "Routine work, making fast another empty barge. How many times do you think Andy helped secure a new one to the daisy chain?"

The older man shuddered. "Worst time to slip, with the new barge nearly in place, those iron hulls ready to crush a man. He well knew that's the time they best like to bite, but it caught him anyway. Sometimes, your number just comes up."

The heads of the stretcher-bearers appeared over the forward rail, and they carried the screaming crewman aboard. Captain Simon and the first mate, accompanied by a medic, rushed to the man's side to inspect his injuries. The man's cries subsided. He must've lost consciousness.

Phillip knelt close as the medic slit the injured man's gory pant leg. The cloth opened to expose a limb covered in blood. The medic dabbed the skin to find the source—but no injury of any kind was evident.

The medic turned to a crewman who helped carry the stretcher. "Were you the one out there with him? I thought you said his leg was crushed."

The pallid crewman nodded. "It was. His shinbone stuck out, and the foot was just danglin' and floppin'." The man covered his mouth before turning away.

The medic crouched to the stretcher and inspected the intact leg again, tipping it this way and that. "Not so much as a scratch," he muttered. He dropped it and slit the other pant leg, only to expose another healthy limb.

The injured man jerked awake with a shout. Eyes showing white, he reached to grab the bloody leg. At first gingerly, then with greater agitation, he ran hands up and down his shin. He sat up, mouth agape, staring at the limb he'd just seemed loath to look upon.

At the medic's prompting, he flexed his knee, then stood, and tested it with his weight. He then began to jump up and down, laughing.

The crewmate who had witnessed the accident went an even whiter shade, then sank to the deck. He rocked and lowered head to knees, repeating, "I saw that leg. I saw it."

Phillip faded back into the crowd, stopping behind Cleeve, a man well past the age of the other deckhands, never having been made mate for he liked to stir up trouble.

When the captain had brought the three on board, Cleeve claimed they were witches casting curses on the crew. He promised a great evil would befall the ship if the strangers remained. Only because nothing bad happened had Captain Simon convinced the crew to ignore Cleeve's ravings. Mostly.

Now, Cleeve stepped onto a tool chest and raised his arms. "This is the work of these witches." He shook a finger at Phillip. "These foreigners are cursin' this ship. Didn't the trouble start when they showed up?"

Phillip harrumphed. The trouble started two days prior, but saying so would do naught but waste breath. Men like this Cleeve were skilled at ignoring facts.

Cleeve grabbed a nearby deckhand. "Danny, you ever seen fish jumping on board as they been since these foreigners came?"

Danny shook his head.

"They're an omen, these fish. Possessed by the evil spirits these devil worshipers brought on our boat!"

Indeed, a steady stream of fish kept jumping onto the lower deck, flopping in the sun by the hundreds. The cook had been overjoyed by the haul. Until hordes of gasping fish, so much more than the crew could ever eat, filled the working space.

Captain Simon spoke of harvesting the bounty and selling the catch at market during port stops. But with no hold in which to ice the tons of wriggling flesh, he'd been forced to assign extra duty, never a popular move, posting two men round the clock, to keep the deck clear. The crew had stopped thinking it funny.

"Mort, let's see that finger of yours. I saw you cut it clean to the bone yesterday. Where's that cut now?"

Mort's face took on a haunted expression. He looked at his finger and then at the ground, tucking the offending digit under an armpit. "Ain't no cut no more."

Cleeve turned a circle, arms outspread. "Any of you ever seen such?" When he received no answer, only troubled looks and shaking heads, he pounced. "Our next stop is Port Ambrose. My brother-in-law is an Order priest at the temple there. I say we haul these three before the tribunal. Make them answer for their hex makin'. Might even be a reward for us, bringin' in some heretics and magic makers for trial!"

The crew glanced at each other. A few heads began to nod. A low murmur of approval spread through the men, growing louder as Cleeve whipped them up.

Phillip slipped away, melting into the shadows with a nearly supernatural act of his own. He must warn the others. In their cramped cabin, Jeremiah was reading while Thaddeus slept on his narrow bunk. Phillip shook him awake. "Trouble comes. Crew want capture us, take to Order on trial for be magic maker."

Thaddeus rose to his feet, instantly awake.

A subdued knock brushed the door. Simon stepped inside and locked it behind himself. "You heard all that, Phillip?"

"Heard. Yes."

"I'll find a way to stop Cleeve from getting to shore." Simon ran a hand across his bristly scalp, grimacing. "If he gets a message out, most I can do is give you a head start. Best you be ready to run. His snake of a brother-in-law is the worst kind of bully and has no little support at the temple."

Phillip gripped the captain's shoulder. "Thank you, my friend. But no. We must go, endanger you no more." He began to stow his meager possessions in his pack.

"No." Jeremiah spoke one word. He sat on his bed, wearing his quiet smile, legs crossed. "No run. Bad man, bad miracle. You will see."

That smile of his. Was the lad that confident or insane?

CHAPTER 18

Maripol ducked beneath the cold running water and let it soak his hair and run over his face. He cupped a handful to his bloodshot eyes. Then he scrubbed fingertips at his scalp as much to invigorate as to wash away the greasy malaise, a result of twenty hours per day at his desk, for all these days since Jeremiah and the *Tikvah* disappeared.

He left the cramped restroom and forced fatigued legs into the semblance of a march down the corridor to the command center. His footfalls echoed from the surrounding concrete and metal, everything painted the variation of mint green favored by governments the world over. Apparently in an effort to more thoroughly demotivate the already laggard security men stationed here.

Outside the big room, he surveyed his temporary kingdom through the floor-to-ceiling glass. A metal wall clock watched over the rows of desks facing the status boards, occupied by men hunched bleary-eyed over documents they'd doubtlessly combed dozens of times already.

But comb them again, they would. And again. Until they found the missing clue, the one that would explain what, exactly, occurred here in Mazkelon.

When he initiated the worldwide manhunt, he circulated the

marina videos, offering a reward to anyone who could identify those on board with Jeremiah. Three of the men had been recognised as highly placed government officials, including the general. None of whom could have been there, if dozens of reliable witnesses were to be believed.

"I put new letters on your desk, sir." A young clerk hustled over.

Maripol scowled at the thought of the growing pile, most of them threatening, demanding redress. Why was it so many powerful people held grudges?

When a local agent joined him, Maripol nodded at the freeze-frame video taunting him from the screens up front, the other two men accompanying Jeremiah strangely blurred. All the cameras that captured their movements suffered similar malfunctions. "It's too distorted for an automated search of the database, but not so much as to preclude identification. If we only had a list of suspects . . . " A list he didn't have as of yet.

The agent sipped his coffee. "Getting any worthwhile leads with such poor imagery has proven difficult."

The video had been altered. If not, how was it only those two faces were blurred? "Any new word from the expert analysts?"

The agent clattered the mug to an overstuffed filing shelf. "So far, none can detect any tampering, at least not by any known technology."

Who had perpetrated this act, and how? It required elaborate and sophisticated preparation, so why couldn't Maripol find the first hint of evidence? He shut down that thought. That was a dead end, and more pressing matters required attention. He *would* return to this trail and follow it to the conclusion. Would find those responsible . . . but at the proper time.

The agent yawned. "We've had multiple new leads on the boat come in."

Indeed. Too many. The Order had called in extra investigators to chase them all down, at massive cost. Maripol had better have definitive results to justify the expense.

Within the circle of search, that being the ever-expanding radius the boat could have traveled, they had chased down dozens of false leads. "This pattern of failure becomes repetitive."

The man stiffened. "Our men are working hard, sir. Agents have boarded and searched innumerable vessels of every description, from fishing trawlers to luxury motor yachts. We've hauled in a score of craft, their names ranging from *Tivah* to *Timah*, even a small sunfish sailing skiff by the name of *Tinah*."

"But no sighting of the boat we're looking for."

Maripol waved off the annoying little man, then weaved through the command center, nodding as he passed those present. Their grim boredom transformed into straight-backed attention at his appearance. Once at his desk, he reviewed the file again, sifting through the data for any vessel matching his search criterion. Buried in the stack was a report from the other side of the world, a distance the *Tikvah* could never have crossed in such a short time. But he never left a loose end, no matter how unlikely. He dashed off a message, requesting the local authorities inspect the vessel and eliminate it as a search candidate.

As he finished this dispatch, his attaché appeared in his doorway. "We found him."

"Who?"

"Hilkiah's mole, the one we suspected was operating from within our staff."

At last, some good news.

Finding any thread to pull on in Hilkiah's orbit had been a waste of time. The man was a widower, and Jeremiah had been homeschooled, had few associates. Hilkiah's colleagues at the university had been thoroughly interviewed, all under truth drug. Not one suspected Hilkiah of subversive activities, much less had taken part in it. None provided any worthwhile information.

Now, perhaps, Maripol had gotten a break. He would squeeze every drop of information from this traitor, would use that information to exact justice.

He marched to the interview cell, boots clipping a reenergized tattoo on polished concrete. He stopped in the observation room and watched the suspect through the one-way glass, gauging baseline behaviors, then took a seat to watch for nonverbal clues the others might miss. He then nodded to the pair of interrogators, who collected their case files and slipped out.

"Are we recording?" he asked the tech.

"Yes, sir, and no chance anyone can alter this feed however they managed to at the marina."

No need to comment on *that*.

The two operatives entered the room, sitting opposite the suspect in silence, checking their notes, and staring at the suspect. The better to heighten his anxiety before the real work began.

A slight bookish man in his midthirties, light-skinned and bespectacled, the prisoner rocked in his seat. Sweat sheened his face and dampened his rumpled shirt. His knees bounced, the handcuff chain vibrating between his jittering hands.

The questioners began with the basics. When asked if he was Hilkiah's associate, the man flinched, paused, then answered, "Yes."

"What is the nature of your association with Hilkiah?"

The man inhaled, head laid back, closed eyes tilted heavenward. He gave a sideways glance toward the observation glass. "I—" He gulped and raised his head, straightened his spine and squared his shoulders. "I helped him avoid scrutiny from the Order. I passed classified information to him and planted false information on his behalf."

The interrogators both jerked backward at the forthright answer, then recovered. "You admit aiding and abetting a fugitive and a heretic?"

The man remained rigidly straight in his chair. "Yes, and to being a heretic myself. The Order is a fraud and a pox on humanity." He faced the one-way glass. "I will answer any question you put to me, and I will answer honestly."

"Do you understand you are accused of and are admitting to heresy and espionage against the Order and the State? And these crimes are punishable by public torture and death?"

The man bowed his head, then clasped his hands before his chin, seeming to whisper something to himself. He straightened again and faced the window, ignoring his questioners, seeming to look Maripol straight in the eyes. Impossible, of course. He couldn't see through the mirrored glass, but a shiver still ran down Maripol's spine.

The man's voice, weak and quavering before, now rang out strong, vital, as if giving a speech, not a confession. "I understand. I also understand that you can do nothing to me that is not allowed by Creator God. I understand that you can kill my body, which is destined for death at any rate, but you cannot touch my immortal soul. I commit my life into the care of Creator God, and if it is His will that I suffer and die on His behalf, I accept that with great joy."

He smiled at the window, at Maripol. A winsome smile, melancholy flavored with fear, yes, but also with a confidence, a certainty that no one in his position should ever possess. Didn't he know what horror he faced? Surely, he had witnessed the public tortures? Everyone had.

The man leaned closer to the one-way glass, confidence radiating. "Before you kill me, may I first tell you the truth about your false Order and the true Creator God?"

CHAPTER 19

Multiple heavy footsteps climbed the stairs toward the executive offices, conversation loud as the group traipsed past Lars's door. One of the voices was Dad's, and he was in a high mood, unusually chatty. Cheerful, even.

Dad's head poked through the door. "Lars, come to the conference room and have lunch with us. I'd like you to meet someone."

The fine hairs on Lars's neck began to stand. Probably just the draft coming through his open door, right? He marked his place in a thick document and stood. When he entered the dark-paneled conference room, Dad sat with two other men.

"Lars, this is Diggs and his assistant, Snow."

Diggs, a middle-aged man, skinny except for a perfectly round potbelly, which could've been half a basketball beneath his shirt, claimed a chair. Thinning dark hair fell over bulging eyes, and broken capillaries spiderwebbed across his ruddy drinker's cheeks. Snow, a gravelly complected man, broad-shouldered and large-knuckled, inclined his head, and his nose that might've been flattened one too many times cast a shadow over his mouth.

"Diggs's the new consortium manager. You'll be seeing him a lot."

"Consortium?"

"Our new mill-worker's consortium."

Diggs spoke up. "We're creating the first-ever industry cooperative for woodworkers in the Republic. We call it the Organization of Woodworking Enterprises. Your dad has been instrumental in its creation. You should be very proud."

"Created for what?"

Dad leaned back in his chair and spread his arms. "Well, lots of things, eventually. Educational programs, for instance, but initially to facilitate cooperative efforts between mills, to help small companies work together on projects too large for them individually."

Something like a spider crept up Lars's spine, the fine hairs on his neck now at full alert. And not from any draft. "Like our new contract?"

"Yeah, like that." Dad nodded, his smile self-satisfied.

Mom walked in, followed by a girl from accounting, carrying sandwiches and drinks. As they ate, Dad and the newcomers reviewed a list of small mill workers, discussing which of them had or had not committed to the new combine, how to entice the resisters, what capabilities each mill offered, various strengths and weaknesses.

This combine wasn't in the early planning stages. Today represented the final touches on a campaign long in the making. These men spoke of agreements already in force, already signed by many companies, Northwoods included.

The contract for the Events Center was about to be, possibly already had been, carved up into pieces, shared by the other members of the Combine. Even worse, this Diggs guy claimed a stake as well.

What did Dad think he was doing? They'd worked hard, taken great risks to land that job. Now these shysters cut the competition in on the pie?

With every word, the skin on his brow tightened. Snow was obviously some kind of goon, used to taking, not earning. And Diggs was just too glib, too smooth.

When Mom stood to clear the empty plates, Lars helped, then caught her alone outside the conference room. “What do you think of these guys?”

“They seem to know what they’re doing.”

“Why is this the first I’ve heard of it?”

She dismissed that with a wave of the hand. “Oh. Well, that was Diggs. He’s organized other industry groups, has lots of experience. He said if word got out before the mill stewards had been briefed, the rumors would start, only causing problems. As it is, he’s done all the legwork and gotten most of them on board already, long before any whispers made the rounds.”

“Are you sure this is a good thing for us?”

“How could it not be? We need help with the Events Center job. We could never do that alone.”

She seemed so casual. How to get through? “Sure, but we can contract out portions as needed. Why do we need this guy in the middle? Seems like an unnecessary complication, another unproductive hand in the pot.”

Mom continued giving him her untroubled smile.

A frustrated breath exploded with his next words. “Mom, seriously. He strikes me as a gangster.”

She laughed. “Gangster? You always had such an imagination.” She laid her hand on his shoulder and gave a squeeze. “Trust your dad. This was his idea. It’ll do us nothing but good, having the small mills work together. And we need the leverage against the big companies.”

Lars put down his irritation, groaning with the effort. But what say did he have in the matter? He was just an employee, son and potential heir or no. He wasn’t going to make the mistakes Leif had, fight battles he couldn’t win. He went back to his office and his work.

All he could do was hope for the best.

Phillip couldn't sway Jeremiah, his only answer to repeated entreaties was: "Faith. Must have. God keeps promises. Believe, my brother."

As the night wore on and the first pink feathers of morning winged across the eastern porthole, the ache in Phillip's tensed muscles, and the throbbing in his temples increased. He worked the pressure points in his neck, at the base of his skull, forcing himself to relax. Wearing himself out, anxiously waiting, would help nothing. And something portended this would be a bad day, one not to be faced burdened with fatigue.

For the hundredth time, he evaluated their options. They were trapped, nowhere to hide on this ship if the Order came in force. They could run. They were not yet into Republic territory, still far south of the border. He had no allies in this area, no contacts.

If they were forced to flee now—and there may well be no other option—they'd be doing it in unfamiliar lands with no aid and no resources. It wouldn't end well.

Thaddeus had gone to keep watch on deck. He now burst through the cabin door. "Cleeve's gone. The night watch says he flagged down a small motor craft. He's headed for Ambrose."

Simon arrived on Thaddeus's heels. "I see you heard. I sent the mate and the sergeant at arms after him. They'll bring him back. Cleeve has disobeyed a direct order, not to mention abandoned his post. We're within our rights to put him in irons and haul him before the maritime court. That'll keep his troublemaking mouth shut plenty long. 'Specially if we keep him in the brig for, oh say, another port call or two." He grinned, bared teeth seeming eager to latch onto Cleeve.

Helping Jeremiah pack, in case flight became necessary, Phillip looked over his shoulder. "Where we are now? How long before out of Ambrose District?"

"Just under two miles from the lock and dam, south side of port. Should be there in ten, fifteen minutes. Depending on traffic, could wait in line for an hour or two. I'll cancel our port call. No empties to drop, just a chance for the boys to stretch their legs, so no damage done. And the boys'll live. I'll make it up to them later. Once through the lock, we'll keep motoring past." He laid a hand on Phillip's shoulder. "It'll be fine, lad. Cleeve didn't have much of a head start."

Once packed, Phillip and Thaddeus returned to the deck, holding the rail with white-knuckled grips as they urged the lumbering flotilla on, focused on the coming trouble.

Thaddeus groaned, then spoke in their mother tongue. "This snail's pace upriver, the whole time in sight of Ambrose, in sight of the temple spire—it's agonizing."

Indeed. At any moment, Cleeve could be betraying them.

Thaddeus flexed his grip, his shoulders inching toward his ears. "Every craft leaving dock could be the one, secretly filled with armed goons, headed our way."

Then the boat—slowed. Stopped. Now they waited stationary within a stone's throw of the dockside market for their turn through the lock.

"Is it my imagination," Thaddeus asked, "or are those people glancing our way?"

Phillip shaded his eyes, squinting to focus. *Were* there more people on the docks than when they'd arrived?

Thaddeus edged closer. "I think the crowd is drifting our way."

Phillip's gaze darted here and there, seeking the flash of a hidden weapon, the expected rush in their direction.

And then he chided himself. "Try to relax, Thaddeus. Remaining this tense, for this long, will leave us spent, our energy wasted." No need to say they might need said energy should any real threat materialize. He sank to the deck and worked through his usual warm-up, stretching to release overtense muscles, concentrating on heart rate and breathing. Thaddeus joined him, and he passed the time by teaching Thaddeus a simple sequence. Soon they had both fallen into rhythm. Muscle memory took over, and his body warmed to the flowing dance-like forms.

Beneath his feet, the gray steel deck plates throbbed, and they inched toward the dam. As the barges approached the narrow lock compartment, it appeared they wouldn't fit. Majestically, they edged the entirety of the barges, including the towboat, inside. The flotilla was over a thousand feet long and a hundred wide. With row upon row of barges tied into one massive whole, the men stationed on the furthest barge forward were little more than specks in the distance. Yet the space between the barges and the sidewall was no more than two or three feet.

He returned to his perch at the rail and leaned far forward, as if by inching closer he could better see the far distant prow. "Amazing. How can Captain Simon slide this monstrous construct into such a tight space so effortlessly?"

Thaddeus grunted. "But now we're trapped." He waved to the solid steel gates penning them in front and rear, the high concrete walls on either side, towering above their heads.

Yes, if Phillip were the Order, this was the time he'd strike.

He bounded up the ladder, past the level of their quarters, and up another where the captain's berth was. He sprinted onto the captain's walk, then rounded to the port side. Leaning against the metal railing and stretching high, he could just see over the concrete wall.

Other than one of the lock workers, who waved, no one took notice of him. He stayed there, on constant guard for any suspicious movement ashore.

Footsteps approached, and Thaddeus took position at his side. "Anything?"

Phillip gripped his hips and rocked off his heels. "Not yet, but you're right. This is a terrible spot to be caught. Does it seem to you this lock is taking longer than usual to cycle?"

Thaddeus pursed his lips, eyes narrowing.

Just then, the forward gate began to open. The big diesels thrummed, and they were moving, the concrete retaining walls creeping past. Then the nose of the lead barge again pointed into open water.

They had cleared the dam when a boat appeared, prow high and motor churning a deep foaming wake in the muddy brown waters. The ship's tender sped toward them. Phillip's muscles tightened as if for combat. But only two men were in the boat. No sign of Cleeve.

He met Simon at the ship's ladder. As the first mate climbed aboard, the captain asked, "Where is that snake?"

The mate stepped from the ladder and took a deep breath, expression grave. "Cap, we weren't able to intercept him before he arrived at the temple. He ran inside and threw himself at the feet of one of the priests. They wouldn't let me make the arrest." His shoulders slumped at the look Simon gave him.

Captain Simon's normally affable face set like granite. "Did you tell them you were carrying out lawful orders and he was called to stand trial?"

"Of course, sir, but the priest, Cleeve's brother-in-law, granted him asylum. Said my warrant wasn't valid on Order property."

The captain shook his head, eyes closed and lips tight. "I'm sorry, Phillip. You best initiate plan B and get yourselves off the boat. Run for it. I'll do my best to stall 'em."

"Hold on." The mate held up a hand. "There's more, sir. Cleeve wasn't able to talk."

"They wouldn't let him talk? Why?"

"I mean, he was physically unable to speak. All that came out was . . . noise, no words. They got him pen and paper, but his hands didn't seem to work right. He just made these scrawling marks, like a two-year-old trying to write or something."

Captain Simon squinted at Phillip. "What do you make of all this?"

"Creator God has protected. He is faithful. Always faithful." Heat rose to his neck. His faith was so lacking compared to Jeremiah's. Now, he was beginning to sound like the lad. If only his faith could begin to resemble Jeremiah's as well.

The mate still stood before the captain, shuffling uncomfortably, gaze on a point beyond his shoe tips.

"What is it, First Mate Jespers?" asked the captain. "If you have more to report, then out with it."

"Well, sir. I'm not sure how to explain this. It's, well, weird. When we started the interview with the priest, Cleeve looked fine, just like he always does. Right in the middle of our talk, he fell to the ground and writhed around. And these—I don't know—these marble-sized boils popped out all over his body. He was covered in them, he was. I think Mr. Phillip is on to something."

He moved to stand before Phillip. He took a knee, hat in hand, and looked up at Phillip. "Can you tell me about this Creator God of yours?"

CHAPTER 20

Evening arrived. Lars was still at his desk, working through a mountain of contract documents. He stretched and rolled his head to relieve the tension in his neck.

Since yesterday, his mind had returned to that meeting with Diggs. Working with that man was a mistake. There was no advantage to it. Was he missing something, some reason Dad thought it necessary to involve other people in their business, people like Diggs? Needing to bounce the whole thing off someone else, Lars headed toward Leif's house.

Leif hadn't been in the office for weeks, but talk around town said his brother had been busy with his timber scheme. It'd be interesting to compare notes.

When Lars arrived, Diana was cooking dinner, and he attempted to start a conversation. She was unusually distant, but she'd every right to be distracted with the room full of hungry, crying kids.

He grabbed the four and wrestled with them, getting them out of her skirts. He then got down to the business for which he had come. He descended to the basement where Leif made his office. A kerosene lantern cast shadowy yellow light across a makeshift desk, an old door propped on cinder block pedestals. Lars crossed the bare concrete floor and grabbed Dad's metal drafting stool, a memory from childhood which had once graced Dad's own basement office.

He dragged the stool, legs clattering on the hard floor, then placed it across from Leif's, and perched on it. He clapped Leif on the shoulder. "Hey, brother."

"Hey, Lars." He lowered some papers, gaze distracted, voice distant.

"Problems?"

Leif snorted and threw his pencil down. "You could say that. Nothing *but*, really. The Burr Oak deal will work, I know it will, but at every turn, I hit a new roadblock. It's like fate's against me. Now, Dad's cut me off from the resources I need to bring it all together. Doesn't he see this could turn things around for us, and for good?"

Lars shifted on his seat. "This is way out of his comfort zone. None of us have ever been in the logging business. You can't blame him for being scared."

Leif threw his arms wide as if for support. "You guys still don't get it. This isn't just another contract. When we get a job, we finish it, then have to go out there and fight for another. It's a vicious cycle, never-ending. I'm tired of working my butt off to scrape by, aren't you?"

He rapped a knuckle on a ledger. "This is a long-term play, one that could make us so much more money than the millworks, and the Burr Oak timber could keep producing profits for generations, forever really. Break that hand-to-mouth cycle once and for all."

"I get that." Lars gripped Leif's arm, squeezing to still his agitated brother. "Really, I do. Plant two trees for every one you cut, and it *does* last forever, as long as you don't cut 'em faster than they grow."

"Right. And that's the beauty of it." Picking the pencil back up, Leif jabbed it in Lars's direction. "We never need to. There is enough product to supply the mill in perpetuity, with plenty extra to sell on the open market. All we've gotta do is secure the logging rights. Haman's already on board. Well, mostly. But what we have in store for him when he finally comes up will ice that cake. It's gonna work."

Lars pushed aside the pencil before it made another pass too close to his face. "Didn't Tunne tell you the advisor over there would never assign the rights? How's Haman gonna fix that?"

Leif waved that away, the pencil again nearly grazing Lars's cheek. "Oh, that wasn't Tunne. The old man died. That was some jerk relative named Junior. There's some complication with the stewardship. Haman's gonna fix all that. Besides, Tunne's family should have no problem with the deal. All we're doing is managing their forest, not clear-cutting it. We'll make it better, healthier. They'll get that when we explain."

Of course, Lars should be supportive, but Leif was taking another blind leap. When would he learn to slow down, quit assuming all risks would pay off? "Sounds like you have a lot of unsolved problems."

"Of course I do, and Dad caused the biggest ones. He doesn't like any idea that wasn't his own."

"That's not fair. He tries to poke holes in ideas to test them. You take it personally."

"You know better." Leif leaned over the table, fist thumping the papers. "He tries to poke holes in our ideas to keep us in our place."

Lars held up his hands, palms out. "Look, he's more of a glass-half-empty kind of guy, sure, but can you blame him? He's taken some hard knocks and wants to be careful. Tries to avoid bad decisions. Those lead to bad consequences, or haven't you heard?"

"Yeah, well, if we miss the boat on this, just because it wasn't *his* idea, that will be one very big, bad consequence."

Great. He was getting nowhere. "I have some news for you. Dad has started a consortium of small mill workers. He and some professional organizer have been working on it for a while, already a done deal."

Leif shrugged. "Not my concern now. I have bigger fish to fry."

"Well, they're set to carve up the Events Center contract. These guys strike me as mice studying to be rats."

Leif swiveled his chair back to his desk and bent over his work. "Dad let me know in no uncertain terms that I am no longer part of the team. I'll run my show, and he'll have to run his own from now on. It's his baby, just as he wanted it."

What a letdown. Lars's belly went hollow. Leif had always been his ally, someone he could bring his concerns to. "Don't you even care?"

Again abandoning his work, Leif leaned back in his chair. "Of course I care, little bro. I care so much it hurts, but what can I do? He's cut me out."

"You should never have walked off like you did." Lars rubbed at his hollow core. "You were our ops guy, and you threw it on his desk and ran off. Now look where we are. I'm dealing with this alone, and you're out in the cold and can do nothing to help."

Leif raised empty palms skyward. "I had to do what I did. He'd never let me run things. He gave me all the responsibility but never any authority. I worked my tail off and never got anywhere."

Lars stood, spinning away, swinging an arm as if throwing it all to the wind as Leif had. "Great. So you left me to deal with it alone. Thanks."

"Whoa, there." Now Leif rocked in his chair. "If I was still at Northwoods, I'd be as helpless as you are. You know it. At least now, I have a chance to help the family in a big way. In the end, Dad did me a favor, cutting me out. Now I answer to no one, not him, not anyone." His gaze focused on something beyond Lars. His voice gained a softer, more contemplative tone. "It is freeing, if I can only work out how to pull this off."

"How, exactly, *are* you going to pull it off?"

Leif slumped forward, elbows on the desk and fists buried in his hair. "I have a few ideas. Once Haman arrives, we'll see if any of them pan out." He let out a long breath. "As far as this consortium thing goes, you need to learn what I did. Dad is the steward. He can do whatever he wants. You have no say in the matter. None at all. Get used to it, 'cause it'll never change."

Lars left. His instincts screamed that they were careening down a dead-end road, making the wrong choices, causing more problems at every turn. And no one ever listened.

What would it take for Leif and his dad to wake up?

A KNOCK SOUNDED on the cabin door and Phillip called, "Is open."

The mate peeked his head inside. "It's my off shift. Mind if we do another lesson?"

After the incident of the miraculous crushed leg, the mate had been coming regularly, to join Phillip and Thaddeus for Jeremiah's lessons, his teachings of what he remembered from the scrolls. What he remembered about Creator God. Which, as it turned out, was a lot.

Jeremiah took his customary seat atop the desk, ready to begin, and waved the mate inside. "Come, we begin."

Jespers opened the door wider but didn't enter. "Yeah, the thing is? You might need a bigger space."

Behind the mate, their bodies filling the companionway, were a number of other crewmen. When Jeremiah continued to sit, silent and tongue-tied, one said, "We've been suffering the miracles too. And First says you knows something about such things. Why they're happening."

Another shouted over his shoulder, "It's only right we're told what's going on."

From further down the passageway came another. "And them dreams we're havin'? Them's not natural."

A mutter of agreement went round, and the bodies pressed closer before the mate shoved them back. "Just hold on. Give these gents some air. Maybe we best find a clear space on deck where there's room for all." He raised his brows at Jeremiah, head cocked. "That okay with you fellas?"

Once settled on deck, Jeremiah began to teach, but he was so peppered with questions that the quarter watch passed before he'd gotten to them all. The boatswain's call signaled change of watch, and Jespers got to his feet, dusting his backside. "Time's up, boys."

At the complaints, the men hemming Jeremiah into a corner,

Jespers turned on those crowded around. "I said time. Give these boys some air. We can do this again tomorrow. Not like any of us are going anywhere."

The crowd dispersed, but when Phillip went on deck to exercise, several men accosted him, all asking questions he couldn't answer. He gave up on the workout and retreated to the cabin, ignoring the repeated rounds of knocking.

Once all had gone quiet, he gave Thaddeus and Jeremiah a rueful smile. "They give up, maybe?"

Sliding off his bunk and grabbing his duffel, Jeremiah huffed. "Hope this is true thing. Is my day for bath." He cracked the stateroom door and peeked his head out. Then, apparently satisfied, he disappeared down the passageway.

When Jeremiah hadn't returned in what should have been plenty of time for the bath, Phillip stood and began pacing the two steps from desk to bulkhead and back. To Thaddeus, he said, "I think our friend's in trouble. I should go find him."

A thumping then echoed from the closed stateroom door, and he opened it a few inches. There stood Jeremiah, head wet and glancing over his shoulder where two more crewmen appeared in the open hatchway, running in his direction.

Phillip grabbed Jeremiah and drew him inside, then locked the door. "What is this thing? There is new trouble with crew?"

Hands waving as if in negation, Jeremiah stammered, "Is–is only little trouble. Man finds me in bath, ask question, question. Will not go. Water gets cold, so finally I run."

Phillip set his jaw and strode from the cabin, instructing the other two to lock it behind him. In the wheelhouse, he approached the captain where he sat cradled by the padded control station chair. "Captain Simon, something we must do about crew."

"Oh? Is there a problem I'd not been aware of?"

"Not problem. Maybe little problem, sometimes. Men want Creator God. Want talk, have question. Many question, all times."

"Ah, I think I understand." Stubby fingers cupped a salt-and-pepper bristled chin. "I've seen the men chasing you three like lost puppies every minute they have off duty. Can't blame them. I've done the same, hogging up your evenings. We've only had a short time with you, only just learned of the existence of Creator God. The men are thirsty to know more. Surely, you'd not deny them?"

Gaze out the side window, eyes not registering the blue sky, the puffy white clouds, but only the memory of that one glance he'd had of those precious scrolls, his hunger for anything, everything Jeremiah could teach him about them, Phillip shook his head. "No, but must control. No more chase into bath, okay?"

Simon scratched a bristly chin. "I'd been thinking about this. Maybe we can land both those fish with a single net. Would you fellows be willing to provide a formal time, an appointment you might say, to teach and answer questions? We'd need two sessions a day to give every shift a chance to attend. Would ya?"

Welcome more brothers into their little band? What would it be like, to be surrounded by fellow believers, not isolated and hiding? Could such a thing be? "Yes. Of course. To know Creator God is greatest blessing. Not deny any man."

But to expose their faith, their devotion to Creator God might be one thing, not that they'd had any choice in the matter. To hint of their mission or cargo was quite another.

This, above all, he must warn the others. The scrolls must remain hidden, unspoken of, until they could be delivered safe to their destination.

And in the meantime, they only need hope that no other crew members decided to turn them in.

What odds, that?

CHAPTER 21

After weeks of painful anticipation, a gleaming fast transport bearing the Committee seal at last topped the railroad tracks. It paused before descending into the yard of Old Bob's sawmill. The approach was slow and majestic. Gravel popped as it advanced, the creeping pace accentuating the day's gravity.

So many dreams hinged upon what happened this morning. As Leif stood waiting, his intestines knotted. *Please don't let me need the bathroom, not right now.*

The driver exited the vehicle and opened the rear door. Haman climbed out and surveyed the yard. From the intensity of his visual sweep, the man probably could now list the entire facility's inventory in detail.

Leif approached, bowing as he drew near. "Sir, it's such an honor to have you here today." He bowed again, too jittery.

"Yes, yes. How are you, young Leif? You have something to show me?"

"Of course. Right away, sir. You'd like to see the mill in operation, I assume?"

"That *is* why you called me here, is it not?"

"Yeah. I guess it is." Leif tried to chuckle. It came out as a giggle. Why did his wits abandon him at this moment? Regathering them, he gestured to Young Bob and the six men with him. His men now? "Right. Places, everyone. Young Bob? Would you like to explain the operations as we watch?"

Unlike Leif, Young Bob wasn't cowed by Haman. "Sure thing, Mr. Leif, my pleasure." His grin wide, he dispatched the crew to execute the tasks they'd practiced, as evidenced by the pallets of sawed boards near the outflow conveyor.

Engines fired to life, and equipment reverberated beneath the galvanized tin roof. Fresh-cut pine scented the air. Then the mill spewed a steady stream of sawdust, turning logs into pallet loads of planks. With a wave of his hand, Haman ordered a halt. Young Bob began shutdown procedures. The noise abated as the machines spun down. The men gathered behind Young Bob, watching Haman and Leif.

Haman gave a tight-lipped nod. Almost a smile? "I must admit I am impressed. When you described this facility, I didn't have much hope, given such antiques, but here we are. Your idea shows some small merit, young Leif."

Excitement stirred the men.

Haman raised an open palm toward the operation. "This was the linchpin of the concept. Without a working mill, it would be futile to harvest timber. It does appear you have produced, as promised. Now, where are we to find the timber with which to utilize said mill? I believe you had a plan in mind?"

"Um, yes?" stammered Leif.

Haman swept an arm toward the car. "Come with me, my ambitious friend. Let us visit said timber, shall we?"

PHILLIP AND JEREMIAH were on deck, faces raised to a hazy sun just beginning to burn through a thin overcast, now midway up the eastern sky. Ahead, the long columns of barges narrowed to the horizon, the furthest still shrouded in the last of the stubborn vapors, rising like tendrils from the rippling waters.

Phillip stretched, continuing to bask in those yellow rays, their warmth now strengthening, so much better than the biting, damp chill they'd faced on waking.

This distraction almost allowed Jeremiah to catch him off guard. Almost. When the lad's tiptoed footsteps neared and the flutter of clothing telegraphed the strike, Phillip made a half step aside and away, spinning as he did.

Jeremiah's body was horizontal to the deck, windmilling in what would have been a decisive leg sweep, if Phillip had remained to suffer it. Instead, Jeremiah had overcommitted. Now, off-balance, he couldn't defend when Phillip slid in behind him and placed him in a choke hold.

Hand slapping the deck in submission, Jeremiah slumped in Phillip's grip. "This time I think I have you."

Phillip bounced to his feet and drew Jeremiah up with him. "Almost, you did. Not many weeks, maybe you land blow."

A grimace crossed Jeremiah's placid face. "I think maybe never I learn this thing."

"No, you think this not." Phillip cuffed his shoulder. "You learn fast. Is good. Better, I think, than I learn Ibrim."

That brought out Jeremiah's familiar smile. "Is true. Hearing you speak Ibrim makes me think of camel Father once had." Then a dark shadow crossed his young face. He shook himself, and it disappeared. "But is good thing, we trade knowledge as we do. You teach me fight. I teach you talk, read. Very good thing."

Phillip clenched a fist as if grasping for something that slipped through those fingers. "But even more I love when you teach of Word of God. This is marvelous thing." If only they could study the actual texts. But still Jeremiah taught from memory. To remove the scrolls from their hiding place, to expose them to view should a crewman intrude into the cabin? Even with their newfound friendship, this was a risk not to be taken.

"One day, we study actual scrolls," Jeremiah promised. He must've been thinking along the same lines. "By then, maybe, you are ready to read in Ibrim." He stretched toward the sun, rolling shoulders in obvious pleasure. Then, with lightning speed, he reached for Phillip's arm and pivoted his hip in readiness for a throw. But fast as Jeremiah's attack had been, his hands grasped only empty air before he himself was airborne, cartwheeling across the deck.

Later, finished with the workout, Phillip and Jeremiah bowed to one another before snagging towels. They settled at the stern rail to bask in the now brilliant yellow rays, towels wrapped around shoulders against the chill wind. But Phillip's gaze flitted downriver, looking for pursuit on that muddy brown sheet of water.

Jeremiah leaned into his line of sight. "Still, no one chases." He smiled a gentle reproof. "Faith, my brother."

Phillip again studied their backwaters, checking the far curve for any vessels newly appeared. "I hear, my brother. Yet there is job to do. One I must do. Trust God but do job. But where is one of these end, the other begin?"

Rocking his head, Jeremiah sank back in his seat. "Hard to divide, sometimes. You say before you have plan, yes?"

"Had one. This"—Phillip waved at the boat—"not it. Now near my peoples again. Still safe for to contact them? I wonder."

"You ask where job end, trust begin. When plan worked not, did best you could. Now you again have plan. Follow it. If Creator God is in this thing and idea is bad, He tell you. Sometimes stop you. You try, try, try, cannot do because He is stop. This way for Him tell you, sometimes. Listen, then all good."

Ahead, a massive iron bridge crossed a narrow section of channel.

Hand to his brow, Phillip narrowed his eyes against the sun's glare, searching the marshlands now off the port side, patches of cattails waving in the breeze. Geese were gathering, circling low over the water. Long necks pointed like spears preceding their flapping wings. Their honking chorus called him as if to a decision.

He slapped a thigh and unfolded his legs to stand. "Yes. Okay, we now begin to follow original plan. Next stop Plumbsburg. Where am to meet those who help. We do this, or Creator God stops, then tell me new plan." He slapped Jeremiah's back. "Come. Pack. Very near."

Once packed, they went to the wheelhouse where Captain Simon hunched over the controls, brow furrowed. He was guiding the leading row of barges into a berth. The daisy-chained vessels formed a floating mass so long Phillip could cover the entire width of the far end with an upraised thumb, yet the space between barge and pier was but a few feet.

How could anyone steer something so huge with such precision? When the furthest barge was so distant? Yet with sure movements of the controls, he glided the barges into position. Now only inches off the pier, all forward movement stopped, the barges centered within the berth markings.

When he'd given his final orders, Captain Simon swiveled out of his bucket seat and crossed to them.

Phillip reached to shake his hand. "This our port, Captain. We go now. Came thank you. Thank much. Saved lives, much more."

Simon grasped the offered hand. He didn't let go but answered a crewman's query over his shoulder. Then he turned back to them, still gripping his hand. "I want to tell you—you're welcome on board anytime you need. I speak for the crew when I say we want to learn so much more."

"We find answers, we give you. Promise."

Simon clasped each man's hand in turn. When Simon again reached for his, Phillip drew the man into a great bear hug, slapping him on the back. "Brother. We meet again."

"Hold you to that." Simon mopped his dry forehead with a bandanna, coincidentally dabbing the corners of his eyes.

The crew formed up at the gangway, two lines through which they were to pass. When they approached, the men snapped to attention and saluted as one of the deckhands blew shrill tones on a metal whistle.

This was an unfamiliar custom, but that this was some traditional honor was obvious. The men stood rigid, gaze fixed, but tears gleamed in more than one eye. His vision grew foggy at the edges. Probably just the change in the weather.

The three filed down the gangway, reluctant footsteps dragging.

Phillip resisted the urge to stop and look back. Never good to look back. On mission, eyes must remain on the task.

Their footfalls left the echoing metal gangplank before the solid footing of the concrete dockside replaced it. Still, their bodies continued rolling side to side with the river's remembered motion.

They were in a city they didn't know, facing a future they couldn't guess. Ignoring the dockworkers' stares, Phillip put one foot forward, then another, moving toward that unknown fate. Surely, the ill will, the unseen threat he sensed, was only his imagination.

CHAPTER 22

Leif had never ridden in a fast transport. The naked fields zipped past so fast they were no more than a gray blur. Trying to keep up with the fence posts whirring past made his eyes cross. But inside the sleek machine, it was silent—no wind, no sense of movement, no roaring motors. And neither Haman, sitting rigid next to him, nor the driver in the front seat broke that silence. No small talk. Not even a grunt.

But with all this so exciting, Leif might not have heard them, anyway. His head swiveled left, then right, his jaw aching with the goofy grin he couldn't lose, paying no attention to the route, only the experience. What luxury. When he made it big, this was how he'd travel.

He jerked back to reality when the car decelerated, his weight pressing the safety straps into his chest. They pulled before an unfamiliar government building, joined moments later by two other vehicles. From them, a squad of uniformed men fanned out on the street, hands on holsters.

The sign identified it as Esther County Administrator's Offices. Why did they come here? Weren't they going to look at the timber?

Standing outside his open car door, Haman waited. Leif sat,

gawking at the building, then jerked when Haman again cleared his throat. Right, he was expected to get out of the car.

He scooted across the long leather seat to exit on Haman's side, just in time to catch the older man's eye roll. Oh, shoot. Yeah, there was a door on Leif's side. Way to look like a rube. This would take some getting used to.

They entered the office lobby, joined by the armed squad. Aside from more uniformed men, three other people occupied the space, one of whom he'd never seen before.

Junior and Kat scowled at him, hands cuffed behind their backs. Haman took a seat behind the lone desk as though a judge assuming his bench. He addressed the third person, who was also cuffed. "Administrator Warren, I am saddened and shocked to learn of Advisor Fegan's seditious activities. I had heard so very many good things about you, so I hope you can assure me you were not party to his schemes?"

Warren licked a bloody lip. "I got nothing to say till Fegan gets here." He snarled a nasty smile to Haman. "Do you have any idea who he works for? You might want to cash in. Run to the islands while you still can."

Leif recoiled, moving away from Warren before the inevitable lightning could strike the man where he sat, catching Leif in the area of destruction.

But Haman just smiled. "That may prove difficult as Fegan lost his head, quite literally." He checked his watch. "Almost an hour ago now." He beckoned one of the armed men. "Officer, I am saddened to report that Administrator Warren has admitted his culpability in Fegan's plot against the Committee."

At the uniformed man's signal, two of his squad lifted Warren by the arms. He screamed. "You have no idea!" His shouts faded into more screams, these of pain as he was dragged out by the cuffs. Then came a single muffled gunshot.

Haman signaled another uniform. Then a pasty-faced man was hustled into the room and dragged to stand before the desk. Haman looked up from a notepad to address the man. "Assistant Administrator Kyle, I regret to inform you that former Administrator Warren has been involved in illegal activities and was shot while attempting to escape. Do I have your assurances that you had no part in the criminal behavior of your superior?"

The man stammered, forcing barely coherent words through trembling lips. "No, sir. I know nothing, sir."

"Oh, good. I cannot tell you how relieved I am to hear that." Haman stood, walked around the desk, and placed a hand on the man's shoulder, who jumped as if burned. "We need a reliable man, a man like you, to continue the important work here, no?"

The man nodded, his chin quivering.

"Excellent, Administrator Kyle. I will have Warren's effects delivered to you as soon as he has surrendered them." Someone dropped a bloody bundle of keys on the desk. "Oh, here they are now. Please accept delivery of your new keys, Administrator. There is some business you need to attend to right away."

Kyle picked up the ring with thumb and forefinger.

Haman gestured the guards toward Junior and Kat. "Bring them." He stepped behind Kyle. "Please lead on to your office."

Kyle began walking toward a cubicle in the corner of the lobby.

"No. Your new office." Haman pointed to the glass-enclosed corner room, labeled Administrator in golden stenciled letters. When Kyle stumbled and changed direction, Haman took Leif's arm and steered him to follow.

Once in the expansive space, Kyle sat behind the big green metal desk, looking uncomfortable, his eyes still bugging. The others took seats facing him. Kat, across from Leif, fixed him with a glower.

He gave her an I-didn't-do-it shrug, but her look only darkened.

Haman opened the proceedings. "Administrator, it is my duty to inform you that your predecessor, in addition to being a traitor, was also a sloppy administrator. He mistakenly assigned stewardship of the Burr Oak properties to the son of Tunne"—he nodded toward Junior—"instead of the named successor of the deceased." He pointed at Kat. "It is imperative to correct this miscarriage of justice. Don't you agree, Administrator?"

Kyle's mouth worked. His head dipped another nod.

"Administrator, please procure the needed documents and make this correction."

Kyle was still nodding, seemingly frozen to his chair.

"Now, Administrator!"

Kyle flinched, shot out of his chair, and waddled from the room, sweat flying from his second chin. He returned with record binders and forms. He scribbled. "I'll need the recorder to witness these signatures. I think your men have him outside?"

Haman waved a finger toward an officer, and a young man was ushered into the room. Kyle presented the forms to Kat for her signature. She picked them up and read the first before signing it. As she began to study the second, Haman sighed. "My dear, simply sign the documents. You are being granted your fondest wish. Show a little trust if not gratitude."

Over the top of the papers, she fixed Haman with narrowed eyes. "All due respect, sir, but my grandpappy told me never sign nothing without reading it first." She continued her perusal. Then, apparently satisfied, she signed the remainder. Kyle picked them up and stacked them before presenting them to Junior. He held a pen toward the grizzled man. "And now your signatures, sir."

But Junior crossed his arms, shaking his head. "Not gonna let you steal my rightful property."

Haman's gaze flicked toward the man stationed at the door. "Did you say Junior was implicated in Fegan's malfeasance?"

The man nodded, mouth set in a grim line.

Junior put his hands in the air, handcuff still dangling from one wrist. "Okay, okay. I'll sign. All I ask is this. Give me a lifetime lease for that little plot I live on. Can you do that? I got nowhere else to go." With that last, his voice morphed from a surly snarl to a whine.

Leif grunted his disgust. This performance would be convincing, evoking sympathy, had he not seen the predator in action. The man was a snake and deceptive as one too.

Haman pursed his lips. "How many acres?"

"Only four. Just bottomland and a few broken-down buildings. Nothing you're gonna miss."

Haman waved toward Kyle, who made the revision before handing the forms back to Junior for his signature. He signed. But a gleam lit his eyes as he did so. Was that a gleam of triumph?

With the forms properly signed and witnessed, Kyle pressed them into the binder. "Okay, that's done." He practically leaned toward the door. "Are we all finished here?"

Haman drew a new document from his sleeve. "Not quite. One final order of business, Administrator. Kat, I need you to sign one last time." He slid the sheet in front of her, indicating with a fingertip where she was to sign. She grabbed for the paper, but he didn't relinquish it. "Not this time, dear Kat. Sign."

She crossed her arms. "What is it?"

"It is an agreement between yourself, as the new steward of Burr Oak, and the newly formed Burr Oak Timber Company, assigning logging rights to said organization. You shall be well compensated, I assure you. Now sign."

She ripped the paper in half and threw the pieces at him.

"Tut, tut." Haman slid a second copy from his sleeve, holding it aloft. In a singsong voice, he said, "Is it true, Miss Kat, that you conspired along with your uncle and Fegan to enrich yourselves at the expense of the stakeholders of this great Republic? I cannot imagine the fate awaiting the two of you once the Bureau of Peace finds out about that." His face lost the mask of false urbanity. "The timber will be cut, my dear. The only question is whether you will be cut with it. Now sign."

She signed, lips compressed, face white. She glowered at Leif, eyes hot, before turning back to Haman. "Are we done here? Don't you have some kittens to drown somewhere?"

Haman laughed a genuine-sounding laugh. That laugh was worse than the venom. Was he that good of an actor? Or that callous? "Quite done, Miss Kat, for now. If further assistance is required, we know where to find you."

Leif stood to follow Kat and Junior, but Haman put a hand on his arm. "One more item of business, young Leif." He handed Leif another sheaf of papers.

Leif read. And then reread. He began to wobble, his vision blurred. He remembered himself and gulped a lungful of air. He'd forgotten to breathe. "I'm named . . . steward? Of Burr Oak Timber Company?"

"Of course, how else would you accomplish all we have set out to achieve, you and I?"

Haman reached across, black robe sleeve brushing the desktop as he flipped to the next page. It was a letter of credit drawn on Republic Bank, in Leif's name. He read the limit and gasped.

Haman laughed. "Oh, young Leif, your lack of pretension is so very refreshing. Yes, you have a liberal line of credit"—his voice hardened—"of which every penny will be accounted for, every penny to be repaid from profits. You, my lad, will be held responsible for it. Make certain every expenditure advances our mutual cause, or you will answer to me, your sixty percent shareholder, in this new venture."

This money was an answer to prayer, more than he'd dared dream of. His mounting obligations, obligations he had no means to pay, had begun to keep him up at night. With the swipe of a pen, that worry vanished. It didn't even matter that Haman had just taken majority ownership in the new venture, with no effort on his part. He was welcome to it. Just get Leif his share.

It was a miracle. All his problems were solved. *I'm rich.*

CHAPTER 23

With heavy heart, Phillip turned his back on Captain Simon and his boat. The entire crew having become like family, Captain Simon more than most.

The gruff old badger had taken Jeremiah under his wing, becoming a de facto foster father, teaching him the ways of the river, and then turning novice student to Jeremiah's tutelage about Creator God. A strange match.

Watching the pair had warmed Phillip's heart, though it was a melacholy reminder of his own mentor, Professor Reuel. How long before he would see home and his adopted family?

Thaddeus edged closer. "Do you know where we're going?"

"Yes." Phillip responded in their mother tongue, low enough no passerby could hear. "My work for the Seekers brought me to this port city a few times." Now, he led the way as they snaked through the crowded open-air dock market, dodging milling bodies. Longshoremen working, barkers hawking wares, and other voices chattering mixed.

"Sure don't remember a port smelling like this." Thaddeus crinkled up his nose as the less-than-pleasant mélange of rotting fish, stagnant river water, and penned animals converged.

Phillip smirked. "Keep your breathing shallow. We'll soon be past the worst of it." Just a few hundred yards up the waterfront, the market gave way to waterside shanties, and he waved to the shacks, moldering porches facing the water, rickety ladders descending to makeshift docks. "Why would anyone choose to live in such a location? The shoreline always smells *bad*."

Once on the side streets, the crowds thinned.

"Remember I taught." Phillip spoke now in Common to both men. "Draw no attention. Speak not to stranger. Stay close."

His hands fisted and unfisted, arms jittering at his sides. They had discussed the danger they were now approaching. If they were to be betrayed, it would happen here. And worse, if such a thing happened here—with no way to travel, no safe place to which they could fall back—they'd have little hope. A narrow, dangerous path this. Only a single misstep, and they'd fall.

He ground his teeth. The original contact on the east coast beyond reach. Now, his only hope was to revert to an alternate plan, make contact with the Seekers here and hope the pieces for this last leg of the trip were still in place.

If no, then what? How could he transport his charges across the Republic? So many unknowns, so many ways things could go badly, and him with so few options. And fewer resources. He unclenched his jaw and walked on. Still, his muscles kept tensing, his mind conjuring threat around every corner.

Jeremiah must have felt it too, repeatedly looking at their back trail.

"Look hunted, attract hunters. Stop looking," Phillip scolded. Still, he caught Jeremiah glancing over his shoulder. Understandable, if irritating. He could feel eyes boring into his own back, the muscles between his shoulder blades jumping at the anticipated bite of some unseen blade.

"Very close now. Prancing Panther, see?" Phillip pointed at a painted sign swinging above the door of a three-story white-sided building. If not for that sign, the building appeared no different from the warehouses lining the street.

He cautioned, "Inside, not speak. Not look. Eyes on floor or on me, yes?" When Jeremiah nodded, wide eyes showing white, Phillip groaned. "Make that only the floor. Keep eyes down."

He entered the inn and stopped inside the door until his vision adjusted to the dim interior. The gray wood flooring and rough-sawn wall panels somehow absorbed the sparse lantern light while huge square wood columns throughout betrayed the fact that the building had, indeed, once been a warehouse.

At his side, Jeremiah gasped. The vast dining room was mostly empty, except for two tables of peace officers. This must've frightened Jeremiah. Phillip stepped in front of the lad to shield him, signaling Thaddeus to take the young fool in tow.

He led his company to a corner table across from the raucous officers. Phillip claimed a chair with his back to the wall. Thaddeus steered Jeremiah into one with his back to the room, then slid in beside him. Now if Jeremiah could keep himself from glancing over his shoulder all night and if we are very blessed, we may escape attention.

Once seated, Jeremiah *did* glance over his shoulder. Under the table, Phillip stomped on Jeremiah's foot. Hard. At Jeremiah's injured look, Phillip shook his head in warning.

A young woman had been dashing from the serving window to the thirsty officers. She now stood, blowing a stray lock of dishwater blonde hair out of her face and surveying the room. Phillip caught her eye, and she scuffed across the bare wood floor, snagging a handful of printed menus on her way. "Evening, gents. Can I offer you something to drink?"

"Water please, madam. Can you take for pay this?" Phillip handed her an odd coin, which he'd slipped from the secret pocket in his belt.

She inspected it before handing it back. "Nope. That coin is worthless."

"But silver that money changer discards, this is beginning of fortune."

"I prefer treasure that moth and rust don't steal."

"This is wisdom." Having finished the recognition phrase, Phillip sighed. With a conscious effort, he let the tense muscles in his shoulders relax. What a blessing. His old contacts remained, at least at this one inn. He'd been haunted by visions of returning to this dining room day upon day, those he sought nowhere to be found, waiting hapless as the hounds which Cleeve had surely called down on them came in for the kill.

"I seek Butterman."

"I assumed. He's busy in the kitchen. I'll send him out when he's free. Want to eat while you wait?"

The officers were becoming louder the more they drank. "Rather not. You have room?"

She produced a key from her apron and pointed to an open wooden stairway on the rear wall. "Second floor, last room on the right."

Haman was talking, and Leif had missed what he was saying. "I'm sorry, sir. I didn't catch that."

"I have identified a candidate for logging superintendent. I understand you have already completed hiring at the sawmill, yes?"

"Uh, yeah, I think so." How could Haman know that?

"Good. Then we should be making for Burr Oak. The man I have in mind is waiting there."

The drive was such a pleasure, the transport so sleek, so silent. And now, as the steward of a new venture, such luxury was his future. His due. Leif sat back, letting the plush cushions, the supple leather mold to his body, as the wide plains transitioned to rugged hill country.

The leaves were beginning to drop. The woodbine had taken on the deep reds of fall. Winding through the underbrush and climbing the occasional sapling, it reached high in a spray of russet splendor among the mass of yellowing forest leaves.

They veered onto a gravel access road, and an ancient jeep had already parked in the turnaround.

Standing next to it was a mustachioed mountain, a man over six and a half feet tall, with arms crossed, huge and well-muscled, beefy forearms popping from the cuffs of rolled-up red-flannel sleeves.

Haman stepped from their car. "Maurice, I presume?"

"Right you are, but the name's pronounced *Morris*, though my momma spelled it fancy-like. And you be Advisor Haman?" He offered his hand, but Haman looked at it with evident disdain, so he pivoted the ham-sized palm toward Leif.

First hesitating, Leif glanced from that intimidating grip to the man's eyes. But there was a gentleness there, and a glint of—what? Humor, yes. But not the humor of a bully laughing at his inferiors. This was more like a smile between old comrades, sharing an inside joke. These were the eyes of a man he'd like to have as a friend.

He grasped the proffered mitt. "Leif."

"Nice to meet ya, Leif. It's you and I'll be ramrodding this shindig?"

Haman interjected, "*Assuming* we agree to retain your services. Leif is the managing principal."

"Not sure who else'd be up to the job, all due respect, Mr. Haman. This here is a special case. Not many men know how to handle high-value timber like this, much less how to harvest selectively without tearing up the entire stand. Add the complexity of the terrain, and you have a widow-maker here." His brown eyes twinkled. "Or a pile of profit, if I happen to be the guy running the show." Beneath that bushy mustache formed an infectious grin. "Up to you though."

Haman pursed his lips. "So you are able to overcome these obstacles?"

Maurice crossed his arms and leaned a hip against his jeep. It rocked beneath his weight. "No problem if you know what you're doing. Big learning curve if you don't. I do know what I'm doing, sir."

"So enlighten us with the wealth of your experience. What other challenges will we encounter?"

Fists on hips, Maurice turned. "Aside from the terrain, your biggest problem is logistics. Transport, to be exact. Felling the trees and grappling them onto flatbeds in these hills'll be a trick, but one I know how to beat. Gettin' those flatbeds to Northwoods is gonna be even trickier."

Haman's eyes widened. "Why so? The site is riddled with good roads. Why could we not drive the timber to the sawmill?"

"Oh, you'd think so, wouldn't ya? Ever harvested woods like these before, Mr. Haman?"

Drawing himself up, Haman straightened his robes. "Address me as Advisor Haman or as advisor, not mister. And no, I have not, *Mr.* Maurice."

Maurice nodded, his smile unwavering. "Well then, I can see why the problem isn't obvious to ya. In this terrain, gotta fell the trees after the ground freezes but before the snowpack gets too deep. Don't want equipment negotiating these hills in the mud, and ya don't want timber heavy with sap. So, when time comes, ya get in there hard and fell 'em, sort 'em, and stage 'em. Then in the offseason, the crew keeps busy movin' 'em to the mill, week by week."

Haman waited as if for him to continue. When it became obvious Maurice thought he was finished, Haman asked, "So what does that have to do with the roads? You hinted that getting flatbeds to Northwoods was going to be a problem."

"'Course, it is. Ever seen these gravel roads in winter? Even worse, when the frost goes out in spring? You bring in a wagon train of flatbeds, they'll get stuck so deep you may never get them back out again."

Haman lifted his hands. "So, what is the solution?"

In answer, Maurice turned and pointed.

He seemed to be pointing at the road. Was Leif missing something? His gaze alternated between the two men, Haman scowling, Maurice beaming. Finally, Leif ventured, "The road?"

Maurice raised the aim of his pointer finger. "Nope, that's the road." He lowered his aim a few degrees. "That's the solution."

Leif searched the indicated area. He was definitely missing something, but what? Then it caught his eye. Between the road and the turnaround where they had parked was an area of raised grade. One exactly like that at the sawmill, further down the highway in Northwoods. Or more appropriately, further down the line. "The railroad."

Maurice gave him a broad grin. "I can see you and I'll make a great team. Yep, the tracks."

Haman peered in the direction Maurice pointed, but his head was shaking. "I see no railroad. What am I missing?"

"No, sir. You're not missing it. The rails are gone now. This spur was abandoned a long time ago. I scouted on down to the active railway. The bridges are still intact. We lay new rails, and we're good to go all the way to the main line, which runs straight to the sawmill."

"Hmm, and I suppose you are also experienced in the construction of rail lines?"

"'Course, Mr. Haman. That's why you hired me."

CHAPTER 24

Settled in the room, Thaddeus and Jeremiah having each taken one of the two cots, Phillip unrolled his pallet on the floor. He'd sleep in front of the door to guard against unwanted night visitors.

Whitewashed rough board ceilings were bathed in light from two windows—one facing north and overlooking an alley, one facing east and offering a street view. Across the way, another warehouse remained dark. The sign above its entrance advertised a boat builder.

He grasped one end of the desk. "Thaddeus, need help move this."

Once Thaddeus helped drag the desk to the center of the room, Phillip stacked the chair on the desk and stood, balancing atop it. "Hand me please mending tape."

After rummaging in Phillip's pack, Jeremiah tossed a roll of tape to Phillip, who tore free a section and pressed it to the ceiling, covering a loose knot in one of the boards overhead. Then he climbed down and, with Thaddeus's help, moved the furniture back into place.

Jeremiah cocked his head. "Why you do this thing?"

Then came a knock. Phillip cracked open the door, keeping one booted foot against it as he peeked into the corridor. He then opened it wide and grabbed the visitor's plump hand.

"Butterman. Is good thing, see you again."

Over six feet tall and as wide as the doorway, Butterman beamed. His ruddy cheeks rounded, and his ample belly bounced in merriment. "Phillip, good man, how long has it been? Never mind, don't answer that. What brings you here? No, no. Don't answer that either. Did I tell you how very nice it is to see you again?" The old innkeeper swallowed Phillip in a massive embrace. "I hope you're planning to stay awhile this time? Mrs. Butterman will be cross if she doesn't get to see you."

"Not sure how long, my friend. Must hurry, but need send message."

Butterman slapped his thigh. "Message. I knew I forgot something." He fumbled in his stained apron for a crumpled envelope. "This came for you. Been holding it, assuming you'd show up."

Phillip accepted the offered paper.

"Can I get you boys something to eat?" At the unanimous consent, Butterman turned. "Back in a jiffy. Got bouillabaisse in the pot if the supper crowd hasn't already finished it off. Real fish, not the protein cake they sell at that place down the street. Bet you don't get that where you come from. Wait here." He lumbered away, wiping his hands on the dirty apron.

At the rickety desk, now back in its place, Phillip inspected the envelope before producing a knife and slitting it. With a flick of his wrist, the knife disappeared again. He slid out a paper, glanced at it, then reached out a foot, to snag the straps of his pack, and dragged it next to the desk. From a book in it, he decoded the letter.

Then Thaddeus at his shoulder groaned.

Jeremiah crowded in. "What does it say?"

Phillip placed a hand on the lad's arm. "Am sorry. Your father."

"What about Father?" Jeremiah's voice rose an octave.

"Very sorry." Phillip squeezed Jeremiah's thin forearm. "Father has died."

Jeremiah dropped onto his cot as still as stone, his face as expressionless and unreadable as if carved from said stone. His eyes closed, and his head bowed.

Phillip and Thaddeus remained silent, gazes downcast.

Jeremiah wiped a tear, then took a deep breath before raising his head. "How this thing happen?" The throatiness in his voice belied his emotion.

Phillip caught Thaddeus's eye, but the other only shrugged.

Yes, this was Phillip's decision to make. How much should he reveal? Would knowing the whole truth be worth it to Jeremiah?

He gripped the lad by both shoulders. "You man—good faithful man. My brother. Between brothers are no lies, but some knowing is only more pain. You deserve things be told if you wish. If you wish the pain."

Tears pooled in Jeremiah's eyes. "Please, I would know all."

A tear of Phillip's own burned the corner of his eye. He blinked it away. This was always so hard. Why'd it never get easier? No, the opposite seemed to be. How many times must he be thrust into this position, feel this gut-tearing pain? At what point would he become numb? Would that be better?

He raised the note and read of Hilkiah's final act of valor.

When done, he let the letter slip from numb fingers, seeing not the room, but that cloud of unseen witnesses, Hilkiah now added to their ranks. "Hilkiah was hero. Led Order men on fine chase in desert. When caught, final act did protect you, buy time for escape. Was close thing, very close. You come to Mazkelon only because of him, only live with time Hilkiah buys with sacrifice. Great and heroic sacrifice for you, for scrolls, for all world. This thing be always remembered. Great love, I see in this. No greater love than this."

Jeremiah's face screwed up. Then he clenched his jaw, breathed deeply, and relaxed his face, a hard expression concealing whatever emotion was beneath. When Phillip embraced his young friend, Jeremiah remained rigid, gaze locked on something in the far distance, whispering something in his native tongue.

And then even that ceased.

Phillip had seen men, victims of terrible trauma, battered beyond their ability to cope, driven into catatonic states. This was how it always started. Were they now to face the same here?

Thaddeus again caught his eye, seeming to harbor similar concerns.

Jeremiah still sat on the edge of his cot, gaze fixed.

No doubt about it. The lad was slipping away.

It always started thus.

MARIPOL strode down stone corridors deep inside the temple prison's infirmary wing, accompanied by a squad of operatives. And the priest who happened to be the afflicted's brother-in-law. They trooped along, barred cell doors passing by on either side. Their lantern light chased striped shadows across dank cell after dank cell, each then returned to its former gloom behind them.

Stopping before one of these barred doors, the priest removed a key from his robes. After peering through the bars, he unlocked the door and gestured Maripol inside. "Not that it'll do you much good. Off his rocker, poor sod."

Maripol entered the padded cell, wrinkling his nose at the stench while the guards hung back, kerchiefs wadded over faces, eyes watering. In a filthy deckhand's uniform, the man stretched on a cot. Leather straps secured his hands, feet, and even his head, precluding the smallest movement. A gag silenced his mouth, and he had soiled himself—more than once if the puddle beneath the cot was any indication.

"Why is this man tied so?"

The priest remained in the corridor, his robe sleeve covering his nose. "He's a danger to himself and to others, sir. When he's loose, he charges for the door, attacking anyone who stands in his way. He's uncontrollable."

"And the gag?"

"If you heard the awful noises he makes day and night, you'd understand. Eerie. It unsettles the other patients."

Maripol leaned closer to inspect the man. "Has a doctor examined him? Has there been a diagnosis? Do we know the cause of those boils?"

"Doctor says there's no obvious malady. Says they're a manifestation of his mania." The priest hesitated. "Some say he's under a curse."

Maripol snorted a humorless laugh. Not that he didn't believe in the supernatural. He served an organization steeped in it, had seen more than his share of the unexplained—but these simpleton priests overspiritualized everything. They'd sold too many fake charms and started believing their own hokum.

He waved the priest to his side. "Ungag him."

"Don't say I didn't warn you." The priest crept to the cot, moving slowly, whispering as one would to a growling dog. "It's okay, Cleeve. It's just me. Remember me? I'm your friend. Don't bite me. Be good now." He removed the gag.

Cleeve let out a wordless howl followed by a stream of gibberish.

The priest jumped back as if bitten.

Maripol took position at the foot of the bed. "I can see in your eyes that you're not mad, Cleeve. If you wish to be set free, do as I say. Now be silent!"

Cleeve quieted.

The priest's eyes widened, mouth agape.

"You say this man is family to you, but you abandoned him to this state? Unconscionable. He's not mad, as you can see. He is simply unable to speak. Get me pen and paper that he might communicate in writing."

"But, sir, we attempted that on the first night. He couldn't write or speak."

Maripol cut the priest off with a slap of black leather gloves on palm. The crack of it echoed down the dark corridor. "Do as I say. We will proceed."

His expression dubious, the priest produced a pen and notebook.

"I'm about to untie your hands, Cleeve," Maripol said. "You will lie still, not thrash or grab. I'll ask you questions, and you will write the answers. Do you understand?"

His eyes were wide, jerky, like those of a trapped animal. But Cleeve nodded.

Maripol untied his hands and placed the pen in one and the notebook in the other. "Ready?"

Again, Cleeve nodded.

"Tell me why you came here."

Pen to paper, Cleeve traced random shapes across the page, hand shaking. He let out a moan, one sounding as if it contained all the despair in the world.

"It's okay." Maripol patted his shoulder. "We won't give up yet." He took the notebook and pen back from Cleeve, who grabbed after them as a man fallen overboard might grasp for a lifeline.

Maripol wrote. "I am writing the letters of the alphabet. Using the stylus to point at them, you will spell your message to me one letter at a time. If you point to the box at the bottom of the page, that will signify a space. Do you understand?"

Cleeve nodded, then spouted gibberish until Maripol bade him be silent. Over his shoulder, he said to one of the security men, "As Cleeve points out letters, I will call them to you. You will record them."

He handed the notebook and pen to Cleeve. "Are you ready?"

Another nod.

"I will ask you questions. You will spell your answers. When you are done with an answer, you will place your hands in your lap. Now, why did you come here, to the temple?"

Letter by letter, Cleeve spelled out his message. T-O—R-E-P-O-R-T—W-I-T-C-H-E-S—O-N—B-O-A-R-D—D-O-R-O-T-H- Y

His hand fell to his lap.

The priest looked as if he was about to vomit.

"Witches?" Maripol asked. "Explain."

T-H-R-E-E—M-E-N—H-E-R-E-T-I-C-S

Again, his hand fell to his lap.

"What are the names of these men?"

Cleeve picked up the pen. P-H-I-L-L-I-P—T-H-A-D-D-E-U-S—J-E-R-E-M-I-A-H He paused. A-L-L—F-O-R-E-I-G-N-E-R-S

Maripol's feral grin caused the priest to flinch and pace backward. "Do you know where these men came from?"

Cleeve's response was one word, the one word in all the world Maripol had been hoping to see.

T-I-K-V-A-H

Tears spent, Phillip picked the slip of paper off the floor and held it beneath the candle. There had been more to the note, a short addendum tacked to the end. "Lucky thing for us, this part of original plan still stands. Butterman has for us new identities."

He stood to find the innkeeper. He hadn't gone far down the dim corridor before the man himself topped the stairs, arms laden with trays. Phillip relieved him of one and carried it back to the room.

Butterman set down his haul and wiped his forehead with his apron. "Sorry I took so long. Bet you boys are hungry."

The stew now in Phillip's hands became the center of the universe, vision narrowing until the bowl occupied all awareness. The rich aroma of the fish, huge, white, flaky chunks of it swimming in a mélange of tomato, celery, and onion carried him far from this room, the vessel in his grasp warm, like his chair before Reuel's fire. Oh, that he might someday return to those happy times of bubbling stew in wooden trenchers, hot spiced cider in earthen mugs.

He shook himself, regaining his surroundings. "Hungry, yes. Thank you, Butterman." He held up the note. "You have for us papers? Plans for travel, yes?"

"This I did not forget." Butterman tapped his forehead. "I remember the important things, eventually." He lifted a leather folio from the tray and presented it. "Voilà."

Phillip opened the folder and checked each set of documents. Exactly what he'd expected. But not what he needed. "Thank you, my friend. Truly. But one problem. Three documents but wrong peoples.

Hilkiah, no longer. Thaddeus now here." He jerked a thumb toward his friend. "Not old man. Not close match. How we get him papers? How long?"

The big man's smile faded. "Oh, I don't arrange these things. They were only delivered to me for safekeeping. My contact will be coming by on Monday. I can pass the word along. But then?" He shrugged round shoulders. "You know how these things work."

Phillip did know. The Seekers were organized in a cell structure, each composed of three people, similar to those used by revolutionaries in centuries past. This arrangement offered protection against vast exposure upon the capture of one member.

But it took time to pass messages up and down the chain. Phillip rubbed his forehead. "Travel plan no good. Must have papers for all. I prepare message for to send. Please, he knows this urgent, need speed."

"I will, Phillip. Just get the message ready. He'll make haste, trust in that." Butterman then brightened, the jovial smile returning to his doughy face. "Now you boys best eat before the stew gets cold. I have a kitchen to clean and prep to do for morning."

"I have letter for tonight." Phillip settled before the desk, already mentally composing it.

Thaddeus laid a hand on his shoulder. "You are wrong, my brother. You go, leave me here. Mission more important than single man."

The operational parameters Phillip had been taught when in the Eye would have prescribed exactly this. To abandon any team member who couldn't further the success of the mission. One more reason to hate the Order. Phillip met Thaddeus's intense gaze, the heat of his own overshadowing Thaddeus's. "This thing we do not do. Team is not broken. We leave no one."

A grunt came from the corner of the cot where Jeremiah remained hunched. "We are together for reason. Trust God." The usual strength was lacking in his voice, the quiet smile missing. But yet, resolve firmed that broken visage.

"You see?" Phillip spread out his hands. "Is settled." He changed to their shared language. "So you can forget about getting out of it. You're enlisted for the duration."

Thaddeus dipped his head. But a smile curved his lips.

What other unforeseen circumstances was Phillip failing to anticipate?

Experience proved the old adage—there is no perfect plan. His job was to eliminate pitfalls in advance and battle the unexpected when it appeared. "Adapt and overcome" was drilled into him during his training. One of the practical lessons he'd taken with him that day he had left the Eye and its evil agenda.

His lips curled in a grim smile, eyes narrowed. Now he used those skills against his foe, the organization that provided that training. Eventually, maybe he could bring an end to the hated Order and the Eye.

Thaddeus interrupted these thoughts. "How long you think is wait?"

Phillip shrugged. "Can be weeks. Hope not longer."

Lips forming a frown, Thaddeus surveyed the cramped space. "Is long time three men stay in room. This thing be noticed, I think."

"Yes." Phillip grunted. "And to leave room is for more eyes to see. Only bad choices, no good. I speak to Butterman about this thing."

He sat on his bedroll. After the candle was snuffed and the deep breathing of the other two sleepers drifted his way, he still lay awake, staring at the vague outline of the ceiling in the moonless dark. His head churned with all these unknowns until he fell into a fitful sleep, yet wrestling with the sure knowledge that, when things went wrong, he would bear that failure.

And of the lives lost as a result. His own among them.

SIMON NEVER SLEPT well when at dock, but it was worse tonight.

Time in home port brought a swelling melancholy, the loss of his Dorothy still too recent. He dreaded these surrounds, this place where he once celebrated so many happy homecomings.

Unlike his crew, who were now enjoying leave with their wives and families, he never left the towboat to sleep in his own home. That empty house was a ghost from another lifetime.

He sank into a leaden sleep only to wake, trembling and covered in sweat. He had recollected where he was, if not the memory of the dream, when his cabin door flew open. His first mate stood there, clad in a sweaty nightshirt, eyes wide.

“Oh, bilge.” Captain Simon fell back onto his now-soggy pillow, his head shaking from side to side. “Not again.”

CHAPTER 25

Leif struggled up the steep rise, gasping for breath. Man, was he out of shape. Far ahead, nearly topping the rise, Maurice's long strides threatened to take him out of sight.

The gorgeous hills of the Burr Oak Moraine offered a great place to hike. Just not at the pace Maurice maintained. How was a guy to keep up with a man like that?

They'd started out at daybreak with the air still brisk, the chill causing their breaths to hang in vapory clouds. Deep forest loam cushioned their steps, their passage noisy with the swishing crunch of new-fallen leaves.

The place was a cathedral stippled with dancing light. The ancient trees were columns, the canopy above a stained glass ceiling. The mosaic of fractal colors filtering through the leaves so resembled those impressionist landscape paintings in Father Curtis's books, but no painting could compare to this magical reality.

They began on the southern end. Here, the main highway bordered western hills while the river bracketed the east, the two forming a sharp triangle of land that widened as it progressed north.

A good fifteen miles upstream, the river pivoted west, chopping off the hill country. There, a steep yellow-clay slope guarded the far bank, atop which the prairie regained control of the land and marched northward for mile upon featureless mile before it gave way to the lake country, the northernmost reach of the Republic.

Over several day hikes, they'd cover the entire Burr Oak. Today, they'd survey the southern third, the only two developed parcels in the holding—Junior's acreage in the river bottom and the main ranch in the hills further north.

According to the map provided by the highly cooperative County Administrator Kyle, the only other structure was a shack in the far northern reaches, adjacent to the abandoned rail line. The parcel featured a corral and loading chute, presumably used by the original ranch family to load out their cattle.

As he crested a steep ridge, he stopped dead. What a view! From the hilltop, the heights fell straight in a terraced cliff face to a table-flat floodplain. The river shimmered in the sun, nearly a mile further east.

Beyond that, a bluff rose. Then plains resumed their flat, barely rolling journey to the east. The sun's wavering yellow orb peeked over that ridgeline, the horizon effect making it look as if it was moving rapidly. A line of blinding light flashed first in his eyes, then down the front of his jacket, past his scuffed boot toes. It crept down the terraces and continued east.

That bright dawn revealed a group of structures tucked into a grove on a low terrace, the last before the slope emptied onto the wide river flats. "That must be Junior's farm."

Maurice nodded. "Mighty private, that. Look how the hills curve closer to the river north and south of here, making a crescent around his land. Tucked right into the vale like he is, you'd have to know the place was there to find it. You can't see it from the road *or* from the river. Makes sense. He struck me as a man who likes his privacy."

"You met Junior? When did that happen?"

They continued the hike northward, following the rim. "Last night. Took my foreman to look over the layout. Junior comes up and started orderin' us off the land. Said it was his property. You warned me he might be trouble, so I wasn't surprised to meet him."

"What happened?"

Maurice grinned. "You might say he and I came to an understanding. I doubt he'll give the boys any more trouble."

"When do you begin installing rail?"

"Equipment will be showin' up by first of next week. Machines are already en route."

"Yeah, I saw." And already got the bill.

As he sidestepped a fallen log, Maurice leveled a thick arm, finger aimed somewhere in the distance. "We'll start loggin' toward the middle parcel while they lay the rail. Tomorrow, we'll mark a few weeks' worth of timber for the cuttin'. Tell the sawmill to be ready to take delivery."

"Why not work from one end to the other?"

"The hills toward the middle are a bit less challengin'. It'll give the boys a good warm-up before tacklin' the rougher terrain. 'Sides, we've got good road access there, so we can be hauling right away while we wait for the rail to go in. Tell the sawmill to be ready to take delivery within two weeks."

Leif pulled up short. Wait. Two weeks? Maurice's long strides carried him a fair distance up the trail before he stopped to turn, bushy brow raised. Leif scrambled to catch up. "You'll have loads showing up that fast? I thought it would take longer."

That thick black mustache quirked up on one side. "Nope, and they better be ready and better stay ahead of us." That mustache now arced up on both ends, a twinkle in those brown eyes. "Seriously, though, we'll start off slow, let all the kinks get worked out. But I do aim to move fast as we can."

Maurice raised his gaze past the far horizon as if studying something there. "You know, I've never seen a project move so fast. When I mention Mr. Haman, people start scurryin'. Handy, that. Good thing too. If not, we might have missed all the good loggin' this fall. That would have been bad, sitting on all this cost with no output."

Leif's knees went weak. What would he have done? Once more, luck had been with them. Everything was falling into place. He'd not even helped Maurice manage any of it. The man already had a plan and needed no assistance.

Good thing, too. Leif would be absorbed learning sawmill logistics from Old Bob. Leif had assumed hiring one crew for the operation would suffice. Old Bob had corrected that error. "Well, you could do that, I suppose, seeing's how you got money to burn."

"Uh, excuse me?" Leif did *not* have money to burn. The line of credit Haman provided once seemed so large as to be inexhaustible. But he could project how the balance would dwindle as operations began. More so as Maurice placed orders for rail stock, ties, a road crew, heavy equipment, and a myriad other purchases.

The rate of projected expenditure woke Leif in the wee hours, set his mind racing, pulse going thready anytime he thought about the sheer magnitude of this bet. And the tab that would come due if his gamble failed to pay out.

On top of that, the breakneck pace overwhelmed him. Was it all about to spiral out of his control?

Of course, expenses were necessary to achieve the goal, but the endeavor had already taken on a life of its own, a pace and direction of its own.

Had he created a monster? Why bother wondering? He was in too deep to stop now.

Besides, for once fate was smiling his way. Look how easily Haman had acquired the logging rights, albeit brutally? How a stewardship and a massive line of credit had been handed to him? And what a coincidence Maurice had come along, both a master lumberman and railman—in a part of the world where logging was never, ever heard of. What were the odds of all this?

It was as if an invisible hand orchestrated the entire play, moved the pieces into place, led him along this path, swept along like a leaf in some powerful river current. And with as much control of his destination as that leaf had.

He was thankful. Though some part of him remained fearful, uncomfortable to be at the mercy of these forces, forces he sensed, unseen, eddying beneath the surface.

Forces for which he was unable to answer the question—what, exactly, were their intentions for him?

PHILLIP HAD AWAKENED at first light and coded his messages before Butterman arrived, carrying the breakfast tray. Phillip handed the envelopes off. "Where is better place hide until answer?"

The innkeeper rocked back a step, then drew himself erect. "Well, that is a question. I don't know why you wouldn't just stay here."

"Not good place for long wait. Many come, many go. Cannot stay three men in room all day, all night. Cannot leave without many eyes see."

Butterman put a finger to his lower lip, gaze rolled toward the ceiling. "I see your point. Old Jack runs the boat works across the way. He often lets out the upper floor to crews waiting for repairs. Let me check with him." He raised that finger in the air. "I'll warn you, the space is large, but much more primitive than our fine accommodations here."

"He is to know we are boat crew, yes?"

"I'll give him the cover story. You stayed behind to take extended shore leave while your boat made the trip to the upper reaches and back. He'll ask no questions." Butterman tapped the side of his nose. "He's a friend."

The innkeeper departed on his errands, and the three of them tore into the breakfast. Butterman set a wonderful table.

A rap sounded at the door. Probably Butterman returning for the dishes, so Phillip called out around a mouthful of egg and scones, "Is open." After a slight delay, the door stirred an inch or so, and a face appeared in the crack, a meek little redheaded girl.

"Sirs? A man is downstairs asking for you. Should I show him up?"

"A man. Who is this man?"

"I know not his name. He came asking if we know where to find you. He brought this." She poked an envelope between door and jamb, apparently too timid to enter.

Phillip opened it. "Strange. It's from Simon." He told the server, "Please to send man to us."

He waited, watching through the cracked door. A form appeared at the top of the stairs, and Phillip's tensed shoulder muscles relaxed. He whispered to his companions. "Is Danny."

Danny, the youngest of Simon's crew, had been a favorite and interested pupil of Jeremiah. Phillip ushered their young friend into the room, rechecked the hallway, then closed the door. "Why Simon send you?" Phillip asked. "Letter say you explain."

Face flushed, Danny dropped onto Jeremiah's cot. "It's the dreams, you see. We all had 'em again."

Jeremiah's face remained blank while Thaddeus shrugged. So Phillip stepped closer to their young guest. "Please explain."

"Last night, we was on shore leave, excepting the captain and the first mate. Neither of 'em have families, least not no more, so they took watch while we went off to see our moms and dads or wives and kids and such."

Almost bouncing on the cot, Danny ran a hand over his sweating brow. "I had an awful nightmare, and rememberin' what happened last time, I hightailed it, right there in the middle of the night to tell Captain. But I wasn't the first man there. They were all streamin' in from their houses. All had the dreams, even the big man."

With a hand on Danny's shoulder to calm the boy, Phillip asked, "Please, what is dream?"

"I was gettin' to that. We all had real bad dreams. I don't know what's fixin' to happen, but it ain't good. But we all knows to trust them dreams, now anyways, so the captain made his plans and sent me off to find you."

"What plans?"

A shrug. "Dunno. He be comin' after 'while. He asks you wait for him, don't go nowheres till he gets here."

Thaddeus's brows knitted, but he wore a half smile.

But Jeremiah beamed.

Phillip instructed his companions to nap in shifts while they waited. He'd long known what all soldiers learned—to eat when the opportunity presented itself and to take every chance to nap.

One never knew when circumstances would preclude either. When the next disaster would strike.

CHAPTER 26

Maripol strode toward the Bureau fast boat as it made a tight turn that terminated in a full-power quick-stop maneuver. A flood of icy water washed across the dock and over his boots. With a single jerking hand gesture, he ordered Cleeve's guards to load him aboard the still-rocking craft. Then Maripol followed.

He shouted an order to the pilot. The prow turned upriver and pointed toward the dark sky as the inboard motor roared. Wind whipped hair, freezing spray misting eyes, and he leaned into a huddle with Cleeve, back turned to block the worst of it. Maripol handed Cleeve an electronic tablet. "Know how to use this?"

When Cleeve shook his head, Maripol showed him how to operate the thing. Then he asked, "Where will the *Dorothy* be right now?"

Fingers tapped on the tablet, one agonizing letter at a time.

But Maripol should thank Eternal the deckhand was literate. When Cleeve turned the screen Maripol's direction, he read aloud. "'In dock at Plumbsburg for three-day leave.'"

He waved the man on. "And if the towboat isn't there, what was the next stop?"

Again, the slow wait for words to form. "Will be there. Is home port. Crew visits families."

All that wait for nothing. From between clenched teeth, Maripol again asked, "And if not? What is the next stop?"

Another wait. Again, he read aloud, "'Upper reaches, then back. But will still be in Plumbsburg. Guaranteed.'"

The man's hands were shivering, pale with the cold. Maripol's own were icy, even inside his gloves, so he waved the man to take a rest.

Cleeve tucked tablet and hands into his coat pocket.

Maripol tapped the guard on the elbow. "Target is reported to be in Plumbsburg. Call ahead and order the Dorothy and all aboard to be held there under armed guard. How long to get there?"

The guard conferred with the pilot, then returned. "He says counting a stop for fuel we'll arrive shortly after sunup."

Maripol found a corner of the seat sheltered from the increasingly frigid wind and huddled in for a nap.

His sleep was fitful, but apparently, he did sleep as he woke, chilled to the core and aching when he sensed movement nearby.

One of the guards had left position beside the pilot. "Almost there, sir. What are your instructions upon landing?"

"Has the Plumbsburg Bureau staged the forces I requested?" At the man's nod, Maripol bared his teeth in a grin. Finally. "Have them meet us at the docks.

Then the port came into view. Only two lonely barges nestled into the concrete anchorage. No towboats. No *Dorothy*.

The fastboat rolled into position, last in a line of Bureau vessels. A platoon of uniformed Bureau men milled on the dock, hands tucked into armpits, stamping their feet.

Maripol launched himself from the still-moving vessel and charged toward the officer in charge, shouting over his shoulder for the guards to bring Cleeve. Still several paces distant, he stopped before a junior lieutenant by the bars on his shoulders. "Where's my quarry?"

"Sir?" The man's face paled white against his uniform's high collar. "I've no such information. Only orders to meet you here."

A short distance away, abutting the concrete dock apron, stood a squat building, also of concrete, the word Harbormaster stenciled on its side.

He jerked a hand toward the officer and the guards flanking Cleeve. "Follow me."

Inside the harbormaster's offices, Maripol ignored the pudgy clerk's interception attempt. He rounded the front counter, stiff-armed the office door, and stopped before the green metal desk. He loomed over the mouse there, pencil-thin mustache quivering above a mouth working to form words. Maripol cut him off. "The *Dorothy*. Where is she?"

Again, the sparse whiskers fluttered. "Why—she left last night. Strange, though—"

Maripol's gloved fists slammed onto the desk. The deep-piled papers in the inbox jumped, a few sliding loose. "Why, in the name of the Eternal, did you not hold her here?"

"Hold her?"

Snatching up that overflowing inbox, Maripol poured the documents to slide across the desktop. His fingers blurred as he flipped first one, then another. Papers fluttered about the room. Then he stopped, crumpled one in his fist, and thrust it hard into the man's midsection. "Read."

He'd sent the message yesterday before his fast trip upriver, dispatched as soon as he'd learned of the *Dorothy*. An order to detain the ship and all aboard. He picked up another flimsy and crumpled it into a ball, then hurled it toward the man's face. "And this, from only hours ago, flash traffic to your office, demanding the same."

The little man gawked. Then his pasty complexion went green. "I . . . but . . . I—"

Maripol threw the heavy metal basket, only at the last moment putting it through the window instead of the worm's head. He needed this man conscious. For now.

"Don't you read your incoming?" It was moot at this point. Let the inquisitors deal with it. "Why did they leave?"

"I–I don't know. Night shift said the boys filed in from all over town, and they up and left. And on a moonless night, to boot. Must have been important. Otherwise, what kind of fool'd navigate from moorage to channel in such dark?"

Eyes closed, Maripol breathed in, then out. Throwing the inbox hadn't been an act of temper, but of intimidation. The Eye had a reputation to uphold, after all. But now his temper dared assert itself, which couldn't be allowed. Cold steel was the way of the Eye. Both in the operative's character and in their dread trade's utensils.

"Any passengers on board?" Voice again eerily calm, he leaned in. "Anyone unusual?"

"George, bring the log." The harbormaster's quavering call wobbled toward the front room.

The pudgy clerk entered, black book in hand. He set it on the desk and retreated.

The harbormaster paged through it. He stopped, pointer finger on a page. "Here it is. Arrived yesterday, observed to disembark normal crew complement, plus three. Must be new hires."

Maripol spun the book to face him and flipped to the entries for the previous night. "Did those three men reboard?"

The harbormaster reached to retrieve the log, then froze. "May I?" At Maripol's nod, the mouse repositioned the book and studied the hash marks. "No. Only the normal crew complement reboarded—less one, for some reason."

Maripol strode to his waiting platoon. "Lieutenant, send a squad via boat upstream. The *Dorothy* is headed north. Board her and bring her back. No one is to be allowed to escape. Use the remainder of your men to seal off the city. No one in or out."

To his credit, the young officer dispatched his men before adding, "Our forces here are understaffed. To properly secure the area, we need more men."

Maripol pulled the electronic tablet from his inner pocket. "I'll request the support of the local Order troopers. They should take the lead on this, anyway."

"But, sir. There is no complement of Order troops stationed here."

Maripol cursed, then grabbed the lieutenant by his sweaty collar. "Do—what—you—must. I don't care if you press every dockworker into service—find the men to seal this city." He released the officer to stumble two steps backward.

Again, to his credit, he snapped a salute before sprinting toward a group loading pallets.

Now, accompanied only by Cleeve and the two Bureau guards, Maripol started his interviews with the street vendors. No matter the city, it was these who saw all that occurred. What little they didn't see, they were the first to hear.

Apparently, the three young strangers took up lodging at an inn named the Prancing Panther. So he stationed himself to observe the greasy dive's entrance and sent one Bureau guard to watch the rear. He then summoned the lieutenant, who arrived shortly, sweat-soaked and breathless. "Sir?"

"Is the city sealed?"

"Sir. Yes. I . . . think so, sir."

Maripol rolled his eyes but let it go. If the intel was correct, it didn't matter. The fugitives would soon be in his grasp. "Have a squad form a perimeter around this building while I enter."

The officer goggled. "I have no more men to deploy. Unless I wake the night shift, that is."

Fist clenched to his lips to stifle the outburst, Maripol affected a hauntingly calm voice. One that should terrify anyone within hearing. "Oh, I'm so glad you didn't disturb their sleep. Critical operations can be so . . . noisy. Especially ones already short manpower."

Eyes widening, the whites now showing, the officer sucked in breath. "I need the commander's authority to do such a thing."

Unbelievable. "And why is the commander not already part of the operation?"

"He went fishing, sir."

Nose now pressed to the lieutenant's, Maripol leaned in and forced the man to fall back a step. "Wake the night shift. Seal the city. Then get—me—my—squad."

Once the perimeter was well secure, he entered the establishment, several Bureau men and Cleeve in tow.

Ignoring the wine festival's busy dining room clamor, he found the owner in his kitchen. Maripol faced him down in the pantry, two of his men holding the big lump, aptly named Butterman, up by the arms. "Three young men, dangerous fugitives, are known to have taken a room here. They may be going by the names of Phillip, Thaddeus, and Jeremiah. Where are they now?"

A dark look crossed the fat man's face. "Eternal be blessed! Those rascals! I knew there was something fishy about them. They owe me for room and board. Kindly confiscate that from them before you take them away. I'll be happy to pay you, er, for your services in that regard, good sir."

"Collecting rent is your job, innkeeper. I asked you where they were."

The doughy face paled. "They took a room and haven't ventured out of it since." Double chins jiggled with his headshake. "Strange bunch. Come. I'll show you the way."

Butterman lumbered up a narrow wooden stair. They crowded down a cramped hallway, whitewashed plywood walls dingy and scarred.

He stopped before a numbered door, handed Maripol the key, and sidestepped out of weapon range. Maripol pocketed the key before signaling a lackey, who readied a pistol and kicked the door free from its hinges, an explosion of splinters flying.

The rumpled bedcovers, carelessly flung, draped three packs, contents spilling from their mouths. Strangely, there were three sets of clothing, complete with boots, one in the desk chair and one on each cot, stretched out as if they had recently been filled with the body of a sleeping man. They still bore something of the shape of the missing members, buttoned shirts tented around absent chests, pant legs ballooned in the shape of missing thighs.

A curdling cry came from the doorway. Maripol whirled. Butterman was peeking around the door, shrieking in the voice of a frightened woman.

"It's happening again! The demon's come again!" The innkeeper fled the length of the hallway, his heavy bootheels hammering the wooden floor slats. Then came the *whump-whump* of a large man bouncing down a flight of stairs.

Maripol shook his head, lip wrinkled, and signaled his men to stand guard while he searched the room. Nothing noteworthy remained in the packs, just personal items and old clothing, no papers, and more importantly, no scrolls.

He beckoned his men to enter, to complete the more corporeal phase of the search, the kind the Bureau forces enjoyed. Shredded mattresses and pillows flew. A billowing fountain of feathers drifted about the whirling men. Those men continued making kindling of the room's contents, breaking each stick of furniture, then snapping those sticks into smaller pieces until they stood, hands empty and flexing, searching for something more to break but finding nothing.

Giving an eviscerated mattress a final kick, yielding another satisfying explosion of feathers, the senior man reported, "Nothing here, sir."

Cleeve had been standing in the hallway, his face white, refusing to enter the room. His trembling hands composed a message on his electronic tablet.

He held it up to Maripol, who read it and groaned. "Just what we need. More hick superstition." He started toward the stairs, but Cleeve didn't give up. He grasped Maripol's sleeve, halting him. He composed another message.

Maripol read it aloud. "'Ask anyone in town about the *Celeste*.' What's the *Celeste*?"

A voice answered. Across the hall, a muscular dark-skinned man, a deckhand by his attire, leaned in an open doorway. "Something beyond your worst nightmare, mister policeman, sir. The demon of the *Celeste* took these men." He indicated the empty clothing strewn about the room. "And if that demon be after you, no escape. A good clean death'd be better than what *it* has planned."

Maripol's men, all common troopers drawn from the local bureau, looked askance at one another, their movements jerky as the superstitious lot edged toward the door. Their fear was so strong he could smell the reek of it.

This was going to be a problem.

CHAPTER 27

Across the street from the Prancing Panther, in the second-story windows of the old boat works, they stood.

Through slitted curtains, they watched the scene now unfolding in what had so recently been their room. All three jumped when bootsteps echoed on wooden floorboards, crossing the shop below.

Phillip took up position alongside the open stairs, holding aloft an oar shaft to brain any unwanted visitor. He relaxed when the old badger, Captain Simon, came into view, short legs pumping like pistons up the stairs.

On the landing, the captain leaned over his knees, panting. "Got out of there just in time. Close as I ever want to cut it."

"Why, in name of all things good"—Phillip's voice carried an unintended heat—"take such chance? For what?"

Simon's brow rose, wrinkling the thick hide on his forehead. "You, of all people, know the value of psychological warfare, my good and stealthy friend. Don't pretend you don't. We both know where you got your training."

Phillip and Thaddeus had spent time with the crew, teaching them hand-to-hand defense. During one over-the-shoulder throw, a man had grasped Phillip's shirt collar, pulling it nearly over his head.

Captain Simon had been the only one positioned to get a look at Phillip's tattoo. Phillip had never been certain if he had or if he was aware of its significance. Apparently, the answer was yes—to both. He nodded, both in acknowledgment of his point and in thanks for his discretion.

"What psychology? Explain please this thing," said Jeremiah.

Simon sauntered to the crude table, pulled up a stained chair, and dropped into it with a guttural sigh. "Folk who live on the water are a jumpy, superstitious lot. Many an unexplained thing has happened on a black and foggy night, and anyone in these parts has heard of the *Celeste*."

He grabbed the stoneware pitcher and poured himself a water, downing it in one gulp, then wiped his mouth with the back of his hand. "She was a luxury paddle wheeler, and way back in the olden times, she steamed up and down this stretch of river. Rich folks'd ride in style, sometimes just for the pleasure of the cruise, eating fine foods and gambling, watching live shows. She held over two hundred souls and was always full up, just like she was that new-moon night."

He leaned in on both elbows, narrowed eyes staring from under beetle brows. "That was one dark night, and folks reported strange howling noises up and down the bluffs. The next day, the *Celeste* didn't make dock as she'd been scheduled to do.

"Fishermen found her mired on a sandbar, about three miles north. When they boarded her, there wasn't a body to be seen anywhere, just empty sets of clothes lying everywhere, like the folks had evaporated right out of them. No blood. No sign of struggle. Fires, even the candles, were still burning all merry-like, the dining room tables set for a feast. Plates were all lined up, pretty as you please, partly eaten, not a spoon or a drumstick out of place. And none of the passengers or crew were ever seen again."

His voice dropped to a near whisper, as if to speak this thing too loudly invited unwanted attention. "Legend has it, a demon haunts these waters, takin' folk on new-moon nights. Been plenty of strange happenings on such, to be sure, and the wagging tongues of folk have created a few that never happened, but which they believe anyway."

He poured another water, pausing with the unglazed earthen mug half raised. "The butt of the matter is this: anything queer happens on a new-moon night hereabouts will have the whole county blaming the demon of the *Celeste*. We just added to the legend, might say." He gave a grunting chuckle and took a deep quaff.

Phillip crossed his arms. "How we do this, add legend?"

Simon pointed through the window, toward the Prancing Panther. "Butterman and I set your room up to look like you disappeared, just like the folks on the *Celeste*, empty pants and all, then planted an old river rat across the hall to spread the rumor you were taken by the demon."

"But why you do this thing, take such risk?"

With a huff, Simon lowered his glass. "Look here. If a man were to disappear around these parts, the whole county'd turn over every rock and bush in the territory until he returned safe to his family. Unless, that is, they think they might turn over a rock and find the *Celeste* demon hiding under it. Folk'll not be so likely to come looking if they think the demon got us."

Thaddeus began to speak, but Simon raised a hand. "That won't stop the Order troops, but in this country, without the willing help of locals, they'll be lucky to find their way home in one piece, much less find us."

Thaddeus smiled. "You master strategist, Simon. Many thanks. Now we find safe place, hide until Phillip peoples come."

"Don't thank me yet, lad. Those Order boys are about to tear this town apart, and they'll find us if we don't get a move on."

"Move on where?"

"That's the question." Simon pulled a map from his breast pocket and unfolded it on the scarred wood table. He jabbed his finger on the river. "We're here. Plumbsburg. You need a spot to lie low until your friends come to get you. Any idea how long that'll take?"

Phillip rubbed his temples. "Weeks, probably. Months, maybe. All has changed."

"Weeks or months." Simon traced the river's line. "That be a problem. No town'd be safe. Those boys will rip through every settlement from here to West River. Anyone hiding us'll talk. Seen this before."

His forefinger made a slow circle around Plumbsburg. "So, no towns, no people. That's the long and short of it. We need a place, a quiet spot, to hide the whole lot of us. Happens I might know of such." His finger landed on a tributary at the northern edge of Plumbsburg and followed it upstream. For several miles, it wound northwest before straightening its course. Further on, it branched into two watercourses. One of which continued northward. The other veered west and terminated at its apparent source. "Yellow River Canyon."

Phillip cocked his head. "Canyon? Not mountain country, how is canyon?"

Simon tapped the map, his stubby finger making a wooden rapping on the tabletop. "That's rough river-eroded bluff country. Limestone hills cut so deep they formed cliffs fifty, hundred feet tall, just like those here on the main channel. Point is, Yellow River Fort lies right here."

He pointed downstream of the headwaters. "Built in a wide spot of the canyon. Strategic. Only way to get at the fort is to come up the stream, leaving the attacking forces negotiating a narrow choke point. Waters are only navigable as far as that spot, even for canoes."

The captain covered a swath of the map with an open hand. "Know the area well. As boys, we used to canoe up there and spend weekends prowling the old ruins. Beautiful place. Plenty of fish, game, and firewood. Easy shelter. And no one goes up that canyon these days, 'cept hunters, but my clan is settled all around those hills. I put the word out, and we could hole up there for years and never be disturbed."

Short, stout arms across his middle, Simon sat back. "I say we hightail it up there pronto. What say the three of you?"

Thaddeus gestured to Phillip for direction. "Must leave fast. Soon, all of town is cordoned off. Some place better than no place, yes?"

Phillip nodded once, decision made, and pulled out paper and book to code a hasty message. "Ask old boat maker Jack. He makes

Butterman get this soon, yes?" He handed the sealed note to Simon, who agreed and stuffed it into a side pocket. "We need two canoe take four men to fort. Where we find this thing?"

Simon said, "Four men? Aren't you forgetting my crew?"

His crew? Phillip blinked. What was the guy saying?

"Oh, Eternal. I forgot to finish my story. We heard you missed us too badly, so the crew decided to keep you company for the remainder of your journey."

Phillip closed his mouth, drew in a slow breath. "Is true. You are missed, but what is this join journey?"

"We join you wherever that may lead. Creator God warned us off that old tub, just like He told us to find you. We broke moorings in the middle of the night and took her upstream to the sandbar that mired the *Celeste*, all those years ago." Laughing, he slapped his thigh. "We staged our empty uniforms and such, just like they found on the *Celeste*. Left the *Dorothy* wallowing there, a new legend about to be made. Just like we staged your clothes across the way." He chuckled. "They'll be telling this story for another three hundred years, is my bet."

"So is this you do in room?" Thaddeus asked. "And peoples believe this thing?"

Simon lost his smile. "Folks around here seen plenty enough dark happenings. You bet they'll believe this. Just sorry I'm adding to their fears." He shook his head. "But is needful, and now we best be off before the whole production is wasted." He stood and waved for them to follow.

Phillip caught his elbow. "Still need boats for men. This is thing you have?"

Simon regained his smile. "All is arranged, my friend. You're in for a surprise."

CHAPTER 28

Leif held a hand to the stitch in his thigh, then hurried to catch up as Maurice cleared the tangled stand of upland pecan trees and stopped. He leaned against the wide bole of one, facing their back trail.

Leif came alongside. This vantage gave another view of Junior's place, and Maurice was again studying it, his frown deepening. "What is it?" Leif asked.

Maurice bit on his toothpick, then shifted it to the other corner of his mouth. "Nothin', prob'ly. Just thinking to myself. Somethin' I noticed earlier. That man must be an outright fiend for fish, huh?"

"Huh?" What fish?

"Why, look at the path he beat down between his place and the river. He must stomp back and forth a dozen times a day, at least, to leave a trail like that."

Leif searched the valley. Then his gaze lit on a dirt track winding over the flats toward the distant river. The game trails he'd seen in the wild were never this wide or well-worn. "Weird."

"Well, it explains that there outbuilding of his. He must need it to store all the fish he catches."

Leif shifted his gaze to the indicated building. Most of the structures on Junior's place were on the downhill side of decrepit with peeling paint and missing shingles.

Not this metal building. Large and new, it must've been expensive. The anomaly stood there without obvious explanation. "What's he up to here?"

Maurice spat. "No good, would be my guess. That hombre smells like trouble, and we best leave him to his mess, not get caught up in it ourselves. I'll let the boys know the same."

Maurice inspected the place once more, snorted, and pivoted north to trudge along the hilltop into a thicker stand of trees, now weaving between the dark trunks of black walnuts. The scent sharpened the air as they stepped on the baseball-sized fruits, the rotting hulls tearing under their bootheels.

Soon sweating under the rising sun, Leif called a stop and sat on a flat-topped boulder to remove his day pack. He stripped off the wind shell he'd layered over his wool sweater, rolled it, and tucked it into the pack.

Maurice needed no such preparations. He'd arrived wearing a wide-brimmed wool felt hat and a red-checked lumberjack flannel over a T-shirt. He carried a simple leather satchel worn cross-body and appeared unfazed by either the early morning chill or the heat of sun and exertion. An enigma, larger than life, he seemed expert at anything he needed to be.

Leif drank from his canteen, the water delicious, slaking his parched tongue, so cool as it washed down his throat. He tipped the canteen skyward again for one last glug before slamming the cork home. "How much further to the ranch?"

"Not far, another mile and a half or so. There's more sign of cattle the closer we get."

Leif cast about, brow furrowed. What sign?

Maurice jerked a thumb to their left. "Check the ground over there, under that tree."

Ah. Some disturbed soil near a patch of tall grasses populating an open glade, black scuff marks in the otherwise unbroken brown leaf litter.

"Those are hoofprints, cattle, probably headed into that grass, and look at the bush over there. See where they grazed off some of the branches?"

Sure enough, there, on a low shrub, the cleanly cut ends of twigs showed bright, obvious once he knew where to look. "How do you know to spot this stuff? I'd never have noticed."

"I spend so much time in these woods, I'm used to what's normal, so the not-normal sorta jumps out. Looks like she's just running beef cattle. You'd think she'd rotate hogs in here with all the acorns. Not so good for cattle, but acorn-finished pork?" The big man smacked his lips. "Well, that's a treat, I tell ya."

"That's the plan, eventually." A high clear voice called out so close to Leif's head he fell from the boulder. "I have to reconstruct the hog buildings first."

And there was Kat, looming over him. Those golden-brown eyes narrowed. Turned dark. Dark, that is, except for that flame burning deep inside.

He crabbed backward out of kicking range. "How'd you get so close without us seeing?"

"No trick to it. You're dumber than my cattle and louder when you move."

Leif stood, hands held high in a sign of peace. This woman was too good with weapons. "Hey, I'd like to start over. We should be friends."

Her gaze snapped to his. The fire was still there, unmistakable, and danger flared within.

He stepped back a pace, hands raised higher in the air.

"Friends?" she scoffed. "I'm supposed to be friends with the man who stole my timber? Who's going to raze this beautiful forest? No thanks."

"Hey, wait. I stole nothing." When she advanced toward him, he backpedaled. "Whoa. Hear me out. Please."

She stopped moving and crossed her arms, grudging assent, but assent nevertheless.

"We're going to manage this forest, make it even healthier, better for your cattle." He pointed at an oak near where they'd seen the cow sign. "That tree is at the end of its lifespan, half of these are. Soon they'll begin falling, filling the understory with deadwood."

He spread out his hands. "Look around. It's already started. Any place there's enough light, shrubs and bushes are choking each other out. The whole thing is an invitation to fire, one that'd run nonstop through these hills."

Her eyes flickered at that, so he chanced moving a step closer and dropped his voice to a lower tone. Friendly. Persuasive. Pleading. "Years past, your family managed this forest. They rotated goats and pigs and cattle through it, which kept the brush at bay. They selectively logged timber too. You can tell. Just look around. You can see the old stumps. This forest doesn't have generations of fallen trees. The only downed timber is from the last few decades or so. This was managed open forest, not left wild."

Her body language softened. Her arms slid limp to her sides. "What makes you think you know anything about my forest?"

"I'm right, and you know it." He wouldn't smirk. "But to answer your question, one of your grandfather's men once worked with my dad. He used to take me to the river bottoms, showed me some things about those woods. He told me the history of this place. It fascinated me." He shrugged. "So that's how I know about your forest and why I want to help you bring it back to its former glory."

She again folded her arms, hugging them to her, hands fisted. "How'm I supposed to trust someone who works with a crook like Haman?"

"You worked with a crook like Fegan."

Her nostrils flared, and she advanced a step.

He backed up, hands inching up again like a trainer facing a spooky stallion. "Besides, your uncle and Fegan stole this land from you. Now you have it back because of me. And you can only trust me once I've earned it. Give me a chance to do that. Please."

A barely suppressed smile tilted her mouth. She jumped toward him, shouting, "Boo!"

He fell backward over a log and landed flat on the ground. The air exploded from his lungs while his rib cage made a sound like a broken bass drum thumped for all one's might.

He lay there, sucking for a breath that wouldn't come while peals of unrestrained laughter, high and clear, echoed through the forest.

Maurice joined her, then offered him a massive hand, and pulled him up, still chuckling.

On his feet and backside dusted, Leif asked, "Friends?"

She looked him up and down. "No. Friendship you earn, just like trust. Are you gonna give me a say in how you manage the logging? That'd be a start."

Leif glanced at Maurice, who gazed back, his brows drawn up. "I have no problem with that. Do you, Maurice?"

Removing his toothpick, Maurice gave a slow nod. "Best we be good neighbors. But, missy, understand one thing. I've been doing this my whole life. I know what I'm about. If you and I disagree about something, you remember that. Don't be thinkin' you know more than I do about how to make a forest thrive."

He turned a slow circle, thumbs tucked in his belt. "Leif and I aim to do right by this land. We'll plant two trees for every one we cut. We'll manage the health of these woods so they're still producing timber, generations to come."

"And meat," she cut in. "Don't forget that."

"And meat. Ruminants and pigs helped make this place a garden spot, and they will again, done right. Work together. It'll make things easier for everyone. We all want the same thing, don't we?"

Kat looked away, expression pensive. "You're saying the right things. That's a start, but sayin's a far cry from doing. Come down to the ranch. I need to hear details."

CHAPTER 29

Phillip and his entourage followed Simon through the boat works, vacant on this festival day, and into the basement. In the far corner, Simon slid a stack of empty crates aside, leaving a man-sized gap between wall and crate. He handed Phillip his candle. "You fellows first. Don't let that flame go out."

Phillip, then Jeremiah, and Thaddeus squeezed through a narrow wall opening. The space beyond was damp and smelled of rats and mildew. Cobwebs adhered to his face as he pressed deeper in.

The cellar's dim light was snuffed out as Simon pulled the crates back into position. "Smuggler's tunnels," he explained as he caught up. "Town's riddled with 'em. Best let me lead." He squeezed forward until he was the point man, candle held before him. As they shuffled forward, he counted aloud each time they passed an intersection. "We go left at the third passage. Help me keep track in case I miss count."

Despite Phillip's experience in subterranean ways, the journey seemed impossibly long. Who would have dug so many miles of tunnels and why? By now, they must be beyond the town limits, even allowing for the skewed perspective such things can have underground. Yet the tunnel crawled on, suffocating with its stuffy rancid air, only a short section of passage visible in the flickering candlelight.

Then Simon stopped and indicated an upcoming intersection. "Quiet now. We'll be passing beneath the Bureau barracks. After that, it's a short jaunt to our exit." He held a finger to his lips and slipped into the left-hand passage, this one so low they stooped, the arched brick ceiling replaced by rough wood planks.

They moved into the cramped space, the way forward obscured by a wall of cobwebs. Simon used the back of his arm to wipe his forehead and stumbled, kicking an unseen bottle. It went skittering along the brick-lined tunnel floor with a heart-stopping clatter.

A gruff voice sounded from above. "What in blazes was that?"

Simon flashed a panicked hand signal, and they froze. Then he blew out the candle, the only light now the dim gray penetrating the floorboard seams so close overhead.

Another voice groaned. "Quit with your jokes, Baker, and go back to sleep. Sun's almost down, and we're on shift next."

"I'm tellin' you, I heard something. Those fugitives are tryin' to sneak into the barracks, bringin' that accursed night demon with 'em."

Heavy boots hit the boards over Phillip, and a cloud of dirt and grit showered his face. He resisted the urge to spit, to blow the offending matter from his eyes, but held stock-still as the footsteps moved away. Shafts of light pierced the floorboards, flaring bright, accompanied by the whine of rusty hinges.

Bedsprings creaked. "Oh, for the sake of the Eternal! Shut that window. Let me get some sleep, you oaf."

"No, sir. I hears what I hears. Take a look around. Think of the points we gets if we're the ones what captures the sneaky little critters."

Another set of feet began stomping. Beside him, Jeremiah had been furiously rubbing a finger under his nose. A final fatal stream of dust filtered into his face, and he let loose an explosive sneeze. All movement in the room above stopped.

A voice whispered, "You sees now? I told you I heard them sneaky sneakers. They's right outside. On three, I takes the door, and you dives out the window. We'll trap 'em where they sit."

"No, sir. You take the window. I'll take the door."

"Oh, fine, quiet now. On three. One. Two. Three!"

Violent motion exploded, vibrating the boards above.

Simon grasped Jeremiah by the arm and hustled him along the tunnel to where Thaddeus waited, far into a section where the ceiling had gotten taller and was again solid stone.

Phillip followed.

Simon relit the candle, then passed Jeremiah a handkerchief.

"I'm sorry." Jeremiah began to blubber as he tried to wipe away the muddy snot running down his upper lip. "I'm so—sorry."

"No, lad." Simon put an arm around him. "Was naught but bad luck, and we be in the clear. No harm done. Might be a blessing in disguise." He gave a soft chuckle. "How d'ya think those ogres will sleep from here on out, thinking they're haunted by invisible demons?"

A few hundred yards or so further, the tunnel terminated in a blank stone wall. Simon blew out the candle, and a dim glow shone from a circular shaft overhead. Embedded in the side were iron ladder rungs, the first nearly nine feet from the brick floor.

Phillip squatted before Jeremiah, lacing his fingers into a stirrup. The lad put his toes in the makeshift perch and vaulted onto Phillip's shoulders. From there, he grasped the first handhold. He clambered up until his feet rested on the bottom rung. Then he looked down.

Moving to position himself before Simon, Phillip again squatted, fingers laced.

Simon laughed. "Don't be daft. With the ballast I carry, I'll break your pinkies." He cocked his head upward and hissed a whisper. "Looped on the top rung. See a rope ladder?"

Jeremiah nodded, and he scrambled up, unwound the rope, then lowered it into the shaft.

Simon called up softly. "Stay put, son. I'm coming up. You'll need to let me past, so I can get at the hatch." He climbed, agile for a man of his heft, and soon perched on the ladder's top next to Jeremiah where he fiddled with a catch.

After a soft scraping, a sheet of blinding sunlight caught Phillip square in the face.

"Close your eyes. Give 'em a chance to catch up."

Phillip did so, the painful bar of yellow aftervision boring into his brain.

"Way's clear," came Simon's whisper. "This hatch opens below a bridge abutment. Scurry yourselves double-time down the bank. Wait at the water's edge. My people should already be there in the boats. Stay under the bridge. Don't be seen from above."

Upon exiting the burrow, Phillip followed the others down the steep slope to the water's edge, stopped by a low stone retaining wall, the river below. Phillip peeked over but snapped his head back. He lowered his lips toward Simon's ear. "Have trouble. Many peoples here."

Simon leaned over the embankment, then sat back, smiling. "Oh? Did I forget to mention our families?"

"Families? What family? Bring where?"

"Creator God ordered us to join you on your journey. We're doing just that. Think the crew would abandon their wives and kiddos?"

CHAPTER 30

Kat's ranch lay in the loving embrace of a hollow surrounded by steep hillsides. From here, on the peak of one, all the valley, around twelve hundred acres, spread out below. A sandpit dominated its southern half, sparkling blue in the afternoon sun. That water was so inviting. Wouldn't it feel good to dive right in, clothes and all? To wash himself free of the dusty sweat that caked his brow and soaked his shirt? But of course, that water must be even colder than his bathtub at home, despite appearances.

A dead-end road cut through the northern end, terminating at the ranch drive. The acres that weren't taken by the waters were split into multiple fenced areas, each connected to the next by a swing gate. Ancient maples flanked the white two-story house. Its south face boasted an open two-level porch. Attic dormers with leaded glass panes overlooked the acres like watchful eyes.

A red hip-roofed barn stood at the far eastern edge while a low hog shed bordered the south. Outbuildings dotted the grounds. All appeared well maintained and freshly painted except for the weathered gray hog shelter, its roof in the early stages of collapse.

"Got the rest of the place up to snuff. Hog barn's my next project." Kat led the way, knees bent, down the steep switchback trail and onto a footpath through a pasture, boots parting knee-high brown grasses and legumes. They entered the farmyard. “Take a seat at the picnic table while I fetch refreshments.” She waved to the picturesque thing beneath an old maple tree.

While Leif and Maurice waited, cattle grazed in one penned enclosure. Next to the nearest fence, beehives sat covered and dormant beside garden plots blanketed in thick fall mulch. Chickens clucked from a coop, the south side of which abutted a metal wire-and-post construct, an outdoor run.

Kat carried over a tray with glasses and a pitcher of pink liquid, sweat beading its sides.

“My grandpa loves his sumac lemonade.” Leif tested a sip. “And yours is really good.”

She aimed her glass toward a mass of the gnarled trees. Just past the entry road, red cones lifted skyward amidst a tapestry of scarlet-tipped palmette leaves. “Help yourself. More than I can use there. I can send you back with a comb of honey for him too.”

Leif swiveled his head, cataloging the buildings, all the activities evident. “How do you do all of this by yourself?”

“A couple high school boys come out from town. They help as often as they can, take their pay in produce. I can’t afford to pay cash. Fact is, nights I do seamstress work myself, just to pay the bills.”

Heat rising to his cheeks, he covered it by glugging more lemonade. “Do I see corn stalks in your chicken coop?”

“Yeah. I have to keep the girls behind wire, or foxes’ll wipe ’em out. Coons always got my sweet corn too.” She wiped condensation from her glass. “So I built a two-sided run and alternate the chickens one side each year. In the off year, I grow corn in the empty one. The corn loves the chicken poop, and the coons can’t get at the crop.”

Maurice cleared his throat. “Very impressive, Missy Kat. You do right well for yourself. Right well.” He finished his lemonade. “But daylight’s wastin’, and a cold night comin’. What did you want to talk about?”

She pushed aside her empty glass, leaned in, and folded her arms on the weathered tabletop. “Let’s discuss your game plan. Where and when do you start logging?”

"First of next week. As to where, you know the old turnabout?"

"Of course."

He took pencil and paper from his satchel and drew a crude map. "Just north of there, the two largest sandpits, the ones next to the old stone railroad bridge. With me?" When she nodded, he tapped the pencil on the map. "We start right here. Easy terrain and a short haul to the road."

She uncrossed her arms. "You've marked the timber you're taking?"

"Yep."

"Can I ask that you notify me when you scout out an area? I'd like to approve the selection before cutting starts."

"Surely, missy, as long as you keep up. I won't leave the crew standing and waitin' on ya."

She reached across the table and shook Maurice's massive paw, eyes level and expression grave. "Thank you, Mr. Maurice. I will keep up."

The big man cleared his throat. "That brings me to a favor I'd like to ask of you. We need to set up nursery operations. Eventually, we'll grow in three locations to keep stock close to where it's needed, but winter's hard upon us, and we've gotta set seeds out before hard freeze. Most specie we'll grow here need to stratify over winter to germinate."

The black-and-white cows in the closest pasture had wandered to the near fence line. They craned their heads over the top board, attention seemingly on the picnic table as if listening. Those beasts were big. What did they weigh? Thousands of pounds each? No way that fence would hold if they decided to charge, and they seemed about to do just that, their eyes rolling white even now, staring Leif's way.

Kat gave a sharp laugh, then covered her mouth. "They're harmless. It's about time for their daily treat." She nodded toward a wicker basket half full of spotted apples. "They get the windfall fruit. They don't mind the spots."

Maurice cleared his throat. "Like I was sayin', settin' seeds out in time's a tall order, and we've other challenges. The base material for my grow media is wood chips. We'll have no shortage of those. We seem to make 'em for a livin'." He snorted. "But the chips need to compost for a year or more before we can use it, or they'll hog up all the nitrogen. I've made do with a mix of green-wood chips, manure, and sand in the past with reasonable success."

One of the cows gave a bellowing moo and raised her tail. A fresh cow pie plopped to the meadow grass.

Kat sat up straighter. "You want to set up your nursery here and use my sand and manure?"

His fist bumped the table as if settling the deal. "Yes, missy, I would like to ask that of you."

"I can't lose pasture." Her lips pressed into a thin line. "Flatland is in short supply hereabouts."

"We needn't inconvenience you. Trees are perfectly happy growin' on hill terraces. Most of 'em like it better, truth be told. I'm just askin' for your sand and manure and access to this here valley. We'll stay up in the hills and out of yer pastures. Promise."

"And your men? Trustworthy? No scoundrels?"

"On my honor. Any of 'em so much as looks at you crosswise, you tell me about it."

She nodded once. "Just show me where you intend to set up before you break ground. And I want to approve of any men who will be working around the ranch."

"Deal, Missy Kat." Maurice's wide grin curved his mustache. "I do believe this is the start of a beautiful friendship."

PHILLIP STRUGGLED to find words while beside him Jeremiah maintained his quiet smile. Phillip again looked over the embankment and then sat back. "Simon, we owe you lives, many times we owe. Pardon, I must say this thing. Cannot take childrens and womens. Rough danger is our road."

Simon held up a forestalling palm. "You well know what the

Order thugs will do to these folks. Folks who've harbored heretics. That'd be you, in case you wondered."

His chin firmed, obviously ready to "badger" his point. "No death on the road that lies ahead, no matter how bad, would compare to what they'd face at the hands of those torturers. They'd wring our location out of 'em, then the life from their bodies for the sport of it. I've seen this thing."

When Phillip moved to speak, Simon cut him off again. "They choose this path. Their choice to make."

Phillip's pent-up breath, drawn for a heated rebuttal, burst past his lips, to be carried off on the evening breeze. "But to travel silent, quick, this is our need. How is this thing to be done?"

Simon tapped a finger to the side of his nose, so much like Butterman, then again smiled his feral badger grin. "You leave that to me and the boys. This won't be the first time they made this trip, fast and silent-like."

He stood and offered Phillip a hand up. "Come now. We best be well gone before full dark. Past Eagle's Bend, it'll be safe to run with lights. Till then, we make our way with what sun we have left. But being almost dusk now, it'll be a close thing."

They slid down the steep embankment, and Simon assigned the trio positions in the boats. Behind the string of passenger vessels were several more, piled high with bags and packages. And was that a china hutch strapped into one?

The watercraft themselves were flat-bottomed affairs fashioned of a light metal and powered by surprisingly silent outboard motors. Danny manned the boat Phillip boarded, and when asked about the machines, Danny flashed a knowing grin. "Our clan makes a fair number of fast trips up Smugglers' Run."

"Smugglers' Run?"

"Let's just say there's a need for goods the Republic'd like to monopolize, and a bunch of us well and able to meet that need. Just so happens these boats are fast, quiet, and can navigate shallow waters their patrols can't."

Danny had been dividing his attention between Phillip and the river ahead as he steered. He now said, "Sorry, Mr. Phillip. This part's gonna take my full concentration." His young face set in serious lines, gaze locked on his task.

The course was so difficult to pick out in the poor light as they raced through hairpin turns, spray flying, their sure movements, their concentrated calm proving the men piloting were skilled and familiar with the route.

The gray dusk slid into a deceptive twilight, the sky overhead still bright, bracketed by the dark outlines of trees on either side. The woods had become places of impenetrable darkness in contrast to the silvery blue sky mirrored in the glassy water, like a bright tunnel between leafy black walls.

The wind stream hit Phillip's brow like supercooled air, the combination of speed and cold river humidity numbing exposed skin. He pulled his parka hood tight and ducked his neck deeper in the collar.

As they left the floodplains, bluffs closed in on either side. Maples crowded the banks and grew out horizontally over the river, reaching for unclaimed sunlight, blocking the sight of that ribbon of light above, except for winking patches of silver. The pilots, however, zoomed the shadowy tunnel as if doing so in broad daylight.

An hour later, the zigzagging stream transitioned into a gentler course. A light appeared on the lead craft. At this signal, lanterns were lit on the remaining boats, and the dim yellow penetrated the gloom a few yards.

This seemed worse than no light at all. The tree-lined banks beyond the orbs of light, once deep in shadow, were now lost in impenetrable blackness. It was as if they floated on the dark waters in a strange, small world of their own, in another dimension peopled only by the line of boats.

Danny had to repeat what he'd been saying. "We're safe to run with lights now. Nearer town, houses covered those hills up there." He pointed where the bluffs, in theory, still existed. "No more this far out, or at least any woods hermits out here know it's wisest to take no notice of strange doings in the night."

He released the throttle to wave forward. "Up around the next bend, you'll see an old icehouse and dock. From there on, we'll take things a lot slower. This first stretch is our normal run, and most of us could probably make it blindfolded. We rarely travel further upstream, though I've explored up there a time or two."

The boats decreased power. The prow, previously slanted into the air, settled low on the water. The roar of wind in Phillip's ears died to a light breeze, almost warm in comparison, bringing the humid, fishy scent of the river mixed with the gassy exhaust of outboard motors.

At the lamplight's left edge stood a double row of wooden pilings. A moss-covered ladder rose into the darkness. "That's our dock," Danny whispered. "Where we would stop to unload. We'll follow the main channel another thirty miles or so, then head up Yellow River. Name's a joke, I reckon. That there trickle's no river." He chuckled. "Ain't yellow neither."

Phillip yawned and shook his head to lose the heavy fogginess creeping toward his mind. During the breakneck flight, adrenaline had substituted for missed sleep, but now in the rocking, his eyelids grew heavy.

"Might as well get some shut-eye, Mr. Phillip. Me and Jock have the helm. This trip's gonna take all night. Better to be rested when it's time to unload."

Phillip lay back on a soft stack of baggage and a blanket warm around his shoulders. Was it certain all threat of pursuit had passed? With nothing to do about that now, he did the most productive thing he could.

He slept.

CHAPTER 31

In the days since the submittals were rejected, Lars reviewed the contract documents. As he suspected, there was no doubt, and even less wriggle room.

If work orders didn't hit the shop floor this coming week, Northwoods would fail to meet schedule. Not only would they forfeit the fat on-time bonus Leif somehow wrangled out of Haman, but the Committee would be well within their rights to hire another mill—Artisan's, anyone?—and back charge Northwoods any amount the substitute supplier cared to invoice.

This was bad. End-game bad. He couldn't let it happen.

He'd worked around the clock since, sorting through the mess, correcting the errors. Satisfied he had an accurate shop drawing, he encountered another problem. There was no time to make the submittal using normal procedures.

Nine copies were required for the submission packet. In the usual course of events, in-house draftsmen would make the multiple copies, which would take days at the very least. He would then send the packet off to the contract officer where it might languish in an inbox for weeks before being reviewed and, if approved, sent back to Northwoods by slow boat.

On a gamble, he boarded the first train out this morning and made his way to Capital, the sole copy of his labors stowed inside a drawing tube. As the wagon train rolled and bumped along, he slept the fitful, unrestful slumber of the sleep-deprived, the tube hugged to his chest like a precious child.

He arrived in Capital after midnight. Not stopping to check into a hotel, he made inquiries, gaining the address of the largest printing house. He caught a bike taxi to their offices, then camped on the cold cobbles before their doors. They'd better be able and willing to create reproductions of his shop drawings.

Everything hinged on it.

His body leaden, his heart like stone, he huddled in the doorway's shallow recess. Something like a dark wave rolled through his soul, colder even than this bone-chilling wind. Why did he bother? It was hopeless. What did he think he'd accomplish?

It was all for nothing. He'd already failed. Tomorrow, he'd be called on his fool's errand. Everyone would know him for the incompetent he was. And what would Mom and Dad say, once they learned what a fraud he was, what an impostor? Even now, he could see Dad's face turning away in disgust, hurt disappointment in Mom's eyes.

He might as well give up now and find a warm bed. A bed? It was worse than that. He'd be better off if he'd never been born.

He shuddered, hugging his arms tighter around himself. Where were these thoughts coming from? He was desperate, short on sleep, and overtaxed, sure. But he'd never been a whiner. He never gave up. If fate or whatever wanted to beat him, then it'd have to *beat* him. He wouldn't quit. He stood and danced about to warm his numbing feet, again buffeted by doubt, by mind whispers.

Who do you think you're fooling? You're still just Daddy's boy, playing like you know what you're doing, but you have no idea. Just admit it and go home.

But those whispers now filled his ears, not only his mind. They echoed from cold brick walls, swirled about his head like a winter's night wind gathering leaves. To his left was a blank wall where the lane dead-ended. A trap. To his right, the alley made a slow curve leftward, disappearing out of sight. The lantern beyond that turn wasn't visible from here, but its light cast distorted reflections along cobbles shiny with condensation.

The whispers came from that direction. They grew louder, many voices echoing, each talking over the other, a word here or there perhaps familiar, but more often just strange, sibilant sounds, escaping his grasp yet speaking things secret and dark into his mind. Into his soul.

Despair, self-hatred, fury, nihilistic rage swelled. He should surrender. When had all this ceaseless, pointless *striving* ever done him any good? Done his family any good? Look at them. They were disintegrating, their company crumbling. All this heartbreak, this hard work, for all these years, and all for naught. All is ashes. Nothing in this world is ever good in the end. Everything dies, all turns to dust and blows away, fate never noticing, never affected by any of the desperate life-sacrificing travail.

"No!" He backed into the corner, fist balled and held high, ready to defend himself.

Wind gusted, and the lantern snuffed out, the alley now lit only by a dim sliver of moon. And the whispers grew nearer, now angry, murderous, and something was moving out of the shadows, toward him, its presence palpable even if not yet seen.

He quailed, but then setting his jaw, he advanced on the adversary, fists still raised. "No! I know Creator God, and I don't accept your lies. I reject you!"

The wind increased. Shrieking like some enraged beast, it threw him back into the corner, his arms wrapped about his head against the pelting wind-borne debris.

Then all was still. But somewhere deep in that dark alley, the presence remained.

He backed his shoulders deeper into the corner, keeping his hands up, ready for an attack.

And he began to pray. Drawing upon that recollection of the presence of Creator God, he tried with all his might to once again find that comfort and pour out his heart to that great and wonderful being.

Even though the threat remained, palpable in the shadows, his heart was no longer troubled.

Sleep had come easily, even allowing for the freezing temperatures and the many times a directional change awakened him. Phillip was lying still, awake but doing his best to burrow deeper in the blanket and drift back off when the motor's purr dropped to an idle. He opened one eye. The reddish violet early dawn now peeked through the black tree outlines.

Danny whispered, "You awake, Mr. Phillip? Time for the portage."

Phillip sat up. They were in a canyon. Sheer limestone cliffs rose seventy feet or more on either side, the chalky beige rock pocked with water-eroded channels. Rust streaked where hundreds of fissures emitted seeping trickles.

Just upstream, the canyon narrowed to the juncture of two standing rocks, carved sentinels guarding the valley beyond. At this constriction, the current ran deep and fast, white water boiling over boulders before spreading into the wide, placid flow where the group now waded as they drew the boats ashore.

With the two-foot-deep water so clean, only the surface ripples distorted the speckled stones at the bottom. Then a floating sediment cloud obscured his view as Danny and Jock stepped into the stream, the boat rocking with their departure. He joined them in the frigid water and hauled the boat, grinding on the gravel, until it lodged firmly and would budge no more.

Jock turned to help ground the next boat in line, but a sharp word halted him.

"Jock!" A woman with a pinched countenance, appearing to match Jock's age of thirty years or so, stood in the boat. "Were you going to leave me to fend for myself?"

"No, my dear. How can I help you?"

She said not a word, but extended a hand in silent command. Jock retraced his steps and took her arm, holding her weight as she tiptoed from the boat. “My mother’s china hutch had best not be damaged. Bad enough you forced these poor children on this reckless boondoggle.”

She marched through the sand, cursing as it invaded her pumps. She changed course and stopped, hands on hips, before a young mother who sat on a flat-topped boulder, holding a fussy child. The seated girl’s eyes rounded, and she scampered away. Jock’s beloved sat and arranged her skirts about her with a prim shake of the hem. “Bring me my bag, Jock. The black one.”

“Yes, Clara. Let me find it.” He rummaged through the boat, then lugged a black carpetbag to Clara.

She sniffed. “I told you to keep this at the top. It sat in the water, thanks to you.” She slapped the bag, to which a few droplets of water had clung.

“Anything else I can do for you, dear? If not, I’ll keep assisting with the portage.”

“I bet you’d like that, wouldn’t you, leaving me here, helpless while you run off to make yourself look good? Why don’t you try to impress me, your wife, instead of these people? Help me change my shoes. Then you can guide me over the trail. Children, come.”

Three ragged waifs, a girl and two boys from four to ten years of age, crouched in the boat, three sets of knuckles clutching the edge, wary eyes barely visible over the rail. They now scampered to their mother’s side, stopped feet from her, and huddled together for further instructions. The youngest, the girl, peeked out from behind her brothers.

Her pumps now traded for marginally more practical, low-cut walkers, Clara stood. “Really! Traipsing about in the night like this? The little ones are bound to catch their deaths. You said there was a house. Show me now that I may settle them in their rooms.”

“Now, I don’t think I actually said house, my dear. But, yes, follow me. I’ll take you there.” He scooped the little girl into his arms. He pecked her on the cheek. “Isn’t this a fun adventure, Molly?”

Clara snorted as they walked away on the trail winding through the reeds beneath the bluff and soon disappeared over a cut between the standing rock and the cliff.

The crew was off-loading the boats, piling the contents on the bank. Phillip joined them, hauling baggage, then shouldering the boats, one man under each corner, and walking in the direction Jock and the other civilians had gone.

The trail rose for twenty feet to the easternmost pinnacle, through a narrow cleft between the rock and the cliff, then down again to the canyon floor beyond.

Once they exited the passage, a valley came into view. The far northern end tapered to a sharp vee. There, the blind canyon ended in high limestone walls, topped by lush sun-brightened trees swaying in a brisk wind, a wind that reached the canyon floor as only a mild breeze.

The stream here spread a wide, shallow sheet over a sand bottom. It hugged the western cliff face, the remainder of the valley floor a lumpy plain of flood-deposited sand. Beyond arrow range from the cliffs above, the fort stood guard to the narrow passage formed by the twins.

Dry-stacked limestone walls created a palisade, the stones darkened by time and weather. Its inside showed the rotted stumps of timbers, evidence of where defensive man-walks and towers once stood. One wooden gate hung askew, its mate nowhere to be seen. Several low stone structures huddled within, lonely walls encircling collapsed roofs, broken beams sticking out of rotted thatch like the skeletonized bird Phillip had seen in the reeds, its broken bones sticking out of matted, tangled feathers and mummified skin.

The sun was now cresting the canyon walls, its yellow rays bathing the old fort. Inside the broken gates, Jock stood, arms encircling his youngest, head lowered to hers, legs spread to brace against Clara's verbal tirade.

Phillip was unfortunate enough to pick up the words, even from this distance.

Danny, holding the corner of the boat opposite him, chuckled mirthlessly. "Poor ole Jock. That's why I'm not lettin' myself get trapped by the first pretty lassie that tries to latch onto me."

A man carrying the front of the boat called over his shoulder. "That gal was sweet as pie when they was courtin'. Not a man jack of us saw this side of her till the knot was already tied."

"My point." Danny nodded.

Another said, "Word to the wise, son, meet the mother and sisters. If you like them, the lass will be a fine choice. If the momma's a battle-ax, run for your life." The men roared agreement, hushed to silence when a woman's voice cut through their laughter.

"The same advice could be given to that lass, boys. If the father and brothers are lazy scoundrels like the lot of you, best she give that handsome rascal chasin' her skirts the shove." A middle-aged woman stood balanced on a boulder at the base of the rocks. She had a dignified elegance, her refined features highlighted by fine laugh lines, her gray eyes sparkling.

Necks showing a ruddy flush that couldn't be laid to sun exposure, the men found a need to concentrate on their footing.

As they descended the trail, knees bent against the grade, Phillip whispered to Danny. "This is who?"

"That be Beatrice, the chief's wife," Danny whispered back. "Nice lady, but don't be gettin' on her bad side."

They leaned the boats in a row against the fort's surrounding wall, flat sterns on the ground, bows pointing to the sky. They whittled stakes from green tree branches and drove these between the great flat rocks forming the wall. Then they lashed ropes left and right, tied to the ring at the prow of each boat to secure them in place. For good measure, they drove stakes into the ground and similarly secured the stern of each boat. Then the men made numerous trips to the stream, retrieved the piled baggage, and stacked it below the anchored boats, protected from the weather.

Nearly mid-morning, they finished. As the men had labored, the women formed cook fires outside the fort walls, and the smell of stew and woodsmoke started Phillip's mouth watering.

He joined Danny at the nearest fire and settled onto one of the rocks ringing the cook pit, hands extended to that welcome warmth. A child filled tin bowls with the soup, and another carried them to the seated men, supervised by a cheerful round-faced woman. They passed a loaf of dark Dutch-oven bread around the circle, each man breaking off a chunk.

Phillip dipped his sop into the stew. As he took the first bite, the sweet perfume of caramelized carrot and onion melded with the deep, satisfying tones of barley and well-seared beef. He closed his eyes and let loose an involuntary moan of appreciation.

The woman stopped before him, one hand posed on her hip. "Now here's a man who appreciates the simple pleasures. And a fine-lookin' one to boot. If I was ten—no, make that twenty—years younger . . . "

Phillip covered the heat rising to his cheeks with a question. "You bring carrot and onion on boat?" How could anyone possess such forethought in panicked flight?

"Oh no. Jenny found them growing wild beyond the fort. Luck is with us."

Thaddeus and Jeremiah, weaving their way through the fires and moving in Phillip's direction, apparently overheard the conversation. Jeremiah winked and flashed his trademark quiet smile. "Creator God is good. Make very good luck."

CHAPTER 32

Lars leapt at his attacker, fists still raised. "I told you I won't quit!"

A high-pitched scream resounded. A young man stood before him. His hands rose defensively, a key hanging from one. "Please, I have no money." The man quivered, backing away, the first yellow rays of sunrise shining in his eyes.

Lars opened his balled fists and raised them in a sign of peace. "Sorry. I must have fallen asleep. Are you the printer?"

Midmorning that day, a rushed and red-eyed Lars pushed through the doors fronting the Committee administrative building. At the reception desk, he stated his name and requested an audience with Haman.

"Do you have an appointment?"

"No, but I have important business with him. Can you ring? I'm sure he'll see me."

"Ah, it appears he is out of the office today. Could someone else help you?"

Lars rocked back as if punched in the gut, fighting for the breath that whooshed from his lungs. There was no other person to whom he could appeal.

Then Haman, recognizable by his regal bearing, walked past, headed for the exit.

Lars ran after him, juggling his packages. "Advisor Haman. Advisor Haman!"

Haman turned, bored annoyance slacking his face. "Oh, young Lars."

"Sir. I'm sorry to bother you. But I'm in a bind, and I wonder if you can help me."

"Please make an appointment with my secretary. There is somewhere I must be." He started to go.

"Sir! That'll be too late. Please, I'll only take a second. I just need to know who to talk to, to get this mess straightened out."

"Mess?"

Lars explained his dilemma.

Haman huffed. "Oh, very well. Follow me."

He led Lars back to the reception desk where he relieved the attendant of her phone. He made a few quick calls and set down the receiver. "Kindly direct this young man to conference room 3." Then he spun on his heels and was gone.

A guard showed Lars to a meeting room where Lars fell into a chair. A group of three men filed in, bearing notepads and annoyed expressions.

One of them slapped his notepad to the table. "I have no idea how you jiggered Haman into ordering this, but I hope you have your ducks in order. I don't care how badly Haman wants to help you out. My department will not approve substandard submittals. Clear?"

Lars swallowed against the lump in his throat. "Yes. Yes, sir. I apologize for the previous submission. It was inexcusable, but please, take a look for yourself." He untied the paper wrapper on his printed drawings, courtesy of an expensive rush job.

He unrolled the bundle and placed weights on the curling corners, the fresh ink scenting the air. For the next hours, he led the group, sheet by sheet, through the submittal, noting each exception that had been redlined on the previous iteration, as well as others he discovered during his audit.

As pages turned, the mood changed.

His presentation complete, he spread his hands. "Any questions? Does everything look okay to you?"

The department head looked at both of his men before answering. "Advisor Haman asked that we approve these submittals on a rush basis. That is something our department does not do. His thinking our job to be so simple it can be done in one afternoon, like a round of golf, is an offense."

Lars opened his mouth to answer, but all words fled, his sleep-deprived mind a blank. He slumped to wallow in the cold sea of failure, making no effort to fight back to the surface.

Somewhere deep in that pool of despair, muffled words reached his drowning consciousness and pulled him back, sputtering for breath.

"—however, the advisor is the lead on this project. If he wants approval rushed, far be it from me to deny him his wishes. You have corrected the errors noted, so I find no reason to reject this submittal."

Lars released a heavy sigh, but the speaker interrupted, raising a finger and holding it aloft like a battlefield standard. "But neither are we going to put our stamp on work we haven't properly vetted. I will be stamping your drawings with our provisional approval. If you so desire, you may begin production—at your own risk. We will conduct our normal review and forward our response when the process has been completed."

Lars reached across the table to shake hands. "Thank you so much, sirs. I appreciate your help with all of this. I really do, and if there is ever anything you need from me, please let me know."

The lead man sat back, face bland. "Very well. There is, in fact, something I need."

"Of course, anything."

"Nine more copies."

Maripol sat in a basement interrogation room of the Plumbsburg Temple. The smell of blood and despair tainted the concrete and steel like a greasy miasma.

He finished his report, and the bishop steepled his fingers before his lips, those disconcerting golden-brown eyes probing. Stripping him bare, leaving him naked before that chill gaze, his soul exposed, weighed, inspected, every flaw noted and judged.

He kept his spine straight, face stony, gaze focused on the far wall. There would be retribution, no doubt.

The weasel Lind, at his usual place at the bishop's right hand, spoke. "So? The scrolls escaped your grasp, and you would have us believe it was the local commanders' fault?"

Maripol remained erect, gaze still locked on that far wall. "I neither assigned blame nor found fault. I have presented only the facts."

"The facts?" Lind sneered. "You don't believe these people were taken by demons?"

"Of course not, sir. An obvious ruse. Even a cursory examination reveals evidence of a planned, if hasty, departure. Empty drawers. Missing objects."

After picking up Maripol's report, Lind flipped through pages. "You have a plan to redeem your failure?"

"I suggest we start with a wide radius, checking all modes of transport, working with local informants. A methodical investigation will pick up the trail. It's only a matter of time."

Lind threw down the report, slapped his hand on it, and trapped the pages against the hard steel table. He stood, bracing his weight on the now flattened papers. Then he leaned toward Maripol, his carriage, his bladelike face, almost reptilian. "Time? I'll tell you the time. It is time to exert power. I have ordered the deployment of an additional company of troopers. You will conduct a razed-earth operation, moving house-to-house, applying maximum pressure. Make them uncomfortable, give them pain until someone talks."

The slightest frown escaped Maripol's lips. "Sir, with all due respect, I believe that to be a mistake. This is a river town. These people are a difficult lot, smugglers and sons of smugglers, rebellious and tough, more likely to respond to bribes than threats." To disagree with this man was folly, but duty required the truth. Maybe he could defuse the fraught moment with some folksy levity. He'd seen it work for other people. "More flies with honey, as my grandmother used to say."

Lind's face puckered. "So, you think your grandmother knows better how to deal with rebels and dissidents than I do? What does Grandmother have to say about field agents who repeatedly fail in their missions?"

The levity had missed its mark. Not surprising. Maripol had never been good at that kind of thing. And in truth, he'd never met his grandmother. "As always, sirs, I await your command."

"Do not forget it. Squeeze these river rats without mercy, make them squeal. We expect to hear of your success in the near future."

CHAPTER 33

Curtis stood up from his morning's study to make a cup of tea.

The trapdoor to the room above opened, bringing the thrill of fear it always did. Then an old pair of oxfords came into view. Curtis checked his watch. Had he again lost track of time? Yes, by the testimony of the watch and the candle already burned to a nub. Must remember to replace that before he was left in the dark once again.

He prepared a second cup of tea. "What a pleasant surprise to see you." And it *was* pleasant. Aside from these dark surroundings, the isolation weighed on him so. He'd been a man of the people in constant contact with his parishioners. And now, forced into solitary confinement? It had nearly broken him early on and had never become easy.

The old man reached the ladder's bottom, huffing with the effort. "That climb gets harder every time, I swear. But I made this unscheduled visit for a reason. We have word of Phillip."

"Oh! Has he arrived on the east coast already?" Curtis set both teacups on the table's edge, forgotten, and dashed to his mentor's side. Word of Phillip's escape from Mazkelon reached them, including the devastating news that the scrolls had been lost along with Keeper Hilkiah. "But you said Phillip's arrival home would beat any other dispatches, given the circuitous route those written messages must take."

"Slow down, my boy." Reuel's wrinkled hands patted the air. "He has traveled as far as Great River, but there have been complications. He needs identity papers for an agent who accompanied him from Nob, and—" Reuel grunted. "*And* many dozens of additional personnel for which he gives no explanation. This message appears to have been written in great haste and is all we have for now."

He sat with a creak of his old knees and reached for one of the cups. "This is most troubling. I hope that young man is safe." His eyes narrowed, the lines between his brows growing deeper. "There has been a great stir. Order forces in all corners of Republic have shown unusual activity. Phillip must be the source of this disturbance. I'd ensure his safety myself, could I make that journey. But the days for adventures of that kind are well gone, for me."

He slumped into a chair, forehead to palm.

Curtis sat in the seat opposite the old man, his weight on the balls of his feet. A new thrill coursed through his veins. "But not for me, Professor. Tell me what I might do, and I'll happily go. With my new identity papers, it'd be safe enough, outside Two Rivers." Though faded wanted-dead-or-alive posters fluttered from random power poles, the likelihood of anyone paying him notice outside this town where he'd been well-known was slim, at best.

And what a thrill, to escape the dark existence of this place. It was like being trapped in a cave. The windowless concrete walls, the low concrete ceiling only added to that. Besides, the chance to be a protector, not the protectee in hiding?

He had to try.

"That would be less than ideal. You are no trained operative." Reuel waved away Curtis's offended look. "This is not an insult, but simply a fact. Truth is, at this time, I *have* no trained operatives available. I am afraid while we shuffled our precious fragments, many of us have grown old and frail without our noticing."

Reuel leaned back into the chair. His face receded from the candlelight, retreating into some inner space. "We have never been an organization designed for action. We are academics after all. And dozens of new identities? We can sneak a single record into the system, given time, but dozens? Preposterous. It cannot be done, much less quickly." He rubbed his forehead as if massaging the hurt there, caused by such thoughts. "I must dispatch a message to Phillip. We will expedite new papers for the young agent Thaddeus. This much I can do. But Phillip and Jeremiah mustn't wait for him, must complete the journey alone. I can do no more, and as much as I hate it, the mission takes precedence."

Curtis stood and paced around the massive wooden table, the candle casting his elongated shadow first on one blank concrete wall, then the next. Phillip, trapped out there somewhere, and no hope of help? "We must act. And what of the knowledge in the head of that Keeper? What if something happens to him, something Phillip can't handle alone? With the scrolls lost, he's our last chance. Let me go now. Let me be that help."

The shadowed wrinkles on the old professor's face had deepened as Curtis spoke. "If something were to happen to you or Phillip . . . " He paused as if pained. "But you have a point. Urgency dictates and needs must. And we have no one else."

He swiveled in his chair and caught Curtis's arm. "Are you certain you're up to this? It will be hard travel, and the danger will be great. I cannot exaggerate the peril." He peered deeply into Curtis's eyes as if searching for something there. "It is as if someone kicked a hornet's nest. Order operatives are swarming over this land. This is the worst possible time to test your new identity."

Curtis gripped the old man's bony shoulder. "I can't sit here, knowing Phillip is in danger." A grin pulled at his lips. Heat flared deep within. "Nor can I pass up the chance to pick the brain of that young Keeper." He lowered himself to a knee before Reuel, a knight offering service to his king. "I'd accept any risk to do my part in this. Phillip would do the same for me, has done."

Reuel took a deep breath and seemed to grow in strength, years falling away. "Very well. Let us prepare. Thorough planning will give you the best chance of success." He went to a shelf, selected a box, and placed it on the worktable. From inside, he retrieved a topographical map. He opened it, the brittle paper crackling as venous hands smoothed it flat. Then he began his briefing.

The last wickering flame on the candle snuffed out, leaving the room in near total darkness, the only light the few stuttering flames dancing on the coals, deep in the hearth.

Once again, Curtis had forgotten to replace the candles.

After weeks of breakneck work, Leif stood in the entry of the drying kiln, stacked floor to high ceiling with pallet load after pallet load of newly sawn hardwood planks. Hard to believe it was real. He slapped the nearest just to be sure he wasn't dreaming. A possibility, as little sleep as he'd been getting.

Young Bob had entered the control room to light the burner for this first drying run. Leif closed his eyes in a silent prayer to whatever god might exist, that this would go as flawlessly as the weeks milling had.

No injuries, no damaged equipment, and a kiln full of beautiful oak. Young Bob was a gem and a competent manager. He understood production flow and how to handle his people. They seemed to love him and were enthusiastic about their work. Leif's gaze ran over the assembled crew, a strange warmth growing inside.

The muted *whumpfh* of the burner igniting caused a stir of excitement, and the first wavering fingers of heat-refracted light began to rise among the pallets. Leif grasped the massive door and nodded to Old Bob, who had stationed himself opposite. They swung the doors together in a majestic arc, then latched them with the wooden drop bar. Young Bob joined the group, and Leif dug into his briefcase and pulled out a bottle, handing it to him. "You do the honors."

Young Bob colored red. "Oh no, Mr. Leif, sir. The honor should be yours. None of this could have been done, if not for you."

"Well, by that measure, then, it's obvious." Leif presented it to Old

Bob. “Without you, none of us would have any idea what we were doing. Please, christen her maiden voyage.”

Old Bob shuffled forward, leathery face split in a toothless grin. He gripped the bottle in liver-spotted hands, skin leathery and wrinkled, but fingers still strong and sure. He swung it into the oak beam, and it shattered, splattering the fizzing liquid on door and onlookers alike. “For good luck!” he shouted.

“Good luck!” the men returned. This turned into a chant, and the men started a kind of line dance, arms interwined over shoulders, shuffling an impromptu celebration, laughing at the joyful silliness of it all.

Young Bob draped an arm around Leif’s shoulders, grinning like a fool. “Mr. Leif, it don’t get much better than this, do it?”

“No, it surely does not. Thank you for doing such a masterful job with all this.”

Young Bob ducked his head, but his smile beamed. That’s all folks really want, wasn’t it? To do something good, to be appreciated, and, well, yes, to be loved for it. It was that simple.

The thrill was headier than any whiskey, and the mill yard filled with liquid light, surreal, the energy sweeping all up in its wake, lifting Leif on the swell.

Why couldn’t every day feel like this? He paused, still riding the surge, and stepped outside time for an instant, motes of sawdust suspended in the air, the glare of the sun off the tin roof frozen in shafts of yellow and gold, backlighting those motes.

In his kingdom, laughter warmed every face. His cheeks hurt from his goofy grin, goodwill bursting from his heart. If this was what success felt like, he’d be making sure every day was a success.

Time started again, and he joined the dance, his vow echoing in his ears along with the song of his men.

CHAPTER 34

An arrow stuttered into the signal tree near the cook fires. Phillip whirled, gaze sweeping the valley. His right hand set down the ax as his left reached for his hunting bow. There, halfway between the fort and the twins, stood a scout, his empty bow still raised to the sky. At the valley entrance, a lookout atop the newly constructed gate platform waved a red flag, indicating an all-hands emergency. A rush of blood sang in Phillip's ears as the semaphore signals announced unknown adversary approaching from downriver.

Women scuttled, scooped up children, and rushed to the fort's dubious safety.

He winced. If they were discovered here, those walls would provide little protection.

They'd done all they could to improve their defenses. Still, their hunting bows would be laughable against Order forces. He looped the quiver over his shoulder and sprinted toward the twins. One did what one could with the tools one had.

Phillip climbed to the sentry post at the left-hand twin and took his place alongside the other men. He peeked through a crude firing port.

Below, a single canoe nosed into the beach, paddled by a lone man. The intruder stepped onto the gravel bank, pulled the craft further onto dry land, and stopped when an arrow buried itself next to his right foot. He raised his hands above his wide-brimmed hat.

The sentry called out. "Turn around, face away from me. On your knees, hands on your head."

The man complied and called out in answer. "I'm no threat. I come in search of Phillip."

Phillip put a finger on the new arrow the sentry had nocked, pushing it down. "Is okay. This is friend."

He opened the shambling wooden man door, passed through the barricade, and spread his arms wide in greeting. "My brother, Curtis. Welcome!"

LEIF HURRIED from lighting the kiln to Northwoods Millworks. Lars, Mom, and Dad were where he expected to find them, eating a late lunch in the conference room, the meal doubling as an informal management meeting. Emotion twinged his gut, but he shoved it somewhere deeper. Many lunch hours he'd spent here, discussing problems, solutions, and opportunities.

He entered the room to surprised greetings, sat, pulled a sheaf of papers from his briefcase, and slid them onto the table. "Here's the list of lumber that will be ready in the coming month, broken down by species, board lengths, approximate board footage, and projected date. The price per board foot is listed in the right-hand column."

Lars lifted the paper and whistled. "Are you serious? Our suppliers are quoting us ten times that."

"Exactly. I told you I could harvest and mill this lumber for a fraction of what we'd been paying. Now I've done that, and the savings will be a huge shot in the arm for us—I mean for you."

Dad spun the pages back toward Leif, leaves flapping as the packet scooted across the table. "Take it and go. We don't buy stolen lumber."

Leif's ears began to ring and the room to recede. "What?"

"You heard me. We don't buy stolen lumber."

Was there a transmission error between Leif's ears and his brain? "What do you mean? Nothing is stolen."

Dad stood and left the room. Mom gave Leif a sympathetic look and followed.

He collapsed into his chair, his hands falling into his lap. "What the—?"

Lars took a seat next to Leif. "Hey, don't let it get you down. He's having a bad day. I just got back from Capital after putting in revised submittals. The original round was rejected. Dad thought we were in trouble. I mean, like the there-is-no-way-we-can-ever-meet-schedule kind of trouble."

"What? Seriously? We've rarely even been issued a Revise and Resubmit order, much less *that*. How'd this happen?"

Lars spread his hands. "The old engineering manager walked out on the job. The new guys weren't up to the task." Wincing, Lars put a hand on Leif's arm. "Sorry, I meant nothing by that, just trying to make light."

"Hegemony. Now what? Is someone getting fired, at least?"

"I wish. Just pointing fingers." Lars grimaced. "Dad doesn't think he can afford to lose anyone. He needs every man he has, so no. No one'll be fired."

Leif lifted the crumpled papers his dad had discarded, then smoothed them. "I wish I could help, but what in Eternal is that stolen lumber garbage about?"

Lars waffled his hand. "Rumors, you know."

"No, I don't. What rumors?"

"Dad heard it from this guy, Diggs. He warned Dad you stole the logging rights from old Tunne. Said to stay clear from any deal you were running."

"That's absolute dung. No one stole anything." Leif rolled his eyes. "Well, there may have been some strong-arm tactics in the beginning. And a few misunderstandings. And one body. No, make that two bodies, but never mind. I stole nothing, and what misunderstandings there were have been cleared up. Besides, Old Tunne is dead."

Lars mock glared through lowered brows, his suppressed laughter easily visible. “So Tunne was one of these bodies?”

Now Leif did laugh. That hadn’t sounded good, had it? “Stop it. No. Tunne is long dead. Of natural causes. His granddaughter, Kat, is steward now, and she’s on board, working side by side with us even.”

“Side by side?” Lars waggled his brows. “Leif, you’re a married man. What does Diana think of that?”

Leif waved the suggestion away. “You know better.”

Sitting up, Lars became serious. “I do. I’m glad to hear about the arrangement with Tunne or whoever. Let me explain things to Dad. He’ll come around.” Lars looked at the packet, then reached for it. “And we do need the break.”

A distance in his eyes, dark circles beneath them, hollows in his cheeks, Lars repeated, “Boy, do we need it.”

CHAPTER 35

Phillip fought to overcome the dull ache in his chest, the tightness in his throat. Why couldn't he put warmth into his greeting for Curtis, a warmth he genuinely felt? Something held him back. What?

When on mission, there was no time for self-examination, no room for sentimentalism. These things were reserved for a more appropriate venue, in a time of safety, when such distractions didn't pose a danger to clear thinking, to mission-oriented action.

Now, he indulged himself, the unfamiliar emotions so confusing. He examined these until it became clear. So this was what people called homesickness. But how could he recognize such strange feelings? He'd had nothing he called a home since his family was murdered. At least he hadn't admitted such to himself. But the feeling was unmistakable, the same he'd suffered as a child, forced to stay with relatives when his parents were away on their travels. Homesick, him. Imagine that.

So few years ago, he'd escaped the Eye. Then he'd started his current life with the professor within the same self-imposed, steely isolation that allowed him to survive the death of his family and the brutality of Order training. Over time, those cold walls melted under the professor's ministrations. Now Curtis, a link to those memories, opened a door of awareness. An awareness that Professor Reuel had become home, family. And a deep aching need for that home hit full force.

Since the mission went sideways, Phillip refused to think about home or the possibility he may never see that cherished old man again. He dare not open himself to those feelings, to allow such weakness, such distractions. They were even now causing him to lose focus. So he shoved them back into that compartment from which they'd escaped.

He dashed away a tear.

"Come, tour." Phillip led Curtis along, showing him the hastily built defenses and the double row of low stone cabins. "So little buildings." Phillip waved toward the structures. The number of existing buildings had been woefully inadequate. "Simon take crew, increase living space."

The man, in a stroke of brilliance, had them build new log walls between the stone cabins, connecting them into a single structure. They had chinked the logs and married them to the existing stone walls with yellow clay.

They walked past these row houses and up the stairs to the porch fronting the largest building, a square structure presumably once the fort's HQ. Their boots thumped on the green-wood planks where Phillip opened the door, then gestured Curtis inside. They'd salvaged the few intact glass panes to reglaze one at each end of the hall, the other empty frames now boarded over.

Once his eyes adjusted, Curtis gestured to the four rows of low tables and benches, rude wood constructs but sturdily built. "This is amazing work, Phillip. You must have been here for some time to have accomplished all of this."

"Yes, much time. Almost three weeks."

Curtis turned another full circle. "It's hard to believe this much work could be done in such a short time."

Another voice answered from across the room. "Captain Simon good leader." The speaker sat at a corner table, working on a stack of papers. A single candle cast a dim circle of light, by which could be seen his lean, pale face and his customary quiet smile.

"Come, Curtis, my old friend. Please, you meet new friend, Jeremiah." Phillip indicated a pile of rolled scrolls, one of which Jeremiah had open before him. He paused for effect, watching Curtis's reaction. "And this is True Text of Creator God."

Curtis wobbled as if blasted by a gust of wind, then gripped the table, steadying himself before lowering his lanky frame onto a bench. He tried to speak, producing only a croak. He swallowed hard. "Those were lost with Hilkiah."

A shadow crossed Jeremiah's young face. He took a shuddering breath. Candlelight glinted on pooled tears. "Hilkiah my father. He fool Order with false scrolls. Make safe for me—" Choked off, he bowed his head, breathing the deep, hard breaths of a man washed in pain.

Jeremiah had taken no time to grieve, and day by day, Phillip had watched the building pressure. To hold that pain inside was a kind of poison. The lad used pressing needs, constant, almost frenzied activity, as a screen, a barrier, his answer to Phillip's inquiries always, "I'm fine, thank you."

Now, the lad broke. Phillip came behind him and laid a hand on either shoulder, supporting the young man as he gave vent. Probably allowing himself to feel it for the first time.

As the sobs subsided, Jeremiah gasped out, "I know he plan this thing, do this thing because of me. Beg him escape with me—" Another explosion cut off the words. Once his heaving chest settled, Jeremiah wiped his eyes on his shirt. The tracks of his tears gleaming in the candlelight. "I think until now something might be broken in me, that something wrong with me. Could not feel the sad for Father. Now I feel the sad. Not broken."

"No, not broken." Phillip squeezed the boy's shoulders. "I see this thing many time. Is good you touch this thing, finally."

Curtis moved to sit beside Jeremiah and gripped the boy's hand. "There is a time for grieving. But Creator God gives us the mercy of withholding that grief until the proper season." He patted that hand, then sat sideways on the bench, facing him. "I'm sorry for your loss, Jeremiah. My name is Curtis, and the memory of your father's sacrifice will be honored, and yours. The importance of saving the True Text can't be overstated. This may be the only chance for the world to know the truth of Creator God."

"Yes. Father Hilkiah knows this." Jeremiah wiped new tears. "Always knows this thing. Teaches me my life small thing. To be Keeper very big thing. Creator God is all."

With one hand, Curtis indicated the open scroll. "This is really it?"

Jeremiah's quiet smile now lit his tear-streaked face. "This is Word of Creator God, protected by my family, line of Keepers for generations. This thing we do to save truth for world. Many times, evil peoples make world forget Word of God. Many times, Keepers preserve, wait for time peoples ready. Perhaps now is time for this world. Perhaps peoples ready to hear." He nodded to himself. "Yes. This, I think, is true thing."

"I think it is too, Jeremiah. I'll help you bring this truth to the world. We all will." Curtis sat back. "This changes everything. I doubt the plan Reuel and I put together will work. We had intended the three of us—you, Phillip, and I—work our way south to the main wagon train line and simply buy tickets home. But all passengers are being searched." He reached a hesitant hand toward the scrolls again, still stopping short before he touched them. "This would never pass. I'll have to advise Reuel of this complication. Wait for his guidance."

He cocked his head and shifted closer to the text. "But what language is that? I don't recognize the symbols."

"This writing called Ibrim," Phillip answered, "language of Jeremiah ancestors. Scrolls very old, language more old. Jeremiah teach me this thing, slow. Too slow. Many years to learn, I think."

Curtis rubbed his hands together. "If that is so, then we need a plan. The knowledge of the scrolls mustn't be lost. While we await word from Reuel, we must translate them into as many copies as possible, as quickly as possible. Scatter them to as many Seeker archives as possible." Curtis pressed a finger to lower lip. "First, we need a supply of paper and pens."

Phillip waved toward the boxes lining the wall. "This thing Simon has supplied. Need now many men reading Ibrim. This is problem."

"Maybe not. How many men do you have who can write in Common?"

The thump of a man's boots echoed on the porch, and a stout form filled the doorway, backlit by a rectangle of bright sunlight. Simon's raspy voice called out. "Why, all of my men can read and write, as can their families. I see to that with every new apprentice. Most river rats are illiterate, and most towboat captains are too dim to see how that limits the crew." He drew up his frame, not appreciably adding any more height. "My boys are literate and the best bargemen on the water."

He crossed the room and sat opposite Curtis. "Life on the tow is hard, away from family weeks at a time. You've never seen how much a letter from home raises a man's spirits." He tapped the side of his nose. "One reason I don't have the turnover."

"Father Curtis," Phillip spoke up, "this is friend Captain Simon, man who saves our lives. Captain, this is friend Curtis."

Leaning across the table, Curtis shook the blocky hand. "A pleasure indeed, Captain. Thank you for helping my friend. Your work here is impressive, and I look forward to hearing your adventures when we have time."

Hands laid flat on the rough table, Curtis rubbed fingers over the raised grain. "Can we use your men to write translations of these scrolls? It's important and needs to be done quickly."

"Oh, I know the importance of the Word, Father, believe you me." Simon glanced out the open door, checking the sky as if expecting some incoming storm. "Problem is I need every man jack to prepare this camp for winter, in case we're forced to remain."

Curtis pulled at his chin. "Why would you stay here? We only wait for new instructions from Reuel, which shouldn't take long. Once they're in hand, we can be off to safety, and your crew can go back to their own lives, no?"

"Oh! No siree." Simon gave a barking laugh. "We're bound to these lads and to their mission. Where they go, we go. Besides, we burned our bridges well and good back at Plumbsburg." He chuckled, but that laugh held little mirth. "Burned 'em right to the waterline."

"Seems Creator God make this thing." Jeremiah gripped the captain's forearm as if to forestall departure. "Captain Simon and crew, families have fate with us."

Curtis whistled. "This won't be as easy as I'd thought. Creating new identities for all may be impossible."

"So we wait." Simon shrugged. "Creator God will make the path clear. That much I've learned. Until then, you and I are of a mind—we need to make copies." His fleshy face widened in a smile. "I have an idea in that regard."

CHAPTER 36

Leif left Northwoods and rode his rusty bike to the county administrator's offices, pedaling as fast as he dared, given the worn sprocket. It was all he needed to strip that and be left walking. But what if German had already departed for the weekend? Then what?

Thankfully, the portly administrator was still at his desk, as reliable as the old typewriter he was pecking at.

He greeted Leif with notably less than his usual effusive good cheer.

"German, can I use your landline to call Capital?"

German frowned and returned to his typing. "Your father has instructed me to refrain from taking part in your dealings. I prefer to avoid another visit from him."

"Oh no. It's not like that, nothing to do with Dad. I just need to pass some information along to Advisor Haman." When German appeared to be unmoved, Leif added a lie. "Information he's waiting for."

The old man kept typing.

"Is expecting."

German let out an explosive sigh and pushed the handset toward Leif.

Leif pulled a card from his briefcase and dialed the number. After a few rings, he heard a voice. "Advisor Haman's office, state your name and business, please."

"Um, this is Leif from Northwoods. I have a report for him. That he wants." He glanced at German who was watching him with pursed lips. "That he's waiting for."

"Hold, please." The line went dead for a long minute, during which Leif jittered. His credit was nearly exhausted, and he was trapped. He'd been counting on that first run of oak to bail him out with Dad as a ready buyer.

If he didn't find a fast sale, he wouldn't meet payroll next week. The line clicked. "What a surprise to hear from you like this, young Leif," came Haman's voice. "To what do I owe this pleasure?"

"Oh, hey, Advisor Haman, good to hear from you too." He glanced at German again to be sure his close friendship with Haman was duly noted. "I wanted to give you a report. That you asked for. About the operation."

"Ah, I do not recall asking for a report, but please. I am all ears. Report away."

"Good, yes, good. Logging operations are moving along smoothly, output is ahead of projection, and quality is good. I mean great, actually. The sawmill is operating well, and the first run of white oak is drying in the kiln as we speak. It'll be ready for market by early next week."

"Fine. Anything else?"

Leif gripped the handset tighter to stop himself from trembling. "Actually, sir, the buyer I lined up for the first run of lumber needs to delay the purchase, so I wanted to let you know. We'll want to get it on the market. Soon."

"Why the rush? Is there a problem?"

Leif scrambled for a response. "Well, no big problem, but output has been good. We'll run out of yard space if we don't get the finished product off to market."

"I'm sure I can be of service in that regard. You may be aware of a mill here in Capital, Artisans? They are always looking for high-quality stock. As it happens, I was just leaving for a charity gala hosted by the family. Give the particulars to my assistant, and he will arrange for your line of credit to be increased commensurate to this week's production."

Haman paused. "It *is* your line of credit you are calling about, is it not, Leif?"

At the brittle hardness in those last words, Leif's knees wobbled. "Uh, yes, sir."

"Do you recall our first meeting? In which I said you should never, ever attempt to deceive me again?"

He strained the answer past a dry throat. "Yes, sir."

"You have strayed dangerously close to making that mistake today. Do not let it happen again. Final warning." Haman's voice regained its customary honey tones. "You see, young Leif, it is not deception I object to. Deceive away, to your heart's content, if it means gain for our organization. Just be sure you do not try that with me again. I will not trifle. Understood?"

"Yes, sir. Thank you, sir." The receiver clicked, and another voice came onto the line. As instructed, Leif relayed the details to the man. After a final click, the phone went dead. Leif set the handset into the cradle, avoiding German's eye.

The sharp creases around German's mouth softened. "Son, I know you're trying hard to do a good thing. Just remember, it's worth nothing if you have to be bad to do good."

Leif nodded, eyes averted. Had he been so transparent?

CHAPTER 37

Professor Reuel turned the key in the old brass lock, securing his cottage behind him. He wrapped the wool muffler tighter around his neck and buttoned his long coat. A frigid wind howled across the campus grounds, driving before it a flock of red maple leaves. Fall, so late in setting in, had come. Now, he could smell the icy breath of winter.

Leaning into that wind, he set off down the pathway. No cold would interrupt his customary walk. Besides, earlier this day a particular symbol had materialized, seemingly out of nowhere, scrawled in the corner of the lecture hall chalkboard. As always, it had appeared sometime between class sessions with no sign of who had marked it.

It took an extreme effort of will not to hurry, but to mimic his evening strolls all these many years. Hope rose, lodged in his throat, so very near his heart, throbbing there as if fit to burst from his chest.

Was it the boys? Was all well? As he continued his stiff-legged march, he whispered, "Creator God, let this not be portent of disaster. Let them be safe."

He renewed his focus and then tempered his pace, which had accelerated to match his galloping heart. Must maintain control. So important that an observer—and of course there was at least one—

not find his demeanor or actions notable in any way. Especially this night.

Having reached Central Park, he stopped on a bench near the water as he often did. The seat he selected this evening was well screened by a semicircular hedge of box yew sculpted into fanciful shapes, a project of the topiary club. In addition to protecting him from the harsh winds, the bushes protected his actions from prying eyes as he slid groping fingers under the bench. There it was, a plastic-wrapped spool of paper taped in place. He plucked it free, tape and all, and slipped it into his inner coat pocket, camouflaging the motion by removing a handkerchief with which he dabbed his nose.

He sat motionless for some time, watching the geese on the man-made pond. Overhead, other geese circled, honking encouragement for their annual flight southbound. Yet these remained, uninterested. Complacent. This group, the same species as those now migrating, had found city life so acceptable they remained year-round for generations.

Why would a once free creature trade that freedom, that self-reliance, for false security in the form of breadcrumbs and water kept open year-round by artificial means? No cage kept these birds captive except the self-imposed shackles of dependence, a reliance on easy living provided by the hand of another.

The same dull acceptance, the same invisible chains, bound the local people, and he shuddered at such a life. Men weren't created to be dumb beasts of burden, tamed and trained, lapping up feed from a trough. Creator God had to look upon such a sorry state with tears. Or disgust.

Without thought, Reuel had begun detouring toward the hide-away. Now, he reversed course. He daren't go there, much as he missed the perverse security of his dusty old tomes. Even more strangely, he missed that cold windowless cell. It now, to a greater degree than his cottage, carried the memory of those priceless hours spent in the company of Curtis, the dear boy. But the risk was too great, the Order forces too alert.

So, on feet already numbing, he tottered toward his abode. Inside, shades drawn, he ignored the biting pain in his toes and carried a candle to his writing desk to decode the message. It was, as he had hoped, from Curtis.

But, even for someone as experienced as Reuel, transcribing such a long letter took well over an hour. Once done, he limped to his soft overstuffed chair, the one he'd occupied the night Curtis had arrived. Dead pipe clenched in his teeth and cup of cider at hand, he settled in next to the soothing fireplace. He tipped the letter to the light.

R,

I hope this finds you well and quickly.

I have made contact with our old friend and his many new friends, more than fifty people all told and of every age. I have sent a full manifest by separate, secure means, so keep an eye out for that. Once you have it, let me know how long it will take to obtain proper attire for the entire complement.

I cannot provide a full explanation here. But be advised that, against my counsel otherwise, our old friend and our new friends insist on traveling as a single party. Unless better wisdom prevails, all will remain here, the package included, this shelter being the safest of available options. We will be unable to travel by the means originally specified, due to its presence, as I'm sure you would agree.

He lowered the letter, whispering under his breath. "Blast it!"

The men of this company are stalwart and true, loyal to our friend, and devoted to his mission. Rumors of the loss of the package were exaggerated. It is here, safe, and undamaged. And more complete by far, more than we might ever have hoped. By the time I receive further instruction from you, we will have a good portion of it copied. Should I risk sending one of these duplicates to you? Please advise. I feel an urgency to distribute as many copies as possible, as widely as possible, but will, of course, bow to your wisdom.

He could read no further. His hands were trembling too severely, his vision clouding. Could this be true? Had they recovered the True Text after all? He stilled his excitement and willed his eyes to focus.

I await your instructions and, as always, your good counsel.

May your efforts and ours be guided and protected from on high,

C

His gaze turned inward, no longer seeing his own spidery script on that page. So difficult to snatch any sort of order from his now whirling thoughts. So many new problems . . . Each crowded out the next. If only they'd hold still and wait their turn.

What momentous times he had lived to witness, this, his most passionate desire, the one he had despaired of ever seeing fulfilled. And here was he, griping about petty problems, in the presence of such a miraculous moving of the Creator.

But still, he had a job to do, his duty to serve that Creator. And now, more than ever, great peril crouched ever nearer, seeking to destroy mankind's last hope, this very hope now shepherded by a mere handful of young men, children, really.

Oh, that he were twenty years younger! He'd travel there himself, this instant. Even ten years ago, he'd have chanced it, given the inestimable stakes. He blew out a sigh. But no, he was long ago resigned to, in reality, confined to, the role he now played. He sat straighter in the old chair. He would, to the best of his ability, fulfill that duty.

Reuel tossed Curtis's letter, both the original and the decoded copy, onto the coals, staring into the glow as the pages darkened and curled, then burst into bright flames. He scattered the ashes with a poker and then shuffled back to his desk. He spent the next hours encoding messages, cursing old eyes that struggled to focus in the flickering candlelight.

CHAPTER 38

Leif helped Lars secure the last pallet to the flatbed, then slapped his brother's back. "There you go, little bro."

Punching his shoulder in return, Lars grinned. "Glad we got Dad to buy your stuff." He ran his hands over a slab of walnut. "It's gorgeous. That last load you sent was the best anyone in the shop ever worked with, even Dad said so."

Leaning an elbow on the flatbed, Leif grinned, chest expanding. The compliment from Dad, even secondhand, spread warmth through his whole body. "He really said that?"

Grinning, Lars nodded.

"Wow." Leif blew out a breath. "I'm glad. Is that why he decided to buy from me, after all?"

"That, or he figured out that garbage about it being stolen was bunk." Something shadowed Lars's face. "Or maybe just the discount. And boy, do we need it." His customary grin returned, and he slugged Leif one more time before climbing into the tug's cab. "Be back tomorrow for more."

Leif returned to his work, of which he was further behind than ever. He'd built a company, a successful one, and now he was discovering the price of success.

One of the old shop guys in his apprentice years, long gone now, had warned a young Leif, full of dreams of helping his family create a large, thriving enterprise. "Problem with building a monster," he'd said, "is you gotta feed it, or it'll eat *you*."

Well, some days he felt this place was about to do just that.

A shadow darkened his office, then the door slammed open. His hand spasmed, and the pencil skidded off the desk and across the room.

Haman stormed in, his black-robed form looming over the desk. "Young Leif, perhaps I have given you the misapprehension that I prefer to limit my profits? If so, please allow me to correct this misunderstanding. I want the maximum gain. Do you understand? The maximum."

Leif nodded, mute, eyes goggling. Could anything be more terrifying than a furious Haman?

"Good, then kindly charge the full price to all of our customers. This includes Northwoods Millwork."

Shaking his head didn't stop the ringing in his ears, still feeling as if he was in some surreal dream. "But, sir, I made it clear to you in our first meeting that my primary objective was to provide my family with a low-cost source of lumber, to give them a competitive advantage. That was the whole reason I started this project."

"*You* started this? Really? Did you have the logging rights? The line of credit? You have been a convenient operative, nothing more, and do not forget it."

"Sir, respectfully, that's not fair. You know it."

Haman vented a long sigh. "Oh, very well, but the lumber you sell to your family will be credited to the company at retail price. Any discount you give to them will be taken from your forty percent share. I do not offer charity."

Haman spun on his heel and slammed the door behind him. The glass rattled so it seemed ready to shatter.

Leif leaned back in his chair, breathing hard, eyes closed, concentrating to still his thumping heart.

Why was he so upset? He'd done nothing wrong. And everything would work out. Right?

And then his eyes went wide. He scrabbled on the floor, moving among uncompleted paperwork growing in stacks there, until he found his pencil. Ledger open, he scribbled fast calculations, then sat back to study them.

Under this new arrangement, once the discount for his family was deducted from his share, he netted slightly less than the subsistence wage he earned working for Dad.

Well, so what? He'd just work harder to earn more, right?

But even as he tried to convince himself, a part of him deep inside let loose a despairing scream. He threw the pencil at the ledger.

It cartwheeled across the room to again disappear among the paperwork.

And it was his only pencil.

CURTIS SET DOWN HIS PEN, taking advantage of a pause to stretch his fingers. Though he was no stranger to academic work, this was stretching even his endurance.

Children of all ages lined the tables, pens in their own hands, reams of paper stacked beside them. More stacks, not so neat, were rising as they wrote.

Jeremiah stood behind a lectern, one of the priceless scrolls laid out before him. He read aloud one verse at a time, first in Ibrim, then in Common Tongue, occasionally halting to delve his memory for needed words.

From his seat at a lectern beside Jeremiah, Curtis offered corrections to syntax and grammar, sometimes discussing these with Jeremiah until they were both in agreement. At which time, Curtis would write the verse on his own paper and read it to the room. It was then duly recorded on dozens of simultaneous copies, pens scratching to a crescendo, then fading as first one, then others completed their transcription.

Seated at a table next to Thaddeus, Phillip wrote just as the children did. He did this often after his work shift ended. Captain Simon had organized the adults into duty rosters as he would have aboard ship, and none were spared the responsibility, save Curtis and Jeremiah, whose sole task was the translation.

Once Phillip finished penning the most recent verse in his neat hand, he looked up, alert and ready for the next. This had been a good language exercise for Phillip, as well as for Jeremiah and Thaddeus. Indeed, Jeremiah's grasp of Common Tongue had advanced rapidly. Surprisingly, though, Phillip had begun to pick up Ibrim enough to understand the spoken word.

The scroll paper whispered against Jeremiah's palms as he rolled it closed. "Herein is end of reading, fifth book of True Text. I see we are ready to set dinner."

In the doorway, Beatrice tapped her toes. A line of women behind her leaned under the weight of pots, arms wrapped around baskets.

Jeremiah offered a prayer of thanks, then said, "Thank you all for hard work today. If you have noted questions regarding today's reading, will review these after evening meal." Movements reverent, he touched his forehead and stowed the scroll in the leather case. He smiled at Phillip and joined the men at their table. "Is good you make time, come write word."

Phillip welcomed him with a brighter smile. "Your language increase. Impressed, I am. Jealous."

Shaking his head, Jeremiah flushed. "Still, I put words in wrong order. Forget to use word such as *the* and *of*. Crude talking, but better and better."

A boatswain's pipe made its mournful call. Curtis and the others joined a growing line of men at the outdoor washbasins. They each scrubbed for the meal, then filed back inside, their table already set with steaming platters.

With the wooden serving spoon, Curtis ladled a heaping pile of vegetables onto Phillip's plate, then his own. "I'm going to miss the carrots and onions when they run out." Maybe they'd laid a lot in? They wouldn't be digging any more now, as frozen as the ground is.

Strangely knowing smiles passed between Jeremiah and Thaddeus. What was that about?

Then Phillip gave those two a wink. "Curtis, perhaps you take time after meal, I show you where vegetable are come from."

What are those three up to? To play along, Curtis nodded and pretended to be too busy enjoying his braised trout to answer. Which was not much of a lie. This fish was so fresh.

A man entered and hesitated. He scanned the room, then strode to their table, and handed Curtis a wooden tube.

Curtis twisted off the cap and plucked out a rolled sheet written in Reuel's familiar, crabbed script. Finally. Maybe he'd found a way to get these people out of here, get them somewhere safe.

"Please excuse me." Curtis stood, leaving a fillet uneaten on his plate, much as he hated to. He'd been looking forward to that fish.

Apparently, so was Thaddeus. He winked at Curtis, then scooped the morsel onto his own plate.

CURTIS SAT at a small worktable in the common room's corner. The sounds of the meal still loud behind, he decoded Reuel's letter. When done, he returned to the table, now swept clear of dishes.

He slid into a seat next to Phillip. "We have a letter from the professor. I'm afraid the news isn't all good." He laid it on the table and tipped it toward Phillip.

C,

Good to hear you and our friends are safe and well and in possession of the package. We are rushing to procure proper clothing for the third member of our friend's party. Getting the tailoring right may take weeks, but he must not allow himself to be seen underdressed. He was so seen upon leaving his home, and it caused quite a stir. He won't be able to return there.

As to the manifest you sent, it has arrived, and we are doing what we can. Your request may not be possible, though. If it can be done, it may take many months. I will provide a definitive answer when I have one.

Please persuade our two young friends to reconsider. They can travel with the suitable wardrobes already in their possession, and it would allay many fears to have them here. I have attached under separate copy the name and location of a man who can arrange transport for you, them, and the package.

Make haste. The hornets' nest has been kicked, and the hive's current heightened activity shows no sign of abating. If anything, it intensifies by the day. I fear for your safety. Do this old heart good and prevail on the lads to make for home.

As for your work. Yes, yes, a thousand times, yes. Provide me a copy, by the securest means, as soon as you reasonably can.

As always, accept my love and my prayers that you are guided and protected from on high.

R

"Well?" Curtis crossed his arms. "You know what my next question will be. How about it?"

Jeremiah held up a palm. "Will not go our own way. We follow the way of Creator God. You know this, friend Curtis. I think you agree, no?"

Curtis rubbed his face. What a choice. But in the end, not his to make. "The tales you've told leave little doubt Creator God is doing great things here." He waved to encompass those scurrying about. "But perhaps it *would* be wise to take the professor's advice? Shouldn't we make safe those we can? Especially the scrolls?"

At their hardening expressions, Curtis let his hands fall limp to the table. "As you will. I'll compose my reply before I turn in. Can I obtain a copy of the translated text as it stands? If I have to disappoint my old teacher on the first, I'd rather our refusal arrive with a gift—which makes me think of another thing. Jeremiah, we should copy the original scrolls verbatim, in Ibrim. It's such a risk to have a single copy."

"I have same idea." Jeremiah began to stand. "Pardon for not telling you sooner. Have begun both these thing, Phillip and Thaddeus work with me every night before lights out. Have one copy finished through book five, two copies not quite so far. I go to retrieve now for you. Please send most complete copy to Professor. This is very good idea. Very good to make safe."

Palm moving to cover Thaddeus's own, Phillip whispered. "I'm sorry, my brother. Have faith. A way will be found. We will get you home." Then he stood and stretched his compact form. "Father Curtis, may I show you gardens? Perhaps you join us, Thaddeus?"

Eyes flat and staring at nothing, Thaddeus shook his head.

Curtis stood and paused to lay hands on Thaddeus's shoulders, squeezing them before giving him a last, friendly backslap. "I could do with a walk. All this sedentary work." He glanced toward the podiums and patted his belly, the hard edges of his torso noticeably softened since his arrival. "And the food is too good."

Outside, smoke wafted skyward from stone chimneys. It must be a trick of the air currents, but the smoke always rose straight skyward, to be carried away by the winds aloft. Never yet had he seen it blanket the village. His fireplace exhausted flawlessly, never filling the cabin with the eye-stinging, choking back drafts so common in his parsonage. If only this good fortune would prevail in the howling winds of the coming winter.

They walked past a line of worktables hosting half-finished crude wood furnishings. A lean-to roof was half constructed overhead. Amazing what Simon's crew accomplished with so little. The people living in the moldering Northwoods' homes didn't have it this good. Seeing it made him itch to return, to light a similar fire in his old parish.

Then he shook off such thoughts. It was not to be, maybe never again. Torturing himself with such hopes only dragged his spirits back into that gloom he'd struggled so valiantly to free himself from.

Phillip navigated the rough ground by the rapidly fading twilight. They passed from the fort walls to an open patch north of the big stone structure. Easily accessible, it stood far enough away that the rays of the sun, its track now well south on the horizon in this late season, weren't blocked by the fort's shadow. "Garden plot. See?"

Freshly turned earth evidenced the recent digging of carrot, onion, potato, and turnip. A few plants remained. The leaves, surprisingly green and vibrant, contrasted the surrounding vegetation all the dull gray brown of early winter, the colors barely distinguishable in the dim silver light.

Curtis sighed. “Well, I supposed this day would come. We’ve little left to harvest. Surprised we can still dig them at all, cold as the ground is.” But surely . . . “I assume much has been stored?”

Incongruous mirth crossed Phillip’s face. “Harvest only what is needed each day.”

“Well, that’s that. It was nice while it lasted.” Curtis summoned false cheer for the smile he gave Phillip. But the act probably fell flat. He so hated dry rations. “Gruel and grain mash for the winter, I suppose. It’s hard to make mush appetizing, meal after meal, but it’s preferable to starvation.”

Phillip chuckled. “You and I will take morning walk before breakfast.”

“Certainly. I could use the exercise, and maybe we can find time to do some of those workouts together, like we did in the hideout?”

Still wearing that mysterious smile, Phillip turned toward the fort.

CHAPTER 39

Last night had been an all-nighter, as was happening too often since he'd begun working evenings in his basement office, all to overcome the shortcomings of others.

But over and over, one thing from Reuel's new Scriptures kept echoing in his mind. The admonition to "honor your father and mother." Mom and Dad needed his help. They were counting on him, and this instruction from Creator God only reinforced his passion. This is what it took, to please God. And he was willing.

When he arrived at work today, Benny, one of the shop's lead men, was waiting. "Got a problem, boss."

"What's that?"

"Come see for yourself."

Lars followed Benny to the shop where several men stood around a pallet, shaking their heads.

Banded to the pallet were thousands of oak slats, the rear faces of which were kerfed and the edges beveled and slotted to receive a spline. Similar pallets, bearing identical burdens, rowed up across the shop. No doubt what these were. The manufacturing concept had been his own. "The parts for the table bases. Good. Finally, they showed up. Better late than never."

"Yep. Now try to put them together."

Benny knew this assembly. Why was he acting dumb?

Lars picked up one of the parts and pointed at the slotted edge. "All you have to do is insert the splines and glue eight pieces together to create the octagonal shape. Clamp them with a strap clamp. Just like we talked about."

"We know that. Do one for us, would you?"

"Okay?" He played along, took eight slats to a nearby table, and began inserting splines. He fit the first two pieces together and stopped cold, a hollowness growing in his stomach. "Oh, shoot."

Benny uncrossed his arms. "So you see our problem."

"Yeah, the edges are machined at the wrong angle. Instead of nice big octagonal columns, they gave us pieces to make little square tubes. Which mill was it? I've gotta get on this now. They'll have to work day and night to correct their error in time."

Diggs had handled jobbing out parts orders to the association's other mills. Lars had been much too busy running his own shop to keep track of which order went where.

"You're assuming it's their error."

The hollow, tight drum in his stomach, previously only playing in the background, now took center stage for a long solo. He laid the pieces down as if they were fragile porcelain. "Please tell me it was."

In answer, Benny unrolled a production drawing, a section of the table base, with an individual slat shown full scale, dimensions, angles, and machining instructions in livid detail. What was drawn on the detail appeared to be the correct sixty-seven-and-one-half-degree cut, but the angle written in the notes was forty-five degrees.

This wasn't part of the submittal Lars audited. This detail was part of the packet sent to the manufacturer. He checked the title block, the draftsman's name inked in black. Hector. No name, just a blank space where the final review should have been noted. Had this order been released for production without review?

Lars snatched up one of the slats and the drawing and spun toward the office. Blood thrumming in his ears, he ran up the stairs into Dad's workspace where Diggs was regaling Dad and Snow with another of his tall tales.

Lars slapped the drawing onto the desk. "We have one thousand of these things to deliver. The slats from your friends"—he glared at Diggs—"showed up two weeks late, so we're out of time."

Dad glanced at the part and back to Lars. "Yes, I know. It'll be tight, but we can make it. Everyone in the shop will need to put out for a change."

"No, Dad. No, we won't—because we have eight thousand slats made to this specification." He stuck his finger on the offending angle.

"What's wrong with—"

Lars stabbed the drawing, his fingertip sounding like a hammer rapping wood. "See that angle? Is that the right angle for an octagon?" He held up the slat. "Does that even look like the right cut?"

Dad's eyes widened, his jaw clenched. Good, he'd twigged. Now for the tricky part.

"There's more. Who approved this for production?" Lars's finger stabbed again, this time on the empty approval block.

Diggs leaned forward in his chair. "Are those the slats we had Western Millworks make? I took that packet to them."

Lars's glare now skewered him. "That mistake should've been caught. Who reviewed it? Who approved it?"

Diggs pulled a face and put his hands up in a big shrug. "Search me. I was going to Western. I asked Velde for the drawing. He gave it to me."

As if summoned by that mention, Velde appeared in the doorway. "Something wrong with the table slats? Benny told me you were looking at them."

Lars tossed him the slat. Not nearly as hard as he wanted to.

"Nothing wrong with them at all, if you like lots of tiny squares." Benny said as he stepped in behind Velde, scowling.

Velde walked to the desk and stood over Dad's shoulder. "Well, that's their error. There's nothing wrong with the geometry. The correct angle is even noted here in the small-scale assembly drawing. It's only labeled wrong in this one place. Their problem, not ours."

Diggs sucked his teeth. "Actually, it is your problem. Specifications and notes take precedence over geometry, and larger scale details over the smaller scale. Sorry, you just bought yourself eight thousand bad slats."

"Who's gonna pay for this?" Dad's fist slammed the desk. "What in the blazes are we supposed to do with a ton of bad parts?"

Diggs made a clown's face. "Build flower boxes?"

Lars picked up the drawing and shook it. "Who reviewed this? Or if no one did, why did it get released?"

"Back off." Velde leaned his face close to Lars's. "We've been working like fiends. The guys are way, way overtaxed. You slam us with this huge contract and give us no extra help. I don't know what you expect. Something's gonna give."

Lars's cheeks were heating, but not as fast as his blood. He should rein himself in, remain above the fray. But he didn't want to. "I've been working twenty-hour days. I notice you punch out at five every night, Velde. Who's overworked?"

Velde didn't answer in words. His sneer was enough.

Lars stepped toward him, his fists tightening. "You'd better start caring about what you're doing to this company."

Benny grabbed Lars's arm, holding him back. "Not worth it, little man."

Snow had been lounging against a wall. Now he moved toward Lars, arms uncrossing and fingers limbering.

"Stop." Dad stood. "All of you get back to work. Diggs, make a run to Western, find out how quick they can remake the slats."

Lars balled his fists, fingernails biting. But Dad was right. If he didn't leave, he'd lose his temper for good. He stomped down the hall.

In the office behind, Diggs said, "Your boy needs to learn a little self-control."

Lars spun and charged back toward the room.

But Benny hooked him by the elbow and drew him down the stairs. "Not worth it, I said."

CHAPTER 40

Curtis gave up trying to go back to sleep, guts clenched, the import of Reuel's letter still echoing. No way to get identities for this many people. It could not be done. Would not.

And Simon and his tribe? Just as firm in their resolve to stay with the scroll-bearers.

Phillip and Jeremiah were the worst. Those two already had their papers and no reason to stay—and a thousand reasons not to. But they were as stubborn as Simon's lot.

How could he convince these people to save themselves, more importantly, save the scrolls? Before the Order came down on them and all was lost? It would happen, somehow, sometime. Especially with the locals drifting in and out of camp as they had been.

And Simon kept allowing these outsiders, no matter Curtis's qualms, claiming they were his relatives and, given their peculiar trade, were better than any folk at keeping secrets. That they would not, even to save their own lives, betray the secret as long as they had no mistrust of those hiding in their canyon. That, for this very reason, it was better for the hill people, as Curtis thought of them, to get to know and trust the folks encamped in their territory.

But wasn't it said three people could keep a secret, but only if two of them were dead? The day would come. They'd all regret this. So how to convince the scroll-bearers to flee while they still could?

With it yet dark outside, Phillip tiptoed toward Curtis's bed and tapped his shoulder.

"Time?" whispered Curtis. At Phillip's nod, Curtis rose to pull on his trousers. Together, they slipped into the frigid morning, carrying their boots.

Brisk air nipped Curtis's cheeks and nose. Subfreezing temperatures were now the norm most mornings, and this day had brought a thin layer of snow. As they rounded the corner of the fort, their passage flushed a pheasant from a tuft of brown grasses. Curtis flinched at the explosion of wings, the shrill trilling cry, as the bird arrowed low over the white plain, then locked its wings into a curving glide to disappear in a jumble of boulders at the cliff base.

Phillip established a brisk pace, and Curtis matched him, though not without effort. The lad was a machine. All the better to warm muscles, though, and he needed that with the frosty air cutting through his thin pants. They were walking north, having seemingly taken this direction at random, and Curtis had fallen into the pleasant groove of a good workout when his steps faltered, then stuttered to a halt.

They were in the garden. He squinted to focus, then rubbed at his eyes. The predawn light must be playing tricks. He walked closer and knelt to cup a handful of soft, green carrot fronds, one of hundreds in row after row, waving in a warm breeze. A warm breeze? Shockingly so, not cold. He moved his hand out of the garden and back over the snowfield. The cold bit his exposed skin. Then back to the carrots. Again, the soft warmth soothed the back of his hand.

Further on were plots of onion and potato plants, all growing green and lush where yesterday there had been nothing but craters of disturbed earth.

In every direction, the ground was white with snow. The garden plot, alone, was singularly free of the white covering.

Still kneeling, he checked Phillip's expression. Was this some kind of joke? A prank? But Phillip's face was only a dark outline against the brightening eastern sky, the arc of the predawn glow little more than like the half-moon on his thumbnail. *I'm losing my mind. I'm looking at impossible carrots, and my thoughts want to turn to poetic visual comparisons.*

He shook himself. "I think I'm hallucinating."

"Your eyes see true. Real carrots. Impossible maybe, but real. But nothing impossible for Creator God. Every day, harvesters dig garden. Dig all carrot, all onion. Every morning, surprise, more carrot, more onion, never freeze."

Curtis pushed a hand deep into the soft soil of the carrot bed, then pressed his other hand to the hard, frozen ground outside the garden's border. "I did believe when you told me of your journey's miracles. But believing and seeing are very different things. Amazing. Creator God is blessing your effort. Who has ever heard of such?"

Finger pointed at Curtis's chest, Phillip said. "Our effort. Yours, mine, ours. And yes, is difficult to believe, deep down in soul, until one sees for self. As for who has heard of this thing? Did we not just write book with many miracles of Creator God? Jeremiah tells that coming books have more miracle. Oil jar which pour, pour, pour every day, never go empty." Phillip chuckled. "Remind me to show you where from comes our cooking oil."

"Professor Reuel will never believe my stories." Curtis imagined telling this tale, Reuel's bright-blue eyes shining in delight at the hearing. "Or maybe he will at that."

Phillip knelt, now level with Curtis. "So now maybe you agree? Creator God shows it is His will we be here together, stay here together. Us, Simon, his people. Creator God does great thing, this thing we understand not. But need not understand to see truth of thing."

"Oh, come on." Curtis stood and broke eye contact, tossing a clod of earth to the ground harder than necessary. "Miracles are one thing." He stepped close, took Phillip's arm, and shook it as if to wake a sleeper. "But that doesn't mean we shouldn't exercise good sense. I've seen no secret message from Creator God saying you should stay here, sitting ducks."

Eyes atwinkle, Phillip cuffed him on the shoulder. "Come. Eat breakfast. Then I show you where we find meat."

They walked back toward the fort, which had now begun to wake, the crisp air carrying the burgeoning sounds of morning activity. The *thwack* of an ax splitting firewood echoed, along with the high-pitched giggles of children playing tag among the wood stacks. From inside the fort, a mother called her brood to morning chores.

Later, breakfast and those chores complete, Curtis, Jeremiah, and their young transcriptionists gathered at their tables. Phillip stood waiting at the door as Curtis announced that, before they started their work, they would take a short field trip. The children cheered.

Soon, the entire party traipsed across the snowy plain, the young ones hopping and skipping, their combined voices like the chittering of birds. Their course took them toward the western cliff wall and the shallow stream running along it. Three men were working near the bank, tying rabbit carcasses to a carry pole.

Phillip motioned. "Come. Careful to stay behind. Look for tracks."

Near the flat stretch of gravel along the water stood a line of stick structures. Inside each was a looped snare, empty and reset, ready to catch more quarry. Curtis crouched by one. "I did some rabbit trapping as a lad. You won't catch any like this. The snares should be on established game trails, not lined up on the beach."

Phillip pointed at the snowy ground, wordless.

The prints of rabbits, dozens of them, crossed the new snow, the tracks clear and crisp. The pattern was strange. Normal rabbit trails wandered, zigzagging from one area of browse to another.

These tracks moved in a straight line—toward the traps, not deviating even when the course of travel took the animal near tasty feed. More, not only were all the trails in straight lines, but they radiated in from all points of the compass as if every rabbit in the area had been drawn to this spot.

"Spooky," was all Curtis could think to say.

But it was more than spooky. It was unnatural.

Phillip crooked a finger, then set off toward the twins.

The group climbed the rise at the choke point. There, the

morning guard saluted Phillip, and they passed through the gate. Then they descended to the stream bank where four men were gathering a net. They unfolded it and cast it into the shallow stream, tying the corner lines to stumps. They then sat on those stumps, sharing coffee from a battered thermos.

What were they thinking? The stream here was only inches deep, no place to net fish. Curtis said, "Shouldn't they go downstream to deeper water?"

Finger on his lips, Phillip just smiled and pointed with his other hand.

After a time, there came a glint, an undefined, shimmering undulation below the water, far downstream. As he stood, gaze focused on the anomaly, it moved closer and soon separated into a cloud of fish swimming together tightly grouped. They came on until above the net. There, they stopped and hovered in place, tail fins waving just enough to hold position in the current.

With no sign of hurry, the fishermen finished their coffee and stowed thermos and cups. Then they sauntered to the water's edge and hauled in the net, full to bursting with wriggling fish.

Curtis stared, mouth open for so long, his tongue grew cold. He snapped it shut. No reason to look like a fool, even if he understood nothing at all. About any of this.

Finally, the weight of Phillip's steady gaze was too much. The guy was just watching him, waiting. And smirking. Smirking! "What?"

Shrugging, Phillip raised one eyebrow. "So, my friend? Perhaps Creator God is in this thing, do you think?"

Curtis growled. "I think I need to revise my letter to the professor."

CHAPTER 41

Leif tossed the last production packet into his outbox and rubbed his eyes with the heels of his hands. No sense starting another project. It was so late, and he had nothing more left in him.

As nearly as he could tell, he had spotted all the mistakes in this week's packets. His managers would make the necessary revisions tomorrow before distributing the documents. He locked the shack and mounted the rattletrap bike. When would he ever get ahead? Gather the funds to replace the rusty old thing?

He pedaled home, movements as lethargic as his sleep-starved mind. But what was this reluctance? Did more than the demands of work keep him away? He *did* miss the kids, so badly that even thinking of them felt like a punch in the gut. But he didn't want to see Diana.

She'd developed a studied disdain for him. It made him feel small, insignificant, unworthy. Lest he have any illusions as to why she would find him a less-than-satisfactory husband, she took every opportunity to clarify which of his many shortcomings most disappointed her.

That she was actively unfaithful was no secret, either. The rumormongers would've made him well aware had she not made the fact spitefully clear herself.

And Diana's mother, Corella, reveled in boasting about Diana's cuckoldry and her own strong approval of Diana's new man. A better man. A man with whom Leif should be replaced as soon as possible.

When he opened the door to his home, an even more unpleasant emotion overshadowed the dread of seeing Diana. As if materializing at the thought of her, Corella stood in the kitchen, warming something on the woodstove. The fire was stoked too hot. Waves of overheated air radiating into the already stuffy room, and whatever she was stirring made the sizzling noise of scalded sauce. The acrid tang of burned milk grew stronger by the minute. The kids were at the kitchen island, scribbling with crayons, oblivious to the ruined meal looming in their near future.

Then Leif picked up the picture Suz was coloring and grimaced. Corella had brought them more of those sappy "comics with a message" that the Order pushed on kids.

He disapproved of these brainwashing tracts, but Diana, and to an even greater degree her mother, were fervent cheerleaders for all things Eternal. He just hoped the kids were smart enough to resist such indoctrination.

Better shut down that roaring blaze before the stove melted down. He reached to adjust the damper, but received a rap from a wooden spoon. Sucking a knuckle as he retreated, he adopted a false veneer of good cheer. "What a nice surprise. What brings you here, Corella?"

She didn't greet him, nor feign any pleasure at his arrival. "She's out. Won't be coming home till Sunday. I'll be watching the kids till then."

"That's not necessary. I'll take it from here. Where did she go?"

"To find a better life for herself. At least so I hope. And I *will* be staying. Who knows what could happen if I left you in charge."

A deep, calming breath failed its purpose. But arguing with this woman would lead to escalation, and she had no limits as to how far she was willing to go. "I assure you the kids are safe with me. Why don't you go home where you can be comfortable?"

"Nope. Was told to stay, and stay I shall. The children probably forgot who you are, anyway."

The kids had stopped coloring and were watching with big worried eyes. No sense fighting a battle he couldn't win. He scooped up the baby and took the twins by the hand, headed toward the living room, nodding at Suz to join them. He set up their favorite board game and began to play, catching up on his snuggle time with the little ones.

For their sake, he tried not to let it show, but his belly was a slow burn. What kind of mother left her kids like this, just to run around? And doing who knows what? Did she have no desire to do what was best for them? But then, he'd been neglecting his children too, hadn't he? There was a difference, though, right?

He was working to secure their future, to provide for them. She was stepping out for fun, partying and catting around. Yes. There was a huge difference. He was certain of it.

But even as he worked to fortify these self-assurances, a still, quiet voice, a voice he was doing his best to smother, whispered. *Can they tell the difference? Does it matter to their tender little hearts for what reason they've been ignored and abandoned?*

When Corella called the kids to the dining room—to eat that slop she wanted to inflict upon them, Leif went to prepare himself a bath.

Diana hadn't forgotten to fill the tub. His fingers tested the water. Good. It'd been tempering all day and was now nicely lukewarm. He hated it when she forgot. Cold baths were his bane.

He indulged the remembrance of what it had been like to enjoy hot running water before the Great Collapse. This house had once been so blessed. The old hulk of a hot water heater still sat in the basement, rusted and abandoned.

But this bath was as far from that remembered hot water as this drafty room was from those bygone days of central heat, now only enjoyed by the elites in their glass palaces. He made fast work of his ablutions and toweled off, body covered in goose pimples, and dove into his robe.

Then he groaned at the murky cloudiness of the water. Three

days—or was it four?—had left him filthier than he'd guessed. He pulled the plug and ran a fresh bath, but it would take hours to temper. The kids would have to do with sponge baths tonight.

As he went through their bedtime ritual, his mind drifted again to his work. Perhaps it *was* a good thing Corella refused to leave. He needed the weekend in the office. Maybe this time he could start Monday morning having caught up with his work.

CHAPTER 42

Curtis and Jeremiah each dropped their armload of firewood to rattle into the nearly empty rack. Not nearly enough. The three-sided wood frame not even a quarter full with this load. And it promised to be a bitter night, fingertips and toes already feeling the bite. All up and down the long row house, other families were stacking firewood next to their own doors.

On the return trip to the woodpile, Curtis returned to the topic of conversation. "I still don't get it. You say Creator God can allow no hint of sin into his presence. It's for this reason we are so estranged from Him, right?"

Nodding as he walked, Jeremiah said, "Is for this reason Mankind is banished from paradise. From His presence."

"And that debt of sin can never be repaid. All these rules and sacrifices we're reading about in the scrolls are only pictures of this condition. But you say no amount of rule-keeping nor sacrifice-making ever really makes a man righteous?"

Again, Jeremiah nodded. "No matter the sacrifice, no matter how well lived the life, still we are tainted by sin. This is correct thing you say."

"So it's hopeless?"

Jeremiah stopped midstep and frowned. "Never is hopeless with

Creator God. We read only today of His promise that He provides these answers."

At that, Curtis had given a hard shake of his head. "When. And how?"

Jeremiah answered with his quiet smile. "With God, nothing is impossible. I tell you already this answer, yet you do not hear me."

Enough with these mystical half answers. Curtis wanted verifiable, objective truth. Something real. Something actionable.

This last load topped off the firewood rack. Jeremiah opened the door, beckoning Curtis inside, but he shook his head. "The woodpile is getting low. I'll split wood until it gets too dark to see." And until he worked off this frustration.

The paradox was maddening. All this time, all this work to recover the True Text, only to learn the secret path to paradise is simple. And simply impossible. Just be perfect?

And even more maddening, Jeremiah understood something, was seeing something in these scrolls Curtis was not. But study them until his eyes bled, he couldn't get it.

Was it possible the quest *was* hopeless? But if so, why all the miracles?

LARS WRAPPED HIS COAT TIGHT, arms crossed to keep his body heat from being stolen by the icy gale, so strong every gust rocked his body sideways. Why had he chosen this frigid, wintry Saturday, of all days, for a trip to Two Rivers?

But the glut of miscut parts logjammed the shop, making his presence unnecessary until replacements arrived. Besides, he needed the break. The constant pressure left him no time to work through this confusion, this inner tumult. In Curtis's absence, the mentor Lars hashed things out with, he'd reached out to Reuel. Their letters had been a balm, but face-to-face was going to be so much better.

Or that had been his thought. But now, he'd been outside the terminal, sitting on this bench for hours. Was Reuel even in town?

Was Lars waiting for someone who'd never show? The north wind blew what had to be icicles right through his pants. His nose and left cheek had gone numb, feeling like dead fish beneath his probing fingers. With no corresponding sensation in his face, it was like touching someone else's flesh.

He cursed himself. What made him think an unannounced visit was a good idea? Maybe he should wait inside? But no, that'd be a break in procedure, and he might miss his connection. So he hunkered down and put his ice-bitten fingers into his coat pockets.

Someone was approaching up the sidewalk, hood drawn up tight. A girl, by her size and pink parka. Not that her face was visible through the slit of her hood. When she neared the bench, she dropped a bag, books sliding down the sidewalk toward Lars. He crouched, knees so stiff they would barely bend, and helped gather them up. As he handed them to her, she whispered, "Take the key, same place as before."

A key like the one he'd gotten at the hotel during his last visit now lay next to the bench. He whispered, "Thank you." But she was already gone. Where was that hotel again? This way, wasn't it? But after what was a wrong turn, he couldn't regain his bearings. Now, new images tormented him, images of himself dying of frostbite before he found shelter.

He then turned a corner, and the big building stood several blocks down the street. He picked up speed, limping along on the cold-numbed stumps he was using for feet.

Once inside the room, he sat in a rickety chair, took off his shoes, and rubbed his toes to regain circulation. He winced at the stabbing pain as blood revived numbed nerves. Then a thump came from the closet, not three feet from where he sat, and he yelped, nearly falling from the chair.

He padded on tiptoes and cracked open the closet door, almost yelling again when a thin line of daylight penetrated the inky space, revealing a head lying on the carpet.

But then his frozen breathing restarted, and his thudding heart settled. It wasn't a head, but only Professor Reuel looking up at him from a hole in the floor, his frizzy white hair a halo in the slanting light. His hands gripped the upper rungs of a ladder descending into a dim space below.

"Oh, there you are, my boy. I thought you had gotten lost. Come, come. I have something to show you."

Lars followed Reuel down the ladder. Once in the room below, he shuddered. The lack of windows was unnatural. "Who could live in a cave like this?"

"Oh, many have. I myself work here several days a week, and for some months, circumstances confined Curtis in this place. But that is not why I brought you." Reuel waved toward a table surrounded by tall bookstacks, all crammed with hand-labeled volumes. The other end of the room was set up like an apartment. "Sit, my boy. Sit. I'll check the kettle."

By the light of a single candle on the table. Reuel crossed to the fire and stoked it. Then with the back of one wrinkled hand, he tested the kettle hanging above the coals. "Ah, good. We're in luck."

He hobbled back, kettle in hand. Then he poured steaming water into a cup, added a tea bag, and placed it before Lars, then settled in with his own cup. Blowing on the hot brew, he looked over the rim, his blue eyes sharp and clear, belying his deeply shadowed wrinkles. "Your message was vague. To what do I owe the pleasure of this visit? And be sure, my boy, it is indeed a pleasure."

Lars had been swiveling his head, taking in the curious room. Now, he lowered it to the steam rising from his cup. Why *was* he here, really? But he did know, didn't he? He clamped frigid fingers around the cup's welcome warmth. "Oh, just needed someone to talk to, I guess. I used to talk to Father Curtis. Hashed things through with him. I miss that."

"I am honored you thought of me. What can I help you with, my boy?"

Lars hesitated but then began to tell him, at first haltingly, of his concern for Leif, of the poisonous dynamics in the family business. As he warmed up and the sources of his angst clarified, his soliloquy became more passionate, his words flowing unchecked until he was standing, pacing, and gesturing his frustrations as if to physically expunge them, cast off that dreadful weight.

Reuel let him continue until at last he ran down, spent, and sat. Lars again picked up his teacup his candlelight reflection wavering over its depths. "So that's what's been eating at me. Guess I needed to get it out. Nothing you can do about any of it, but I do appreciate you listening. Helps to know someone cares."

"A sympathetic ear is sometimes the only salve any of us can offer one another. It is true. There is little I can do for your brother. Tragically, he sounds to be descending into a abyss of his own making. The best you can do for him is to keep planting seeds, as you have been, and hope he tires of the dark and chooses to seek the light. Some will." Reuel blew out a breath. "But truth is, some never recognize that they *are* in darkness. And sadly, some love that darkness. Neither you nor I can know his heart or his future. We can only offer him truth and be ready to help if he tires of his course."

He remained silent then, head bowed, porcelain teacup cradled in one palm, a finger tracing the rose vines circling the rim. "As for your father, that is a bit of a quandary, isn't it? Working with family is complicated in the best of conditions. When one member is a difficult person, it is infinitely harder. From your description, it seems your dad is just that sort of person, yes?"

Nodding, Lars grimaced.

Reuel stretched across the table and patted Lars's arm. "Just remember, not all difficult people have malignant motives. Your dad has good intentions, and you both share a desire to do what is best for the company, for the family. You share the same goals, but the two of you differ in terms of strategy and tactics. Yes?"

"Oh, of course." Lars tried to picture his dad as a villain. It didn't fit. Dad cared. Almost cared too much. "He's a good guy. It's just that he makes up his mind how to do something and then sets off on that path, too stubborn to listen to anyone else. That's why he and Leif never got along. Leif would never back down, either, and he was such a jerk he'd set Dad off. The problem is, this time, Dad's wrong, and this is no small deal. I don't want him and Mom to lose all they've ever worked for, including their home."

"The difference between you and your brother seems to be how you interact with your dad. You remain respectful. You do not wage total war to win your point. This is interesting as it regards Creator God. You are aware Curtis has been sending me the text of the scrolls as they are translated? I assume you have read the excerpts I sent you?"

"Well, I've skimmed them. With the workload lately, I haven't had the time I'd like."

"Understandable. Everything has its season, to quote one of my favorite of the recently arrived Scriptures. My point is that you instinctively obey one of the tenets laid out by Creator God, made clear in these scrolls our friends have recovered. He is a God of order, has established that order on earth, in families, in every earthly sphere. Your father has been placed over you in authority, been placed there by God, one could argue. It is your responsibility to respect that authority. This does not mean you cannot disagree or you're not allowed to argue your position. It does mean you should obey as long as your doing so does not force you to disobey God himself. Am I making myself understood?"

"Yeah, I get that, but how do I deal with how I feel"—Lars fisted his chest—"when I can't get through to him? How do I get rid of this?" He pounded his chest again.

One hand gripping Lars's shoulder, Reuel leaned in. Those bright-blue eyes peered into his. "When you have a problem you cannot solve, when something is too overwhelming, too big for you, you do have a friend to whom you can take it."

"I did. That's why I'm here."

With a chuckle, Reuel settled back into his chair and reclaimed his tea. "I am honored. But that is not what I meant. You are not personally responsible for every outcome for every person in your life, nor do you have the power to change them. You do what Lars can do. You obey God in doing it—for instance, by respecting your dad when you disagree. Make suggestions, make your opinion known with love and respect, and leave the outcomes to the One who has the power and the wisdom to do that which you cannot." He clicked the cup onto the table, gnarled finger pointed skyward. "That person is Creator God."

Lars blew through pursed lips. "I'll try. Anything is worth losing all of this . . . this garbage eating me up."

"You be Lars. Let God be God. You'll feel much better once you master that. As to the current dilemma in your shop, the inability to produce those tables in time. Would a larger workforce help?"

"Well, yeah, once we have the right parts, but hiring is impossible. We try all the time but are lucky to find one or two new guys a year. We'd need, I don't know, dozens more people, skilled people too. That's just not realistic."

"How skilled must they be? Isn't the assembly of so many identical items repetitive work? Could you train an unskilled person to do just one or two operations if you had enough people? Create a production line of sorts?"

"Maybe, if they were smart and willing to work, but good luck finding dozens of people like that."

Reuel smiled. "I may have an idea in that regard."

CHAPTER 43

A few days after Curtis learned whence the cooks got their victuals, Captain Simon approached him. "Got something I wanna run by you, Father." The stubby ship captain rolled a log before a cook fire, then brought another for Curtis.

Simon sat, short, thick arms on knees. "Here's the thing. We've been running round the clock since we got here, setting this little fortress up. But now we got 'er making good headway, and it's time we think about the crew's health."

Curtis raised an eyebrow. "Is there some problem with disease? I'm no doctor."

"No, not that kind of health." Simon waved that away. He leaned in closer. "It's their health here I'm talking about." He tapped his head, then his heart. "They've given up a lot. The second the work rotation slacks up, they're gonna start thinking about the homes they've lost, the people they've left behind."

He stared out over the snowy valley, gaze growing distant, then shook himself. "But it's river wisdom. A rested crew is a happy crew, and we can afford it now. They need scheduled downtime, but we gotta deal with those other issues, the issues of the heart, of the spirit, or the whole flotilla is like to come unmoored, if you catch my meaning."

Cheeks chapped from the cold, dry air stretched with his smile, and Father Curtis rubbed his hands together. "I believe I do, and it so happens ministry is a particular calling of mine. Are you suggesting an organized day of rest and worship? I'd be happy to plan it if that's what you're asking."

Simon slapped a thigh. "I like the set of your jib. That's it. Just what the crew needs."

At a company-wide meeting, they chose Sunday as the appointed day of rest, as was the habit in Republic, even though Jeremiah pointed out that the historical Sabbath of the scrolls was on Saturday. But Jeremiah accepted the will of the majority with his quiet smile and a nod at Curtis, indicating all was well between them.

As the previous month progressed, Curtis began pigeonholing Jeremiah after breakfasts on this day, discussing the scrolls they'd translated that week. Jeremiah wasn't only fluent in the language but also schooled as to their meaning.

Curtis often whispered a prayer of thanks for Hilkiah and his ancestors who'd preserved such a wealth of knowledge not only in the scrolls but also in the mind of this young man.

Many others of the crew, and no few of the wives and children, joined this informal discussion. Thus, a new study group had formed. The meeting morphed into a hybrid forum, one part interview of Jeremiah by Curtis, and one part question-and-answer period. Now, pursuant to Captain Simon's request, they followed those informal teaching sessions with formal services.

Today, the first Sunday of those services, Curtis and Jeremiah sat at the head table raised on a rough dais so all could observe the discussion.

Curtis opened with a short prayer, then motioned to Jeremiah. "We've made it through most of the first scroll and a short way into the second. I'm a bit lost, though, with this blood-sacrificial system. It strikes me as some barbaric magic ritual. And most of the scroll has been nothing but the history of a single family, over a thousand-year period or so. Why such a focus?"

He sat straighter. His heart began to thrill. This never failed to energize, the pursuit of the truth of God. "We were promised these scrolls contained the secret way back to paradise. To Creator God. When are we going to get to that part?"

Jeremiah lifted a pointer finger in the air, so much like Reuel. "Ah, but story is all about that very secret, if you would only grasp what God is trying to teach you. Let me explain—"

A disturbance erupted at the room's far end. Several people had been in conversation, and their discussion had escalated into an argument. Clara, the ringleader, red-faced and agitated, now stood nose to nose with Beatrice. "You have no right to stop us. This building belongs to everyone, not just your cult."

Beatrice maintained her customary composure. "Of course, the buildings are for the use of all. What do you need the space for? It will be available this afternoon. Will that work?"

"We need this room for the church. The real church, not the heretical garbage these outsiders cram down your throats. And no, this afternoon will not work. Who ever heard of Sunday afternoon church? Sunday mornings are the proper time for the worship of the Eternal. Even you should know that, Beatrice."

Beatrice closed her eyes and took a long breath. "You are welcome to worship in any way that seems right to you, *as is everyone else*." Her emphasis must've been lost on Clara. "How many of you are there? I see only three others with you. Do more wish to join you in your services?"

Clara drew herself up, lips pressed together in a prim smile. "I imagine the entire settlement will wish to worship properly, given the opportunity."

"I see. Have you put this question to the entire settlement? No? Well then? How many are currently interested in joining you, just these three?"

Clara only glared at Beatrice in answer.

"If that's the case, I'm certain the four of you could conduct your proceedings in one of the residences. Perhaps yours, Clara. It must be quite spacious, housing only one family as it does. The rest of the cabins are forced to accommodate at least two families and are quite cramped. I suggest you give that a try." Beaming, Beatrice clapped her hands. "Everyone gets what they need. Everyone is happy."

A scowling Clara faced the room. "I call for a vote. All in favor that this room be used Sunday mornings for proper worship, please raise your hands."

In the uncomfortable silence, people glanced at their neighbors. Only Clara and her three accomplices raised their hands.

"Jock!" Clara scowled at her husband in the first row, his hands in his lap. "You get your hand in the air right now."

He lowered his head. One hand inched into the air.

Her gaze zeroed in on Curtis, still standing on the dais. "Father Curtis, I understand that you are an ordained priest of the Eternal. Why do you not stand with me?"

Curtis gave what he hoped was a disarming smile. "I'm certain they've gotten around to defrocking me by now, but that aside, I'm sorry, madam. I must tell you a painful truth. The Order is a sham, the Writings are a forgery and a fake, the Eternal an impostor god."

Clara's face darkened, and she drew in a breath to retort.

But he held up a hand. "With all you've seen and experienced, it's surprising you wouldn't want to join *us*. Please, my dear lady, come. Sit and learn about the One True God of the universe. I beg this of you, for the sake of your immortal soul."

Clara marched to the front row, grasped Jock's ear, and dragged him along as she flounced from the room, three lone sheep and one yelping husband in tow.

LEIF RUBBED his eyes and strained to focus, but the ledger remained fuzzy.

He'd chosen this shack for an office, not because it was ideal, but because it was on the sawmill grounds, the better to be close to the never-ending grind he created for himself.

Young Bob stepped in, a clipboard under his arm. "Mr. Leif, it's the middle of the night. What're you still doing here? Thought you promised to stop sleeping at your desk."

Setting the pencil onto the open ledger, Leif leaned back, and the rickety wood chair creaked a warning. "Could ask you the same."

"I knocked off hours ago. Just forgot to turn in today's tally." Young Bob laid the clipboard down, then peered more closely in the dim candlelight. "You don't look so hot. You sick? Need a dose of Pop's tonic?"

Leif shuddered. "No. Just short of sleep." He'd had that tonic once. No wonder Young Bob never seemed to be ill. The threat of that awful concoction would scare the sick out of anyone. "Feel like I'm hungover, and I haven't had a drink in weeks, haven't had time."

Pulling over another straight chair, Young Bob removed the stack of unfinished paperwork there and plopped it onto another growing tower on the floor. Dust billowed. "We need to hire another manager?"

An elbow on the ledger, Leif lowered his head, pinched the bridge of his nose, and pressed against the pain stabbing behind his eyeballs. "We have enough managers. I've delegated everything I can to them. Now I'm spending all my time fixing their work."

Young Bob huffed. "If'n a man in the yard keeps messing up, I find him a job he *can* do, or—" He made a chopping motion at his neck.

Leif dropped his hands to the desktop. "It's not that they're bad at their job. They're not." He lifted the schedules for next week's production run. "These are a masterpiece of managerial ledger domain—"

"What?" Young Bob squinted at the stack. "What kinda ledgers?"

"I was being sarcastic. What I meant to say was these"—Leif again lifted the packet—"are beautiful work. Only they *won't* work. My assistants know their portions of the manufacturing chain. However, they don't understand how their output affects the operations downstream. We're working on that, training them. It's gonna take time. Until then, I'll keep doing this." He rapped his overflowing inbox. "Or we'll have another fiasco like three weeks ago. Remember that day, when you tried to load the kiln?"

"Don't remind me." Young Bob rolled his shoulders. "Still feeling that one. Jammed up the whole works—all the way to the railhead. Another like that'd be real bad."

"Bad? Catastrophic!" Leif stood, arms flying to animate his words. "We don't have the margin to have men standing around, waiting for another mistake to be fixed. And I uncover dozens of errors like that every week."

Now standing himself, Young Bob raised his hands as if to pat Leif's shoulder, but froze short of touching him. "Mr. Leif? I'd help if I could, but not real sure how."

He patted Young Bob's shoulder. "Only more time and experience for the team's going to fix this. You're doing your own job well. Output is fantastic, almost too good." He sniggered. "That's why it's so hard for me to keep up on this end."

Young Bob ducked his head and rubbed the back of his neck. "Well, anything I can do."

"Come to think of it, you could do one thing for me. The lumber buyers keep snatching up the product I've set aside for my dad, shipping it down the rail before I can get my hands on it. Make sure that stops, will you?"

Or maybe he'd be better off letting the timber go out for sale? After the discount he gave his family, not to mention Haman's 60 percent cut, Leif was earning less now than when he'd worked for his dad. And working more hours. For crying out loud, he barely made it home one night in three, with no more than a nap at his desk.

But no. This was why he'd started this operation, to create an edge for his family.

Smiling, Young Bob puffed out his chest. "You can count on me, Mr. Leif."

It was the right thing to do. And even though Leif hadn't turned a profit yet, it was bound to pay off if he just worked a little harder, right?

CHAPTER 44

Curtis rolled to his side and punched the pillow harder than necessary. After weeks of studying the scrolls, he understood less than he had when he started, even with all of Jeremiah's coaching.

How could that be?

This was the text that had promised to answer all the deep mysteries of the universe, of Creator God. Was supposed to hold the secret that would save all humankind from a universe run amok. The secret of how they could all again find that lost paradise.

But these scrolls were, at least to his reading, nothing more than a confusing, meandering history of a family, and not a very nice one at that.

Could it be more confounding? Depressing. How was he to gain the clarity Jeremiah seemed to possess? The surety?

A frustrated groan rumbled free. He rolled onto his other side and again fluffed his pillow, wrapping it about his ears against the snores reverberating through the cabin.

Who was he fooling? The noise didn't keep him awake. His racing mind did.

He flopped onto his back. The guard fires outside the window cast dancing shapes among the shadows on rough-hewn ceiling timbers.

Then those shadows deepened, elongated, and swirled about, coalescing into the nightmare forms of his dreams.

He was again standing atop his steep promontory, surrounded by the barren, rocky landscape, the ground covered with malformed, hungry entities. Scattered about the plain for as far as the eye could see were other peaks, all pushing skyward from the churning dark mass, each covered by people he knew.

Some were his parishioners from Northwoods, but others were of his new flock, these strange, rough river folk he'd become part of. They were besieged on all sides, dark forms milling in the shadowy mists, charging the unwary. The people all showed distress, some falling to their knees, heads bent, giving up all hope.

None were looking to the tallest peak where still that magnificent sword hung, levitating above the rocks, beaming light into the gloaming. As before, Curtis reached toward that light, drank it in. His soul, his spirit, began to heal as the light infused his very being. Why weren't the others doing the same? It was the answer, the *only* answer, yet they seemed oblivious.

In his hunger, his aching need to be nearer the sword's pure, good essence, he stepped closer. His foot bumped into something solid. There, on the ground, an object glowed with an inner radiance not unlike, but not the same as, that of the sword.

He picked it up. It was a breastplate like those worn by ancient warriors, radiating a glow, warm wherever it touched his flesh. That warmth entered his hands, moved up his arms, through his limbs, his head, and penetrated to his very core, healing what it found there, changing it, transforming it.

In his mind, he opened himself to that light, tasted it, breathed it in, listened to its song, and tried to understand its essence. Just as he had with the Belt of Truth, he identified that essence as an element of the chord of light contained in the Sword. But what, exactly, was that flavor? It was tantalizing, something he'd never tasted before, yet something he recognized, as if from some primordial memory.

Then a voice echoed in his head. "This is my righteousness, granted to you by account of your faith."

Curtis gasped. He and Jeremiah had been discussing a passage from the scrolls, one in which the patriarch of the family, whose history dominated the narrative, had "believed God, and it was granted unto him as righteousness."

They'd been arguing this verse for weeks. Curtis, returning to it over and over, couldn't let it go and couldn't understand it.

But now it was all so clear. Jeremiah had been *giving* him the answer. The scrolls had too, but Curtis missed it, had been incapable of seeing it when it had been right there all along.

He again allowed the warmth to flood his mind and swam in it, embraced it. Let it cover him. For the first time in his life, he was in the presence of true righteousness. Absolute and untainted. Pure.

And even though he had no right, no claim to such, he now wore it as if it belonged to him. And in some mysterious way, it not only covered him with a righteousness not his own but was also changing his being, molecule by molecule, thought by thought, bringing his nature more closely in line with its own. More than it could have ever been of his own efforts.

And not only was he *not* the owner of this covering, this righteousness, it was obvious who was—the only person who could ever have been its creator. His Creator. The same Creator God who had shown himself to Curtis in that epiphany so many months before, who had been showing himself to Curtis through the text of the scrolls, even though he'd been too dense to realize it.

A thrill tingled up his spine, and his eyes flared wide. Of course! That's what the scrolls were, their purpose, the reason the story of this strange family from so long ago was important. "It's a story," Curtis whispered. "It's His story, the record of how He manifested Himself to humankind, taught them about Himself."

He held the breastplate high, at arm's length, reveling in the sublime light radiating and warming the very air. What a marvel. What an indescribably precious gift.

A set of golden straps was spaced to match the golden loops on the belt. He slipped it on and tied it to the belt. It rode light on his shoulders, and was a perfect fit. It felt somehow right, as if it completed some lack in him he'd never before recognized. As if he'd always been meant to bear it. And in a way, he sensed he had. Had been chosen before the foundations of the earth for this moment.

He glanced across the plain toward the peak that had housed the cherubs. They were still there, entrapped even more tightly in the tendrils extruded by a false creature of light. Wrapped about his middle, his chest, the belt and breastplate thrummed with energy, with true light. Such power.

Was it enough? So equipped was he ready to charge the dark entities below? Could he make his way to the cherubs, to free them?

But what of those past failures? He shuddered. This light he bore was powerful, yes, yet it wouldn't be enough, not down there in *that* cauldron. The problem was, both these garments were defensive. To push through the enemy, to defeat them, he'd need an offensive weapon.

Again, he cast his gaze toward the sword. He needed *that*. But how to get it? The same enemy that separated him from the cherubs kept him from the sword.

As he stared at the blade, rejecting first one plan, then another, its light again suffused his body, his mind. He sorted the tones, the notes, the threads that combined to create the glorious chorus of light. Some he knew. Some he might recognize, given time. Some were foreign, too alien to identify, much less understand.

A whisper, a breeze blew through his soul, and with it, a thought drifted into his mind, a surety. Someday, somehow, that marvelous sword, that heavenly weapon, would be his to wield.

He again turned to the evil beings on the plain threatening the people he loved.

And smiled.

WHAT LUXURY! In heaven, in a living paradise, Diana's heart sang, and euphoria carried her to lightheaded heights. If only this feeling would never end.

Who could ever have known life could be so beautiful, so intoxicating? Every moment so exquisite, she dare not lose the memory, forget this indescribable sensation when she returned to her gray life.

She sank deeper into a tub of foamy hot—yes, hot—water, sipping champagne and eating strawberries dipped in chocolate. *Real* chocolate, not the bitter, tasteless stuff Leif gave her every Lover's Day. She tipped her head on the enclosed deck, a sunroom, really, atop a high hill overlooking Crescent Lake. Delicious to share such a mansion with Mullman for the New Year Festival weekend. Who knew what the man did for a living? He always answered such questions with non-answers, winking and teasing with something like, "Oh, I am so boring. Let us talk of something exciting, like you!" His buddies—or associates, she couldn't decide what they were—would respond that he was a businessman, a very gifted businessman.

A very *rich* businessman, if the current digs were any indication.

Voices approached from somewhere deep in the house. As they came closer, one was clearly Mullman's. "You tell him I hold him accountable. He is to see to it that nothing interrupts the flow of product. Nothing. We have not made up for that load we lost earlier this year." There came the sound of an impact. A hand slapping a table? "He will not be allowed to delay any longer. We have obligations to meet. He will keep his to us, or it will be his head. His head! Make sure he understands this. I do not care how he has to do it. Tell him!"

"Yeah. I'll tell him, boss," another voice responded. "But my advice to you? Don't trust him and don't count on him. He's one slippery operator."

"We have invested too much time and money into this scheme. He must make it pay."

"Okay, I'll tell him. You're the boss."

Footsteps thudded but stopped when the other man again spoke. "Boss?"

"Yes, what is it now?" Mullman sounded irritated.

The words receded into a near whisper, becoming clear one second, then again fading. " . . . boys are talking . . . not Marguerite . . ."

A door slammed, and distance muffled the voices. But Mullman's excited words, bordering on a shout, still reverberated. " . . . lost my mind? . . . course, she is not . . . but my choice to make, not . . . "

"I get it, boss." The first voice responded, tone placating, now moving closer. "But the appearance. Can't afford—"

"Enough, I said," Mullman's voice snapped again. "I will hear no more. Now do your job, allow me to manage my affairs as I am perfectly capable of doing. Go."

Footsteps approached. Then a fingertip traced the curve of her jawline, inching into that sensitive place under her ear. She shivered, eyes closed, and smiled. "Come on in. The water's fine."

"You must be part mermaid. I fear that, would I let you, you would pull me into the water, never to be seen again."

"Oh, wouldn't that be nice? To stay right here in this beautiful bath, eating berries and sipping champagne for the rest of our lives? What a delicious thought."

"I take it back. You are no mermaid. You are a lotus-eater, intent on enticing me with languid pleasures. Mission accomplished, my dear. I am hopelessly mesmerized." He cupped her chin. "I am captured. Yours to do with as you will. Only make me one promise, lovely siren."

"Only one?"

"Only one. Come here and live with me permanently."

Her shock must have shown for he pressed a finger to the base of her chin, fitting her mouth together once more. "Oh, come. Don't be so surprised. Have we not enjoyed weeks of bliss? But the parting grows more painful each time. I'll not survive another week of separation. Come, make my happiness complete."

Where had this come from, and so quickly? A few days of stolen pleasure were one thing. But permanently? "You know I'm married. And the children?"

"You are married in name only. You have made that clear in speech and in ways more eloquent than speech." He grinned. "The little ones love me, and I, them. We will make a wonderful family, and our children to come, yours and mine, will only add to the joy."

She broke free of his gaze, lowering hers to the lathery bubbles, each holding a rainbow reflection of his face. Did she want this? Of course she did, more than anything. Guilt jabbed over leaving Leif, taking his children. But only briefly. He'd brought this on himself, hadn't he? Ignoring her, abandoning her for his mistress, for his real love, his work.

More importantly, what was her heart telling her? Mother always said to follow your heart, and hers no longer held any love for Leif. Hadn't in quite some time. The only thing keeping them together was habit, and a bad one at that. Time to break that habit.

"Oh, Mullman, are you sure?"

"More sure than I am of anything else in this world."

"Then so am I." She scooped her wet hands around his neck, drawing him to her. Overbalanced, he fell atop her, ejecting the water in waves. It spread to cover the white marble floor in a sudsy froth.

He laughed. "I knew you would tempt me into your watery realm."

She whispered into his ear. "Yes, and I am planning to keep you here forever, just as you promised."

CHAPTER 45

The ship's bell was ringing. Curtis rolled his pillow over his ears, still half asleep.

But Phillip pulled it from his hands. "Is big emergency. Hear bell? Up, up now." Not waiting to see if he was heeded, Phillip dashed out the door. It banged in the bitter subzero wind. If the urgency of the alarm bell hadn't roused Curtis, the need to shut that blasted door did the trick.

He dressed, now alert enough to allow concern to creep up his spine. The bell was reserved for the direst emergencies. In the long months, it never rang. Not for the fire at the gatehouse, not for the midnight arrival of the injured messenger, not for the bears raiding the meat stores.

Curtis ran out, careful to close the finicky latch. Still pulling on his coat sleeves, he joined a line of bleary folk streaming toward the guard post at the twins. He pushed through to the center where Captain Simon stood over a man to whom the first mate was ministering. An unconscious man. A trickle of blood seeped from a head wound, his arms unnaturally twisted under his body.

The mate rolled him over, exposing hands tied behind his back with a length of sisal cord. The mate flicked open his case knife, sliced those bonds, rolled him onto his back, and tapped Derek's cheek—calling for him to wake.

Beatrice pushed to his side, carrying a canteen. She tipped it to the unconscious Derek's lips.

When drops of water trickled into his mouth, he choked, moaned, and swallowed. His eyelids fluttered.

Simon, previously issuing orders to scout for the attackers and reinforce the lookout towers, now knelt and put a hand on Derek's cheek. "Can you tell me what happened?"

Derek croaked, groaned, and leaned toward the canteen. Once Beatrice trickled more water, he swallowed, wet lips with tongue, and spoke in a husky voice. "Was Jock. Jumped me when we was on guard together. That harpy, Clara, gagged me and tied me up. Then it all went black."

Simon stomped a foot. "First! Take two men and check their cabin. Danny, find the scouts, tell 'em to keep an eye out for Jock and Clara."

Danny disappeared into the dark.

Soon, the first mate returned, scowling. "They're gone, Jock, Clara, and all three kids. Looks like most their clothes are gone. No sign of struggle." He spat. "China hutch is still there, just fine as you please, in case you were a'wonderin'."

"Okay, folk." Simon raised his voice. "Looks like Jock and Clara went off on their own. No reason to think there is any more to it. You can go back to your beds, all except you men. You'll reinforce the guard posts for the rest of the night. I want all watches doubled and extra patrols. Now go!"

Curtis's battle station was as aide to Captain Simon, so he followed the man into the great hall. Simon first stoked the fire, the new logs sending curls of smoke up the flue, hung a kettle for tea, then settled in to wait for developments.

Curtis paced from fire to door, then back. How could Simon sit there, so calm? "What do you suppose Jock is up to?"

Mouth puckering as if he'd bit a lemon, Simon shook his head. "Don't think it was Jock up to anything. He's not the kind. Now that

Clara? She is. She's been stomping about, pawin' the ground all winter. Only surprise is she didn't do something foolish sooner. I just hope we get hold of 'em before they can do any real damage."

"What kind of damage do you think she intends?"

"Who knows? Oh, I doubt she has malice in mind. She just wants what she wants, and what she's been bellyachin' about for some time now is her nice, cozy little house in town. She heads back there, malice or no, we'll be in for it. How long do you think it'll take the Order to haul her in, get our location out of her?"

Curtis shivered. *Creator God, can Simon's men please forestall any such possibility?*

Danny ran into the room, trailing snowy footprints, followed by the first mate. "Cap'n, sir, we found 'em. I mean, we found their tracks. They be travelin' on skis, maybe a sled with 'em."

The mate growled and whirled, striding from the room. Simon dispatched a second team of trackers to join the chase. To ensure best speed, he ordered them equipped with skis.

The trackers returned minutes later, along with the mate, his face twisted and blotchy. "They stole our skis. Our skis! Every single one. And the small sled. Maybe some snowshoes. I have the men countin' to be sure."

Betraying no emotion beyond the stony glint in his eyes, Simon kept his voice level. "Send the scouts after them as best they can. They must be taken, or it seals the doom for us all."

Dawn came, the sun failing to penetrate the gray overcast, the biting wind alone piercing the damp. That gloom matching their mood, the group huddled in the great room, shoulders hunched, arms across knees, gazes inward. There'd been no word. Still no word nor food came at the noon hour. The cook fires hadn't been lit. No one had any appetite.

The day wore on. The people returned to their tasks in half-hearted effort, gazes darting toward the gate in the hope of seeing some sign the trackers had succeeded. All understood the consequences if they didn't.

Early in the afternoon, Simon called for his senior officers along with Curtis and Jeremiah, Thaddeus being out leading patrols. In the great hall, the captain chuffed, face drawn. The flickering yellow firelight highlighted new wrinkles shadowing his forehead. "Gentlemen, it's time we made a decision. It's been over ten hours since Clara and Jock left. If our men haven't prevented them by now, Clara will be reaching Plumbsburg sometime tonight or, at latest, tomorrow morning."

He passed a hand across his forehead, rubbing at some irritation physical or mental. "We must face facts. Having no word yet is a poor sign. At this point, it's unlikely our men will catch 'em, not having skis. The Order will waste no time extracting our location, and *they* can be here in a matter of hours on those snow machines, the river iced be like an open highway for 'em. We must, by any means necessary, not be here when they arrive. I've already given the order. All personnel are to pack for fast travel, one pack per person. My scouts long ago prepared and provisioned a few hideouts, all within a day's travel, one in each direction, a contingency plan."

Simon's gaze circled the group, eyes shadowed beneath his jutting brow. "The question now is not whether we should run, but in which direction? Where are we to go from here? Where are we to find another permanent base?"

When no one else spoke up, Curtis said, "I suspected this would be necessary and already prepared to depart, as has Jeremiah."

"Scrolls safely packed, ready." Jeremiah patted a leather satchel at his feet.

"As to where to go . . . " Curtis paused while the captain shouted for quiet. "Our best option would be to make for Two Rivers. There we have allies. If we notify them of our coming, they'd create a safe hiding place for us, if not proper identities. The question is how do we get there with no papers? Leaving that aside, how can we keep these children safe in this weather?" He pointed out the window where icy flakes swirled, driven before the wind.

"It's midwinter." Simon bounced a fist on a thigh. "No good time to be traveling on foot, much less in the wild, and there's a storm brewing."

Jeremiah buttoned his coat and raised his collar. "I can feel this in air. Peoples could die, exposed to these elements."

Simon dipped a slow nod. "Which brings me to the obvious point. You *do* have papers—you, Jeremiah, and now even Thaddeus. You could hoof it to the nearest town. Walk right up and buy tickets on the wagon train, ride wherever you please. This would be best. Your survival and that of the scrolls is of the highest importance. The rest of us will get by, somehow."

"No." Jeremiah set his jaw, his quiet word firm.

"Come now, man. Be reasonable. You can't throw everything away."

"Creator God has placed our company together." Jeremiah held up a hand, forestalling Simon's coming protest. "Remember story of King Asa? When he relied on Creator God and was obedient to his leading, God defeated great army threatening his peoples. Later, when threatened by another army, resorted to worldly defenses did he, dealing with problem his own devious way. Did not turn to God, and many awful things result. In his old age, he had terrible affliction of feet. Again, failed he to turn to God for help, but instead turned he to human physicians and dies without relief. Explain I cannot, why a man—one who has seen blessings of God, who has seen consequences of failing to do so—would refuse to turn to great and mighty God next time in need is he. Can you?"

There was only silence.

He asked again, "Can explain any of you why?"

The men shook their heads, mute.

He leaned in, gaze intense. "If cannot explain why Asa is so foolish, please then to me explain why would repeat this mistake? Trust God, not own wisdom. The wisdom of God is as foolishness to men, says the Word. We cannot always understand. To follow His leading seems sometimes to be folly."

His hands balled, and he shook them. His intensity electrified the room, the air seeming to vibrate with it. "But we *need* not understand." He then pulled those balled fists into his chest, arms crossed, as if hugging some precious treasure to his bosom. “We need only trust. We need only obey.”

CHAPTER 46

When the bell had begun to ring, Phillip was one of the first to respond. He assembled his team, and once he ascertained there was no apparent danger inside the walls, he took select men on a patrol around the outer perimeter.

He came upon tracks—skis and a sled, by their appearance and a few hours old at most, the wind-driven snow only now beginning to soften their edges. He was squatting next to the trail, looking for anything to tell him who had made them or why when Danny ran up.

"It's Clara. She and Jock tied up the night guard. Cap'n says you're to keep an eye out for 'em."

Phillip pointed. The tracks continued in a straight line into the gloom. "Tell Simon they headed downstream. Have skis and small sled." While Danny spun and sprinted back toward the fort, Phillip motioned to his second-in-command. "Putting you in charge. Do not let others trample tracks. I go now, follow trail."

"We should go with you if you're going."

"No. You wait for orders from Captain. I move quickly, only chance to catch man on skis. Your men cannot move this fast, I think."

Phillip loped off, running beside the clear ski trail, long flowing strides blurring the snow on either side with his speed. He could maintain this pace for hours and would have to, given his quarry's head start. He kept near to the trails but never destroyed the tracks with his own. Jock and Clara had kept to the flat, easy going of the frozen river. At the main channel they'd turned south toward Plumbsburg.

Shortly after sunrise, he removed a strip of dried meat from his pack and shed a wool sweater. The sun's rays, added to this exertion, were too warm for comfort. His hairline had begun to prickle. The beginnings of sweat ran between shoulder blades. He drank from his canteen, topped it off with snow, placed it in his parka's inside pocket to melt, then set off again.

At his current rate, catching a man laden with a heavy sled should be easily done. He'd have them in sight in six hours, double their three-hour head start. He had only to move at twice their pace to accomplish such, after all.

But by midmorning, when this six-hour mark had come and gone, he'd made only a slight gain on them, judging by the tracks. How could an overloaded man pull a sled at such speed?

When he still hadn't made contact by late morning, the first pang of alarm added a new note to the throbbing of his already thudding heartbeat. He increased his pace, now edging toward a level of exertion he couldn't long maintain. Expending himself at this rate, he must catch them in the next few hours before his body gave out.

By midday, he'd made significant gains, the tracks now much more recent, the edges crisp and clearly defined, no more than an hour old. He was tiring, his steps less certain. But, if he kept pushing himself, he had an excellent chance of catching them before they reached populated areas. And before he collapsed from exhaustion.

He had been picking his path as best he could, avoiding both the deep snowdrifts and the glassy windswept ice, choosing instead the better traction of the shallow hardpack skiffs. Then he came to a straight stretch of river. The prevailing winds had taken advantage of the open course, blasting down this section of frozen waterway with nothing to slow those frigid gusts, leaving the ice bright and glossy, scoured free of snow.

With no more time, he dare not slow his pace for the sake of safety. Instead, he kept to the river's edge where the occasional rock peeked above the ice, and the frozen surface itself had a rough rimey texture.

But then, one of his long strides landed in a slick patch. His front foot skidded. To compensate, he slammed his rear foot to the ice. But it, too, failed to find purchase, and he flew sideways, feet in the air. There'd be no getting them back under himself in time. He'd hit hard, shoulder first. So many times today, the ice had betrayed him, causing similar falls. Like all those other times, he tucked, prepared to roll once, then pop back onto his feet.

But midtumble, something dark appeared in his peripheral vision. The tip of a rock, no larger than a cabbage, hid in a finger of snowdrift. The snowdrift he was set to land upon.

He twisted in flight, bringing an arm up to curl about his head. Time slowed. He hung midair, the sun reflecting from snow crystals so perfect, like fine grains of sugar. His arm was still shifting from where it had been tucked into his chest. But then too soon, time restarted, the world now moving with lightning speed. Too fast.

He felt nothing, but heard an unpleasant crunching impact. Saw a flash of expanding yellow before he fell headlong into the waiting blackness.

CHAPTER 47

A sound didn't shatter Leif's focus, but rather the cessation of sound pierced his concentration. His head jerked upright. Those machines don't stop running for anything—unless there was a problem. A serious problem.

He jumped from his desk and dashed into the sawmill yard, gaze darting from machine to machine. It better be a cheap fix this time. The last breakdown cost a week's profit to repair.

Men were leaving workstations, their equipment still, crowding to watch the low, sleek, fast transport glide past. It stopped near the shack where he stood open-mouthed.

The driver exited the vehicle and opened the rear door to usher into view Advisor Haman and another man, short and thin, with a dark complexion much like Haman's. But unlike Haman, who had the regal carriage of a pinnacle predator, attracting attention wherever he went, this man faded into the background, overlooked and unnoticed.

Leif strode toward his guests, bowing in greeting, his stomach tight. What had gone so badly wrong that it brought Haman here in person?

But Haman showed no sign of concern. He almost even appeared to be smiling. "Ah young Leif, kindly show us to your offices, if you would. We have much to discuss and a short time in which to do it."

Leif ushered the two men into his cramped office shack and emptied piles of paperwork off two straight chairs, the only furnishings in the crude space, aside from his own desk and chair. Haman wiped the seat with a handkerchief before sitting. He then dropped the cloth to the ground in lieu of returning the filthy thing to his pocket.

"Um, to what do I owe the honor?" Leif shifted on his chair, failing to find a position that didn't feel unnatural.

Haman looked about himself before answering. "What is the status of those negotiated contracts you promised to produce, all these many months ago?"

Leif grimaced. *That* pile of documents on his desk, one pile of many, displayed the thickest dust buildup. "Well, to be honest, sir, I've had little time to spend on that. The mill operation—"

"Unacceptable. When I am promised a thing, I expect it to be delivered."

"I'm sorry sir. It's just that I can't seem to keep things running smoothly unless I check every detail. We can't have this operation jammed up with mistakes."

"I am aware of your situation. I always am, which is why I brought you your new executive, Nicollo. Nicollo, meet your new superior, Leif." Haman pointed at the stack of unfinished work. "You will train Nicollo to perform the tasks upon which you have been expending your own time. Then you will apply yourself to securing these contracts, as we originally agreed. In the future, do not force me into such direct action. I expect my subordinates to manage problems, not be managed by them. If resources are required, you are to communicate your needs. You are not to make me identify and solve such things for you. Have I made myself clear?"

"Yes, sir. Sorry, sir. And thank you."

Haman stood and exited the building, leaving Leif to reintroduce himself.

He reached out a hand. "Hey, Nick. I'm Leif. Nice to meet you."

The man brushed dust from his well-tailored suit before shaking the proffered hand. He then retrieved Haman's discarded handkerchief from the floor and used it to wipe grease from his palm.

Leif glanced at the smudge on his own hand, then shrugged. "Sorry. I was helping Young Bob with one of the machines this morning. You'll get used to a little grease working here."

"No, I assure you, I will not. I manage mill workers. I do not intend to be one."

Leif's smile faltered. "Well, okay. I guess we need to get you up to speed on what we do here. Once you get the hang of things, in a few weeks, we can work up to the kind of problem-solving I'll need you to handle."

"I suggest we dispense with the gettin'-the-hang-of-things phase. Why don't you show me the prollem-solvin' part now?" He mimicked Leif's northern dialect perfectly. Was he being mocked? But the man's face was an unreadable deadpan. "I have already studied your work packets dating to the day you began operations, both before and after your edits, and I am well aware of what is needed here and how to accomplish it."

"How in the blazes did you get ahold of those?"

Nicollo didn't answer but returned Leif's stare with his gaze flat, his mouth expressionless..

A laugh grated Leif's throat. "Okay, then. Let's get started. I can tell you and I are going to have great fun together."

Nicollo was as good as his word. Leif needed only to show him where things were. The man already knew how to perform Leif's customary tasks.

His presence no longer required, he packed up his neglected prospective designs and stuffed them into his briefcase. "Not enough room for both of us to work here. I can do all this from home. You know how to get ahold of me if you have any questions?"

Nicollo didn't look up. "Yes sir. In the unlikely circumstance I require your assistance, I will dispatch a messenger."

A strange sense of displacement overcame Leif as he left the mill and cycled home. Before the end of a normal workday. In the daylight. As he pedaled, his heart began to thrill. Imagine what this might mean to his family. He pedaled faster, visions of Diana's surprised joy spurring him on. Imagine how much greater her happiness when he broke the news that he would be working at home from here on out. With her.

This had been his goal when he'd first dreamed of freelancing. Now, the dream might be coming true. The small profits he earned from the sawmill, added to the more lucrative earnings from these new contracts, would ease Diana's mind about their troubled finances. And for once put the lie to Corella's assertions that he would never amount to anything.

CHAPTER 48

Excited voices buzzed in and out of focus, intruding upon this warm, pleasant dream. Phillip didn't want to be interrupted, just wanted to float here in this cottony bed he'd found.

But something refused to let him rest. Something he needed to be doing, something urgent. Now, he swam against the foggy weight trying to pull him under. He struggled, grappling toward consciousness, toward those voices. Where was he? And why were snowflakes falling on his face, sharp pinpricks on cold-numbed cheeks?

He cracked one eyelid and snapped it closed again, the light having stabbed through his eyeball to the base of his skull.

Footsteps crunched snow, coming nearer. The voices were those of his scouts. Then it all came back, his body flooding with adrenaline at the remembered need to catch Jock and Clara. He managed to roll, bracing his arms beneath himself, and pushed into a sitting position. Before toppling sideways, face slamming into the ice.

His men rushed to his side, kneeling about him. The visage of his best scout appeared, backlit by the gloomy overcast. Phillip winced against the light which, even so muted, pierced eye sockets, throbbing deep in his brainpan.

"Phillip?" asked Robinson. "You okay?"

Phillip opened his mouth, but nausea gripped him, stealing the words, cramping his belly. Gorge rose up his gullet. Now his entire head throbbed, and Robinson's face spun in slow circles. Phillip retched. When the spasms subsided, he laid his forehead on the ice, the cold bringing a modicum of welcome relief. He scooped a handful of snow toward his mouth and let it melt on his tongue. Blessedly cool water trickled down his throat. He motioned for Robinson to come close. "Concussion. Leave me, get them."

Robinson's gaze shifted downriver, then back, brow furrowed. "Think we lost 'em by now, boss."

Phillip caught himself about to shake his head. Mistake that'd be. "Nearly had them. Close now."

"Tracks tell a different story. I'm guessing they are three, maybe four hours ahead. Tough to tell with this snow coming down as hard as it's been last couple hours."

Phillip sucked in a sharp breath, cold biting his tongue. How long had he been out? It hadn't been snowing when he'd taken the fall. "Time. What is time?"

Robinson tilted his head to the sky. But the sun was obscured by swirling snow, so he removed his gloves and fished out a watch. "Nearly four p.m."

Shivers raced through Phillip. He'd been out for over three hours? Too long. No way would they catch the fugitives now. What to do? He clenched his teeth, forcing some sort of sense into his muddled thoughts. How long would it take the authorities to haul Clara and Jock into custody? How long until operatives streamed upriver to capture all in the settlement? Not long. Maybe a few hours. Tomorrow morning at the latest. The families must be informed. "Leave me. Go warn them. Must leave fort. Order coming."

Robinson sat back on his haunches. "I'm sorry, boss. I can't rightly do that. Leave you here for 'em." He stood and called over the youngest tracker. "Head to the fort fast as you can. Warn them, tell them soldiers are comin'. They gotta make for the north redoubt, fast!"

The young man spun, sprinting back the way they'd come, only to skid to a halt. Two figures had materialized from the blowing snow. Two more of Phillip's trackers.

Robinson waved the messenger on. "It's okay. It's our boys. Keep goin'. Run. We'll follow as best we can." He returned to Phillip's side and knelt, face grave. "You're not gonna be able to walk, not for a few days at least. We gotta find a place to hole up till then, get a fire goin', and warm your bones."

Phillip shook his head, forgetting himself in the urgency. Plans must be put in place, and already his grasp on consciousness was growing weak. When the world had again righted itself, teeth gritted against the effort, he rasped out, "No. No fire. Must prepare, then must hide, wait. Ambush soldiers. Protect families."

Robinson gave Phillip an unbelieving look. "Ambush? You plumb knocked all your brains out on that rock?"

Phillip crooked a finger, beckoning him closer. To raise his voice against the rising wind was becoming too much effort. When Robinson's ear was next to his own lips, he whispered detailed instructions.

Having trouble keeping his train of thought, he gripped more tightly to his hold on consciousness, on clarity. But his tongue was becoming too thick to form the words. His lips seemed to belong to someone else. Things grew so fuzzy he couldn't be certain he completed his directives, or, for that matter, if Robinson had understood them before the world receded.

As Leif entered his house, his boot steps boomed hollowly on the dining room floor. He danced in place, pulling off his shoes, grinning goofily. "Shoes off here. Diana hates shoes in the house," he said to himself. Then he shouted, "Diana! Kids!"

The silent house answered him with only his own echoed words.

"Wow, what happened here." The normally cluttered countertops were strewn with toppled containers, some of Diana's collectible antiques missing.

Wait. His forehead wrinkled.

He walked into the formal dining room. Naked walls stared back at him, Diana's family pictures gone. Also empty was the living room wall where that awful painting had hung, the one Corella had given them as a wedding gift.

He dashed upstairs to check the bedrooms. The kids' dressers were empty. In his and Diana's bedroom, her scattered clothing littered the floor.

"What the—"

Voices rumbled outside.

He parted the curtains. There was Diana, accompanied by several other men, just now exiting the cab of the small freight car blocking the driveway, pulled by a tug from which two more beefy men appeared.

One of the men put an arm around Diana. She lifted her face to his and kissed him, smiling sweetly. Leif wobbled on his feet, the blood draining from his face. He'd not seen that smile in years.

He snapped into motion, bouncing off the wall when he overshot the corner into the corridor. He fairly flew as he more skied than ran down the carpeted stairs. He was approaching the door between the kitchen and the garage when it opened and a face appeared, only to disappear again as Leif, still running full tilt, straight-armed his palm into the nose of the man who kissed Diana.

The man catapulted over the railing and landed hard, flat on his rear. The impact, like a side of beef hitting the concrete, a meaty smack, was perversely satisfying.

Diana started screaming in Leif's face. He shouted back, not hearing a word she uttered. When she cocked her arm back to strike, her fingers clawed, he backpedaled into a large man entering the room. The man wrapped Leif from behind in a bear hug, trapping his arms as another caught Diana by the wrists. The man holding Leif sat him down in a dining room chair, the impact jarring his molars.

The man Leif struck reentered the house, dabbing a bloody nose with a dainty silk handkerchief. He approached Diana and flicked a hand toward the man holding her. "Permit her to say farewell to her ex-husband."

Fire flared in her eyes, and her mascara ran down her cheeks. But she allowed herself to be steered into a chair facing Leif.

The man said, "Talk."

Leif spread his hands to Diana, a plea in his expression, in his very being. His throat closed like he was being strangled. "What're you doing?"

"What does it look like?"

"But . . . why?"

She averted her face. "Because I'm not in love with you anymore."

"Married people feel not in love all the time. That's no reason to throw it all away. You just work through it!"

"Well, I don't want to *work* through life. I want to be happy." Her arms rose as if trying to describe that happiness. Then, giving up, they fell to her lap. "I want that thrill I had when we were first together. We lost that a long time ago. I found it again with Mullman."

"How could you do that?"

Her narrow shoulders hunched. A weak shrug followed. "I can't help who I fall in love with. He swept me off my feet. I'm in love with *him* now."

"We can get the thrill back if we try." His voice came out like the whine of some beggar.

A slow shake of the head, black hair caressing her brow. Her green eyes met his, now firm. Gentle. "I don't think we can. There's nothing more to say."

Blinding white heat exploded, all thought drowned out by the deafening static in his brain. "If you're going, then get out. Get! You take nothing else, and I want my kids back."

She sprang to her feet, finger in his chest. "I'm filing today. You'll get the papers." She then marched for the door.

He was on his feet, following, only to be stopped by a huge arm barring his way. That arm was like an iron I beam pressing into his chest as he struggled to pass, finger jabbing in her direction. "I said I want my kids!"

She stopped and turned. A smile twisted her face. In falsely sweet tones, she said, "What makes you think they're all yours? Just try taking them. You may find out how few rights you have."

On the way out the door, she tossed over her shoulder, "Oh, and by the way, if you want to see them again, you'll be telling the kids we both agreed this was best. I'll let you know where and when."

She was gone, and he gawked at the closed door. The man shoved him back into his chair.

Mullman approached and stopped several paces away. "Be a good boy and cooperate. If you don't, the result will be the same, only much more painful." He pivoted on the balls of his feet and his upper body exploded into motion. His fist burrowed deep into Leif's stomach as if it had gone all the way to his backbone.

All the world was hot, red pain. Time slowed, allowing him to swim in that agony for some undefinable, endless period before he surfaced, the world reappearing. But the pain continued, rolling through him in an irresistible wave, and he remained doubled over, hugging his belly. Something important there seemed to have torn loose. In slow motion, he fell sideways, landed hard, and bounced once, not even feeling the impact. The chair clattered on linoleum a world away.

He gasped, lungs sucking only vacuum. The edges of his vision faded, and a high-pitched whine intruded. As he lay helpless, the patio doors showed a clear reflection of Mullman, taking a long skipping sidestep and kicking him in the kidneys. Then again.

Leif's face pressed against the cool glass patio door, eyes now closed, red agony his only vision. Unprotected back to the room, he waited for another blow.

Footsteps faded into the distance. A door closed. Yet he wheezed, unable to move. Consciousness receded and returned, keeping time with his shallow breaths. Were those stabbing pains in his back broken ribs?

Then the blackness retreated, and his breaths calmed, deepened. Should he try to stand?

Not wanting to explore the new pain any attempt to move might bring, he remained as he lay. Outside was the deck table where he and Diana had whiled away so many happy evenings. Beyond was the kid's swing set. The afternoon sun played bright notes on the drifting swings. The orchard further on lay under a perfect carpet of new-fallen snow, some of it still resting atop the fruit trees he'd planted last spring.

It was like a picture. A perfect winter day.

CHAPTER 49

The snarl of some unworldly feral beast, distorted by distance, faded in and out with the wind. Phillip jerked against bonds trapping his arms.

Clarity returned, blurred, and then consciousness jolted him. His eyes snapped open, his startled intake of breath cold in his lungs. A heavy fur someone had wrapped about him trapped his limbs. He struggled to loose it from around his arms, even as he tucked it tighter beneath his chin. He was so cold, chilled to the core, his entire body shivering, teeth chattering, though sweat tickled his underarms. Hot and cold at the same time. Not a good sign.

And those growling shrieks were no fevered hallucinations, but growing nearer, now distinct. Taking in the bare trees, the empty snow-covered hillside, he worked to recover lost memory. Where was he? Those were snow machines, motors revving, screaming ever closer.

He tensed to sit, but a hand pressed his shoulder, easing him back down into the cushioning embrace of snow where he'd lain. Next to his face was the rough bark of a tree trunk, above him dark branches that disappeared into vague, smudged shapes in the dusky gray blur, obscured by blowing snow.

"Stay put," Robinson whispered. "They're almost on us. If you peek under this here log, you can watch the action. But don't you move from this spot, no matter what happens. Hear me, boss?"

Phillip grunted his assent, throat dry, raw, as if the skin had been flayed from the tender flesh. He angled to see through an open space below the fallen tree where broken stubs of branches held the trunk a foot or so above the snowy ground. Beyond the slope, the river spread out in a flat sheet of ice, disappearing around a bend to the south, to his left. There, a group of four snow machines, each carrying two men, appeared through the hazy snow curtain, their bouncing headlights bright in the deepening gloom.

As the machines drew abreast of their hiding place, the snowdrift on which they had traveled buckled and collapsed into the now-exposed river current. In a spray of snow and water, the lead machine pitched sharply nose-up, capsizing and then cartwheeling on the ice, riderless. The second, unable to stop, followed its fellow, to be swallowed in the widening flow of dark, bubbling water. The third swerved left. It avoided the trap, only to enter an uncontrolled slide and roll, spilling its occupants. The last machine dodged onto clear ice, engine screaming while it accelerated upstream. As it passed his position, both riders flew off their perches and into the air, arms and legs snapping forward in a sudden stop. They hung motionless, then toppled, landing hard on the ice.

Above their unmoving bodies, a rope still vibrated with the force of impact, stretched taut and spanning the river where the men's torsos would have been, had they kept their seats.

Robinson shouted, "Go!"

Four of Phillip's trackers vaulted over the concealing tree trunk, clubs raised, and charged the fallen figures. During the melee, Phillip struggled to gain a standing position. Two shots rang out. He broke a thick branch from the tree and, using it to steady himself, levered to his feet.

He stood, catching his breath. Then the horizon tilted upward. His nose mashed into the snow. Wet slush clogged his eyes and mouth, and his skull rattled. Stabbing pain radiated, blurring his sight, the universe, with a flashing sickly yellow light.

He had remained upright, as far as his senses were concerned. Instead, the world had gone crazy, the ground racing up to strike him in the face. It was unfair. If a person couldn't trust the world to remain sane, what could be trusted?

By the time he crawled onto the ice, this being the only way to prevent the ground from betraying him again, the battle was over. His men were tying up the last troopers, Bureau of Peace men by the uniforms. Had they been Eye operatives, the outcome would have been equally one-sided. In the other direction.

One of his trackers writhed on the ground, hands clutched to his thigh. Phillip crawled to him. "Let go. Let me see."

Another held the man still while Phillip slit the pants leg to expose a perfect round hole high on the outside of his thigh. A single trickle of blood ran from the dark puncture.

Phillip turned the leg, eliciting a shriek. The exit wound was ragged, blood sheeting down the thigh. But it wasn't spurting, and Phillip exhaled.

"Thank Creator God. The bullet pass through. Miss bone and femoral artery," He struggled out of his pack, fought down a moment of vertigo, and scrabbled with numb fingers for his first aid kit. First, he sprinkled the wound with his sole packet of antibiotic clotting powder. Then he applied gauze pads and secured them with a length of rolled fabric, followed with a layer of tape.

Robinson, who'd overseen the after-battle, now crouched at Phillip's side. "He gonna be okay?"

"He not walk for maybe weeks. Take time to recover. But he lives. Is this only casualty?"

"Oh, there's lots of bruises and scrapes and such. Nothing to worry about. We best hightail it, though. Bound to be more of those boys on foot behind this bunch. Plumbsburg had a full garrison of Bureau men. Dozens of them."

"Yes, you go. I stay with injured man, lay low until healed. Leave signs at north redoubt, tell where are you go. We follow when can."

Robinson scratched a stubbled cheek. "Reckon I have a better idea."

Two snow machines roared up Yellow River Canyon and halted near the twins. Two men rode astride each beast, more clung to a sledge behind one. Behind the other trailed a crude travois, fashioned from tree limbs and cordage. It had been a fast trip, if not smooth, the travois jarring airborne at every ripple in the ice. The injured tracker was oblivious, unconscious, and tied in place on his side of the stretcher. That spared him unnecessary suffering.

Phillip had tensed, wedging into position, refusing to protest. Speed was of the essence. He could take the pain. He used every ounce of will power to remain conscious, to keep the world pinned in the upright position, to stop it from spinning.

Robinson dismounted. "Stay here. I'll take a look. Appears they already left. Barricade is unmanned, and the man-gate is standin' open." He returned in minutes. "Yep, all gone. They packed up in a hurry, but I see no sign of battle. They must have figured out the way of things and hightailed it."

Phillip fought the cottony fatigue slowing his movements, his thoughts. With lips seeming too stiff to move, tongue thick, he wheezed. "North?"

"Hope so. The plan was to move that way if we were threatened from Plumbsburg. Only one way to know for sure." Robinson swung his leg over the machine and settled into the saddle. Gears clunked, and motors revved. They swung about, headed back toward the main channel, which would lead them northward toward the fallback shelter.

The world wobbling, vision spinning again, Phillip laid his head down and closed his eyes.

He'd rest, just for a minute. Just until he gained a little strength.

Curtis shook his head. The drowsiness retreated, but it crept back almost immediately. His watch partner nudged him, offering a thermos. He removed the cap and tilted the opening to his mouth. The rich, aromatic steam wafted past his nose, and he drank, sighing. "I'm grateful someone thought to bring the coffee."

The other man was about to answer, but he went still, head cocked. "Hear that?"

The man's fear infected Curtis, and he had to still his surging heartbeat to hear anything over the throbbing in his ears. Somewhere out there in the snowy night, something growled. Motors whined, revving, the sound surging in waves distorted by distance.

The guard moaned. "They're coming for us."

Curtis sent him scrambling to alert Captain Simon. Curtis maintained position behind a tree, guarding the trail to the crude shelter. There, the families slept, exhausted by hours of hard travel, much of it in the dark.

This shelter was a rock overhang, a depression more than a cave, hollowed by floodwaters from the lower layers of a limestone bluff. Simon's men had stacked fallen logs across the open face to provide crude protection from wind-driven snow.

From behind his tree bole, Curtis peered across a floodplain dotted by sparse trees toward the river only fifty yards distant. The gloom and snow, whirling nearly sideways now, thwarted any effort to locate the machines. But they had grown near indeed, the only hope now that the snow had covered their tracks. That the hunters would pass them by.

The motors cut off, the last vestige of that hope silenced with them. Now, only the wind's whooshing moan resounded in the treetops above.

A flicker of movement rippled the snow-blanketed darkness.

A voice called out, "Ahoy, the camp."

Snow crunched behind, and Curtis risked a glance over his shoulder.

Simon trudged from the shelter, high-stepping in the knee-deep snow. "That'll be Robinson. Stand down."

Curtis had no memory of picking up his club, but he held it in a high ready position, his shoulders aching from long-tensed muscles. He lowered the weapon, swinging his arms to ease the cramps.

With one hand cupped over his mouth, Simon called, “Come on in slowly, hands over your heads. How many are you?”

“Six men, Cap’n. Not quite a full watch.”

Simon visibly relaxed. This code phrase indicated all was well. “Come on slow, Robinson, until we can see you all clearly.”

The figures of three men emerged, hands over their heads.

“I thought you said six men?”

“Got two injured, one on watch.”

Simon stepped forward and inspected his three crewmen, sending two others to check the river approach. “Looks like you tangled with something.”

“Yep. Bureau of Peace came upriver on snow machines. We ambushed ’em, took ’em out. But more’ll be comin’. We need to put some miles between us and them, fast as possible.”

One crewman who had been dispatched to the river returned. “Need more men down here, sir. Two injured need carrying, and we got two snow machines to hide.”

In a flurry of activity, additional manpower ran out to complete the task. Simon and Curtis joined the procession to the river where sat two snow machines, each tied to jury-rigged sleds.

Curtis made a beeline toward the injured men. He knelt beside the first stretcher and put the back of his hand to Phillip’s forehead. It radiated an alarming heat. “Phillip, can you hear me?”

Phillip stirred, wheezed something incoherent, and struggled to rise, only to fall back again, still mumbling.

Curtis sat up taller. “Robinson? Where’s Robinson?”

A figure detached itself from a group at the other stretcher. “Right here, Father.”

“What are the nature of Phillip’s injuries?”

“He took a bad knock on the head.”

“Help me with this stretcher, will you?” They carried Phillip to the shelter and laid him near the fire. “Where’s the medic?”

“Out with the other man. Want me to fetch him?”

A group of men squeezed into the cave, carrying the other stretcher, so Curtis called the medic over. "Phillip doesn't look good. Blow to the head."

The medic knelt next to Phillip and checked his pulse at the jugular, the back of the other hand to Phillip's forehead. "Bit of a fever. Can be normal with concussion. Pulse is a little off. That can happen too. Where's the site of injury?"

Robinson faltered, hands worrying his fur mitts. "Never looked at it, doc. Told me he was concussed before he went all wonky, and we kinda had our hands full from there on out."

Another figure materialized out of the dark, knelt beside Curtis, and laid a hand on Phillip's shoulder. It was Thaddeus, who set to work, helping Curtis and the medic untie Phillip's parka hood. They peeled it back, eliciting a moan from Phillip. The front and top of his head appeared to be fine. As they pulled the hood further, they met resistance. Phillip moaned louder.

"Help me roll him," the medic instructed.

Once they had him on his side, the medic lit a flashlight to inspect the site. Dried blood matted Phillip's unruly dark hair, adhering the hood in place.

"Canteen." The medic held out one hand into which a woman placed a flask. "Clean water?"

She nodded. "Boiled. We had it ready, just in case."

The medic trickled water onto the back of Phillip's head, catching the runoff on a towel at his neck. The warm liquid dissolved the blood, and the hood released, exposing a lump with an open gash running down the center. Loosening the hood reopened the wound, and fresh blood streamed down Phillip's face. The medic placed a compress against the area, saying over his shoulder to the woman. "In my kit. Alcohol in the flask, then the needles, and gut. I'll need to stitch him up."

He then glared at Robinson. "Why wasn't this wound treated in the field? Tommie's leg was tended. Why not this man?"

Robinson shifted, avoiding the medic's gaze. "Was Phillip tended Tommie. Like I said, things got real hairy, real fast."

The medic snorted, muttering. “He took care of Tommie, but no one bothered to take care of him. Nice. You’ll all be lucky if this isn’t already infected. Shouldn’t even close it up, but I can’t stop the bleeding otherwise.”

Simon tapped Curtis’s shoulder. “Can I steal you away? Phillip is in good hands, and we have decisions to make.”

CHAPTER 50

Lars had spent too many days wondering if Diggs would come through, would deliver the replacement parts this week.

But now Lars stood on the loading dock, shoulders hunched into his jacket, breath fogging in the lantern light as the first pallet of table parts wheeled off the freight car. They'd actually made it. A new fear clenched his guts. Would they be correct?

Lars waved the men steering the pallet to follow him. He led through the dark warehouse and into the shop, then pointed next to some workbenches. "Right here. Let me check them before you unload any more."

Lars broke the bands and selected eight random slats. He fit each with a spline and then pieced the assembly together, and secured it with a pair of strap clamps.

He stepped back and crossed his arms, almost closed his eyes, even. "Okay, Benny. You do the honors. I'm too scared to look."

Wood rule in hand, Benny spent several minutes taking measurements, inspecting joinery, and selecting more slats from the pallet for spot checks. "Thank Eternal. Now we just have to turn out a thousand tables in two weeks. Let's hope your plan works, boss."

Lars waved to the men on the pallet jack. "Line them all up in a row, right here. Benny, you go ahead and get the men started on assembly. We have a few more hours before this shift is done. Let's get as much accomplished as possible before then. I'm gonna go grab the new boys. I'll run the overnight shift with them."

He bundled up, adding the wool muffler his mom had knitted before he braved the quarter-mile walk to the barracks. The wind was howling out there tonight.

He winced. Barracks? No, an old Quonset hut at the small airport near the mill. Earlier this week, they'd transformed it, moved out pallets of machine parts to make room for a double line of bunks.

Worse, thirty-odd men would be forced to share the single shower and toilet in the airport offices. But he could find no better alternative. The unused locker room in the rear of the Northwoods mill had been out of service for decades and couldn't easily be replumbed. They'd have to make do.

He opened the door to the temporary lodgings and stepped inside, stamping the snow from his feet. The smell of old grease still hung thick in the air, but he shook his head at the scene. He'd expect a collection of bachelors in their early twenties to be raucous and rowdy. But here, the mood was subdued, thirty-some young men reading, writing, or chatting in groups.

"Hey, guys, the parts are here. Ready to get to work?" A chorus of ayes and you bets greeted him. They wrapped up and, heads bowed into the increasing wind, walked to the mill. Once inside, he guided them to the assembly area. "You'll be watching for the next two hours while the day shift does assembly. Try to pick up as much of the operation as you can. When they go off shift, you'll jump in and keep the process going, okay?"

These had been provided by Professor Reuel. All were his senior year seminary students, all slated to perform an extended missions trip overseas. As they were about to embark on their journey, the Order restricted international travel permits, stranding them with a two-month hole in their schedule. When it came time for the young men to take their turns, he walked from station to station, making suggestions, correcting errors, but soon could find none to fix.

Benny had been leaning against the far wall, arms crossed. He now pushed off and sauntered toward Lars. "Guess they have what it takes after all. Hats off to ya. I had my doubts."

Hands on his hips, Lars rocked onto his toes. "Yep, me too." When Reuel had suggested this solution, Lars had been uncertain. "But it's looking good so far."

No longer needed as a coach, Lars manned a workbench himself. At the end of eight hours, they had assembled twenty tables. Although well short of the number needed per shift to deliver in time, he had hope for the first time in a long while. Tonight, they were learning something new. Speed should come with practice. Tomorrow's production numbers would tell the tale.

THEY FORMED a circle across the fire from where the medic set up shop—Curtis, Simon, Jeremiah, the chief engineer, the first mate, and Beatrice. Thaddeus had refused to leave Phillip's side, but instead watched from where he remained, fingers on Phillip's neck as if monitoring his pulse.

Simon crossed his arms. "We're in a tight spot. We can't go back to the fort, and we can't stay here." He rocked back on his heels. "Thanks to Phillip and his men, we dodged the Bureau, for now, but more hunters will be coming. They'll find us if we don't put a lot of miles between them and ourselves. There are only two questions as I see it. Where are we going, and how are we to get there?"

A crowd had grown outside the inner circle. Now, a voice called from behind Curtis. "What I want to know is why you brought us out here only to freeze to death or be murdered by Bureau men. We should never have listened to you. Should have turned this lot of outsiders into the authorities and been done with it from the start."

Another man shouted, "We could still do that. Maybe should."

More raised voices answered, a few in agreement, more in opposition, and shoving matches began. Someone fell onto Curtis's back, and it seemed the situation would escalate out of hand.

Fingers in his mouth, Simon issued an earsplitting whistle.

The shoving, the shouting stopped, and in that silence, Simon strode into the center of the circle, turning, meeting the eyes of the people gathered round. “Did you all forget how we burned our bridges back there when we staged the taking of the *Dorothy*? Forget we all agreed to this, voted on it?”

The man who started the commotion cut in. “Making a bad move don’t mean we gotta keep making more. I call for a vote. Who’s for turning the outsiders over to the Bureau? Take a vote.”

Simon raised his hands, cutting off another shouting match. “Wouldn’t work, even if you tried.” He searched round the circle. “Robinson. Tell ’em what you learned when you interrogated those Bureau men. Tell us how it’s working out for Jock and Clara, this idea of turning informant to the Bureau.”

Robinson wrung a fur hat between his hands. “Yeah. We tied up those Bureau men, like you said, left ’em on the river for their buddies to find. But first, we questioned ’em. Jock and Clara are in the dungeons, havin’ their confessions wrung outa them. Officers we laid hands on say they’ll string ’em up when they finish working ’em over.”

Letting the silence hang, Simon pinned the most vocal with his gaze. “So, any of you feels like running to the Bureau, you have my permission. Go to it.” He swept his arm toward the cave opening.

No one moved.

“Well? Who wants to give it a try?”

Still, no one moved.

Simon spat into the coals. “Well, then. If we got that outa our systems, let’s get down to it. We’ve got decisions to make.” He took a lungful of air, then let it out. “First question first. Father Curtis suggests we make for his old stomping grounds. He has contacts there, people who can help hide us, maybe even get us new identities. Anyone have a better suggestion?”

Heads around the fire shook.

Beatrice stepped forward. “We all have family who’d take us in, but the authorities are sure to look there first.” She cocked an eyebrow at Simon. "You have, um, shall I say . . . a lot of friends in this area? Perhaps they have a hideout they could offer?"

Simon rubbed his chin. "I do have a number of, ah, associates hereabouts."

Around the fire, smirks appeared on a few faces.

"Family too. They do have a unique skill set which might be helpful if we were trying to get a few crates moved across country, but this many people?"

He waved around the dozens of faces who'd drawn up about the inner circle, silent, concerned spectators. "If we were to smuggle ourselves across the country, what then? We've nowhere to go. We've all disappeared, at least the families and crew from the *Dorothy* have. We're dead as far as the world knows, all of us wanted if found alive. Our old identities are worthless. We need new names, new documents, if we're to work, travel, to do anything but hide. If we're to remain free."

He squinted, mouth pulled into a frown. "Besides, we need to be well clear of this country, double-time. The Order'll rip this whole area apart looking for us. Doubt even my folk could hide us long from that. Any other suggestions?" With none offered, Simon began to speak, but his voice had gone hoarse. He accepted a canteen from one of the women, took a swallow, and drove the cork home. "Should we put it to a vote? I'm loath to give orders to anyone when it comes to a decision like this."

There were some nods, and no dissent.

"Okay, a vote it is. All in favor of making for Two Rivers—"

"Wait," a man interrupted. One of Simon's hill people who'd joined the exodus, whether to help or to spectate, who could say? He stood tall and lean with deep-set eyes. "I'm thinkin' *how* one is to get somewhere might have some bearin' on *where* one might go. If the best means of transport only had the capability to go certain places, wouldn't I be right in thinkin' that?"

Simon wobbled his head side to side. "I suppose it could, cousin. What were you thinking?"

"You remember the stories old Uncle Hank used to tell us about the Before Times? How he talked of the runs he and Pa made on that old express line?"

Simon squinted into the air as if trying to recall such stories. He shook his head. "Sorry, Henry. I don't."

Henry scratched one darkly stubbled cheek. "Well, at our house, us boys heard 'em plenty."

Thumbs tucked in overall straps, Henry rocked off the balls of his feet. "Leadin' up to when the Bad Times hit, it was gettin' harder and harder to move cargo. Uncle Hank knew about this railroad just north of here. A long time back, the Hegemony put in a high-speed line across this part of the country, kinda like an interstate for nonstop, long-range trains. They ran it through the most remote parts they could, keepin' clear of towns, just like the interstate highway did, back in the day, but more so."

Henry spat a long brown stream into the fire and wiped his lips with the back of his hand. "Government work, a boondoggle, and the first year they were runnin', bridges started crackin'. One did collapse back East, and that there high-speed line got shut down and never got used again. Uncle Hank and Daddy spent a few years during the Bad Times runnin' contraband down that rail on their handy little carts. They made an art form of it."

Danny sighed, eyes wide. "That musta been sumpthin'."

"It were, boy." Henry released a deep sigh of his own, seeming as if he, too, wished he were there, part of that great adventure. Then he clucked his tongue. "Well, anyways, the Bad Times came and went. After a while, the Committee started runnin' wagon trains up and down the roads, and things got real civilized. The family business stopped usin' that old rail. Pumpin' that there handle up and down was real work, I tell you. Why do that when you can just pay off an engineer and send a full freight car on down the road, straight to where you need it? But those carts are still there, and they still work. I rode one a few times when I was younger. So I'm sayin' the how might be a bit more important than the where if our first priority is to get lots of miles behind us fast. That's all."

Simon pulled a map from an inner pocket and motioned Henry

to his side. "Show me where that rail is, where it runs, and where those carts are."

"Well, the first and last part of that's easy. The rail runs through Uncle Hank's farm, and the carts are there in his barn." Henry jabbed his finger on the map. "No more than three, four miles upriver from here, I'm guessin'. The middle part is harder. I'm not rightly sure where the rail goes. I know it runs east and west. All I can tell you."

Curtis leaned in over Simon's shoulder. He tapped the location now identified as Uncle Hank's farm, then traced a line across the map. "If that line runs straight west, it passes well north of Two Rivers." He kept moving his finger. "But it must cross just miles south of Northwoods."

He snapped his fingers. "I know where that line is! I've seen an abandoned rail bridge south of town when I canoed out there. This might be a good option. My friends in Northwoods will hide us, maybe even transport us to Two Rivers."

Simon pursed his lips. "Best alternative offered yet this morning."

Firelight shone from the smudged, sweaty faces. Flames reflected in their eyes. Behind them, the limestone cave walls were nearly lost in shadow, the rough grain highlighted in the occasional flicker. The contrast of yellow flame and darkness made the colors all the more vibrant, almost surreal, like a painting by one of the old masters.

The expressions, once drawn and frightened, had taken on a cautiously hopeful cast.

Simon raised a hand. "You all heard the discussion. All in favor of Henry and Curtis's plan, raise your hands. Opposed?"

There were no opposing votes.

Curtis narrowed his eyes, glancing sidelong at Jeremiah. Just as in the histories of the scrolls, it was easy to get unanimity from desperate people.

Murmurings and trouble came later when all danger had passed.

Always, the trouble came later.

CHAPTER 51

Leif dunked his head in the kitchen sink. Maybe the cold water would clear its throbbing. Yesterday's bender had caught up with him more than usual. Of course, he was out of practice, not having had time to drink these last weeks. Or maybe that deep ache was from when that creep had kicked him . . . or the way his family had been ripped from his life, leaving a soul-torn hole where his heart had been.

He popped another painkiller from the bottle and chewed it dry. It might help with the headache and bruises. Nothing would help the rest. He dug through the dirty dishes for an unfinished beer. Something, anything, to take the edge off.

His back door burst open, and the doorknob slammed against the wall. One of the sawmill workers rushed in, doubled over, hands on knees. Between heaving breaths, he said, "Come quick. Mill. Hurt."

Leif didn't wait for the man to regain his breath. Hangover drowned beneath a roaring adrenaline wave, he mounted his bike on the run, already pedaling toward the sawmill. The messenger would have to catch up as he was able.

Leif disregarded the icy streets, pedaling with all his might, taking advantage of the downhill slope for even greater speed. Snow-covered hedges blurred by. The icy streets provided no friction, so he leaned around corners with one foot planted, tires sliding, bounding off curbs, then popping back onto fishtailing tires.

At the mill, he slid to a sideways stop, throwing gravel. Then he let the bike fall and sprinted to where a group formed an impenetrable circle around the big saw. He elbowed into the tight mass. "Let me through. Move." His fogged brain couldn't interpret the images. It was all blood and incorrectly assembled pieces, like a bad, gory abstract painting.

One of the mill workers lay on the ground. What initially looked like a sagittal crest came into focus as a section of the huge saw blade intersecting his skull, the saw teeth looking for all the world like the rippled comb on a reptile's skull. Other sections of blade were sticking at random from the roof timbers, and a severed arm lay on the conveyor. Next to it sat Young Bob, propped against the steel framework. A man worked on the stump of his arm. Young Bob was white and clammy, and while Leif watched, frozen, Young Bob slumped to his side, his head bouncing off one of the metal conveyor legs.

"Grab him!" shouted the man, tightening a tourniquet with his teeth. "Help me get him on the stretcher."

Leif staggered, bumping into a wood corner post, which he grabbed for support.

He vomited, and then all went dark.

MARIPOL WRAPPED his cloak around his shoulders. The day was again cold and damp, as it had been the whole week he'd spent aboard the *Dorothy*. Almost as if the gods of weather were taunting him, the ever-present gloom a constant reminder of his exile.

The big towboat remained beached north of Plumbsburg, her power plants dead. All aboard smelled of mildew and sweat, the ship's ducts no longer circulating the now stagnant air. No local towboat captain would pilot the *Dorothy* to dock or brave the supposed *Celeste* curse.

Maripol strode through the corridors to the wheelhouse. *Replaced, replaced, replaced*—the ghostly word seemed to toll with each step. After fruitless months, he'd been replaced. Abandoned to rot in the eddying backwaters of the Order hierarchy, far from the mainstream of political favor. Accused of being too softhearted, failing to exercise the necessary barbarity.

Now, stripped of authority, he was left to reexamine old files. But some clue must be here amid the boatload of records, discarded belongings, and artifacts. He opened the ship's logs and sank into the captain's chair, flipping back, back, back—there, the week the *Tikvah* arrived.

The captain had duly reported the *Dorothy* docking at the gulf port. Maripol slowed his reading through a spate of unusual occurrences that plagued the boat for three days, including the dreams the captain and the crew experienced. What a surreal account. As the logs recorded the trip upriver, the captain noted more happenings, things bordering on the magical.

He tapped a finger over words written in a shaky hand. If, in his long career, so many things hadn't defied rational explanation—all the more so since his assignment to this case—he would've considered these accounts the ravings of a madman.

But something was happening here, something strange, and something connected to these three young men and the scrolls they carried. What, after all, was the reason for all of these . . . these *what*? Miracles? There was no other word for it. But miracles created by whom? And for what purpose?

Boots clanging on the stern ladder reverberated through the ship. The approach of a small motor had impinged upon his awareness, but he'd ignored it, intent on his reading. One of his men knocked on the wheelhouse door. "Messenger arriving, sir." His man stepped aside to allow a flushed young man to approach.

Maripol pivoted the captain's seat but kept finger on the line he was reading. "Report."

"Sir, there has been a development. Field Agent in Charge Stein has asked that you be kept abreast of the situation, as a courtesy."

Maripol braced himself. That man would have extended no such courtesy had there been good news. Perhaps another oversight for which he was even now pinning blame on Maripol? "Yes?"

"Two of the fugitives appeared in Plumbsburg yesterday. They were apprehended and questioned. FAC Stein sent squads of Bureau men to check out a location where the remainder of the rebels are alleged to be hiding."

"What?" Why send those buffoons? "Did they find the *Dorothy*'s crew?"

"That is unknown at this time, sir. It appears there was a battle on the river. There were casualties. No other information has yet been released."

Maripol shot to his feet, beginning to pack his valise. "You will take me there."

"Sir, I'm sorry I can't."

Hands frozen midair, Maripol raised his gaze. "Are you refusing to obey a lawful order?"

The messenger retreated a step, hands extended. "Oh no, sir. Sorry, sir. I should have been more clear. The water is open only as far as the port. The tributary in question is frozen. I can take you to HQ in my boat. From there, FAC Stein will need to authorize other transport to the site."

"Very well, take me to Stein." Maripol latched his briefcase. He hesitated, then opened it, and placed the ship's logs inside before latching it again. "Ready?"

WHEN LEIF AWOKE, ears ringing, a large concerned face swam above his.

"Hey there, lad. Just lie still. Take a sip." Maurice lifted Leif's head to a water jug, then held it back when Leif drank too eagerly. "Slow, you don' wanna puke it right back up, now."

Leif laid his head back onto a thick carpet of sawdust, dark timbers and rusty tin roof high overhead.

"Better now?" Maurice asked.

Leif nodded. His head was no longer spinning, and the ringing in his ears had stopped. That had to be a good sign, didn't it?

And then a heat washed through him, rising to his cheeks. He couldn't lie here like this, couldn't let the men see him acting like some weakling. He levered himself up, pushing with strangely limp and prickly arms.

"Shock like that will level many a hard man." Maurice must have anticipated what he was feeling. "Most the boys lost their lunch, and they all know how much you love Young Bob. Nobody thinkin' anything of how anybody took this here mess today."

Leif shook his head. "I embarrassed myself, set a terrible example. A weak sister."

"No, ya di'nt. Besides, everyone here has heard how you single-handedly organized the rescue of all those poor folks. Them who was at that big rail accident that never happened. How you pulled that poor baby outa that burnin' car. Nobody gonna think less of you today."

Leif, his head clearing, winced at a pang. Why had his concern been about what people thought of him? His priority should have been for the injured. Now he jerked upright, weak arms or no. "Oh, good golly, where's Bob? Is the other man, okay?"

"Bob's gonna make it, more than likely."

"And the other man?" Leif's cheeks went hot. What kind of leader was he? He didn't even know the man's name.

Maurice's voice went soft. "Ronald di'nt make it. It was real quick like. He never knew what hit 'im. Good that. If'n a man's gotta go, that'd be the way to go."

Head lowered, eyes closed, Leif focused on his breathing. His stomach again threatened to rebel, his limbs still so tingly. "How many others hurt?"

"Oh, a few, just flesh wounds, but the blade's shot. Shattered in a million pieces. We'll hav'ta check the shaft. If she's bent, we're in a heap of trouble. If not, just gotta swap out the blade. We've got extras, though we better be lookin' for more."

"What in the blazes happened?"

Maurice beckoned Leif to join him at the log jammed halfway through the big straight-line saw. Maurice pointed where the clean saw cut terminated into a jagged eruption of splinters. Deep inside the cut was a gleam of metal.

With surgical precision, Maurice used a hatchet to clear away the wood surrounding the spot. He soon exposed a gray metal rod embedded in the log, at least five-eighths inches in diameter. As he removed more wood from around it, a diamond hatch embossed pattern emerged.

That pattern. "Rerod!"

Maurice set the hatchet aside. "Yep, appears so, and fresh too. No rust." He eyed the rod's trajectory and followed it to the other side. He probed with a belt knife.

With a dull clink, the knife struck something hard.

Leif leaned in to see more closely. After a moment, he picked out a neat round hole, the exposed fibers in the entry wound still white and fresh.

"Bark's not even started healin' over, not more than a few days old. This log's been spiked. Somebody killed Ronald and crippled Bob on purpose!"

A circle of men had gathered. Now, a dangerous mutter went around the group. Another voice, old and wavering, stopped all other speech. "You find out who tried to kill my boy, Mr. Leif. You find 'em, and you put 'em in prison, or so help me I'll hunt 'em down my ownself." Tears streaked Old Bob's cheeks, and his hands shook, not with the palsy but with barely contained fury. "They'll *wish* for prison compared to what I'll give 'em."

The crowd erupted in hearty agreement.

Leif raised his hands. "We're going to track this thing down, and I swear to you, on my honor, this will not go unpunished."

Maurice stepped up, his big voice booming over all other sounds. "All right, boys. We gotta job to do. These snakes aren't gonna shut us down if'n that was what they were after. You men"—he pointed at the mill crew—"break out the spare blade and check the shaft. Get this old girl runnin' asap. You"—he motioned others forward—"check every log on this site and find every one of 'em that's spiked. Sort 'em out and keep a record of the tally marks. You others gather up your mates, get up to the railhead, and do the same. The rest of you get back to your jobs."

He turned to another man, one of the superintendents. "You got a copy of the register with ya?" After the man handed over a rolled sheaf of papers, Maurice strode to the butt end of the log and compared the painted markings there to the columns of notes. "What I suspected. An' what I was afraid of."

Leif sidled close and read the line where Maurice's massive pointer finger rested. "South Crescent. Is that where I think it is?"

"If'n you think you smell a skunk named Junior, reckon you're on the right trail, lad."

CHAPTER 52

Before acres of polished mahogany was the narrowest sliver of space. There, Maripol sat on a cheap plastic chair, back tight to the rough concrete wall and knees pressed to desk panels, staring at the new FAC, mouth agape.

Stein himself was a big man. And , his physical power had taught him an unfortunate life lesson—the shortest distance between any problem and its solution was the liberal application of brute force. Often enough, obstacles crumbled beneath his overpowering attacks, reinforcing his belief. Now, he seemed incapable of foreseeing any situation in which it might not.

"The squad was wiped out? All men disabled?"

Stein's jutting brow furrowed, gaze hardening. "The locals have been aiding the rebels. The criminals knew when and how we were approaching. They ambushed the mounted squad, destroying or stealing all available snow machines. But rest assured, those responsible will pay a high price. Very high indeed."

"But you sent the entire garrison." Careful not to show judgment, Maripol folded his hands in his lap. "Surely, the remaining Bureau men continued the mission on foot. They should be at the site by now."

Those meaty lips, a match to the rest of the man, let loose an explosive huff. “There was a miscommunication on the part of the Bureau commanders. Incompetent, those men.”

A long, deep breath loosened Maripol’s jaw muscles. What was the bishop thinking putting this man in charge? “What sort of miscommunication?”

“When the unmounted forces found their fallen comrades at the ambush site, they stopped there, set up defensive positions, and sent back messengers requesting additional orders.”

Lids closed to conceal his eye roll, Maripol tried again. “Okay. That was yesterday evening. Surely, they have reached the rebel position by now.”

“Why, surely? ’Course they haven’t.” Stein pursed his lips. “Was a mistake to trust the Bureau with this. We’ll be using our men, here on out. I’ve ordered a contingent of snow machines rushed here, enough to allow a fast-moving force to attack the rebel stronghold. They’re due any moment. The fugitives are holed up in an old stone fort. We’ll have heavy weapons to make quick work of such defenses. Gonna show those heretics what for.”

“How do you know they’re still there, waiting for you?” *Can you be such a fool to think they are?*

Stein leaned back in his overstuffed padded-leather executive chair, chest puffed, smile self-satisfied. Even with his chair reclined, there was plenty of space on *that* side of the desk. Order lore maintained that anytime Stein received a long-term assignment, he arranged for this desk to be shipped to that location. And here it was, another unlikely fable confirmed.

“Of course they are. Where else would they go? If a few did flee, we’ll run them down. They can’t match our superior numbers or mobility. You should come and watch. Gonna be great fun, I tell you. Exciting to be in the field for an operation like this one, don’t you think?”

Maripol searched for words. He settled for an anemic. “I do believe I will join you on your, ah, adventure.”

LEIF PRESSED fingers against a fresh white wound in the bark. How many of the mature trees, already marked for logging, had been spiked? This made the tenth he and Maurice sighted. The footprints surrounding each impaled tree were still visible, their outlines softened by one light snowfall.

Leif's anger, at a low burn since the incident, now kindled to a roar. Fist clenched, he pivoted. "Let's go get that bastard. He needs to pay for what he did."

Maurice laid a big mitt on Leif's shoulder. "Lad, we got no proof. You gotta have a slippery eel like him nailed down good and proper before you move in."

Leif pulled off his stocking cap, bunched it up in his hands, and wiped his brow with it. "How do we do that? And what more do we need?" He tossed the cap at the nearest wounded tree. "He's the one that spiked all these. You know that."

"You and I may know it. Provin' it good enough to lock an eel up is another thing. Move slow and sure, lad. We're not gonna stampede ourselves here. We're gonna take him down real careful like."

Maurice had instructed his crews to inspect the timber throughout the Burr Oak spread, but neither he nor Leif expected similar tampering elsewhere. Maurice scooped up Leif's cap, then knocked a knuckle against the rough bark. "The trees were spiked at this specific location for a specific reason. But what was Junior's motivation?"

Maurice passed back the cap, took off at a fast clip to the South Crescent, then on his belly, scuttled to the ridge's edge.

Leif followed. Could he truly be in the same place where he'd stood with Maurice just months ago? It may as well be a different world entirely.

When he was here last, the trees were beginning to color, the arch of branches overhead like a stained glass cathedral. What a contrast to this wonderland of sparkling winter white, the midday sun in a clear blue sky reflecting off snowfields too blinding to view even with sunglasses.

Before the wide bowl of the river bottom stood Junior's place, its grounds exposed to view. They stayed well back in the tree line, using the cover of a leafless wild plum thicket.

"See the trail to the river?" Maurice pointed, the fog of his breath more likely to give them away than the whisper of his words.

The last time they had been there, a heavily used trail wove through the marshy flats between Junior's place and the river.

"It's even wider, and the fresh snow of a few days ago . . . "

It appeared now beaten by what must have been hundreds of pairs of feet.

Maurice then signaled that they should withdraw. Once far enough back from the ridge, they stood and hiked well into the trees before speaking. The still, cold winter air carried voices amazing distances, and they had good reason to keep their presence covert.

Back turned to the Crescent, voice still kept low, Maurice said, "Did you see what I saw, lad?"

"Someone has been moving between the river and Junior's place."

"Lots of somebodies, be my guess, but there's somethin' else. Lots of tracks goin' to the place. None comin' out. Whoever it was is still holed up there." Maurice's eyes narrowed. "What say we have a few of the boys take up a watchin' post here, see if we can find out who is comin' and who is goin'—and why?"

MARIPOL STOOD ALONE in the old stone fort, aside from the single aide Stein grudgingly left for him. Snow stung his face, driven by a howling wind that prowled circles about the empty structures. Its eerie moan suited his mood.

Stein and his men had searched the fort before roaring off upriver to catch the outlaws. Stein's parting words still rang in the frigid camp air: "How far could a bunch of women and children have gotten?"

Maripol searched the row houses, empty except for crude timber-framed furniture and scraps of clothing. Anomalously, one cabin boasted a china hutch, neatly polished and oiled.

He scouted the snow-drifted yard, also empty, then clomped up the wooden steps of the porch fronting the main building, the aide shadowing him.

How could Stein have been so foolish? Once again, the quarry was nearly in Maripol's grasp and, once again, slipped through his fingers. He shook his head. No, not *his* fingers, not this time.

But the terrible luck of it all. If the bishop had only left him in charge, this would be over. He would be vindicated, his derailed career on track again.

Inside, a chaos of scattered papers littered the big room. He inspected some. Work details, inventories, and the like. These would merit study, and he signaled the aide to gather them.

At the head table, a cardboard sign perched atop a stack of bound documents, the words clear—*Free, take one. Regards, Jeremiah*.

Maripol flipped through the pages. Then, with a lightning sweep of his arm, he gathered them all into his evidence case. After one more glancing inspection of the building, he sprinted toward the door.

CHAPTER 53

Professor Reuel strolled across campus toward his cottage. A gray melancholy gripped his soul, a grating unease exacerbated by this bitter January weather.

At his door, he stooped to retrieve a special delivery package, groaning as cold-stiffened joints protested. Ignoring the raised stoop, the deliveryman had set it on the sidewalk in a muddy puddle, the cardboard already soggy, the waterline working up its sides.

"To tarnation with these slovenly workers." He shook it to dislodge a few stubborn water droplets. The contents gurgled. He turned the key in the brass lock, keeping the muddy package clear of his overcoat. What could it be? He'd ordered nothing, at least nothing he recalled.

Inside, he shed his coat and boots, went to the kitchen, and spread a towel on the wooden counter before setting the box atop it.

He inspected the scrawled return address, squinted, then tilted it toward the window for better light. "Ah, old Butterman."

A paring knife made quick work of the strings and brown wrapping tape. He pried the top flaps open. A glass bottle labeled Butterman's World-Famous Fish Sauce nestled in a cushion of crumpled papers. Was this a jest?

He despised the stuff, as Butterman knew all too well. Reuel set the bottle aside and unfolded the note.

Professor Reuel,

It has been far too long since you favored this house with your presence. As you requested, I have enclosed a jar of the sauce you love so well.

It pleases me so to hear from you and to know you have missed the repast of our table. Alas, travel does become difficult at our age, and time does fleet away.

In answer to your kind inquiries, Mrs. Butterman and I are well and enjoying the quiet life granted to us in our modest little inn, although our lives have been turned quite upside down in the past months.

First, there was the visitation of the Curse of the Celeste, of which I informed you in my previous letter. So sad. I still haven't decided whether it is a blessing or not, that when the crew of the *Dorothy* were devoured by the demon, their families were taken in their homes, as well. Would it have been kinder for them to remain, their fathers and husbands having vanished? I'm not sure.

To add to that disturbing incident, our little city is now overrun with Peace officers and temple troopers, as well as many men of less certain origin. Shadowy men and dangerous looking. Very secretive and not given to small talk. Several have taken lodging in our fine establishment, and they do give Mrs. Butterman the shivers, I can tell you.

It seems the authorities learned of a nest of heretics living in the hill country somewhere in the Yellow River Valley, north of here. Rumor has it that these hoodlums have managed some sort of escape and are being hunted with great fervor. Mrs. Butterman has begun double bolting our doors at night, in fear of these dangerous men ravaging the countryside. My family and I pray these will be brought to answer for their crimes forthwith. Please rest more easily with the sure knowledge that all that can be done is being done.

We also pray that no unwary traveler would think to sojourn in these parts, at least not until these unsettling times have come to an end, which I anticipate I'll be reporting in my next communication, and soon.

As always, I look forward to hearing of your good health.

Your old friend,

Butterman

Reuel's breaths sped in sympathy with his beating heart. What extreme circumstance would cause Butterman to send this note, both the need for such and in this form? An unencrypted letter, disguised as idle gossip, indicated the man was too closely watched to risk a coded message, lest it be recognized as such.

Terrible tidings. Terrible, indeed.

Reuel slammed the sauce into the garbage, then groaned. Once again, he vented his displeasure on an innocent target. He stooped to fish it back out. Phillip loved the nasty concoction.

Elbows on the old wooden kitchen table, he reread the letter.

Given the time it had taken the package to transit, by now, either Phillip and Curtis were in custody along with the precious scrolls or else they were—what? Injured and friendless, somewhere in the wilds? Safe and warm? But where? How to find out? How to assist?

Reuel prepared coded missives to be sent far and wide, querying his contacts for anything to determine the team's fate. If not for the cursed brittleness of age, he wouldn't play such a passive part in this, the most important mission of his long lifetime, of many lifetimes.

Staring into the fire, he muttered to himself, the dying orange-blue flames flickering, arthritic knuckles clenching and unclenching as they gripped his traveling stick. With a sharp nod and an oath, he leaned on the staff and stood, his jaw set. He went to his desk, dashed off a few more short letters before packing a bag. His house in order, he snuffed out all candles before he left, double locking the door behind himself.

CHAPTER 54

Lars helped load the last one onto the freight car and rubbed spread fingers across a smooth, dark tabletop aglow in the lantern light. Good stuff. He wrapped the shipping blanket around it, strapped it in, and stepped out. Swinging the big freight door closed, he eyed the driver's cab. So tempting. It'd be great to ride with this load, to feel that thrill of accomplishment as they delivered. But he had more pressing matters.

As Lars shepherded the completed product onto the transport, Benny set up for the next task.

The contract included multiple freestanding concession counters, all of identical design, and the problems with the tables had eaten a huge chunk out of the time scheduled to build them. If they were to deliver this next phase before the deadline, all hope rode on the seminary boys. But these counters were more complex. Would they be up to the task? Untrained and inexperienced as they were?

He shook himself to dislodge such doubts. Of course they'd succeed. They had to.

He handed off the lantern, left the loading dock, and headed through the rear warehouse toward the shop. As he passed pallet after pallet of lumber, each waiting for the alchemy of his craft to breathe new life into the dormant stacks, the essence of the once-living hardwood reached out to him. The nuttiness of oak filled the air. At the cheery, sharp bite of it, his chest expanded. The deep sweetness of chestnut called to him, hinting at ancient secrets that might be his if only he'd tarry. The rich juglone bite of walnut enervated his being, enlivened his step.

He was still walking between the looming dark shapes when raised voices echoed from the shop. He picked up his pace as much as he safely could in the gloom, flinching in anticipation of a shin barked on a protruding block. He swung open the door and stepped into the lit shop.

Benny stood, hands on hips, scowling at a stack of newly-arrived material.

Lars moved up beside him, stomach already lurching at what he somehow knew he was about to hear. "What is it now?"

"Those lousy—" Benny stomped a heavy boot. "They did it again!"

"Did what?"

"The counter assemblies. The doggone counter assemblies. They're all screwed up! We've got nothing but a jumble here, and when I started pulling out parts, the first one I touched, the studs for the main walls, were made too short."

"Slow down, man. Show me what we've got. Let's see what we can figure out."

Normally, freestanding counters like these would be manufactured one-off, meaning the team of carpenters building it would fabricate the needed component parts one at a time, cut to fit as they built.

Because these counters were a repetitive assembly, Lars had come up with the idea to standardize the components. This would allow the parts to be jobbed out to other mills and made in advance, decreasing the man-hours required for construction.

His belly twisted, and he swallowed hard on a rising sourness. He'd checked production drawing after production drawing, intercepting and correcting errors, but had never seen the final packet for this assembly. How had it slipped through?

Late afternoon rolled into evening. The day shift checked out, and Lars's seminary boys arrived. Lars put them to work, helping to sort the mess. Well into the night, they processed the parts.

Finally, Lars said, "Okay, Benny. How many were cut wrong?"

Benny consulted his notebook. "Thirty-four wrong for each assembly. Luckily, most of these were made too big, so we can recut them. That leaves about a dozen per counter that are scrap."

"Their shop error? Or was it our engineering team?" Little doubt where the fault would lie, but a guy could always hope, right?

Benny gave him an ironic look. "Do you really have to ask?"

Lars closed his eyes and tried for a cleansing breath. He rapped a miscut piece on the concrete, the hollow, steady rhythm like a clock ticking down. Time running out. "Do we have the raw materials to remake them?"

"Should. Want me to get a team started on that?"

Lars gave the lumber one last sharp rap, then threw it on the pile. "No. I'm tired of fixing other people's mistakes, aren't you? Do you know where Velde lives?"

Benny grinned. "I like where you're going with this."

REUEL STAGGERED round the corner and stumbled on a loose cobble. It was almost too hard to lift his soggy leather oxfords for even one more step. He trudged on, then paused, squinting at the faded sign overhead. With a sigh that was more groan, he approached that sign. At the entrance, he hauled himself up one and then another of the mud-soaked stairs, leaning on the handrail, then clomped through the Prancing Panther's door, sweaty and rumpled.

He doubled over in a coughing fit.

Had to be the diesel fumes from that broken-down freighter with which he'd hitched a ride. He'd been forced to such extremes once it became clear no wagon train would soon depart the terminal he'd been marooned in . . . and for three days no less. If the Order intended to strand travelers in such a manner, the least they could do was provide lodging. Or at least more ergonomic seating. To sleep in such was sheer impossibility. Intolerable.

Or maybe it had been that long, final stretch he'd been forced to walk, slush filling his shoes, cold air raking his lungs raw. He was far too old for such, of a certainty.

He let the door bang closed and collapsed into the nearest chair. Butterman hurried from the kitchen, wiping hands on apron. The innkeeper stopped in his tracks, horror tautening his ample face before it transformed into a bland smile. But the lines around his eyes never relaxed.

Butterman rumbled over. "Good morning, Professor Reuel. It has been many moons since you graced our inn. How may I be of service?" Beneath his breath, he murmered, "What are you doing here? It's not safe. Didn't you get my message?"

Reuel whispered, "Upstairs, later." In a normal speaking voice, easily overheard in the nearly empty dining room, he said, "I found myself wishing to revisit the places of my youth one last time. I may be unable to accomplish such a journey again. Age catches up with us all, you know. I hope you have a room available?"

"Of course, sir, of course. It is an honor. Follow me."

Butterman was halfway up the stair before Reuel levered himself onto the bottom step, head spinning with the effort. The big man reversed course, slung Reuel's limp arm over one broad shoulder, and more carried than led him up the steep stair, then to the last room on the right. Inside, Butterman closed the door and put his hands on his hips. "What in Hegemony are you thinking, old friend? This town is crawling with Peace officers, Order men." He shivered. "And worse."

Reuel patted Butterman's chest before sinking onto one of the cots. "I couldn't stay comfortable and warm in my cottage, not knowing if my friends were safe, not knowing if they needed my help. I came to find them, to assist if I can. What can you tell me of them?"

Butterman huffed. "Last I saw any of them was in this very room, the night of the Curse. As it is, that's the only reason I had this room available. We're full up, but folks won't stay in this devil-touched room. As for those poor boys, all I know is what can be heard about town, as reliable as that may be. As my letter said, the Bureau men mounted up on snow machines and tore off north, toward Yellow River—what was that? A week, ten days ago? Anyway, next thing we heard, they came walking back into town, all beat up. You've heard, I assume, that your friends were holed up in that old fort in Yellow River Canyon?"

Reuel gave a weak nod. "I remember the place well."

Butterman chortled. "Aye, there's many a tale in *that* memory." He then gave an update on the empty garrison. "Since then, this town's been afire, Bureau men and Order bigwigs and some"—he put his hand over his mouth to whisper—"from the Eye."

"Any sign of my boys?"

"Those Order men have been turning over every rock from here to the north country, if you're to believe what folks say, but no sign of our fugitives. That's all there is to know. You should've stayed where you were safe. Mark my words, the fact that you're here has already been noted."

Reuel began to answer but was taken by another coughing fit, hacking into a soiled handkerchief. Once the spasms subsided, he leaned against the headboard, wheezing for breath.

Butterman's flaccid face twisted up. "You don't look well. You had best get into bed and get warm before you catch your death, my friend. I'll have Mrs. Butterman make some of her chicken soup."

Reuel let Butterman peel off his trousers, his own fingers too numb, too weak to handle the fastenings. He flopped onto the mattress, hugging himself to still the shivers. He lay his throbbing head on the pillow and curled into the blankets.

He was cold. So very cold.

He fought against a new certainty, one he'd denied these past, arduous days. That something was fearfully wrong with this old body of his. Something powerful even now stealing the last dregs of his life force, his breath.

The room began to fuzz in and out of focus, and he struggled to maintain hold on reality, on his mastery of this traitorous flesh.

There was so much he must do. He owed succor to those poor boys, alone and hunted in that cold.

He must overcome. Must prevail.

But his vision continued to blur, his breaths to grow more labored. Finally, even his wits abandoned him, and he wandered lost in a world of shadow and mist and nightmare visions.

Wasn't there something he must do? If only he could remember what.

And then even the terror of his inability paled, dwarfed by some unseen entity, one whose advancing presence could be discerned only by the ravening hatred it radiated into the void.

It circled ever nearer, a shadow prowling the periphery of those blurred mists into which his soul had been cast. That presence then pressed upon him, surrounded and suffocated him, until his heart no longer had strength to overcome, to beat. It slowed, slowed, ever weakening, approaching the final spasming shudder that would precede release, then stillness.

Through lips that refused to respond to his commands, he tried to pray, to call out to Creator God. Tried and failed.

A hellish glee shrieked from the mists now encroaching upon his vision, and now even the gray empty place disappeared, to be replaced by absolute, total darkness.

As usual, Maripol remained in his office when all others in the wing were dark and vacant for the night. He checked his inbox. Still no return messages. He'd sent repeated dispatches to the bishop. The import of the documents from the fort couldn't be overstated, so why would the bishop ignore this vital intelligence?

He squared his spine and strode toward the executive wing, the document tucked beneath his arm. He'd be put off no longer.

He used the weight of his position to bluff his way through layers of gatekeepers. But in the vestibule of the private offices, the two troopers guarding the door barred his way.

As he stared them down, the private secretary was sputtering, pulling at his sleeve. "I insist you remove yourself, or I will have you removed."

The adjoining conference room door opened, and the dome of Stein's large skull poked out, followed by the craggy face. "Oh, Maripol. Just the man we were looking for. Please enter."

Maripol removed the secretary's plucking fingers from his robe, strode into the room, then pulled up short at the other men already seated.

The bishop spoke into the silence, voice a deep purr. "Well, my faithful servant Maripol. Thank you for so kindly joining us."

"Your grace. What a pleasant surprise. I've discovered troubling documents at the old fort where the heretics holed up. This is a situation we must address."

The ever-present Lind pulled a crudely bound book from a stack of papers. He thumped it on the table. "Are you referring to this?"

Maripol riffled the pages of the tome, the text from the fort. He concentrated on his tone. On keeping the excitement from tinging his voice, especially here. Especially now. "Yes, sir. I believe this to be a translation of the scrolls I was sent to Nob to find."

Dry lips wrinkled. "You mean the scrolls you failed to find?" The prosecutor let the silence hang, pregnant, then waved a hand. "Oh, well, that is old news. Let us overlook past failures and turn our attention to the future, shall we?"

"Um, sir? I don't understand." Maripol raised the book as if presenting it as evidence. "This is dangerous material, subversive. This document must not be allowed to get out."

Lind leaned back in his chair and rested chin on one fist. "Of course, this material must be intercepted and all who purvey it destroyed. Stein has been tasked with that mission and supplied with the resources to complete it. The heretics are in panicked flight, hiding in caves. Soon, they'll be run to ground and wiped out."

He scooted forward, metal chair legs screeching on concrete. "But that is his concern, not yours. I have another task in mind for you, one for which your training is well-suited."

He laid a thin folder on the table and slid it toward Maripol, manila whispering across the metal surface. “Our interrogators have been interviewing the heretic defectors. Here is the information they extracted. Release your spiders. All of them. They are to sniff out any persons who may have assisted the rebels in any way, may have been in contact with them. And we must know of any persons who may be aware of this.” Lind tapped the crudely bound translation. “If we do not identify and cut out the rot, every whiff of it, that rot will infect the entire body. Am I clear?”

CHAPTER 55

Lars sat on a worktable, concentrating on his breathing, on his thudding heart. It couldn't be good for a guy to be so keyed up and so short on sleep for so long.

His seminary boys found their seats nearby and settled in for the wait. Then one broke the silence. "Mr. Lars? Are we going to get all this made in time?"

"I don't know how, Tatten, but we've got to. That's all."

"Would more workers help?"

"Well, sure, if they were as good as you guys, but where to find that? You don't have more classmates that could come, do you?"

"No, not exactly, but I do have an idea."

Another student, Fritz, spoke up. "I already told you. It's a bad idea. Don't bother Mr. Lars with it."

Lars raised a palm to forestall the objection. "Let him talk. I thought *you guys* were a bad idea, but look how wrong I was."

"Well, he might be right." Tatten hunched into himself. "It might be a bad idea. But it *is* an idea. I know where we can get another twenty students. They could do this work."

Fritz shot Tatten a glare. "Tell him the rest—"

The outer door banged open. Velde slunk inside, and his lips curled beneath slitted eyelids. Benny still had his collar bunched in one fist, but Velde shook him off. "Let me go, you jerk. Just wait till tomorrow. You're going to be in a world of trouble."

Jumping down from the table, Lars dusted the sawdust from his seat. "Why would he be in trouble, Velde?"

"For jerking me out of my bed like this, that's why."

"Oh, I doubt anyone will find fault with an employee working late hours, trying to recover from another disaster. One caused by you and your people. I'm sure, had you realized the seriousness of the situation, you would have jumped at the chance to come in and help, right?"

Velde didn't answer.

Lars waved him over. "Come see what we've found, would you? You need to understand what sloppy engineering is doing to these guys out here. It's got to stop, or we're not going to make it."

MORNINGS WERE TOUGH, but Monday mornings were the worst.

At least Monday-morning *hangovers* were the worst. Weeknights —well, to be honest, weekdays too—Leif tended to drink only enough to banish the loneliness. The pain. During the week, he had to maintain at least a minimal level of focus. Had to do his work.

On weekends, there were no such compunctions. What happened to Young Bob, and his own failure to find Diana, to find out where she'd taken the kids, left him with nothing but an earnest desire to make the world go away.

So, again this weekend, he drank in earnest, carousing with his childhood buddies at the local tavern, scouting for some girl to provide companionship, something to fill the void in his heart.

Some had been willing. None had filled that void. The experiences left him ashamed and even more sad and lonely. His friends and even Diana seemed energized by a playful little tryst, cheered by the thrill of the chase.

So why did it leave *him* so depressed? So empty?

He gave up on sleep and padded downstairs to plop into his office chair and sat, head in one hand and the fingers of the other jittering on his desk. No longer having a family, he'd moved his office into the well-lit family room.

Sitting at his workstation, chin on palm, he stared out the picture window into the predawn gloom. Fat flakes streaked sideways in the wind, lit by his candle. But then headlights emerged from the curtaining snow—Maurice's jeep bumping into the driveway.

Leif met the big man at the kitchen entryway. "Hey. What brings you to town?"

Maurice rubbed his hands together, blowing on them for warmth, melting the frost on his whiskers.

"You look cold. Let me get you a toddy to warm your bones." Leif reached for the whiskey bottle conveniently on the breakfast island.

"No, lad." Maurice's upraised hand interrupted him midstride. "And I wish you'd stop nippin' like you been. Gonna lead you to a bad end."

"Coffee, then?"

"Tea, if you got it, thanks. Came to let you know 'bout a development at South Crescent."

"Oh?" Leif lifted the kettle from the woodstove, sloshing to make sure water was in it, then poured it steaming over a tea ball.

"I think we know what ole Junior was up to, why he was tryin' to drive us off that there ridgeline." Maurice accepted the hot cup, sighing as he slurped. "Give ya three guesses. You guess right, you get my allotment of jerky."

Jerky? Better make this good, but the answer was simple. "Smuggling." Of course, that was it. What else made sense? Leif clenched his fists, just as he did anytime Junior's name was mentioned. It'd been all he could do to restrain himself from taking action before now. Make Junior pay. Only respect for Maurice held Leif back. A volcano built deep inside, and he wanted to erupt all that ire on Junior.

"Ding, got 'er in one, but you only get half a point unless you can tell me *what* that ole boy was smugglin'."

This was the question. He settled on the most likely, the most lucrative he could think of. "Untaxed liquor or tobacco or both."

The Committee didn't discourage these vices. In fact, they rewarded good behavior with extra allotments of both. Such contraband was profitable to smugglers because of the system by which the Committee dispensed them. According to the government's fat-happy-and-dumb strategy to keep the population from unrest, every stakeholder received a liberal allowance of liquor, at least liberal for one consuming it in moderation.

For people who preferred their libations in more generous measures, there was a problem. To use part of one's cash earnings to purchase additional liquor was highly expensive. The Committee discouraged overconsumption, yet profited handsomely by it through exorbitant taxes. Hence, the market for smuggled liquor.

Maurice finished his tea. "There may be some of that indeed, lad, but no. That isn't the main of it. Try again."

Leif grunted. "I don't know. What?"

"People. To be specific, Northerners."

Leif twigged. "They bring them down the river from the border." He screwed up his expression, brow furrowed. "But it's frozen solid. I could see them using it the rest of the year, but in winter?"

"Yep, in the dead of winter, to be sure. Our boys saw 'em comin' a ways off. Heard 'em too. They pulled big sleigh-like contraptions right down the river, towed with snowcats."

"Snow cats?" Like mountain lions?

Maurice guffawed, perhaps discerning the catsled image akin to a dogsled in Leif's head. "Seen some of 'em out West. They be a sort of machine with skis on front and treads on back. Anyway, the whole lot of 'em unloaded right there in South Crescent and walked as easy as you please up to that big ole metal buildin'."

Leif smacked his fist into his palm. "We got 'em. Come on. Let's get German. He needs to call out the Bureau of Peace." He started toward the door. "Nail him right now while he's stuck with the evidence."

Maurice stopped him with a hand to the chest. "Whoa there,

laddie. Take it easy. They already loaded outa there last night. In and out, all the same day. The only evidence you're gonna find is footprints, and last time I checked, a man can't be hung for that."

"That fast?" Leif slumped. "How're we going to nail that jerk if the illegals are there and gone before we can call in the law?"

Maurice's teeth flashed in a feral grin. "Let me finish the tale. You'll see for yourself."

LARS ARRIVED extra early this morning. Velde would make his play, catching Dad's ear first thing to sway him once again.

This time, Lars would be doing the preempting.

As usual, Dad was in his office and working well before sunrise. Everything normal. Lars filled him in on the previous evening's events. Instead of laying out his plan and browbeating Dad into agreeing to it, as Leif would, Lars stated the facts, ending with a simple question. "How do we get Velde and his people to understand the cost of their sloppiness? How do we create natural consequences for this?"

All night, worrying over his approach kept Lars from sleep. In the wee hours of the morning, he'd flashed back to similar moments in his training. When he made dumb mistakes, as he often did, Dad ordered him to work after-hours, correcting those mistakes—in other words, making restoration. Could he prompt Dad's memories of those times, sway him into applying the same logic now?

"Best way a man can understand the impact of his mistakes is to make him clean them up himself, on his own time." Dad said what he'd told Lars so many times. Thank Creator God.

Velde rushed into the office an hour earlier than he had ever appeared before and stopped cold. His eyes went wide, and his steps faltered at finding Lars already there, enjoying a coffee with Dad, the drawings in question laid out.

"Oh, hey, Velde." Lars beckoned him in. "Glad you're here. Dad and I were talking about last night. Grab a coffee and take a seat, will you?"

The jerk looked daggers at Lars but greeted Dad with his usual obsequiousness. Velde accepted the offered coffee, his sneer concealed behind Dad's turned back.

Dad leaned forward on both elbows. "We've got a real mess on our hands. How are we going to fix all this, Velde?"

Velde cleared his throat. "Well, it's not all that bad. Only a few parts to be remade. The rest are only recuts. No big deal, really."

"But, Velde," Lars cut in, "we're already behind schedule and short manpower. How will we do all that?"

Seeming to think, Velde looked up. An obvious pretense. "I suppose the guys could work a few extra hours after their normal shift, doing the remakes."

The chair springs creaked as Dad rocked back, posture relaxing, a smile spreading across his face. "Excellent idea, Velde. I knew your heart was in the right place. Besides yourself, how many of your draftsmen do we need to have that done?"

"Me? No, I meant the shop guys!"

Lars suppressed a grin at Velde's priceless shock. He should feel guilty for enjoying this, but the man was such a weasel.

Dad scowled. "You wouldn't ask another man to clean up your mess, would you?"

Face reddening, radiating hot resentment, Velde set his mouth in a tight line.

"Good. Figure out the number of guys you'll need. Start at five p.m. For sure, use Hector and that girl he always hangs with—what's her name? They were part of that table fiasco. You pick the rest. Maybe rotate all of your people. It'll do them good to get some hands-on training. Too many of them don't understand the nuts and bolts of this work."

It was a start. But would it be enough?

CHAPTER 56

At a light scratching on the door, Reuel looked up from his reading. "Come, my child. Enter." A tousled head of bright-red hair peeked around the door. "Ah, Tuesday. It's safe. I am decent."

The teen elbowed in, carrying a tray.

Reuel lifted the serving bowl's lid and sighed. "Didn't you tell Butterman I was well enough to eat something aside from chicken soup? It is wonderful, to be sure, but after all these many days, I'd like a bit of change."

Her fists went to her bony hips. "You're like to get bread pudding if you don't watch out."

He made a face.

"Then eat your chicken soup."

"Tell that woman I want red meat for my next meal."

"I'll try to get you eggs, and you'll thank me if I can do even that much. You're still weak, sir. You must build strength."

Reuel grumbled.

"What was that, sir? I need to hear your words so I may accurately repeat them to the missus."

Reuel scowled. "Tell the old battlewagon thank you. No. Strike that. I'm irritable from being bedbound. Tell her how much I appreciate her kindness and her fine food. And thank you, Tuesday, for the marvelous care you have shown me. I do appreciate it."

"You can tell her yourself once we have you up and walking again."

"I have been up and walking, twice about the room this morning."

She stomped a bare foot. "Now, sir. You know you're not to do that unless I'm here to help you. What if you fell and hit your head again?"

Reuel fingered the healing scab at his right temple, lips drawn in a petulant frown. But he needn't argue with the girl.

A voice boomed from the doorway. "My, but Mum's soup is putting color back in your cheeks faster than I would've thought possible." Butterman squeezed his substantial bulk into the room and patted Reuel's leg. "I shall tell her she's cured yet another of the infirm with her magic broth."

Tuesday bowed to Butterman, dipped a curtsy in Reuel's direction, and scampered from the room.

"She thinks she'll be reprimanded for dallying in your chambers, old friend."

"You would never. She has been a great help to me, a balm for my soul. You know she spent her off-hours here, reading to me to brighten my spirits, do you not? What a gem she is, so bright."

The fat man chuffed an overdramatic sigh. "Yes, too bright to be a scullery wench, but sad as it is, that's the lot life has dealt her. I've educated her to the limit of my own poor learning, but have no better life to offer." Butterman narrowed his eyes, failing to hide their twinkle. "Now if some fine fellow were to take her in, further her education? Who knows what she might become?" He shook his head. "But there are so few with the heart to make such an investment, even fewer with the compassion to help."

"Don't you try to shame me, you old codger. I would make a place for that child, in a heartbeat, if not for the current danger. As you should well know. But the path ahead is not for such a one as she. Who'd want to share such a future?"

Tuesday's muffled voice interrupted from outside the not-quite-closed door. "Oh, but I would!"

Butterman reached around the jamb and hauled the squirming redhead into the room by an elbow. "What have I told you about eavesdropping?"

She wriggled free, then stood, gaze on the floor. "I didn't mean to, sir. I just realized I forgot my tray. I was coming back to get it and couldn't help hearing your words through the door." She raised her head enough to peer at Reuel through lowered bangs. "You'd take in such as me?"

"Oh, my dear girl. Of course, I would, in other circumstances. But the future holds only pain and trouble for me and those who associate with me. I would not wish that upon you. I care too much about you to do such a cruel thing."

A tear crept from the corner of her eye. "You care for me? Really?"

He reached a crooked finger and wiped the tear from her chin. "I do, my sweet child. But that changes nothing. The danger."

"I don't care about that. I'd slay dragons with you." At his wince, she insisted, "I would! Just never stop calling me your sweet child."

"I do believe you would." He gave her a sad smile. "But to selfishly take you into peril would be unfair. You wouldn't thank me for it."

Butterman cleared his throat. "I remember a time, when I was but a young lad not much older than this girl here. A certain someone I looked up to then told me it was my right to choose my path, to do what I felt Creator God leading me to do, danger or no. Doesn't this girl have the same right?"

Reuel gawked. "But that . . . How can you? Oh, that is fighting dirty!"

Butterman smiled. "So do you agree Tuesday should have some say in what danger she is and isn't willing to face?"

"In theory, yes. In practice, I, well, I . . . "

Tuesday walked to his side. "If there were no danger, would you have me as your child?"

"In an instant, I would."

She beamed through wet lashes and took his hand, kissed it, and turned to go. "Tonight, we can finish that book together, the one about that boy sold into slavery. I like him. I'll be back when my work is finished." She looked over her shoulder as she left the room, eyes bright. "Daddy."

IN HIS OFFICE, Maripol battled a mountain of data for a lead, any lead, to hint at the fugitives' location.

There came a knock on the door. A temple servant stood in the hall. "The bishop's office would like a word with you."

"I'd asked to be notified as soon as he arrived, but I've heard no word. How long has he been on site?"

The servant stood, still and wordless.

"Okay, then. By all means, take me to him."

At the bishop's drawing room door, Maripol marched in, brisk boot steps silent in padded carpet. Prosecutor Lind sat at the carved desk, the bishop not in evidence. Maripol swallowed, forcing down a bitter lump. Not the bishop. "Sir," Maripol began, "I have grave concerns about tomorrow's spectacle. All of our troopers are in the field searching for the fugitives. We have little strength left. Few to guard against any civil disturbance. The local Bureau men are less than useless, as you well know."

With more force than was necessary, Lind dropped a heavy pen onto the blotter. "I am well aware as to the posture of my forces."

Maripol moved back a step, then forward again. If only the bishop had been in residence, but this was a serious oversight. He'd not allow this bureaucrat to ignore it. "Then you know we are unprepared for any problems, should they arise? I recommend either recalling some of our troops from the field or postponing the trial."

Lind reclaimed the pen and perused a document without a glance his way. "I've heard your concerns and taken them under advisement. What of your assignment? What information have you extracted from the population?"

Heard his concerns? Taken them under advisement? He almost

attempted another foray, but a sharp look from those cold glittering eyes stopped the words. Apparently, there was no interest in his opinion. He cleared his throat. "I assume you've seen my reports?"

"Of course. They are disappointing. I hoped you had gotten actionable information since then?"

"Nothing new, sir."

Those wrinkled lips twisted, leaving no doubt what Lind thought of his performance. "Ah, well. Stein will turn something up. In the meantime, I want all the prisoners ready for the trial tomorrow."

"All of them? Only Jock is to stand. You granted Clara immunity for her testimony."

The Prosecutor chopped the air. "Testimony which has led to no arrests. No scrolls. I have it in mind to ratchet up the pressure on Jock. Perhaps he would see his own neck in a noose, but his wife, his children? That is a price he won't pay. If he is hiding anything, we'll see if he is willing to allow them to die for his secrets."

Maripol goggled. "But, sir, you know as well as I do, no man could have withstood the questioning he underwent. We've extracted all he has to offer. Why, the drugs alone would have seen to that, not to mention the . . . other methods we employed. He has no more secrets."

The man inspected a cuff, flicking a speck of dust with a fingernail. "This is not about breaking the man—or not exclusively. This is about teaching lessons. The people of this province have been troublesome to me, headstrong and rebellious. They need discipline, a reminder of who is master and who is servant. They need to remember fear."

Not allowing it to show, Maripol squirmed inwardly. Was this man so out of touch? "Um, they may not stand by to watch children being harmed, sir."

"They have no choice but to obey, swiftly and completely. If they have any inclination otherwise, they are indeed due for a harsh lesson, one I will provide. Am I clear?"

Heart now pounding, jaw grinding, Maripol took an instant to calm himself before answering. "Sir, I don't believe—"

"Am I quite clear, Field Agent?" Lind stood, hands planted on desk, his dry aloofness having evaporated. It seemed someone—*something*—else was looking at Maripol from deep within those cold black eyes. Something hungry.

He gulped. "Yes, sir. As you say, sir." He spun and retreated.

As his heels clicked a cadence, the echoes rolling down the gloomy concrete corridors, the memory of his arduous service to the Order played through his mind.

For the first time in all those years, an inkling of regret twinged. Maybe, just maybe, he'd have been better off as a professor of literature as, upon his entry into the academy, he'd intended.

Along with that regret came something else. Something like a premonition, a sense he might have even more reason to wish he'd chosen another course, to wish so much more fervently in the days to come.

Something was in the air, an undercurrent, a vague feeling that a greater danger lurked below the surface.

Then he scoffed. What danger could there be to him? To the Eye?

They were the pinnacle predators anywhere they went. What could there be, anywhere in the world, to cause them fear?

And yet . . .

CHAPTER 57

Reuel lay upon his bed, floating in a hazy half sleep, his partially open eyes focused on the leaden clouds outside the window. They looked much as he felt. "Enter, child," he wheezed, sleep-laden voice still scratchy. He sat up and fluffed a pillow behind his back.

But Butterman, not Tuesday, elbowed a breakfast tray into his room. "Good morning, Professor. How is the proud father this morning?"

Reuel gave the innkeeper a dark look. "Don't you pile on. That fool girl was calling me Father this and Daddy that all night. I'm not certain if she is serious or just likes teasing me."

"Oh, she's serious. She's been telling everyone who will listen all about her new father, what a wonderful man he is. Of course, she's just met you, so she can be excused for her misapprehensions." Butterman chortled, running down when Reuel didn't join in. He set the tray up at Reuel's bedside. "You like your tea black and hot, no? And voilà! Eggs over easy! Tuesday insisted you be given these for breakfast. She cooked them herself."

Bliss passed over Reuel's soul. He dipped the corner of his toast into the golden-yellow yolk and waved the sop under his nose, breathing the bouquet as one would a fine wine. Taking a delicate bite, he thought for a moment he might swoon, his eyes rolling back in his head. "Heaven! Now if she can only finagle that beef for my supper."

Butterman had remained where he stood, obviously enjoying Reuel's appreciation. But now, he fidgeted.

Reuel swallowed, then sipped his tea. "What's wrong? If you have things to do, feel free. Just leave me here to partake of this bounty. I assure you I can eat it without assistance."

Now Butterman studied his fidgeting hands. "It's not that. A big announcement was posted in the town square this morning. I thought you should hear about it from me first."

Reuel dipped another strip of toast into the yolk and spooned the golden nectar to his waiting tongue. "What sort of announcement?"

The big innkeeper strode to the window, not meeting Reuel's gaze. "A trial and execution. Of captured heretics. They are making a great spectacle, even the bishop is attending."

Reuel dropped the toast on his plate, then pushed the tray aside. "No. Dear God, please, no. Have they released the prisoners' names?"

"No, and none of my contacts have further information. The local Bureau men aren't involved, just the Order men working out of the temple. They're not the talkative sort. The spectacle will be held in the square this afternoon. Guessing they're doing this on a Saturday to get the biggest crowd, it being a market day."

Reuel pulled back his covers and swung his legs off the bed. He wobbled on his feet.

"Whoa, my friend." Butterman caught his arm. "Where are you going?"

"To the square, of course." Reuel shook him off. "I must see what has happened. We must do what we can to rescue them."

"Now hold on. Hold on. It's *the Order* has them. There's no hope of saving them. Besides, you're in no condition to walk to the square. Mum just nursed you back from death's door. She'll scalp me if I let you catch it all over again, out there in the weather."

Reuel tottered, the room spinning before Butterman eased him back onto the bed. Reuel put a hand to his forehead. "I have to go.

Those are my men, people who trusted me to bring them home safely. I have betrayed their trust."

He covered his face with both hands and groaned. There were no words.

"My friend, it's not safe for you to do this. I'll have a trusted man observe and report to you. You'll learn all there is to know without taking risks."

"I must be there, must see their faces." Reuel raised a bony finger. "If I have to sneak out of that window, mark my words, I will not dishonor their sacrifice, hiding to protect myself." His lips trembled. "I will be there."

Butterman scowled at the ceiling. "You're going to force me to go against my better judgment once again, aren't you? Well, I have a wheelchair somewhere in storage. If I take you to the square myself, do you agree to stay bundled up in that chair? Do you agree to do as I say, do nothing crazy?"

Reuel unclenched his jaw. "Of course. Thank you, old friend. If only something could be done for my boys."

"If there were, I'd be doing it. Let me go prepare." Butterman paused at the door. "I have your word of honor?"

"Word of honor. I will be here waiting for you, just do not be overlong. I must see all."

CHAPTER 58

The crowd had grown to several thousand by noon. Butterman rattled Reuel along in an old wheelchair, really little more than a wooden straight chair to which someone had added two cart wheels. His passenger sat cocooned against the gray blustery day in layers of thick quilts, a borrowed wool stocking hat on his head. Unable to see from the rear of the crowd, Butterman had allowed himself to be convinced, against his better judgment, to push through to the rope barricade, thirty feet or so from the elevated platform.

A dozen dignitaries, all dressed in foppish finery, sat on stage, sipping wine and picking dainties from silver trays. They might as well be on hand for a theater performance, not an execution. He stilled himself, reading the mood. These folks were his people. He'd lived among them his entire life, was one of them.

And, in this assemblage, vibrated an undercurrent, an unquiet discontent, that tickled his small hairs. The contrast between the display of privilege on stage and the worn, patched clothing of the commoners, often inadequate for the piercing winter cold, spoke of a shocking lack of awareness. Given the level of disillusionment long fermented in the back alleys, what a mistake that was. If he were one of those dignitaries, he'd be double-checking his personal protective teams when it came time to carriage back to those hilltop mansions.

The temple door opened, and a squad of armed men in black robes marched out. They formed a double line facing outward, creating a corridor to center stage. A man in fine black robes stepped out, the fabric shimmering in the breeze. He was exceedingly handsome, his hair and skin, even his eyes all of warm golden tones.

A shiver started at Butterman's core, radiating outward through his ample flesh, shaking his body like a dog shakes a rabbit. His knees trembled, and he fought an urge to run away. Even as he was taken with this fugue, as if from some great distance, a vibration came beneath his hands, the handles of the wheelchair jerking, the result of Reuel's own shudders, the old man's lips twisted in revulsion.

He bent to Reuel's ear. "What was that?"

A shadow crossed the professor's face. "That is the bishop. Stay well clear of that . . . man, but I think you have already sensed this."

Butterman grunted. "I'll be needing no encouragement on that account."

He stood, focus again on the stage where another man was emerging from the temple bowels. He wore ordinary black robes, the opposite of the bishop in every way. Where the bishop was tall and glamorous, this man was short and plain. Where the bishop drew every eye, this man seemed to melt into the shadows. If he hadn't followed the bishop's wake, his arrival may well have gone unnoticed.

About to ask Reuel who the new entrant was, Butterman gasped. Framed in the door stood a man he had known for years, one of Simon's crew, if only barely recognizable in his current battered state.

Jock's arms and legs were clamped in heavy black irons. His face was bruised and badly swollen, his body naked and wounded, his skin and hair matted with filth and dried blood. Two men in masks, dressed in tight-fitting unmarked black uniforms, dragged him to the stage's front left corner and attached his leg irons to a steel ring. They dropped him there, his chains rattling a metallic glissando as he fell.

The crowd muttered.

A uniformed bailiff strode onto the stage and faced the crowd. "Quiet! You will be quiet now. We call this special court to order to hear charges of heresy and conspiracy against the Republic. These charges have been brought against Stakeholder Jock, who is present today. All rise."

The dignitaries rose. A robed and wigged judge walked to the center table and sat. The bailiff called out, "You may be seated. This court is in session, the Honorable Judge Pilsbrock presiding."

Turning to peer up at him, Reuel asked, "Why only this one man? Where are my boys?"

Butterman could only shrug. "Maybe the Bill of Writ will tell us something?"

The judge nodded toward the line of men at the bishop's table. "You may present your case."

A black-robed man with a pinched face and narrowly set eyes carried a folder to the lectern.

Reuel put a hand to his mouth. "Lind, the Bloody Prosecutor."

Aides now passed out printed handbills.

Butterman grabbed two and handed Reuel one while he studied his own. He leaned into Reuel's ear. "Bill of Writ says nothing of your boys, only lists Jock, Clara, et al. Seems your people are still on the loose?"

"On behalf of the Temple," Lind had begun speaking, "we hereby request sentence be carried out with utmost haste on this heretic and insurrectionist. He has admitted to his many and heinous crimes as are set forth in his signed confession."

An underling distributed a manuscript, first to the judge, then copies to the assembled dignitaries.

The judge inspected the document, then held it up to Jock. "Is this your signed confession? Do you acknowledge the crimes set forth in this document?"

Jock blinked dumbly, his eyes searching but seemingly unable to focus.

The prosecutor raised a bony finger. "If I may, Your Honor?" At a wave from the judge, he walked to Jock, the paper in his hand. "Is this your sworn confession? Did you testify to this with your own lips and sign this with your own hand?"

Jock's face screwed up, and he squinted. He began to speak, choked, then tried again. His raspy voice barely carried to where Butterman stood, feet away. "My confession. You promised you wouldn't hurt the children. Yes, I remember."

The prosecutor stood. "You have heard the criminal confirm this is his sworn confession. It is the desire of the Temple that sentence be carried out immediately, with great prejudice. Enemies of the Order and of the Republic must know there are consequences for such behavior." He bowed. "Your Honor, we rest our case."

The judge raised his gavel and clacked it on the bench once. "Pursuant to his sworn testimony, the court finds the prisoner Jock, guilty of multiple capital crimes against the Eternal and against the State. We hereby—"

The bishop stood, regal hand held in the air. All murmurings ceased. "Your Honor, pardon. As the prosecutor has shown, this is indeed a dangerous man, one who has demonstrated vile intentions. Had he and his accomplices made good on their plot, many innocent lives would have been destroyed. This is true, yet the Eternal is as merciful as He is just. I believe this man can be rehabilitated, as can any child of the Eternal, if they would only turn to Him and submit to His commands. I would like to offer this man clemency and the chance to repent, to restore his soul in the eyes of the Eternal. He need but reveal the whereabouts of his co-revolutionaries, reveal their location and plans, and we would move that his death sentence be commuted to reeducation. He may yet become whole in the loving arms of the Eternal Brothers."

During the bishop's speech, Jock gaped, the beginnings of hope dawning in his eyes. With the last, he collapsed, sobbing, forehead to the ground. "I told you—I told you everything. I know nothing more! Please! Mercy, I beg you."

Reuel said something that couldn't be heard above the rising murmurs. When Butterman crouched closer, Reuel was repeating to himself, over and over, voice trembling. "Oh, praise Creator God. They've not yet found my boys! Thank You, thank You . . . "

On stage, the bishop was shaking his head, his face a study in compassion. "Oh, poor sinner. Even yet, you refuse to let go of the evil which has gripped your soul." He sat and twitched a finger toward Lind, who signaled the masked men.

The temple door opened once more, and Clara emerged, flanked by two more guards. Seeing Jock, she gasped and planted her feet, struggling to turn about. The guards carried her bodily along, her feet kicking ineffectually, one of her pumps dragged off in the effort.

The guards stood her before Jock, holding her upright as she tried to shake free.

Behind her, Lind spoke, and she stilled. "Jock, you involved your wife in your schemes. If not for yourself, then repent for the sake of your precious wife, who is guilty of the same crimes, her guilt proven by your confession. Do this for her. Save her. All you need do is tell us where your accomplices are. Tell us the nature of their plans before they hurt more innocent people."

Wide-eyed and weeping, Jock locked gaze on Clara. He crawled forward, chains rattling until they went taut, bringing him up short. He knelt, hands clasped in appeal, head bowed to the bishop. "Please spare her. Take me. It was all my fault!"

She began struggling in her captors' hands, then shrieked, "Wait! You promised. I was the one who came to *you*, who told you of the heretics. I am friend to the Eternal. I'm loyal! It's not fair!"

The prosecutor sighed. "Can both of you be so unrepentant? The poison of your cultist beliefs runs deeper than I feared. Oh, Jock. I want so badly to help you. If only you would help yourself, give over this misplaced loyalty, your attachment to that coven of witches." He stood tall, arm raised, finger pointed heavenward. "I will give you one final chance before your eternal judgment." Lind's voice dropped, and the crowd edged closer. "Where are your friends?"

Jock remained on the ground, his head shaking from side to side as if to deny this could be happening.

Tsking, Lind turned his back on Jock and strode to the head table where he picked up a folder. He raised it for the crowd to see. "Jock, you not only included your wife in your rebellion against the Eternal but also poisoned the minds of your three children. Our laws are clear. *All* heretics are to be eliminated, no matter their age. I had hoped to see some sign of remorse. If not in you, Jock, then at least in your wife. But in both of you, I see only rank rebellion, hate for the Eternal. Perhaps I have been too softhearted, too easily swayed by my love for the little ones of the world. If you are so devout in your idolatrous and superstitious beliefs, I must reconsider your three little children. I fear they may be so corrupted as to be as irredeemable as the two of you."

Clara gave a scream, her words unintelligible.

Three children were hustled out of the temple door, manhandled toward the front of the stage. Lind was speaking. But the crowd's swelling roar drowned him out.

The prosecutor may have misread the rising emotion, thinking it to be anger at the so-called heretics, the righteous anger of the fervently devout. But Butterman's hair stood on end. These cries were a crowd in passionate dissent, ready to riot.

Many supposed him to be a big dumb innkeeper, forgetful and forgettable. This misreading served him well as he gathered information for the Seekers. While others overlooked him, he missed nothing.

Of the things he noticed today, one remained front of mind. During the trial, numerous men, all of sour countenance, elbowed to the front of the crowd. Many were associated with the Sons of Freedom.

This group had grown in recent years, their missives against the oppressive Order finding sympathetic ear among the working poor, especially in the past months, in direct proportion to midnight raids inflicted upon the population.

Their rhetoric had taken a revolutionary and violent tack. When the first short clubs began appearing from coat sleeves, he leaned to Reuel's ear. "Hold on. We need to get clear of here—quickly."

He wheeled the chair too late. Shouts erupted, mixed with the cracks of clubs meeting batons, with the sickening sound of truncheon encountering skull. The mass of people became an eddy current, some rushing into the melee, others attempting to flee, many falling to be trampled underfoot. Butterman spun and pulled the chair backward through the smothering throng, using his ample backside to bull his way through, his shoulders hunched over Reuel, elbows akimbo, to protect the old man from errant blows.

Then the weight pressing against his rear disappeared, and he broke into the clear, nearly toppling backward with the release. He turned to orient himself. Just to the right was a clear path. In a lumbering charge, he bowled the wheelchair through the streets. He ducked into a side alley, slowing as his eyes adjusted to the gloom, then ran. He weaved the wheelchair around stacks of rotting refuse, moving away from the square. The shouts of combat receded.

When he'd cleared the riot, he'd been on the square's side opposite his establishment. He now circumnavigated the temple grounds. He stumbled, legs weakening, down a final side street. His breath came in hoarse, heaving gasps as he unlocked the gate to the inn's rear courtyard.

Once inside, he braced against the white picket fence, ragged breath tearing his throat but not satisfying his lungs. His heart pounded in his temples. He bent over and retched before sliding to the ground, forehead on knees. His skin was prickly and his head spun, his vision swimming. He shut his eyes tight against a world so unbearably bright, painful to look upon.

A young voice wavered as if from far off. "Sir, sir? Are you okay?"

A high-pitched sound grated his ears. He opened his eyes, searching for the speaker, only to have his field of vision contract into a decreasingly small tunnel, and then to a point, before all became black.

Butterman jerked his head. Something wet his face. Then he started awake and would have believed he was rousing from a restful sleep in his feather bed, if not for the gray sky overhead. And the gravelly ground biting into his buttocks.

Where was he?

Tuesday bent over him, patting his forehead with a damp cloth. "Sir?"

He sat up, reassembling the day's events. "I overdid it. That's all, girl. I'm fine." Reuel was watching him from the wheelchair, his wrinkled face shadowed. Butterman laughed. "Look at the two of us. Not those same boys who played cat and mouse with the gendarmes, are we?"

Reuel smiled. "I, for one, am still that same young man on the inside. My body, however, seems determined to impose upon me the unwanted limitations of age. You had best remember *your* age before attempting another marathon of this sort. Let us step aside and allow the young men to take their place, performing the strenuous tasks of our trade, shall we? We'll do our part, supplying them with wisdom and experience, but from a safer vantage point. Perhaps a nice comfortable seat by the fire. What say you?"

Butterman pushed himself up, levering against the fence. His knees wobbled. Every pound of excess weight bore down on his faltering limbs, conspiring with gravity to pull him back to the ground. "I must lose a few pounds," he muttered as he reached for the chair's handles.

"Oh, sir. Let me get that." Tuesday intercepted.

Reuel had been watching Butterman, had apparently noticed how tentative his steps had been. "My girl, why don't you help our friend inside? I am fine here, in this chair. You can come back for me, after."

The girl came to his side and took his arm, draping it over her shoulders. Together, they lurched into the inn.

REUEL REMAINED IN THE COURTYARD, shivering in the damp breeze. He pulled the shawl tight around himself. As Butterman left, that slip of a girl somehow supporting his limping weight, Reuel passed a hand over his forehead.

Oh, Creator God, how did that big man get so old, so quickly? How did I?

So many plans yet unfulfilled. So many dreams still nothing but the hot wind of an old man's ramblings.

An image hovered foremost in his mind, one he'd been unable to erase since the day of Butterman's letter. An image of his young wards, out there in the snow, hunted by Order wolves. And nothing he could do to help. With all the hopes and dreams of humankind riding on their survival.

Is it already too late for them? For all of us?

CHAPTER 59

Maripol exited the temple behind the bishop who took center seat at the big table, Maripol standing behind, studying the crowd as the preliminaries were read. What he saw—or more importantly, what he felt and heard—sent a tickle up his spine. An undercurrent thrummed in this crowd today.

The bishop leaned toward him. "Who is that man in the wheelchair, front row, next to the fat one? I should know him but cannot place the face. Is he local?"

Maripol scanned faces, then located the person indicated. "Professor Reuel, currently teaching at our training institute in Two Rivers. We surveilled him for some time last fall, in connection with that missing priest, Curtis."

"Why would he be here, in the midst of all this? Strange."

"I'll make inquiries, sir."

During the proceedings, Maripol studied the crowd, intent. What was it, in particular, that had him so on edge? The crowd's ugly tone was to be expected. Was it the many rough men in attendance? Again, this was to be expected. Longshoremen and fishermen weren't the collar-and-tie variety.

As the prosecutor baited Jock with threats toward his wife, what

Maripol had been picking up clarified. A subtle change came, a filtering, a percolation in the crowd's composition.

Women and children had drifted toward the rear while men moved to the front. Many of these were surly, glowering with undisguised ill-intent.

When it became clear the prosecutor was about to introduce the children, using them as pawns in his ill-considered play, Maripol signaled his remaining troopers to heightened alert. But he was too late.

Releasing their rage, men charged the stage, clubs and pipes appearing as if by magic. They swept across the raised platform, weapons swinging, bowling over the delegation of elites as they closed on the bishop, their primary target.

Maripol barked orders to his troopers to create a cordon around the man, to rush him into the shelter of the temple. The troopers didn't respond, too busy defending themselves.

He fought toward the bishop amid the melee. Seemingly unaware of the danger or unconcerned, the bishop showed no hint of fear, instead exhibiting offended anger, wrath, boredom, and somehow, overlaid over all was a sort of hunger, of glee in the violent exercise.

When rushed by one club-wielding man, the bishop flicked out a hand as if swatting a fly. The man reeled away, clutching the side of his neck, which was now spurting blood. The bishop's fist encircled the throat of another, then tossed him away, his body cartwheeling to land amongst the combatants' churning feet. He lay there, writhing, struggling to breathe through a ruined larynx. The bishop flowed languidly among the attackers, and bodies flew like leaves before the wind, sheaves before the scythe.

The entire episode, so unexpectedly begun, was even more suddenly over. The square had emptied, the last fleeing people disappearing around distant street corners. Of the attackers, there remained only scattered piles of broken bodies and moaning men.

The bishop cast about, looking for more victims, teeth bared and eyes hot. With no more opponents to be found, he stomped the face of one lying nearby, silencing his cries with a sickening wet crunch.

He then drew himself up, adjusted his blood-spattered robes, and strode into the temple. "Maripol! With me. We have a full night of activities to arrange."

Once he was certain Butterman wasn't in danger, but only winded from the chase, Professor Reuel had gone to his room. The excitement and his weakened condition left him bone-weary, aching in every joint, enervated, barely able to swing his legs onto the bed.

He woke to dim twilight painting his dust-encaked windows. A light knock tapped at his door and must've wakened him. "Enter."

The door swung open, and Tuesday backed in, followed by a tray. "I thought you'd like tea."

"Oh, thank you, my dear. How is Butterman?"

"He has regained his strength, though it took a platter of pastries to do so." She set the tray on the bedside table and poured. "It was all I could do to snatch one for you. I almost feared he'd gnaw my arm off. He had a messenger, asked that I check to see if you were awake. I'll go let him know you're available."

One pastry and half a cup of tea later, the heavy creaking of floorboards came from the hallway, the same as always presaged the big innkeeper's arrival. The man's ample bulk darkened the open doorway, and then Butterman stood at the bedside, inspecting Reuel with narrowed eyes before slumping into the straight-backed chair. "Glad to see you looking well. In truth, you look better than I feel, and you are the recuperant."

Butterman indeed looked wrung out. "Are you sure you are quite well, my friend?" Reuel asked.

"The question is, are *you*? I know you're still weak. But have you beaten the illness? Could you travel if needed?"

Reuel raised an eyebrow. "Is such a thing needful?"

Butterman's face creased. "I've had a visit, a go-between to one of my garrison contacts. A major crackdown is planned for this night. The authorities have a list of persons targeted for capture, of places to sweep during a series of midnight raids. My friend, this establishment is on that list. And though your name is not, as a stranger you'd certainly be detained. They mustn't take you to that temple dungeon of theirs. In your health, you may never come out again."

Reuel wobbled to his feet. "Is there a wagon train scheduled to depart soon?"

"They stopped incoming and outgoing traffic. They even shut down the river locks, leaving no way in or out of the area. They don't intend to let anyone escape."

Reuel turned his gaze upward toward that little window, high in the eastern wall. The one he'd so recently threatened to escape through. If only. "Is it too late to put the next phase of our plan into action? Is all ready?"

"I had anticipated the possibility things might become more interesting. I have set up a deadman's switch, so to speak. The materials are ready. Preparations are complete, final instructions distributed, and our cells standing by. I've been sending a simple code every day, holding off final implementation. The organization was told to initiate the plan at any time that message was not received. In short, I need only *not* send a message to start the process."

Butterman locked eyes with Reuel, one eyebrow raised in question. "I await only your orders."

Reuel nodded, relief escaping his lips. "Good. That is good. Let the operation begin now. If we do not survive this night, I will rest easy knowing the plan lives on."

The big man drew himself to his full height. "Oh, you *will* live to fight another day. You must. I'll be seeing to that." He put a knuckle to double chins where it sank to the first joint. "But what're we to do with you?"

"What are my options?"

Butterman sucked his teeth. "I may have an idea. I hope to hear back on that soon. Best you pack and be ready to go."

CHAPTER 60

Leif paced, stump to boulder and back, mashing a muddy path into the snow-covered forest floor.

"Give it a rest, lad," Maurice called to him in just over a whisper. "Or you'll dig a trench too deep to climb back outa."

Leif plunked onto the stump, knees bouncing. "Any movement?"

"If there were, you'd have heard already. Now relax and let this thing play out. We've done what can be done. All's left is the waitin'."

This waiting is agony. He should be part of the action. Of course, Maurice had vetoed that. The plan was already well in motion. Their one shot at Junior had been taken. They'd never get a second crack at such as him.

A man materialized next to Leif, and he jumped from his seat, nearly crying out. He'd been too deep in his glower to notice the approach.

"They're moving out," the logger reported.

Maurice dispatched a runner to the lookout nearest the road. He reappeared moments later with a thumbs-up signal. "All complete."

Leif whirled around, arms waving. "Where in Hegemony are those Bureau of Peace guys?"

He'd used all his persuasive power to convince German and then the Two Rivers Bureau chief, all mustache and growls, to agree to this plan. The Bureau declined to station men in Northwoods, potentially for weeks or months, on the chance of spotting a smuggling operation underway. They had agreed to keep a fast reaction force on call in Two Rivers, able to mobilize and race to this site within ninety minutes of German's phone call. The hope was they would arrive with an opportunity to catch the smugglers in the act.

Now, Leif and crew must keep the illegals, and Junior with them, from disappearing before the Bureau men arrived. Maurice, a gifted strategic planner and a master tactician, ran today's operation like a seasoned wartime general. But would it work? Leif's knee jittered again.

Maurice gripped Leif's shoulder. "Gonna be fine, lad. The call's been made, the Bureau's coming, and these jokers can go nowhere fast. You'll see. Come on and watch the fun."

He followed Maurice toward the road, stopping short of the military crest of the hill where they belly wriggled through the snow and under a thicket of dogwood shrubs. His passage knocked snow from the slender red stems, and it fell down his neck. Beneath him, the slush began to melt and soak through his trousers.

Below on the road, a wagon train consisted of three cars attached to a tug. A line of people snaked single file out of the trees, being directed by armed men. They boarded first one freight car and then another. Many carried liquor boxes. Aha, he'd be collecting that jerky from Maurice.

With practiced efficiency, the cars were loaded, and the rear doors closed and sealed. The armed men mounted the cabs, and the tug engine roared. The tires spun in the deep snow. The three freight cars stayed fast, unmoving.

The tug driver threw open his door and jumped to the ground, stomping to the first freighter where he exchanged heated words with the driver. He repeated the conversation at the three towed cars, even mounting each to inspect the controls. He then ran back to the tug and slammed his cab door.

The engine roared again. With the same results.

The driver reversed gear, budging the line slightly, and then rammed the lever forward, advancing the throttle to an earsplitting bellow. Snow flew from drive wheels, and the cars inched along. Their tires remained locked but were now sliding. They skidded forward, the entire train in a slow-motion descent toward the shoulder, the crown of the road too steep to resist.

The drivers in the freight cabs fought with their controls, jerking levers first one way, then another—to no avail. The inexorable drift continued until the lead cars lurched ditchward and dragged the locomotive with them. All were now off the road and leaning into the snowdrift, buried axle-deep, all progress halted.

Maurice covered his mouth, but deep guffaws broke free in nose-snorting bellows.

Leif flinched, glancing toward those cars full of armed men. Would they hear? How could they not?

Fortunately, the tug driver made several more attempts to power his rig out of the snow, the engine noise covering all others. Maurice had himself under control by the time the engine cut off. Then a deathly silence hung over the valley, the blue-black cloud of diesel smoke drifting away.

Two armed men exited the wooded trail and strode toward the wagon train. After a conference with the freight jockeys, one man sprinted off. Several minutes later, Junior himself blustered along, swearing. He stared at the tug engine, right-hand tires concealed by packed snow.

With a jerk of his head, he shouted orders to his men. They then began unloading the freight cars and herding the people back onto the wooded trail. Leif and Maurice trotted to the other side of the hill to watch. Soon, the line of porters trudged toward the big steel building, heads down and shoulders sagging. Once they were all inside, Junior snapped a padlock onto the big sliding door and locked them in.

Then came commotion. Dozens of armed uniformed men stood from where they had lain concealed in the brown waist-high grasses. Leif shouted a cheer as they latched handcuffs on Junior and his men. He slapped Maurice on the back with the ferocity of long-pent emotion. "You did it, big man. You did it!"

Junior's time troubling Leif was over. He had his revenge.

BUTTERMAN RETURNED TO THE KITCHEN, dinner service having well begun. He was still weak, his legs still threatening to betray him, so he delegated his normal tasks. His underlings knew their jobs. His input not being required, he took a seat in the kitchen, available but enjoying much-needed rest.

The staff busied about their work, but Tuesday seemed quiet. When she refused to meet his eye on her third trip past his perch, he caught her sleeve. "What is eating you, girl?"

She only shrugged, gaze fixed on the floor, mouth in a tight line, then pulled away to carry trays of meat to the dining room.

One of his boys burst through the rear entrance. Seeing Butterman, he ran over to him. "He says there's no chance. Everything's locked down tight. No one getting in or out."

Butterman muttered an oath. "Thank you. Go tell him to have another spot ready in the tunnels, a dry one, mind you. We'll be forced to hide him there if we can't get him out."

He pushed himself erect, moving stiffly into the dining room and toward the stair.

A TIGHT BAND squeezed Tuesday's heart so hard, it forced tears to pop in the corner of her eyes. What the boy had said, coupled with the conversation she'd overheard outside Reuel's door, proved the peril to Reuel. Of course, he planned to leave her behind, to abandon her. Still, she loved that grumpy old man. If only she could do something to help.

One of the chief cooks called to her. "Girl! Stop daydreamin' and go help with the milk delivery. Scat."

She scampered to the rear and through the delivery door. Outside, the old milkman stood next to his horse-drawn cart, an anachronism in his wide handmade straw hat and homespun woolen suit. He was from a colony of farmers west of town atop the hills overlooking Plumbsburg's wide river valley. There they lived lives unchanged for centuries, eschewing modern technology and conveniences, maintaining their own simple, self-sufficient if primitive lifestyle. The Bad Times barely affected them, not having become dependent on modern systems. Now, in better times, they continued in their age-old ways.

Butterman bought much of his dairy and meat from them, a black-market arrangement overlooked by the authorities. Today the milk delivery, due at noon, never arrived.

The farmer bowed. "Howdy, miss. Got your milk. Was delayed by all the ruckus earlier. Many apologies."

She curtsied. "It's no problem, but how did you get into town? I heard the roads were closed?"

He tapped his breast pocket. A yellow slip of paper peeked over the flap. "The head of the Bureau likes his cheese. Got me a pass, long as I'm out before sunset." He glanced at the reddening western sky. "So I best hurry."

Tuesday helped him lower the steel canisters from his now empty cart. He started to remount the driver's seat and take the reins when she grasped his coattail. "Stop. Please, sir, wait here one minute. Don't go!"

BUTTERMAN WAS HELPING REUEL PACK, having explained that the old man would need to hide in the smuggler's tunnels.

They'd strapped the bag shut when Reuel placed a gnarled hand on Butterman's elbow. "My old friend. What of you? When they cannot locate me, you will be at the center of their focus. What good for me to hide, only to transfer the danger from myself onto your head?"

With a careless wave, Butterman hoisted the bag onto the bed, then grasped Reuel's shoulders, holding him at arm's length. "I've weathered many a storm in this place. They'll make a great noise, but will find no rational excuse to do more than bluster. Besides, I've many secret friends among the troops. All will be well, rest assured."

Tuesday burst into the room. "I've found a way to get you out of town, Father!" She flushed and ducked her head. "I mean, Professor."

Butterman and his friend shared a glance.

Then Butterman asked, "And how is that, Tuesday? And why the long face?"

She kept her gaze downcast. "The milkman is here. He has a pass. The professor can hide in his cart and sneak out of town." She raised her face to Reuel, unable to stop the betraying tears. "I know you're planning to leave me here. It's okay. I understand, but I wanted to help."

She returned her gaze to the floor, face again concealed by a fall of red hair. "That's all."

CHAPTER 61

Leif's first stop upon returning from Junior's arrest was a visit to the sawmill.

Young Bob was still bedridden, an infection having slowed his recovery. "Don't you worry about me none, Mr. Leif. I'll be up and ready to work soon enough."

Leif choked back the tears, pretending a cough. What a travesty, the damage done to this good and faithful man. Young Bob had lost at least thirty pounds, and his nightshirt hung limp on his once robust frame. Leif gripped his shoulder. "Don't you worry. You take all the time you need to mend. Just you be sure to mend well. I want you back to one hundred percent."

He stopped short, choking again. Young Bob would never again be any such thing.

Changing the subject, Leif asked, "You still have plenty of the eggs? Enough meat?"

Old Bob gave a brusque nod. Leif had been slipping Old Bob produce from Grandpa's farm, the better to heal the wounds of both men, one of the body and the other of the heart. The old man had aged ten years since the accident, if that was possible for one already so ancient.

Leif then attempted to cheer the two with how Maurice hoodwinked the gangsters, slipping saboteurs under the unattended freight cars and jiggering the brake and steering linkages. Both men laughed, making the effort for his sake.

Leif swallowed against a hollow lump in his throat. "Are you sure I can't bring you anything? More food?"

This was all his doing. He alone bore responsibility for the evil fortune these two faced. And nothing he did now could assuage this awful leaden weight. This guilt.

Young Bob shook his head.

Old Bob answered, "Oh no, we be good, Mr. Leif. I thank you for all you done. Just you have a place for my boy. He won't have his arm back, but he can be of some help to you anyhow, right?"

Leif gaped. These two thought he was going to throw Young Bob over? "Are you kidding? Of course, I need him. I need both of you, now more than ever. It's not your strong arms that matter. It's the things you know. You're too valuable to be running the machines, anyway. I need you to lead men. To train them, keep an eye on the operation. No one knows it as well as you two, and no one loves it so well. You'll always have a place here. Both of you."

The spirits of both men visibly buoyed with the first tentative return of that warm, happy homeliness, the same as had always filled this house. But now heat rose to his cheeks. How could they have worried so? How could they think he would treat them so badly?

What kind of man did they think he was?

It was dark before he arrived home. Something stuck out of his mailbox. A special delivery envelope conveyed a phone message, relayed from German's office. Haman instructed Leif to call by land-line first thing Monday.

He smiled. The advisor had heard of Junior's arrest and wanted to congratulate him.

Leif opened the door to his empty house, footsteps echoing and belly growling. He rummaged about for something with which to make a cold meal. But he was filthy. Too filthy to touch food, hands black with muck, brow sticky with dry sweat, hair gritty. He'd clean up first.

Then he groaned. He'd forgotten to run a bath that morning.
Make that a cold meal and an even colder bath.

THE NIGHT WAS DEATHLY STILL, the normal sounds of the river city absent. So much like how, at the roar of a hunting predator, the chittering calls of forest life could go silent. Against this backdrop, the horse's hooves clip-clopped on pavement, dragging the old milk cart up the miles-long, unbroken slope, dragging Professor Reuel away from the river, away from his friends, a man helpless and hapless, no use to anyone. A failure.

The dank cold of this night, pregnant with the shoulder-hunching anticipation of bad news, well matched his heart. He'd come here to rescue Curtis and Phillip. Instead, Butterman had been forced to rescue him at great risk.

A disgusted grunt escaped. What a fraud he'd turned out to be. Too impotent to save anyone, too old to be of value, more burden than asset. A fool playing with the lives of others. Time to hang it up before any other innocents fell victim to his folly.

Like Curtis and Phillip had.

As they climbed toward the crest, his perch facing rearward offered an exceptional view of the entire river valley. On another night, he might have marveled. Now it was only one last glimpse of this place, the one where he'd once celebrated his youth and now failed his people.

Plumbsburg, visible as a field of twinkling lights, would be indistinguishable from the star field above if not for the glow coming from the temple district where the government buildings clustered in that artificial radiance. Ringing that bowl of glittering jewels were the cheerfully bright windows of the many bluff-top mansions, haughty demigods surveying their domain.

It would have been a breathtaking scene, but for the wrenching awareness of his failings. What of the storm the Order was about to unleash upon such a defenseless citizenry? And not a singular thing he could do about it.

Heart aching, he said another prayer for those innocents. He also prayed for his friend. Butterman's insistence that his influence would keep him was false bravado. But the big old oaf refused to flee. Insisted he was needed to whisk into hiding the targets of this night's raid. Had he succeeded? Were those potential victims now safe? Was Butterman?

A flash lit the night sky. A fireball mushroomed over the temple, city streets and hillsides lit as if by the midday sun, the circular shock wave still radiating from the center of the explosion, rippling destruction in its wake.

He had only a moment to marvel before his ears were boxed by an unseen blow. The intense concussion thudded on ribs, squeezed breath from lungs. A sharp pain pierced his ears, a high-pitched whine, leaving him unable to distinguish the ensuing explosions now enveloping the government district from the distant, almost toylike pops of small arms fire.

Atop the bluffs, more fiery flowers bloomed, one after another, scattering the self-satisfied lights of those splendid hilltop mansions, flinging them to the winds, never again to brighten their former abodes.

Diamond glass confetti expanded outward, glittering in the reflected yellow-orange glow of the billowing fireballs like ephemeral spores blown into the world, riding the winds of this man-made storm, to take silent seed in the fertile soil of other lands, to grow and reproduce more of their kind in the eternal, exponential dance of procreation.

Tuesday sat beside him. Her face glowed in the reflection of those distant fires.

Was that amazed horror in her expression? Or gleeful wonder?

Through the high-pitched ringing in his ears, came her exclamation. "Wow."

CHAPTER 62

His steps light, jaunty even, Leif strode down Main Street. Like some truant schoolboy, he stopped, wound up, and just for the sheer joy of it, kicked the top off a particularly inviting snowdrift. He straightened his coat and continued along the empty street toward German's office.

It wouldn't be open yet, of course. The sun had barely begun pinking the eastern sky, but Leif had been unable to roll back over, had no interest in sleep. His mind was buzzing, the blood rushing in his veins, singing in his ears.

They'd taken down that human debris, Junior. Hah. And Haman wanted to congratulate him personally? No way he was missing that. It was worth waiting out here, even in these subzero temperatures, until German arrived to open the office.

But as he approached, the office windows shone. Long rectangular pools of yellow light striped the snow-covered sidewalk. And the door was open.

Inside, German was in his leather armchair, feet on his desk, cup steaming in one hand, freshly creased newspaper in the other, fresh ink and coffee tinting the air. Leif's head began to buzz, his heart to beat more threadily. He'd been so excited he'd not bothered to brew his own morning cup.

German lowered the newspaper, eyes peering over wire rims. “Need I be concerned?”

Leif jerked his gaze from that coffee. “What?”

The cup thumped the jade-green blotter. The newspaper rustled to rest beside it. The chair springs squealed as German sat upright, the heels of his well-shined black wing tips hitting the wooden floorboards. “I said, need I be concerned for my well-being? Are you here to mug me for coffee? The way you stared at mine was more than a little disconcerting.”

Leif’s gaze again darted to that cup, then away. “No. I mean, you know I wouldn’t.” But he would like some of that coffee, and he again had to force himself to look anywhere but at it.

Sighing, German stood, shoes rapping a brisk cadence as he disappeared into the back room, then soon returned. He held out a second coffee to Leif. “I offer this to you in the name of my continued safety.”

Leif accepted and downed a quarter of the brew. It warmed his throat, his belly, and eased the tightness at his temples. “Good coffee. Really good.” Lots better than the stuff he got. “Thank you.”

Silvery brows rose. “What brings you out so early? Or is this late for you? Is this morning or the end of a long night’s carousing?”

The heat singed Leif’s cheeks. That wasn’t fair. He’d been working too hard to drink lately. Much. But German’s gentle smile showed no hint of insult. “Morning. I mean, it’s an early morning for me. Got a message that Haman wanted a call.”

Reclaiming his seat, German cradled his coffee between cupped hands. “Ah, yes. There was a message. I must say, though, I doubt you were expected to respond so, ah, promptly. But if you like, we can ring, though few start their day quite this early in Capital.”

Leif pulled a chair to the desk, and German handed him the phone. Leif punched in the memorized number. Surprisingly, after he transmitted his request to a handful of gatekeepers, the line clicked, and Haman’s smooth tones drifted through the earpiece. “Young Leif. I’m glad you returned my call.”

Knees bobbing, Leif grinned in German’s direction. Hopefully, the volume was loud enough for him to overhear. Wouldn't hurt Leif's reputation for word to get around about such a powerful man calling to congratulate him.

"I'm disappointed, Leif, baffled as to why you would let such a thing happen."

Mouth agape, Leif stumbled on the humble thank you now sticking in his throat. "Uh, happen?"

"This was a key contract. Critical to our new partnership. How could you allow some other shop to pluck it from your fingers?"

Leif moved further from German's desk, pressing the phone to the side of his head. Maybe German hadn't heard? Maybe he'd heard wrong himself? "Sir, you lost me. What?"

Now Haman's voice thundered. No way German couldn't hear this. The people sleeping across town might. "Bridger Hills. The Bridger Hills contract! Someone has stolen it. And after the investment I've already made!"

Leif had long labored on several contracts, all mansions under construction, but he'd spent nothing on the others compared to what he'd spent on this, the deal of a lifetime, the full package. Very big. Very lucrative. And the millwork, the furnishings so ornate, so exquisite, they would be the talk of the region. Every newly rich robber baron in the territory would be flocking to his door, begging him to provide the same for them.

He'd already finished the designs, even some of the production drawings. Had spent lavishly on dinners at the most expensive restaurants, tickets to the most exclusive venues.

And now Artisans had stolen the deal? The breath rushed back into his lungs and spluttered into the phone. "They can't. We have a contract—"

"*Young Leif*! A contract? Are you so naïve? How do you *enforce* a contract, pray tell?"

The coffee now burned his belly, aching there, a hot lump. "In court, I guess?"

A sigh whooshed over the line, growing distant. "Yes, and they could hire an entire brigade of lawyers, tie you up for years. That mansion will be old enough to remodel before you get a hearing. But they won't bother. Don't need to. People like them *know people*, my young barrister. They need never worry about the likes of your lawsuit because it will disappear and, if you persist, so will you."

"But—"

"No buts. Not one! All I want to hear is how you plan to repay me for the wasted investment."

This couldn't be happening. Repay Haman? Leif didn't have such money. Had never had that much in his life. How to fix this? "But, sir, there has to be a mistake. Bridger Hills is intended to be a work of art. A statement to last generations. No one else can produce this quality. They won't understand the design intentions."

"I'm not the one you need to convince. And it no longer matters. Find me my money." The line clicked, dead.

Eyes unfocused, he held the dead phone to his ear, Haman's words still echoing. Leif lowered the receiver into the cradle, then stood, and walked past a gaping German, barely noticing the man.

Outside, Leif leaned against the building, the rose-gold light of early dawn outlining his reflection in the windows across the way. He closed his eyes, breathed in and out, in, out. Again.

His rampaging heart settled into a gallop. What to do?

Haman was right about one thing. He wasn't the one Leif needed to convince. It was the owners, more specifically Eleanor, the wife of the mogul building Bridger Hills. She was in charge of this, her passion project. Her husband had abdicated the details to her, unable to trouble himself with such minutiae.

But what had happened? She'd always liked Leif. Was a fan of his designs. She wouldn't have thrown him over like this.

Whatever went wrong, he *had* to figure out how to fix it. Before it was too late.

CHAPTER 63

Traveling in his weakened state had been an ordeal, a blur of discomfort and self-rebuke. In the wake of what was already being called The Night, the government clamp-down had made travel nearly impossible. But Reuel had pushed on, resolute in his desire to be home in his own bed. Now, home was in sight.

As he walked the final yards, Tuesday grasped his right arm, steadying his steps. He cursed whoever had initiated such wholesale attacks. What needless loss of life, and to what end? Such actions would only divide the populace when they needed a united front against the oppressors. Who knew what level of suffering and death would rain upon the innocent now.

The attacks had already exacerbated the enmity the Order troops held for the citizenry, and brutality was bound to increase as conflict begat more conflict in a self-feeding cycle.

He was rocked as if by a wave washing through his soul, his vision misting as he placed a palm on the weathered oak of his front door, the portal to his home for so many decades now. Beyond the leaded glass panes, he could almost see Phillip and Curtis, ghosts of days long past.

Where were they right now? Were they safe? Warm? Or freezing even as he entered this cozy abode, to slip into the comfort of his old chair, to soak in the heat of a crackling fire? To lounge in safety while they struggled for their very lives.

He slid his key into the tarnished brass lock and turned it, tumblers clicking. Then he ushered Tuesday inside and locked the door behind himself. “Hold now, girl. Let me light a candle.”

“No need. Let me help you.” A voice hissed out of the dark and into his ear. Hands grabbed him and threw him from the entryway, to crash atop his favorite end table, snapping the legs. Light flared, showing a hulk dressed in tight-fitting black and advancing, cold violence in his eyes.

Another grabbed Tuesday from behind and held her, arms trapped at her sides, her pinwheeling legs soon locked between those of her captor.

A dry voice, like a wind blown from some desert crypt, rose above the struggle. “Now, now. Is that any way to welcome the hero home from his long and arduous journey? Come, Professor. Have a seat. You look tired.”

Reuel’s dangling toes were lifted clear of the floor, and he was deposited in a straight-backed chair as if he were a child. Across the table was the bishop’s unexpected face, looking back at him with disconcerting golden eyes.

Beside him, Prosecutor Lind smirked. “We anticipated your appearance much sooner. Your wagon train arrived in Two Rivers some time ago. But it has become so hard to find a taxi in these troubled days, has it not?”

Reuel stared across at his captors. So was this how it was to end? Had his long-delayed torture, his death, found him? It was well overdue, so much so he’d stopped fearing its arrival ages ago.

But what of Tuesday? What a tragedy that she be caught up in all of this. “Before you say whatever you have to say, may my nurse be excused? She is innocent and is expected elsewhere, should not hear anything of a . . . sensitive nature.”

“On a mission of mercy perhaps?” Lind gave a disgusted grunt.

"Dispense with the subterfuge, Professor. We are aware of who she is. Moreover, we are aware of what you have been about."

At his signal, a brute slammed a beautifully bound leather volume in front of Reuel. He deigned to touch it, tracing the embossed letters on the cover, unable to disguise his delight. This volume, the child of his dreams, was it real? Here was the culmination of his life's mission. Here was proof the plan succeeded, at least in part.

Lind went on. "I see that you recognize this work? Your precious thirty-nine books, the product of your not-so-secret cabal, the Seekers?" He thumped a ragged volume next to it. "I'm sure you'll want to keep the original as well."

Dog-eared pages marked, his first handwritten copy of the Scriptures, sent to him so recently by Curtis. His breathing became ragged, and his hands began to tremble.

If they had found this, they had been in the hideout. They knew everything.

"Oh, please," Lind mocked. "You thought we were unaware of your little club? We've watched you scurry about for years."

Lind leaned in, hands flat on the table. "Professor, dispense with the games. We know who you are and what you've been doing. If we wanted to convict you, we could." He pressed in closer, his breath hot acid in Reuel's face. He withdrew and tented fingers before his chin. "And we both know, if we wanted you gone, we'd not need to wait for even that."

"Very well." Reuel drew himself up and gave a curt nod. "Then what is the point of this charade? Why not make me disappear as you have so many others?" A part of him, a despairing, defeated part, almost wished for it.

Lind pursed those dry lips of his. "Because you have an opportunity to correct your terrible mistake. To serve Order. Avoid the coming chaos."

"Order?" Reuel rolled his eyes. "You mean tyranny."

Lind's mouth thinned to an impossibly flat line. "Come, Professor. You know history. You know the horror humanity is capable of, how all human civilizations ultimately crumble. We were balanced on that precipice—even in your own lifetime. Had the Order not dragged this world back during the collapse of the Hegemony, we would've entered a dark ages rivaling any in history."

Finger poking the well-worn tome, Lind said, "Even these *priceless histories* of yours make this clear." Withered fingers rose, then closed into a fist. "Mankind left to his own devices is inept, knows not what is best for him. He must be led, must be governed, and by a strong hand—for his own good."

Those hands, their gray parchment skin so thin the candlelight nearly shone through it, slapped the table, wobbling the candles. That bony finger extended toward Reuel's face. "And now, you unleash this . . . *whirlwind*." He batted at the book. "Upon our fragile times. You unleash forces you do not understand, and the resulting madness could be the final end of mankind."

Reuel shook his head. "You exaggerate. Besides, truth is no peril. It is light." He fixed Lind's gaze with his own. "Perhaps it's truth, not chaos you fear. Perhaps the only thing at risk of destruction is your temple of lies."

Lind stood, jaw trembling. He scooped up the book, shook it in the air. "*This* was a waste of time. Your friends from the *Dorothy* have died in vain, and all of their accomplices with them." He wiped spittle from his lip, then strode to the far wall and back, hands clasped behind his back.

A cold numbness tingled in Reuel's fingertips, moving up his arms. Dead? Curtis, Phillip, all those precious people were dead? The coldness moved inward, turning all to stone in its wake, now encircling his heart.

From a great distance, Lind's voice penetrated, now in a more measured, reasonable tone. "For so long you searched for the secret way back to your lost God, back to your lost paradise. Searched for this very book, thinking those secrets were revealed within it. Is this not so?"

Lind lifted the volume high as if presenting it to the heavens, then extended it toward Reuel. "Now you have it, right here in black and white. You've printed hundreds of thousands of copies, distributed them far and wide."

He tossed the book in the air. It thudded, spinning to a stop before Reuel. A sneer twisted Lind's shriveled visage. "You broadcast your promise to the world. An old promise. An ancient promise." He rocked forward, head lowered, eyes burning. "A *broken* promise, one your God can no longer deliver. It's much too late. How will the world react to your great announcement when they realize it's all a lie?"

Now, from somewhere deep inside Reuel, a rising heat blossomed, shattering that gripping coldness like a stone vessel dashed to the cobbles. He lurched to his feet. Then leaned across the table, nose to nose with Lind, much closer than he'd have dared had he been of sound mind. "The God of Creation never lies."

Lind gave a dry, wheezing laugh, his hot breath again washing Reuel's face. It carried the same acrid smell. Sulfur. Not like the sweet smell of a freshly struck match, but sour, stomach turning.

From the end of the table, the bishop cleared his throat. Then came a tone gentle, friendly in counterpoint to Lind's raspy antagonism. "That may be. But *you* are *not* immune to error, Professor. And as men of good faith, it's important we correct this particular mistake, for the sake of all. Prosecutor Lind does not exaggerate when he indicates the stakes for our flock. Our beloved people."

The bishop walked to Reuel, placing a conciliatory hand on his shoulder. "I beg of you. Listen and recant of your error, your possibly fatal error."

That warm smile, so friendly, so caring, how could he ever have been so foolish? Who could disagree with such a reasonable man? Then with an effort, Reuel jerked his focus away to the cover of his precious Scriptures. "And that error is?"

The bishop squeezed Reuel's shoulder, then leaned close—voice honeyed, warm, caring. A close confidant. Someone to trust. The one person in all the world who was really on his side. "It's not your fault. No way could you have known."

Reuel brought all his force of will to focus, to grasp the fleeing wisps of reason. Of resolve. He shook himself, shuddering. He stepped away and faced the bishop, relieving himself of that too-familiar hand. "Known what?"

The bishop gave a one-sided half smile and raised a shoulder in apology, a friend hesitant to deliver embarrassing news. "Your God long ago offered your kind the fulfillment of that promise. You rejected His offer, rejected your God, and now He has abandoned you. Have you not felt the distance that has grown between your kind and Him?"

The bishop's benevolent expression didn't change. But something happened deep in those eyes, and Professor Reuel's spine crawled. A dreadful glee swirled in those sucking pools, those golden orbs. So bright. So liquid. So terrifying, yet so enthralling.

Lind slapped the table, jolting Reuel free of the reverie. "The great promise is a lie." Lind rose from his seat and stalked around the table. He accepted a stack of books from a black-robed man. He placed them before Reuel.

"Here is your proof. Read. Study, and then break the bad news to your associates, to all to whom you have spread this unfortunate fairy tale. Disband your sorry little club. Do so, and you may even escape the punishment you deserve."

Those volumes. They were titles he knew, Josephus's *Antiquities*, Tacitus's *Annals*, even a copy of the *Talmud,* among others. Reuel dismissed them with a wave of his hand. "I'm familiar with these. They have no bearing on the subject."

With one wizened hand, Lind spun the tomes, spine-first, toward Reuel, his misshapen finger pointing to a garish red-and-yellow stripe there. "The versions you have read were redacted. These are not. You will find they prove our assertions."

His heart skipped a beat. Red-stripe volumes? From the fabled locked temple vaults? To be in the possession of such bore a death sentence. But why was he even listening? These men were inveterate liars, their entire kingdom a web of deception.

He shook his head and pushed the books away. "I cannot—*will* not—believe this to be true. Creator God is good. There has to be some explanation."

The bishop had reclaimed his seat, but now he moved as a striking snake. More so, he didn't seem to move at all. He was across the room in an instant, and his hand encircled Reuel's throat, lifting him to dangle by the neck, legs kicking. The bishop's mouth was at Reuel's ear, hissing. "Hear this, you old fool. There is a power that prowls the world over, delighting in those it might devour and destroy. Take care, lest you attract notice." Those lips moved closer, now touching his ear, intimate. Invasive. "Disband the Seekers and disown these lies."

The bishop dropped Reuel into his chair, then rammed the forbidden volumes into his chest so hard he had to struggle to regain his breath.

When he again looked up, the bishop was gone. Only Lind and the black-clad men remained. The shortest of these stood at the foot of the table, studying Reuel, his thumb testing the point of a wicked dagger.

Lind straightened and shook imaginary creases from his robes. "The bishop requires your written confession by Thursday morning next, including a list of all involved in your conspiracy. I'll meet you here, and you will deliver it to my hand. Omit nothing and have it credited to you when your punishment is considered. At that time, have ready a document in which you recant this." The man placed his hand on the Scriptures. "You were deceived, mistaken. This old fable, long discredited, was proven untrue eons ago. You will reconfirm your loyalty to the Eternal and to the veracity of the Writings."

Those cold eyes shifted to the man with a knife, then back. "Fail to please the bishop in any of this, and the penalties will be unpleasantly fatal. For you." His hand shot out to grab Tuesday's jacket collar. He spun her to face Reuel as if presenting her for inspection. "And for your surviving associates."

He shoved her stumbling to Reuel's feet.

The men surrounded Lind, and on cat feet, they departed and shut the cottage door, its click barely audible.

The room was empty except for Reuel and Tuesday. His senses

told him this. Yet that hand still encircled his throat, squeezing, hot, hard as stone.

Tuesday raised a palm to his cheek. "Father, are you okay? Did they hurt you?"

Reuel set aside the red-striped tomes and lifted his beautiful new leather-bound edition of the Scriptures. Candlelight played along the gilt lettering, highlighting the embossed cover. This was to have been his greatest victory. Was it just an old man's folly? "Creator God has abandoned us?"

"Don't you listen to that man. If everything he said was true, then why did they hunt the *Dorothy*'s crew for so long? Why bother?"

Reuel slumped to his knees, all strength leached from his limbs. His mind refused to engage, his vision clouded. "They are dead? Curtis and Phillip, all those dear people . . . dead?" A wordless wail escaped. He shoved the Scriptures aside and collapsed to the table, head in arms. "Oh, my poor boys, lost, and for nothing—because of me. All is ashes!"

She knelt, turned his face toward hers, and smoothed his brow with soft fingers. "You don't know that to be true." Her voice then gained a hard edge. "I don't know much, either, but I can tell a liar when I see one. And that man's a liar."

"Bah. Why would he bother? He's already won."

"Has he? Then why is he going to all this trouble? Why do you believe him without checking for yourself?"

He breathed hard, in and out. Then, with resolution, he used the back of the chair to lever himself to his feet, Tuesday on one elbow. Yes. He would do this last duty. His back straightened. He brushed the dirt from his coat. "You are right, of course. It is my responsibility to verify his claims. I owe the boys that much, at least. Poor souls."

He wiped a tear and drifted about the room, plucking up random items only to set them back down. "We must gather a few things, then depart. I will find you a safe place to hide, then determine how deeply he has penetrated our organization."

She shook her head, arms crossed. "Where you go, I go, whether you like it or not."

He exhaled a deep sigh, more a groan. "I am much too tired to argue, though I suspect the effort would be in vain. So I say only this: I do not wish you to be harmed. The chances are very good you may indeed be. Likely tortured, almost certainly killed, should you remain in my company. I beg you to reconsider."

Tuesday organized her bag. "Tell me what to pack for you. I have all I need." When he teetered, dizzy, exhaustion and delayed reaction causing his hands, his knees to falter, she jumped to steady him. "We should rest before we go anywhere, Father. After all, our deadline is days away. We can afford the time."

He put a hand to his forehead. "In truth, for days I have looked forward to a night in my own bed, but my conscience now revolts at the idea. So many have sacrificed so much. How can I think of my own comfort in the face of that?"

"You're going to bed." She towed him by the arm. "You'll be no good for anything if you collapse in the street."

CHAPTER 64

Fritz had never liked Tatten's idea to bring seminary girls into their work groups. He probably regretted it more now as several had outperformed even the best of the boys and shown exceptional attention to detail. They were even on track to complete the counters well before deadline. It was nothing short of a miracle.

Every time Lars came against an insurmountable problem, God seemingly opened a door and sent the solution needed. As he walked from the rear shop, he said a silent prayer of thanks.

Near the offices, Velde's team was performing their nightly penance, correcting yet another round of errors. Diggs had taken to loitering with the group and was with them again. The whole bunch had drawn in a circle, deep in conversation. Before they spotted him, Lars detoured through a less direct route. He wasn't afraid of the jerks, but he'd rather avoid the discomfort. And the whispered comments behind his back. Besides, he'd already heard all their daddy's-boy jokes.

Surprisingly, Benny, who'd taken the most recent load of counters to Capital over the weekend, was in the main office sorting paperwork. With the winter games celebration being held at the same venue, delays had been expected. "Hey, back already?"

"Yeah, was no problem getting unloaded. Getting to the center was a bit touch and go. That town was a zoo all weekend."

"Did you get to go in and see our tables in use?"

Benny's expression hardened, and he looked away. "What kind of *events*, exactly, did they tell you this Events Center of ours was going to host?"

The answer died on Lars's lips. Something about Benny's haunted eyes. "Well, I never asked. I assumed conventions, meetings, weddings, parties, holiday celebrations—that kind of thing?"

"Yeah. That kind of thing. And yeah, I went in to see our work in person. Wish I hadn't."

"Why? Something wrong?"

Benny blew out. "I'm no prude or anything. I barely made it to Father Curtis's teachings once a month, and then only 'cause my wife dragged me there. But, man. Father Curtis would be rolling over in his grave, or wherever he is, if he'd seen what I saw."

Lars pulled up a chair and straddled it, facing Benny. "What happened?"

"I shouldn't even tell you. Some things you can't unhear." He rubbed the back of his neck and scowled at his shoes. "Or unsee, unfortunately."

"What could be so bad?"

One hand pulling his face, Benny groaned, then shook as if to dislodge an unpleasant memory. "You're too young to remember what things were like before Father Curtis. And you keep things all business when you travel, so maybe you can't understand."

Why did people have to treat Lars like he was stupid? Did they think he knew nothing of the world just because he was young? And kept his nose clean? "I know about the time before, and I've heard all about the wine festivals, the wild holy-day parties. I'm not so naïve and uninformed as all that."

"Hah." Nothing in Bennie's barking laugh or expression indicated amusement. "Oh, people were partying-up, all right. I expected that, even expected some would get out of hand later at night. But I was there in broad daylight, and people were doing things right there at the tables—at those tables *I built*, mind you—that no decent person should do, public or no."

Mouth open, Lars lifted a finger.

"No, boss." Benny cut him off. "You think you know. But believe me, you don't. And that wasn't the worst of it. That VIP ticket you gave me got me into the private reception. I was propositioned the second I stepped into the room—by some girl no older than my Elsa! And she's barely fourteen. Okay, bad things happen. I get it. And girls are misused at all ages, poor souls, but the next one to proposition me was even younger. I should have walked out right there and then, but I didn't. That's when I saw him."

Before Lars's eyes passed a vision of Elsa, sweet little Elsa, in such a position. And he wanted to punch something. "Saw who?"

"That bishop, the one that came around when Father Curtis disappeared, the pretty boy. Something about that guy makes my stomach hurt every time he's around. Makes me want to run the other way."

That day at the farm when Lars had met the bishop . . . Want to run away? Yep, he could relate.

"Anyhow, he comes walking through. I figure people would straighten up, but when he comes by, it seems like they doubled down on what they were doing. And worse, he seems to like that, like he was feeding off it, and they off him. Then some of his guards started handing out these green slips of paper, prize tickets like. People who got them went to the bar and turned them in for drinks."

Benny raised a hand in the air as if swearing himself in for testimony. "I admit—I moseyed that way. I mean, a free drink is a free drink, after all. I'm getting close, and they pull out these red tickets and start passing them around." He shuddered. "I'm not even going to tell you what those tickets would buy you."

His jaw set and his lips quivered. He took a deep breath and let it out, visibly forcing calm. "After that, I lost my appetite and my inclination to stick around."

His fist slammed one well-muscled thigh. The impact resounded in the nearly empty office.

A lone draftsman looked up, startled. Seeing Benny's wild eyes and red face, he again ducked his head to his work.

"What's wrong with people, Lars? How can that bishop smile, watching them do all that? It's wrong!"

Lars searched for an answer, but what? He believed Benny, of course, but what to do with that information? Thank Creator God Benny hadn't been any more descriptive. Lars already heard enough. And what Benny said about being unable to unhear it? Man, was he right. If only Lars could wash his brain clean again, right here and now.

This must be something like the corruption mentioned in the first scroll. And now that story held a new level of meaning, that at the Fall, the minds of the first humans, once pure and untouched by the knowledge of sin, were forever after tainted in a way that they couldn't undo.

If only *he'd* never heard *this* story, never imagined these pictures now intruding into his thoughts, unwanted, unshakable, no matter how hard he tried. Disgusting.

This had to be a little glimpse of what those words meant, "the curse of sin." How irreversible it is, how powerless he was to undo the damage. "Benny, we need to pray to Creator God and ask that He cleanse us of this ugly thing."

Benny rocked backward and narrowed his eyes. "What are you talking about, Creator God?"

Lars's heart lurched. What had he done, saying such a thing out loud? But it was the right thing to do, wasn't it? To pray? And to help Benny, too?

Without answering, he knelt and nodded for Benny to join him. After a moment's hesitation, Benny did.

And they prayed.

Reuel sat at his table as Tuesday cooked a light breakfast, preparatory to their departure. How strange to be served in his own house, but the girl seemed to take pleasure in doing it. So how could he deny her this thing, deny her anything after all she'd done? "Tuesday, child, I want to thank you."

"For breakfast? It's easy. Besides, I like bringing you your meals." She smiled at him. "It's how we met, after all."

"Eh? Oh yes, for that too, but no. I want to thank you for so many things, really. I owe you my life several times over, but I was thinking of how well you care for me when I am incapable of doing for myself, such as last night. I did not realize how weary I was, how muddled my thinking. You recognized this and, against my protests, insisted we take the time to rest. This was what I intended to thank you for, in particular. I do not make things easy for you, yet you never give up. Why is that, I wonder?"

"Why? Because you are my daddy. Because you chose to love me. I could serve you for the rest of your life and never repay such a thing."

Reuel helped clean the dishes after breakfast, the least he could do. Then he and Tuesday shouldered their packs and were trooping out of his old cottage. At the outer door, nostalgia stopped him. This may be the last time he saw his home. He turned for one last look at the rooms that sheltered and comforted him for so many years.

As he did so, something white flashed in his peripheral vision. The corner of an envelope stuck out from under the doormat where it must've lodged when it dropped through the mail slot.

"What is this?" He stooped to retrieve it. The address was written in Curtis's neat hand. His heart leapt, and he wavered on his feet, confused waves of emotion washing through him. Joy at seeing that familiar hand. Grief at the reminder of the precious lad's death. The envelope shook in his fingers.

"What is it?" Tuesday craned over his shoulder.

"It appears Curtis sent one last message before the end. I am sorry, girl. I must decode this before we go." He abandoned his bag and shuffled to his desk where he worked for some time. There, his hands, which at first had only trembled, began to shake in earnest.

"Father, are you well?"

"Hush, girl. One moment, let me recheck myself. I dare not hope."

After a few more minutes of work, he spun in his chair. "Curtis and the crew of *Dorothy* may yet live! We must determine their location and make our way to them, but must take care. We cannot afford to be followed."

He gripped her shoulders. "I deceive you not, my child. The danger to you has increased exponentially. Will you reconsider? May I arrange a safe place for you to hide?"

"Where are we going and what can I do to help?"

CHURCH LET OUT JUST after noon. Lars took the scenic path home, following the lakeshore, as was his habit. Why did he still bother to attend services, knowing all he did?

But Professor Reuel's admonitions rang in his ears. So, to avoid unwanted notice if nothing else, he maintained the outward appearances of the devout young student of the Writings he'd always been. But fact was, it wasn't a total waste of time. He'd gained valuable insights in the process, information Reuel assured him to be worthwhile in the greater cause.

The new priest's sermon of today was noteworthy. The man had launched on a diatribe, twice as long as the average sermon, focusing on what he called false teachings. The professor's mass-produced Scriptures had hit the street, so the impetus for this line of teaching was clear. They must have struck a nerve, to produce such an energetic response.

As he walked, his breath's fog drifting before him like some companion cloud, he mentally composed a message for Reuel relaying this newest intelligence, lost in concentration, unseeing.

A burst of movement caused him to start sideways, but not quickly enough. Steellike fingers covered his mouth and dragged him into the brush, then into the deeper shade of the tangled trees beyond before his captor turned Lars to face him. The hand lowered from his mouth. "You know me, yes?"

"Phillip! We feared we'd never see you again. How did you get here?"

Phillip wrapped him in a bear hug, lifting his feet from the ground. Once they finished slapping one another on the back, grinning, then slapping again, Phillip hauled Lars away, still gripping his shoulders. "This is very long story. Now is not correct time for the telling. Curtis waits. Please you come? We go to him."

"Curtis is here? He's okay?" A welling deep in Lars's chest choked off his ability to speak. "There have been so many rumors. Terrible rumors."

"Is here, but many problems must be solved. He says need your help."

"Of course! Where is he? Take me to him."

"Is several miles. Rough country. You change into field boot?"

"Yeah, I should get out of my church clothes. Where should I meet you?"

Phillip pointed across the lake. There, the old railroad trestle crossed the water at its narrowest point, separating the south bay from the remainder of the long lake. "There. I wait."

Lars nodded and hurried off.

As he entered, Mom was at the woodstove, frying the traditional Sunday brunch. "Gonna miss lunch today, Mom. Got something I need to deal with."

"Too important to stop and eat with your family?"

He pecked her cheek. "Sorry. A friend needs a hand. He's waiting for me." He then dressed in hiking gear. As an afterthought, he snagged a day pack and tossed in snacks and a canteen.

With a pang, he walked back past Mom's sizzling skillet, surrendering his chance at this coveted feast. He took a deep breath, which brought the sweet, smoky scent of hand-cured bacon into his nostrils. He stopped in his tracks and glanced at the eggs, the edges of the whites bubbling in clear, clean bacon fat, golden yolks perfect and round, glistening as Mom basted them with more of the hot renderings.

He set his jaw, fortified his resolve, and turned his back, headed for the door. But not before sniping a strip of bacon.

He really was hungry.

CHAPTER 65

Lars tromped along the four-mile hike downriver. Phillip insisted they keep to the difficult going of the thick wilds parallel the riverbank, eschewing both the easy going of gravel roads or of the frozen river. "To be seen we must not." He insisted, so here they were, weaving through the deep brush.

Good thing Lars changed clothes. And thank Creator God there'd not been much snow yet this winter. Here, in the sheltered woods, the sugary snow barely reached above his ankles. It scattered as easily as sugar, too, offering little resistance as his boots described long arcs through it.

Along the way, Phillip recounted his adventures since October. Much of it, Lars had heard from Curtis or Reuel, except the ordeal these last weeks.

Then Phillip wrapped up the story. "Seemed very good idea, travel old rails, avoid towns. Easy, just roll, roll on nice steel road, no?"

"Sounds like an adventure. Wish I'd been there." Sort of, except the damp and the freezing temperatures and the snow and the lack of shelter. Lars had been cold like that before. No fun.

"Good idea. Hard to do. Saved lives, but hard, hard travel. Some days, maybe move twenty miles. Some days move one mile, maybe less. In open plain, many snowdrift must be moved. Brought some food, but ran out in first days."

Lars again studied Phillip's compact frame. The play of muscles moved beneath skin. Nothing new there. But he couldn't see Phillip's ribs. If anything, he'd put on a few pounds, fairly glowing with health, not a starving refugee. "Don't look like you've missed many meals."

"Creator God provides. We stop for night and build fire. When fire ready, deer comes for dinner." Phillip punched Lars in the shoulder. "This is good joke I hear. Deer comes for dinner, means he come to *be* dinner, yes?"

Lars laughed, not at the joke he'd heard hundreds of times, but at Phillip's joy in it. "Creator God is good. I've heard of the miracles you've seen. I'm jealous."

"Yes, God very good." Phillip sobered. "Without Him, many times, we would fail. Many times, we would die. God protects. This is testimony to us, assurance our task is of God."

They had drawn abreast of the old bridge Lars knew of as Four-Mile Bridge. Funny, he'd never before considered where it went, even though he'd hiked or boated past it. But that wasn't abnormal. On the water, it was so easy to lose track of where you were. After floating for what seemed like tens of miles, one could come upon a bridge and realize it was that of a familiar gravel road a short distance from their starting point.

Phillip led up the steep, muddy embankment. As they crested the rise, an encampment came into view.

Still on the rails were five rusty old contraptions, little more than flatbeds on rail wheels, a teeter-totter like double handle mounted to the top. Sheltering in the lee of the rail carts, the company had settled in, luggage and crates stacked around cook fires.

Lars whistled. He'd heard of the growth of the Yellow River group, but seeing sixty or so people in one place ratcheted that idea to another level of reality.

A man stood from one fire and sprinted toward them. Curtis, once his light-skinned and well-shaven priest, was nearly unrecognizable, weather-bronzed and shaggy-bearded. "Lars!" he shouted, white teeth flashing in his grimy face.

Father Curtis collided with Lars and embraced him in a rib-cracking bear hug. Then held him at arm's length. The joy of the reunion gleamed in his dark eyes. "We've so much to catch up on."

Lars grinned back. "I can't wait to hear your adventures firsthand. I've been keeping in touch with the professor, but, wow, what amazing stuff. Unbelievable, and you came here on these?" He pointed at the rail carts.

"Only by the grace of God. I've so much to tell, it'd fill a book. But, Lars, there is so much to do first. We've been out of communication for weeks. The professor has to be at his wit's end. The first order of business is to get this to him as fast as possible." Curtis handed Lars an envelope. "We had to leave the fort in a terrible hurry, and who knows if the letter I sent then ever reached him—I didn't even forward it through the Seekers, but risked having it delivered by regular mail. I'm still worried about that."

Lars followed Curtis to the fireside and took a stool as a seat. "He's been anxious, for sure. I'll make sure he gets it right away."

"Thank you, son. The second order of business is these folks. We need somewhere to hide them, and a way to feed them. I can't just count on God to keep sending miracles if we've some way to take care of ourselves. And we can't stay here. Any ideas where they can go?"

"Oh, wow." Lars scratched his scalp. "They need new papers before they can be seen in public, right?"

Curtis leaned forward on his stump and grabbed a stick, which he began worrying in his hands. "That's the problem. With luck, that'll soon be solved, but for now, they can't camp here forever."

The sick feeling in Lars's stomach must have shown. Curtis touched his arm. "What?"

"If the professor hasn't already solved that problem, things might be trickier now. You haven't heard about the riots?"

The stick broke in Curtis's grip. "Riots?"

Lars ducked his head. "Well, maybe riot is too tame a word. There have been a lot of actual riots to be sure, but more than that. End of

January, someone launched a full-scale revolt, including bombings and assassinations, a real mess. They've clamped down tight. Hard to move anywhere, and it's slow moving at that."

The stick landed in the fire, and Curtis pulled his face, eyes closed as if in pain. "Who in the world would do such a thing? Why?"

"They're blaming you. And this." Lars shrugged off his pack and from it handed Curtis a cloth-wrapped bundle.

Several other men had joined them. As Curtis reached for the package, he said, "Oh, pardon my manners. We have introductions to make, don't we? Lars, you know Phillip. These other ruffians are Thaddeus, Jeremiah, Captain Simon, and Mate Jespers."

Lars stood to shake the offered hands. "I'm honored to meet you all in the flesh. You're famous, you know?"

Jeremiah blushed and lowered his head.

Simon spoke up. "We've heard much about you as well, lad. I feel as if I already know you, and glad we are to have you join us."

As the captain spoke, Curtis unwrapped the package, revealing a leather-bound volume. Gilt lettering caught the sunlight, flashing like some ancient golden treasure. The entire camp stilled, people at other fires seeming to sense something momentous. In the silence, Curtis whispered, "Is this . . .?"

Lars laid a hand on Curtis's shoulder. "This is the printed translation of the scrolls. Your work has been mass-produced and distributed around the land. They won't be able to destroy it this time. The professor made sure of that."

"And this has caused riots?"

"I don't think so. I haven't heard from the professor yet, so I'm just guessing. Things are confused, and there's lots of propaganda and rumor. What I *have* gathered indicated another group is behind the violence. Some people called the Sons of Freedom posted flyers all over, calling for armed insurrection. By coincidence, it happened around when the Scriptures were printed, but they're lumping us in with them."

Curtis scratched his beard. "So, this makes our job that much harder, finding a place to hide. Getting new papers."

Lars let his hand slide down Curtis's arm, then gripped the father's fingers. "In the meantime, I have an idea where you might stay for a little while, but I need to check on it before I say for sure. Are you good to spend the night here, if it takes me till tomorrow to arrange things?"

The young man, Jeremiah, spoke up. "Pardon, but you said printing many copies of this book, yes?"

Lars nodded. "The professor worked real hard to get it out there, in as many hands as he could. He wanted word to spread so far the Order couldn't ever put it down again."

A tear ran down Jeremiah's cheek. He turned away, whispering in some unknown tongue, gaze focused far beyond the empty snowy expanse.

CHAPTER 66

Leif checked his tie for the fourth time in ten minutes, acid burning his belly. His fingers once again strayed to the itch on his cheek. The one he'd nearly made bleed on the wagon train to Capital. That was all he needed right now, to open a wound on his face before his big moment. His luck it'd bleed all over his shirt in front of the clients.

He went to the window, but there wasn't much to look at, nothing to distract his racing mind. Just piles of steel beams in a mud-churned industrial lot. Jameson, husband of Eleanor, had insisted this meeting be held in his steelworks conference room. Apparently, to attend a meeting at some other venue was too taxing on his oh-so-valuable time.

After making this mad dash to Capital, Leif had been lucky to find Eleanor, much less convince her to arrange this meeting. She'd been reticent to broach the subject with Jameson, who for some reason and unexplained fiat, mandated she change vendors.

And to *Artisans*? What was the man thinking? They were the worst choice, their quality nowhere near the level the principals were expecting.

Once Leif demonstrated to Eleanor the quality issues, her resolve renewed, and she'd badgered Jameson into arranging today's meeting. But she'd warned Leif she suspected this was a false gesture, meant only to assuage her feelings. "Jameson recently began business dealings with the family who stewards Artisans," she'd whispered, hand to her mouth.

Murmurings inundated Capital about that family for years. That their business interests were widespread and not a little shadowy. That they were best not crossed.

Leif snorted. And their quality stank. A kindergartner could pick their stuff apart. Give him five minutes and he'd show Jameson a hundred details where Artisans' work fell short, all on a single piece of furniture.

But Leif could hardly use either argument, neither their questionable business practices nor their *more* than questionable quality. Dad always said to make sure it was obvious how much better your product was, and you wouldn't have to point out how inferior the other guy's might be. Try to tear the other guy down and you made yourself look petty and desperate.

For the twentieth time since he'd been escorted into this room, Leif went to the door and cracked it. Wasn't Artisans done yet? It'd been so long. Leif had lobbied for an open meeting, but Artisans insisted on blind presentations, the opposing parties sequestered while their competitor made their presentation. He opened the door a few more inches. Twenty yards down the hall was the conference room's glass half wall, the blinds drawn. Only an occasional flicker of movement visible through the vertical slits. Nothing he could make anything of.

But the door was ajar, and voices now echoed down the corridor. Recognizable were Jameson's booming bass, Eleanor's contralto, and another. He'd know that smarmy, cocksure voice anywhere. Chip, the scion of the Artisans clan.

Leif's heart skipped. His knees went weak. Listen to them. The lot of them joking like old chums. What was going on? Had he been snookered? The deal already set? And him sitting here in this crappy side office, listening to that bunch of shysters laugh, not knowing the joke was on him?

The conference room door opened wider, spilling bright light into the dim corridor, and Chip stepped out, turning to trade one last laugh with Jameson. He spotted Leif, and while he clapped Jameson on the shoulder, he winked at Leif. Not a friendly wink.

Another man squeezed past Jameson and stole toward Leif, who ducked back into the office and hurried to the window to adopt a casual waiting pose, nearly falling when his hand missed the chair he'd meant to lean on.

The door swung inward, and a bland-faced assistant peeked in. "They're ready for you. This way." He accompanied Leif to the conference room where he indicated the door as if Leif couldn't find it for himself.

Farther down the hallway, Chip stood, stance careless. He flipped a coin in the air with his thumb, then caught it, showed Leif one face of the coin, then the other. Again, he flipped the coin high, caught it, and slapped it onto the back of one hand. He peeked under that covering hand and tsked with mock sympathy as if Leif lost the toss, then pointed with thumb and forefinger. The thumb snapped down, the message clear. Bang. You're dead.

So that's it. All was already lost. Leif slumped, his breath wheezing past lifeless lips. Why even bother? Why even go into this room and embarrass himself before these terrible people? People who only brought him here to torment him before casting him out, empty-handed? A cruel joke.

What would Haman do to him? No way could he pay what that man demanded without this contract. Would he then turn to the family? To Northwoods? Take his profit, his revenge on them? Of course he would.

Leif straightened. He couldn't let that happen. Not without a fight. Besides, he had the winning hand. If only he could get them to see it. Artisans shouldn't be allowed to fulfill this order. Not with their junk. He set his jaw and faced the door where the assistant waited, no longer so patient.

With one more deep breath, one more meaningless adjustment of his tie, Leif stepped through the door. Inside were Jameson, broad-shouldered and beefy in a vested suit, Eleanor with yellow suit dress and pearls, and a secretary. They sat at a long metal conference table, the legs made of welded and bolted sections of I beam, the sheet steel top polished to a brilliant shine. Figures. The guy sold steel. Why not make his furniture out of it? As long as you like three-ton tables that rust if you spill your drink. What a soulless room it created. Who'd do such a thing?

At the room's far end was a presentation table, also steel, and Leif's samples were stacked in one corner, Artisan's in the other. Garbage. It was obvious, even from here. The exposed cores of cutaway samples revealed poorly graded stock, the joinery their typical schlock, designed for fast assembly by unskilled workers. Not the works of art his family put out.

He lifted the Artisans sample chair, one of the items Leif had ensured, through Eleanor, they would both provide for this meeting. Nothing showed quality, or the lack of it, more easily than a chair. He moved it further into the corner, ostensibly to get it out of the way, but really just to heft the thing. It even *felt* cheap. When he set it down, it actually creaked, and there was evident play in the joinery.

Hegemony. The thing seemed ready to collapse.

He took a deep breath and faced the table, the firing squad, and resisted the urge to check his tie again. Why would anyone wear one of these things? He was choking, and his neck was raw with abrasions. But Eleanor had insisted, and who was he to refuse?

He opened his presentation, hands shaking, knees jittering. Could they hear the wobble in his voice? And since when did he have stage fright? He'd done this a million times. Reveled in it. He was the guy who drew energy from the room, connected with the audience, channels of empathic communication below the conscious level opening wide, his rapt listeners hanging on his every word, eyes wide and liquid upon him.

His greatest talent was his feel for a room, his ability to tell what got through to his audience, lit them up, turned them off, and then fine-tune his presentation on the fly until he was so tuned in, so *one with* those he spoke to.

It was almost a spiritual experience.

And it was always a success.

So why was there nothing today? No connection. It was like talking to a blank wall. Oh, Eleanor was giving him encouraging nods and smiles, but even she seemed detached, disheartened. Somewhere else.

The room was stone cold. He was getting nowhere.

As he continued his spiel, his mind raced. What could he do that he hadn't tried? Hadn't said?

But there was nothing. He'd used every tool in his playbook, every argument. And then it was too late. Jameson placed his hands on the table, weight pressing down, preparing to rise. To end the meeting.

That day in the restaurant flashed to mind, the day Artisans had gobbled up that contract. As he continued speaking, he sidled toward Artisans' display, ignoring Jameson's cleared throat. Casually, as if he did it with no thought, he dragged the Artisans chair forward, spun it in front of him. Just something to lean on one-handed while he made his close.

But while he spoke, he tested the chair, explored the joinery through the contact of flesh on wood. With a lifetime's experience in the craft, he felt the weaknesses there, just as he could feel his own tendons, his own joints.

When Jameson again opened his mouth, Leif made his move. Just a little more weight *here*, and—*craaak!*—the chair collapsed to the floor, Leif following it. His fall was partly an act, but not much. That chair had fallen apart much faster than he'd anticipated. And much more thoroughly.

As he fell, he positioned the heel of his palm on the seat, and when he landed, he gave it one last, sharp blow. The seat split down the middle, the remainder of the splintered legs sliding across the floor in all directions, no one component attached to another. Kindling.

He rolled to his knees, groaning. All three spectators now open-mouthed. He lifted his hand in an I'm-all-right gesture and stood, dusting the knees of his suit as he did. Then he flashed an abashed grin and walked toward his corner. "Sorry about that. I grabbed their chair by mistake. Should have known better."

Holding his chair by the back, he spun it onto one leg. "You see, Mr. Jameson, we don't dowel our furniture. That's a fast and cheap way to make a chair. Problem is, to the untrained eye, both chairs look the same."

He raised the chair and slammed it on one leg. The joinery wasn't even phased, just made the sound of a hammer rapping wood. "But they're not the same. As you can see." He spun the chair across the room, and it cartwheeled to land at Jameson's feet. "Test it for yourself."

Jameson's face blotched red, but not as red as Eleanor's. "You—"

Eleanor cut him off, finger in his face. "Jameson, you were going to let those . . . *people* . . . fill my house with—with that?" Her finger stabbed at the remains of the Artisans chair before snapping back toward his nose. "My beautiful house?"

Jameson raised one hand, eyes closed. "Very well." He drew himself up, pulled down his suit cuffs, and let out an explosive breath. "Do as you wish, my dear. I'm late for an important call." He glowered in Leif's direction, poison in his eyes. "Good day." And he spun on his heel, his lackey scurrying in his wake.

Eleanor grinned at Leif, fist raised in victory, diamond bracelet glittering on her narrow wrist.

He grinned back and raised his own. No diamonds there, though.

She checked her gem-studded watch. "Oh dear. It's later than I realized. I, too, am now late for an assignation." As her high heels beat a brisk staccato out of the door, she waved manicured nails over her shoulder. "We'll talk. For now, continue as planned. You'll have those color samples for me by next week?"

Leif remained where he was. Chip appeared in the doorway, and Leif tamped down his glee. It was bad manners to gloat, or so Mom always said. But his face refused to cooperate, and the grin remained.

Chip crossed the room and stood looking at the broken chair. "What in the—?" His narrowed gaze snapped to Leif, teeth clenched and jaw muscles bunching. "You have no idea who you're dealing with, do you? You'll pay for this."

"No problem." Leif pulled a one-credit coin from his pocket and showed it to Chip. Then, with his thumb, he flicked it high in the air. It arced across the room, the spinning faces glinting in the light, straight toward Chip's forehead. Not where Leif was aiming. Leif winced, shoulders tensed, and watched it fly, beyond recall now. For a heart-stopping second, it seemed about to impact.

Then Chip's hand shot up and caught the coin.

They stood, facing one another across the room, Chip glaring, Leif grinning.

Then Leif shrugged. "Keep the change."

CHAPTER 67

Over not one, but three days of frenzied work, Lars organized the move. To attempt the eight-mile journey by road would be too great a risk. Even on the back roads, they'd be seen. To hike cross-country was out of the question. The group was too large, with too many children. With these limitations in mind, Lars had settled on the current mode of transportation.

That the company made it to the final destination—in one piece, undiscovered—proved his plan a good one, though by the looks he was collecting from the female passengers, there may be a diversity of opinion on the subject. And on his own parentage and personal habits.

A line of people disembarked via the livestock trailer's ramp, each being greeted by their temporary new hosts.

Grandpa, in his mint-green button-down and black-and-white pinstriped overalls, stood beside Grandma in her perennial gingham dress, apron bearing witness to the cauldron of chili she was dishing out to the newcomers. The passengers, for their part, seemed occupied with dislodging the stubborn hog manure from their shoes.

When a few more cast dark glances his way, Lars ducked his head. Before picking the group up, he'd cleaned the trailer to the best of his ability. But time constraints and the sheer volume of fecal matter defeated him. Maybe, eventually, they'd forget it?

Curtis, Phillip, and the other leading men remained at the rear of the livestock freight car, assisting in the debarkation. They now double-checked that everyone and everything was unloaded before stepping down themselves. Lars slid the ramps into place and swung closed the doors before turning to welcome the company to the farm.

A crooked figure stood to the side of the action, waiting. The breath whooshed from Lars's lungs as if he'd been gut-punched. A shadow of his former self, his loose skin hanging gray and pallid, his once wizened form now so shrunken as to be almost childlike, the professor leaned on his staff. It seemed he'd be unable to remain standing at all, if not for the assistance of the pretty young redhead at his side. Really pretty. Lars's cheeks heated, and he again ducked his head.

Curtis and Phillip, too, had spotted the professor and were rushing to his side. Lars held back as the two embraced the old man, tears visible on their faces. "What has happened to you?" Curtis asked. "Have you been ill?"

"Oh, my boy. To see you is a balm for my soul, and you, Phillip! When they told me you perished in the wilderness, it was nearly the end of me, but now? All is well." Reuel patted their hands, both of which he gripped in his own. "All is well again. And here! You must meet someone. Please let me introduce my adopted daughter, Tuesday, Creator God's gift to me through many trials. Tuesday, please meet Curtis and Phillip, who are sons to me as you are daughter."

Curtis and Phillip bowed to the young girl. Curtis said, "Another orphan comes to the fold. The professor seems to have a habit of collecting us, doesn't he? Well, you're welcome here, adopted sister. You're in good hands, to which I can attest from experience."

Grandpa harrumphed. "Everybody, follow me. I'll show you where you'll be staying. Wish it was fancier, but it's warm and dry." He opened the walk door to the big machine shed. "Men in the loft, women and children down here. Lars made room for everyone. If not, just yell."

Lars had cleared the open shop and lined it with a hasty row of two-by-four framed beds, not much more than raised pallets padded with folded shipping blankets. In one corner, flames danced beyond the glass door of a woodburning stove. In another, weathered picnic tables formed the remainder of the sparse furnishings, all Lars could come up with, on such short notice.

He now raised his hands and addressed the group, though he'd rather run the other way. "I'm sorry. I really am. It's not much, but . . . " His voice cracked. He shrugged. If only he'd had more time.

Phillip gripped his shoulder. "Ritz Hotel, this is. Grateful, we are young friend. Thank you."

A chorus of agreement echoed from the group, even the women who had earlier been glaring at Lars. Though one bent to pry a last manure clod from her shoe.

The former heat in Lars's cheeks now fired into a veritable blaze, hotter than the one in the woodstove. He waved about. "Make yourselves at home. If you have any need, let me know." As people sorted themselves and carried in luggage, he found Professor Reuel. "Professor, I am so glad to see you. I missed you so. We've made a space for you in the main house. Did Grandpa show you?"

"Oh yes, my boy. He showed me, and your grandparents are delightful. Be sure to thank them again for me, for all of us, for hosting us. I hope we can be well out of their hair soon. I must object, though. It's not right, that I take the soft bed in the house when all of these people sleep here."

Tuesday had remained at the professor's elbow. "Oh no you don't, Father. We've had this conversation. I didn't nurse you back from death's door, only to let you catch it again out here."

"She's correct, Professor," Curtis broke in. "Besides, we've been roughing it for so long out in the open, that this is the height of luxury. But as for your health, are you quite well? I can see you've been ill. What happened?"

They settled at one of the tables, and Reuel shared the events of recent weeks.

Curtis gaped, bushy brows rising. "You put yourself in such peril?

Over us? We were fine, but we could have lost you. Nearly did, it sounds like. Please don't take those sorts of risks with yourself again. You're too valuable. We'd be helpless without you."

Then Lars leaned in, hands spread. "About the rebellion you witnessed in Plumbsburg. Are you certain it was the work of this group, the Sons of Freedom?"

"Yes, without a doubt, and a poor work it was. The violence has spread over the whole land, although not to the extreme done there." The professor shook his head. "What a waste. So many innocent people have suffered, will suffer, and for what? Worse, they are blaming the violence on us, on the Scriptures which we printed."

As if in awe to be holding it, Curtis stroked the lettering on his copy. "It's good you printed them. You made no enemies we didn't already have. They may hope to blame us and thus turn the public against us. But is that narrative working?"

"Bah." Reuel scoffed. "Of course not. Other than the usual mindless sheep, no one believes their propaganda, and the Sons made their campaign public and clear. What concerns me is something else the bishop said."

He paused long, staring into the fire, seeming to lose himself there. Then he sighed, his gaze traveling around the table. "The bishop made a disturbing assertion, as I have said. He claims the promises of our True Text to be false. His flunky gave me a number of histories, which he contends will prove his assertions. I have studied these histories. His claim may . . . have merit."

When retorts came from all those around the table, some rising in passionate objection, he lowered his head and waited patiently until Curtis called for silence. Reuel continued, "Pray allow me to finish my report, uninterrupted, if I may."

He filled his lungs. "As the Seekers always knew, God created the universe, created mankind, created a perfect paradise." His wrinkled hand patted his volume of the Scriptures. "From these, we have now learned how that paradise was lost. As human beings, we rebelled and, in so doing, opened our world to a previously unknown corruption. One which changed us, irreversibly insinuating itself into every fiber of our being, our world—in fact the entire universe and everything in it."

Now, Reuel's voice, before weak and wavering, dropped to a whisper. "We all eventually die, and, horror of horrors, this corruption remains after our death. Making us unable to stand before our Creator, as no such taint can survive the pure light of His presence. He would not—by His very nature, could not—tolerate such. It is for this cause that He has separated Himself from us and forever barred our way to that eternal paradise."

Reuel's hand shook as it cupped his down-turned forehead. He propped an elbow on the splintered tabletop. His shoulders slumped as if that reality was too much to bear. Then he took a deep breath and sat straighter. "That we have always known, if only in part. We have also known God promised a way we might return to that lost paradise, though we knew not how. Long have we searched for the key to that secret way. From the scrolls, we now understand Creator God was to send to us a promised deliverer, one who would solve this problem we can never solve for ourselves. Yet we could not fathom how He planned to do such a thing. The Scriptures with which you have blessed us"—he nodded in thanks to Jeremiah, Phillip, and Thaddeus—"not only tell us much of God, of His history with the human race, but also speaks in great detail of one He would send for this very purpose. Nearly every book refers, in some fashion, to this deliverer. Many prophecies are predictions about His coming, describing it to the smallest detail, hundreds upon hundreds of details at my count."

Jeremiah had been listening rapt. He raised one hesitant finger like a shy grade-school student. At Reuel's nod, he said, "Over four hundred, I have found in my own studies."

"Just so, hundreds of specific prophesies. Because of the scrolls, we can now create a detailed picture of the man Creator God would use to save the world from the Curse, even if I do not yet understand how, exactly, such a task might be accomplished."

He motioned to Tuesday, who brought him a leather satchel from which he extracted a stack of old books. "These are the histories the bishop delivered to me, along with his claim. I have studied these at length, have crossed-checked them with other known sources. I invite you all to do the same, but in my estimation, there is no way to refute the bishop's assertion, whether I like it or no."

Reuel trembled as if uttering the next words came at great physical effort, his voice croaking forth from a painfully choked throat. "The long-awaited King, the promised Deliverer, our one and only hope, the one God would send to us bearing the secret way by which we might return to Him, to paradise—has already come." Tears dripped from Reuel's chin and splattered to the wooden table. The drops exploded on impact, transformed by the flickering firelight into a myriad of misty pinpoints, arcing into the darkness.

"He came to us, came to His own, long, long ago, and—" He gasped for his next breath, then again. Finally, he looked up, but his gaze was hollow, unseeing.

"And we killed Him."

CHAPTER 68

Lars had lost half a week helping Curtis and Phillip. He didn't begrudge them the time, but he still had jobs to deliver. And he'd lose his seminary kids at the end of the month, so he had to get done before then.

He pedaled to work, so distracted he barely noticed the bright winter morning, the new snowmelt tinkling down the creek banks as he crossed the old wooden bridge. He gave scarce a glance toward a family of rabbits, flushed from cover by his passage and now scurrying over the snow-covered hayfield toward some new shelter, far from his intruding presence.

And he failed to register the roadblock across the entrance to the family business until he nearly plowed into it. He skidded to a stop, heart skipping a beat. But then his stomach dropped, and a hollowness emptied the spot where his heart had been, a high-pitched tone replacing the birdcalls.

Official vehicles crammed the lot, and uniformed men bearing stubby submachine guns trampled over the lawn. One now strode toward him while a second stayed back, moving sideways to maintain a clear line of vision with Lars, the muzzle of his weapon coming to bear.

"What's going on?" Lars asked.

"Can I have your name and your business, sir?"

"Lars. And I work here, my family owns—I mean, are the stewards."

"I'm sorry. You're not on the list of authorized persons. Please go home."

Now the heat was rising. What right did these goons have to do this? "I asked what's going on?"

"Move along, sir."

Lars hopped off his bike and started for the main entrance. Everything got blurry, and then he was lying prone with what had to be a ton of bricks in the middle of his back. A sharp pain lanced through his shoulders as his arms were wrenched. Then the weight lifted. He struggled, but his hands were trapped behind his back, something pinning his wrists in place.

"Do not move until you are instructed to move."

Lars lurched, flipping his legs to roll over, only to be kicked in the ribs. "I said do not move. Remain face down."

Lars yelled his frustration into the frozen turf but didn't try to move again. The hobnails pressed into the back of his head may have had something to do with that. There came another voice from the road. His brother's. Lars let out a yell, muffled by the mouthful of snow. "Leif!"

The voice grew nearer, now joined by German saying, "Why are you holding him down like that? He's a good boy and no danger to you. Release him!"

The pressure on his neck disappeared, and Lars was lifted to his feet, if none too gently. His hands dropped to his sides, numb and unresponsive, as the restraints were cut.

Leif patted his shoulder, then moved toward the door.

Lars caught up. "What's going on?"

"Don't know. I was at home. German came and found me, said he heard about a raid going on here."

"What kind of raid?"

There came no answer. The door had opened. Armed men exited, escorting a line of prisoners at gunpoint. Dad's hands were tied.

Mom's were not, but two men flanked her, each holding her by an elbow, their body language broadcasting the universal vocabulary of coercive physical force. Behind them, Diggs and Velde walked freely, smiling and chatting with two others. And . . . was that Chip? The arrogant scion of the Artisans dynasty? Yes! And beside him, Nicollo, the manager who assisted Leif at the sawmill.

Lars ran toward his family. "Mom! Dad! What's going on?"

Dad's face was dark red, veins popping in his forehead. Through her tears, Mom whispered, "We've been replaced. We've lost the stewardship."

"What? They can't do that! We're more profitable than ever."

Chip grinned and elbowed Nicollo. "Wouldn't be here otherwise, would we?"

What a bunch of jerks. They weren't going to get away with this. "German!" Lars cried out. "Can we call Advisor Haman right now? On your landline? He'll straighten this out."

Nicollo sauntered up to where Lars stood, bracketed by Leif and German. He stopped before Lars, his disdain evident. "So you're the pup. Haman is no longer your advisor, pup. He was caught accepting bribes from suppliers." Chip guffawed, and Diggs smirked. "Now go home, boy. Don't trifle with your betters unless you want your mother to spend time in prison. Like your father."

Leif moved between Lars and Nicollo, chest bumping the short man until he was forced to back away from Lars. "Nicollo, best go back to work and show my family some respect before I'm forced to reconsider your position with my company."

Nicollo laughed. "What company, Leif? Your stewardship has been revoked along with these other poor imitations." He jerked a thumb toward Mom and Dad.

Lars began to shove past Leif, to throttle the little weasel, but he was too slow. Leif unleashed a jab straight at Nicollo's face. There came a meaty slap as Leif's fist buried itself into the biggest palm Lars had ever seen.

Snow had appeared and interposed his hand between Leif's fist and Nicollo's nose. Now, he twisted that fist with apparent ease, forcing Leif to the ground. "Striking an advisor is a serious offense. Should I take them in, sir?"

Leif gasped, fighting the pain. "What advisor?"

Nicollo bent to bring his face level with Leif's. "Oh, I'm sorry. Did I forget to introduce myself? I'm your new advisor, and you just made the *second* biggest mistake of your life. I had planned to make you pay for your superior, arrogant ways. Now, I'll make your life a living hell. I suggest you kill yourself and avoid the coming agony."

Nicollo stood and, with a final lip-curled glance, walked toward an armored fast transport. Diggs joined him.

Lars called after Diggs. "So you were a worthless snake all along? No big surprise there."

Diggs laughed. As he stooped to enter the limo, he called back. "The money will help me heal from the sting of your disapproval, and it's Mr. Snake to you, you unemployed little twerp."

Lars's heart hurt, real bad, as Mom and Dad were loaded into a van and driven away. Couldn't someone do something? From behind came the clomp of advancing boots. He dared turn. What now?

A line of guards formed between themselves and Velde, Chip, and a few other men Lars didn't recognize. Snow still held Leif to the ground, arm bent backward at an angle that made Lars's shoulder twinge.

Chip shoved through the line of guards to stand over Leif. He reached into his pocket and pulled out a coin, which he flipped high into the air with his thumb. It rose as if in slow motion and hung suspended at the top of its arc before rolling end over end, bright sunlight flashing from its faces. Then it plummeted. Chip snatched it from midair and again launched it with his thumb. It streaked beeline fashion toward Leif where it impacted with his forehead, the slap too big to be made by such a small object. It bounced away in the grass, leaving a swelling welt on Leif's skin.

Chip said, "Keep your own change. You're gonna need it." He then shouted an order. "Guards! Remove these trespassers. If they give you any trouble, feel free to use excessive force. If they don't, use a little anyway on principle."

Lars lifted Leif from the ground and steered him, stumbling, to the road where German's rusted runabout idled. Lars pointed his brother into the back seat before sliding in beside him.

German asked, "Where to?"

Leif rubbed the welt. "Let's head to the sawmill to check on the Bobs. Hope the gorillas left them out of this."

When they squeaked to a halt, two men were already at the sawmill entrance. An older and younger version of each other, except the younger had only one arm, a nub above where his elbow should be.

They stood alone and forlorn surrounded by official vehicles and armed men. The rail embankment hid the sawmill, but heavy diesel machinery roared there. The dust of its movement rose into the blue sky.

Lars followed Leif to the two men.

"Bob!" Leif called. "What happened? Are you okay?"

The older Bob stared into the distance, not answering, chewing on nothing.

A single tear traced its way down the younger man's cheek, leaving a clean, wet trail in the dust. This younger man approached. "Mr. Leif, I'm so glad you're here. You gotta stop 'em. They're takin' all the lumber. They're knocking down our house, sir! You're gonna get this fixed, right, Mr. Leif?"

Leif grabbed at German's tweed sleeve. "Can they do this to Bob? I know they can take my inventory, but how can they take Bob's house? He had tenancy for life."

German held up a finger and waddled to his car. He returned with a file folder. He flipped through pages, some falling to the ground in his haste. He waved one sheet, peering over the tops of his wire rims to read it. "Here it is. They are authorized to take the inventory only. This says nothing about the equipment or the property. I'll take care of this, Bob. You'll be back in your house in a jiffy."

German approached the men guarding the driveway barricade. After a brief conversation, he waved Leif over. "Let's go in and sort this out."

The five climbed the steep driveway and topped out, standing on the tracks. Leif leading, stopped short.

From this elevated position, the entire property was laid out before them. Big machines surrounded the house, the sawmill, and the kiln, some loading lumber onto flatbeds parked on the railroad siding.

But Leif was staring at something beyond the siding. A train of flatbeds sped past on the main line, all of them loaded high with logs. Leif spun to German, hand extended. “Can I have the keys to your car? I’ve got to see what’s going on up at the railhead.”

German scowled and clutched the keys to his chest. “You must think me the worst kind of fool. Let you have my car? I think not. I’ll drive.”

As they sprinted toward the car, Leif yelled over his shoulder at the officer in charge. “You heard German. Bob’s house is off-limits.”

The uniformed man scowled but nodded.

Lars jumped in the car with Leif, and German drove as fast as the old rust bucket would move. Faster than it should have, maybe, given the way it wobbled in and out of the lane. Or perhaps that was German’s driving. The old guy sat hunched, squinting through his coke-bottle glasses, his fringe of hair rippling in the breeze as he peered over the dash, knuckles white where they gripped the wheel.

They pulled into a gravel roundabout. Several vehicles were already here, many official. A large man leaned against an old jeep’s hood. They skidded to a halt next to it and jumped out. “Maurice! Are you okay?”

The big man looked over at them, face pregnant with unspent violence. “They’re rippin’ it all up. Our beautiful forest, Leif. They’re tearing it out by the roots.”

From where they stood, the railroad was visible, a row of flatbed cars being loaded with logs. Beyond the nearest hill came the roaring of big engines and the higher, snarling screams of gasoline-powered chain saws. Leif let out an agonized yell and sprinted up the slope, disappearing as he topped the rise and descended the other side. Lars chased after him, glancing behind to where Maurice had pushed himself off the hood and trudged up the hill, head down, shoulders slumped.

As Lars reached the hilltop, Leif stood a few feet down the slope and next to a younger woman. As far as Lars could see, rolling hill after rolling hill disappearing into the smoke-hazed distance, crews were felling trees, clear-cutting. The landscape resembled a bombed-out battlefield. Heavy tracked equipment moved over the expanse like carrion beetles swarming a corpse. It picked up the scattered, splintered remains of the felled trees, tearing up the snow and the soft, black earth beneath like tender flesh.

Now stood steep hillsides, rutted, naked, and exposed, vulnerable to the coming spring rains. The cloud-borne deluge would rush down, gullying and washing away the fertile soil. Then summer's dry winds would scour ruined crags, the desolation complete, this once verdant paradise a scarred desert, a fitting sacrificial offering to the gods of this world, a monument to them for time immemorial.

Beyond Leif's shoulder, the largest tree Lars had ever seen, an oak hundreds of years old, wobbled, teetered, then accelerated groundward. It could have been the fabled Tree of Life. When it impacted, the old limbs shattered as they plowed into the ground. The snapping and tearing of the living branches and the groan of the splitting trunk combined in a single, slow-motion crescendo, the dying scream of some ancient forest immortal, brought down for the pleasure of lesser beings.

The sound faded but still echoed in Lars's mind. Would he ever rid himself of that memory, that terrible death cry? Certainly, such a thing would haunt his soul year after endless year.

Leif spoke to the woman. "Kat, I'm sorry."

Her answer, coming as it was in a hoarse whisper, barely rose above the cacophony. "I blame myself. You are a destroyer. I knew this, yet I trusted you." Her eyes were dry, her features gray and rigid. She walked away, never looking back.

Fists clenched at his sides, Leif muttered something inaudible.

Lars moved up to stand at his side, Leif's muttered words now clear. ". . . not a destroyer."

Lars put a hand on his brother's shoulder. "You know she didn't mean it."

But Leif let out a scream of his own like some injured forest animal and jerked free of Lars's grip, then stormed off toward the deep forest, head down, body stiff. He began to run.

Lars made to follow, but a big fist wrapped around his elbow.

Maurice shook his head, eyes dark. "Leave be. Let 'im sort it."

From behind came a ragged shout, then another. German, red-faced and panting, plodded up the hill, followed by a uniformed Bureau man. When he came abreast, he whipped a kerchief from his pocket and mopped his sweaty brow.

"Lars, boy. You've got to come with me now. Hurry. There's no time." His grip fumbled at Lars's sleeve, and he made to turn back toward the road.

But Lars planted his feet. "Whoa, not without Leif."

German cursed under his breath. "No time, I said. The entire Republic is on emergency lockdown. If we're not home before the soldiers arrive, I can't say the consequences."

Lars started whence Leif had gone but pulled up short. His brother had disappeared. But which way? There was no sign of him.

A shrill siren emanated from the big machines, earsplitting above even the roar of those motors. One by one, the engines shut down, and operators sprinted toward the road, piled into transports, then sped toward Northwoods. Lars again checked where Leif had gone.

But Maurice's deep baritone broke the newfound silence, muffled by the ringing in Lars's ears, the roar of those big machines still seemingly echoing there. "Best go, lad. Come on." He draped an arm around Lars's shoulders, moving him again toward the road.

Lars spun free and dashed toward the forest.

And then his feet were clear of the ground, and the world turned upside down. He could see only Maurice's big boots as they strode down the hill, German's wing tips at his side. Every jolting step pounded the point of Maurice's shoulder into Lars's midsection, forcing his breath out in a painful *whumpfh*.

Maurice plopped Lars into the open-sided runabout's back seat.

German slid in beside him, and the officer took the wheel. German shouted to the man, "Drive!"

Lars struggled against Maurice's big hands, still pinning him in the seat, but Maurice leaned in, eye to eye. "I'll find him. Just you go now, so I don't have to worry about you, too."

The transport spun, gravel flying, Maurice receded behind, hands on hips, red-checked flannel sleeves rolled above the elbows. Then he, too, turned away, big cleated boots marching toward the woods.

Trees blurred past as the driver sped through the tight curves, Lars thrown alternately into German on his left and the open space on his right where the door ought to be. Only the safety strap stopped him from flying free. Lars barely registered their surroundings, seeing only the image of Leif's back as he disappeared. Where was he going? What was he capable of doing in his current state? To himself? Lars's gut spasmed, the burning cramps filling all the world. A tear ran down his cheek, dashed into spray by the icy wind whipping through the open car sides.

They topped the rise overlooking the wide valley he called home. The vehicle's nose pointed down the slope to the river. Northwoods lay as if in the bottom of a big shallow bowl. The snow-covered roads were crawling with the black vehicles of the Order, the town alive with them, like ants on a picnic blanket. The black smoke from their exhaust stacks formed a flat cloud over the village. A shroud.

At the edge of town, a bunker was being constructed of timbers and sandbags. A barrier stretched across the road. A dozen black-clad men stood before it, submachine guns held cross-body.

German sat stone-faced, jaw clenched. "I'd hoped never to see a day like this again."

Now Lars's heart was racing. The never-flustered German looked terrified. "Wha—" Lars's voice cracked. "What's going on?"

The old man gave a slow headshake. "Someone woke the dragon, son. And whoever it was, Eternal have mercy on them."

His next words were a whisper, nearly lost amongst the roar of distant motors. "Eternal have mercy on us all."

THE END . . .
FOR NOW

Thanks for joining the adventure! I hope you've loved your time in the world of the Seekers.

Don't forget to leave a review at Amazon and Goodreads, or wherever you get your books.

Most importantly, receive our newsletter and be the first to know about new releases, special offers, and exclusive content available only to subscribers. Go to jawebbauthor.com to sign up, and get your free book while you're there!

ACKNOWLEDGMENTS

This book would not exist if not for the many people who played a part:

My precious wife, who lovingly and patiently supports this obsession I call writing.

Deirdre Erin Lockhart, my mentor, editor, and trusted friend, without who's tireless effort and extraordinary dedication to this project, this book would not have succeeded.

Stefan Rudnicki, audiobook narrator and honored friend, whose brilliant performances elevate my stories and brings them to life.

Thank you to the Beta team volunteers who poured through early drafts. Your efforts contributed greatly to the quality of this novel and I'd like to thank each of you personally. Those team members include- A. R. Harrison, Erin B., Curtis D., Birgit, Tina L,. and nameless others.

To you, and to all the others who have made this novel possible but were not listed here- Thank You!

J. A. Webb

www.ingramcontent.com/pod-product-compliance
Lightning Source LLC
Chambersburg PA
CBHW020355310726
48979CB00015B/2600/J

* 9 7 8 1 9 6 5 9 1 5 0 5 9 *